The Dark

James Herbert was not just Britain's number one bestselling writer of chiller fiction, a position he held ever since publication of his first novel, but was also one of our greatest popular novelists. Widely imitated and hugely influential, his twenty-three novels have sold more than fifty-four million copies worldwide, and have been translated into over thirty languages including Russian and Chinese. In 2010, he was made the Grand Master of Horror by the World Horror Convention and was also awarded an OBE by the Queen for services to literature. His final novel was *Ash*. James Herbert died in March 2013.

JAMES HERBERT

The Dark

PAN BOOKS

First published 1980 by New English Library

This edition published 2012 by Pan Books
an imprint of Pan Macmillan, a division of Macmillan Publishers Limited
Pan Macmillan, 20 New Wharf Road, London N1 9RR
Basingstoke and Oxford
Associated companies throughout the world
www.panmacmillan.com

ISBN 978-0-330-52207-6

3 5 7 9 8 6 4

A CIP catalogue record for this book is available from
the British Library.

Typeset by SetSystems Ltd, Saffron Walden, Essex
Printed and bound by CPI Group (UK) Ltd, Croydon, CR0 4YY

Visit **www.panmacmillan.com** to read more about all our books
and to buy them. You will also find features, author interviews and
news of any author events, and you can sign up for e-newsletters
so that you're always first to hear about our new releases.

The Dark

Part One

... And God saw that the light was good;
and God separated the light from the darkness ...

Genesis 1:4
(R.S.V.)

It was a bright, sunny day. Not, you might have thought, the sort of day for hunting ghosts. Nor was the house the kind of house you might expect to be haunted. But then psychic phenomena pay scant attention to time, place, or weather.

It was a nice road, but ordinary, with that mid-morning, suburban quietness that areas only minutes away from high streets have. The houses themselves were an odd mixture of semis and detached buildings; bright new town houses sparkled at the far end, as yet undaunted by the daily grime.

I drove slowly down the road, looking for the right house, and drew into the kerb when I saw the sign. 'Beechwood'. Unimpressive.

This was one of the detached buildings, tall, grey-bricked, Victorian. I took off my driving glasses and slipped them into the glove compartment; then I rubbed my eyes and settled back to study the house for a few moments.

The small area in front, which obviously had been a garden at one time, had been concreted over to provide an off-the-road parking space for cars; but there were no cars there. I had been told the house would be empty. The windows were opaque from the glare of the sun and for a brief, uneasy moment, it seemed the house itself was staring out at me through mirror sunglasses.

I quickly shrugged off the feeling – imagination could sometimes be a hindrance in my job – and reached over to the back seat. The black case was neither large nor heavy, but it contained most of the equipment I would need. The air had a deceptive edge to it when I stepped out on to the pavement, a hint that winter would soon have its turn. A woman whose small child preferred to skip rather than walk gave me a curious look as they passed by, as though my presence in her road had broken a routine. I nodded but the contact made her lose interest.

After locking my car, I crossed the concrete area and climbed the five stone steps leading to the front door. There I paused, placing the case by my feet, and searched for the key. I found it and dropped it. The attached faded address card flapped loosely in the air when I retrieved the key and inserted it into the lock. For some reason I stopped and listened before I pushed the heavy door open, peering uselessly through the leaded glass of its top section. There were no sounds and no moving shadows.

I wasn't nervous, nor even apprehensive, for I saw no reason to be. I suppose my initial hesitation was simply due to caution. Empty houses had always made me so. The door swung open and, picking up my case, I stepped inside. I closed the door behind me.

The rays of the sun shone brilliantly through the leaded glass of the door and windows on either side, casting my own shadow deeply and well-defined along the hallway. A broad staircase, its ascent beginning only five feet from where I stood, disappeared into the upper portion of the house, and near the top, from the overhang of the first floor, there dangled a pair of legs.

One shoe – a man's – had fallen off and lay on its side halfway down the stairs; I could see the heel of the man's sock was worn, the pink flesh almost visible through the punctured material. The wall beside the hanging legs was scuffed and blackened as though it had been marked by the man's death-throes. I remember dropping my case and walking slowly down the hall, craning my head upwards, not wishing to mount the stairs, but strangely curious to see the rest of the corpse. I remember peering into the gloom of the stairwell and seeing the bloated face above the grotesquely stretched neck, the ridiculously small loop of plastic flex, no more than three inches in diameter, biting into his flesh as though someone had tugged at his legs to pull it tight. I remember the smell of death coming to me, subtle yet cloying, elusive but all around. It was fresh, unlike the heavy, pungent odour of stale corpses.

I backed away and stopped when I came into contact with the edge of the open doorway opposite the staircase. I turned in surprise and looked into the room; the others were in there, some lying on the floor, some sprawled in armchairs, some upright, staring, as though watching me. But they were all dead. I knew it not just from the smell, the unseeing eyes, the mutilated bodies. I knew it from the stagnant atmosphere, the stillness of the room itself.

I pushed myself away from the door, sliding my body along the wall for support, my legs suddenly weak. A movement ahead made me stop and I saw there was a small door beneath the staircase. I could only go forward towards the sun-filled front door, not daring to rush back into the depths of the house. The door under the stairs moved again, only slightly, and I realized a draught was disturbing it. I moved closer, keeping my back pressed hard against the wall, and soon I was level with the small opening, sliding past, going beyond it. And then, for some reason still unknown to me, I reached out and pulled the door open, its back slamming against the rising staircase, rebounding so it half closed again. I thought I saw movement but perhaps it was only the shadows receding from the sudden light.

There were stairs leading down to what must have been the cellar. All I could see was the blackness down there, a deep, almost solid darkness. And it was the darkness more than the corpses that made me flee from the house . . .

1

She sat at the kitchen table, lonely, brooding. She knew she had to face up to it: their life together was no good, it never would be. The idea of moving into the new town house seemed fine at the time; she thought a real home of their own would change his attitude. No more drab flats where everything mended, everything painted, was for the benefit of the landlord. A chance to build something solid, a foundation for their relationship. Marriage didn't matter to her, she'd never pressure him. But the house was right for children . . .

They had snapped up the chance of buying the place, for property prices were constantly soaring, reaching an unbelievable level, settling for a few months, then continuing their relentless upward flight. They had been hesitant about asking the agent to repeat the purchase price again, almost afraid he would realize his mistake and add on an extra three or four thousand. He had confirmed the original cost.

Richard had been a little suspicious and she had stepped in quickly with a firm offer. Whatever unseen drawbacks there might be, this was at least a new start for them. Besides, it was mostly her savings that would pay the ten per cent demanded by the building society towards the cost of the property. The existing owners had already moved out – 'Gone abroad,' said the agent – so within a month they had settled themselves in. It wasn't long before the rumours reached them.

She looked down at the empty Diazepam container before her on the table, picking it up and twisting the plastic tube between her fingers. There had been seven left that morning. She had steadily cut down the Valium tablets, making progress, moving away from her breakdown of six months ago, suppressing the memory, coping. But Richard hadn't changed. Her near self-destruction had only stemmed the flow briefly; his old ways had soon come slinking back. His excuse was the house now, the road, the other houses. The place made him uneasy, people were unfriendly. Others were moving away – at least three families in the two months they had lived there. There was something wrong with the road.

She had felt it too, almost as soon as they had moved in, but her uneasiness had been quelled by her new hope. Things were meant to change, to become better; instead they had become worse. His drinking had always been hard to take, but bearable – his job as a rep for a finished-art studio demanded he drank with clients, anyway. The women he occasionally slept with didn't matter to her any more – knowing his inadequacy, she doubted he even enjoyed himself. It was his resentment that had become impossible to live with.

He resented being trapped by the responsibility of owning a home, resented being in debt to a building society, resented her demands, both physical and mental, on him. He resented being the cause of her breakdown.

Now that she had finally come to bear the physical marks of his bitterness – bruising, scratchmarks – she knew it had to end, it was pointless going on. Even though they were not married, the house was in their joint names. But who would be the one to go? Would she come out with nothing after four years of torment? If he insisted, she knew she couldn't stand up to him. She smashed the empty tube down on to the kitchen table. The pills hadn't helped at at all.

She stood, her chair scraping harshly against the tiled kitchen floor, and strode towards the sink. She filled the kettle, water splashing fiercely off the metal side, soaking her blouse. She swore, dumping the kettle on the gas ring. After switching on the gas she reached for her cigarettes, the packet lying open on the breadboard. She snatched one out and thrust the end into the gas flame, then quickly into her mouth, drawing her breath in sharply to make it light. Her fingers drummed against the aluminium draining-board, becoming more rigid as she tapped until it was her fist beating down, harder and harder, the sound echoing around the small kitchen. It stopped when a tear slid from her face on to her thinly covered breast, the single damp sensation more disturbing than the overall tap splatter of a few moments earlier. But one tear was all she would allow herself. She rubbed a hand roughly against her eyes, then drew in deeply on the cigarette, looking out through the window into the street below, the lights casting isolated silver pools along its length. Would he come home tonight? She was no longer sure if she even cared. She would have her coffee and go to bed; there she would decide what to do.

She lit another cigarette – the last one, she noticed with annoyance – before carrying the coffee through the kitchen towards the stairs leading to the bedroom. The town house consisted of three floors, the ground being the garage and back workroom, the second level the kitchen and lounge-dining area, the third the two bedrooms and bathroom. She paused at the top of the stairs descending to the front door: should she lock him out? Steam rose in spiralling wisps from the coffee as she pondered. Abruptly she stepped on to the top stair, her mind made up and, just as abruptly, her hand grasped tightly around the balustrade. It was dark down there.

Normally light shone in from the outside street-lamp through the reeded glass door, bathing the tiny hallway in its diffused light. Now she could only see a heavy blackness. Strange, she hadn't noticed the street-light not working from the kitchen. Twisting her body, she flicked the switch controlling the downstairs light. Nothing happened, but the sudden movement caused hot coffee to spill over on to her fingers. She gasped with shock and quickly changed the mug over to her other hand, sticking her burnt fingers into her mouth to lick the offending liquid off. The pain served to remind her of the pain she might receive if she did lock Richard out. She stepped back on to the landing and walked down the hallway, her troubled mind not noticing the bright artificial light shining through the hall window from the street-lamp outside.

Pinky Burton was still angry. The boys in the house opposite had no right to call him such names. They were nothing more than pimply-faced louts, yobbos. He couldn't understand why he had even bothered to be friendly with the younger one, the one with the long, golden locks. Golden when he bothered to wash his unruly mop, that is. Neither had any respect for their elders, not even their father. Father? God, it was little wonder the boys were so offensive with a big abrasive man like that as a father. It was hardly surprising the brute's wife had run off years ago. She obviously couldn't stand any of them.

It used to be a nice respectable road at one time, before the riff-raff moved in. He could remember when one had to have wealth to live in this road, and every family was respectable. And respected. These two guttersnipes certainly had no respect for him. It was nonsense to suggest he would take the time and trouble to spy on them. Perhaps he had watched them sometimes as they had worked, stripped to the waist, on the older one's motorcycle. What of it? He was interested in machinery, always had been since his RAF days. The younger one wasn't so bad at first – at least one could have a conversation with him – but the other yobbo, the sneery one, had obviously influenced his brother. How dare they suggest ... just because a man ... *how did they find out about that anyway*?

Pinky turned over in bed and pulled the covers up over his ears. The road was full of nastiness. Never used to be. Nasty modern boxes they called town houses at one end, the old, bigger houses becoming dilapidated, allowed to run down; and greasy-haired louts like those two roaring up and down all night on motorbikes. Well, perhaps they were the only two, and they had one machine between them, but they still made enough noise for a dozen or more. And then there was the house further down, the big detached one – what on earth could have caused something like that? Totally unbelievable. Totally insane. Sign of the times. New – worse – atrocities every day. Made one wonder if there was any goodness at all left in the world. But nothing could match the inhumanity he had found in ... Pinky still found it hard to form the word in his mind. Why had they sent him there? Hadn't he done enough for his country in the last war? Had it been necessary to punish him so harshly for one misdemeanour? The child had suffered no real harm. All right, so there had been other minor offences to take into account. But they *were* minor, small lapses on his part. It wasn't as if he had ever actually hurt anyone. The degradation inside that ... place. The degenerates. The vicious, mean bullyboys. To put a man like him alongside such animals. And when he had been released after months that seemed like a thousand years, his position at the club had gone. None of the members had rallied round to support him as their bar manager. No, it was the cold shoulder, them and their bloody tweeds and afternoon golf, their bloody cocker spaniels and crusty-fannied wives. People he had known for years saying nasty, spiteful things. Thank God Mother had left the house – thank God she was long dead before it all came out. The shock would have killed her. He would never have been able to afford the place on the measly sum he earned as a part-time barman. And it was humiliating to be on a 'suspect list' of sex offenders. When any crime was committed in the area that had any sexual connotations he could be sure of a police visit. Routine enquiries they always said. Well it wasn't bloody routine to him!

He turned over restlessly on to his back and stared hatefully at the light patterns on the ceiling. The nebulous shapes shivered as a breeze disturbed the leaves on the tree outside, giving the reflected light from the street-lamp a living, embryonic quality. Pinky swore at the ceiling.

The jeers, the sly insinuations, from the two louts over the road had cut deep that day. His other neighbours had always treated him with respect, had always politely acknowledged his greetings, had never pried into his affairs. But these ... these scumbags had shouted out their obscenities for the whole world to hear, had laughed at him when his own temper had forced him to run back indoors. He did not know what he might have done if he hadn't. Well, tomorrow the police would be informed of the racket they made with their infernal machine. He was still a citizen and, as such, entitled to his rights. Just because he had made a mistake once, it didn't mean he had lost his civil rights! He bit into his lip and choked back a sob. He knew he would never venture into a police station again, not of his own volition. Those bastards, those dirty, little, long-haired bastards!

Pinky closed his eyes tightly and when he opened them, wondered why it had become so dark, why the patterns on the ceiling had disappeared.

She knelt on the bed, a small, huddled form. Susie was small for an eleven-year-old, but her eyes sometimes had a knowing look of someone way beyond her years. At other times they were completely blank. She pulled methodically at the hair of her Cindy doll, the silver strands falling on to her lap. Glass-mounted pictures of Beatrix Potter animals gazed down impassively at her from the blue walls of her little bedroom, oblivious of the sharp snap as a plastic arm was wrenched from the doll's body. The tiny limb bounced off Peter Rabbit and clattered to the floor. Susie pulled at the other arm and threw this, too, across the room, towards the closed window. It fell on to her toy chest beneath the window and lay there, the hand bent back supplicatingly on its swivel-joint.

'Naughty girl, Cindy,' Susie scolded in hushed anger. 'You mustn't stare when you're at the dinner table! Mummy doesn't like it!'

The doll's expression did not change as her leg was pulled back and tugged. 'I've told you time and time again, you mustn't smirk when Uncle Jeremy tells you off! He doesn't like it – it makes him angry. It makes Mummy angry, too!' The leg came away with a sucking sound and was tossed towards the door. 'Uncle Jeremy will go away and leave Mummy if he gets cross. Then Mummy will send me away. She'll tell the doctors I've been acting bad again.' Susie drew in a deep breath at the effort of tearing the last limb free, her small body sagging into a relaxed position when her exertions were rewarded.

'There! Now you can't run away and you can't get into mischief.' Susie smiled triumphantly, but her happiness lasted only seconds. 'I hate that place, Cindy! It's nasty. And the doctors and the nurses are nasty. I don't want to go there again.' Her eyes became tearful, then her face suddenly screwed itself up into an expression of spiteful anger. 'He's not my uncle, anyway. He just wants cuddles from Mummy. He hates me and he hates my dad! Why doesn't Daddy come back, Cindy? Why does he hate me too? I wouldn't touch matches ever again if he came back, Cindy, I promise I wouldn't.'

She fiercely hugged the limbless doll and rocked to and fro on her knees. 'You know I wouldn't, don't you, Cindy? You know I wouldn't.' There was no reply from the doll and Susie thrust it away from her in disgust. 'You never answer me, you naughty girl! You never show you love me!'

She pulled at the pretty plastic head, her arms quivering with the effort, a scream building up in her throat. She suppressed her cry as the head popped free and laughed when she threw it at the stars outside the window. Her body went rigid as the doll's head rebounded off the pane and rolled to the floor. She dared not breathe for a few moments as she listened for footsteps to come thumping along the corridor. She sighed with relief when no such sounds came. They were both asleep. Him, with her, in Daddy's bed. The thought made her angry again. It wasn't just cuddles he wanted. He did other things. She knew, she'd heard, she'd watched.

Susie sprang from the bed and padded towards the window, careful not to disturb the toys lying scattered in the dark on the bedroom floor. She examined the pane of glass which had been struck by the doll's head, looking for a crack to show up against the stars outside. It would mean more misery for her if the glass had been broken. She grinned when she saw there was no damage.

Pressing her face to the window she tried to pierce the gloom of the garden below. She spent most of the summer days there when she wasn't at the special school; a prisoner, not allowed to go out on her own. Susie could just make out the shape of the rabbit hutch, weather-beaten and empty, not understanding why they had taken the rabbits away. The baby ones had been gorgeous, lovely to hold, to squeeze. Perhaps if she hadn't squeezed so hard they would have let her keep them.

She returned to the bed and squatted on it, ankles crossed, her arms hugged around her raised knees. The blankets lay rumpled around her. If Uncle Jeremy went away, perhaps Daddy would come back. They could all live together again and be happy, like before. Like before the time she'd been really naughty. Before the trouble.

Susie lay back in the bed, pulling the clothes up around her. She gripped the silky edge of the blanket and brushed it rhythmically against her cheek, staring out into the deep blue night framed by the window's edges. One by one she began to count the stars, determined this time to number every one in the rectangle before falling asleep. And one by one, as she silently counted, the stars went out, until only blackness filled the window-frame.

2

Bishop glanced discreetly at his watch and was relieved that the two-hour lecture was nearly up. Usual mixed bunch, he thought wryly. Most of them deadly serious, several just curious, one – maybe two – sceptics. And, of course, the token headcase. He smiled generally at the gathering in the lecture hall.

'So you can see by my list of equipment on the blackboard, parapsychology – the study of paraphysical phenomena – uses technology rather than the more unreliable and, if I may say so, the dubious spiritualistic methods. Graph paper will usually tell you more about strange disturbances in a house than self-imposed mental trances.'

A nervous hand fluttered in the air from the second row. Bishop noticed the man wore a clerical collar. 'May I, er, ask a question?' the equally nervous voice said. All eyes turned to look at the cleric who steadfastly kept his eyes riveted on Bishop's as if embarrassed by his own presence.

'Please do,' Bishop encouraged. 'In fact, we'll spend the last ten minutes discussing any points you might want to raise.'

'Well, it was just that for someone whose profession is the investigation of the paranormal or paraphysical . . .'

'Call it ghost-hunting – it's simpler,' said Bishop.

'Yes, ghost-hunting. Well, it hasn't really been made clear by you whether or not you actually believe in ghosts.'

Bishop smiled. 'The truth of the matter is, having been involved in the study of parapsychology for some years, I'm still unsure. Certainly I've come up against the inexplicable time and time again, but every day science is uncovering new facts about our own powers. Somebody once said that mysticism is just tomorrow's science dreamed today. I think I'd go along with that. For instance, we know concentrated thought, or often unconscious thought, can physically move objects. Scientists throughout the world, particularly in Russia, are now studying the psychokinetic power. Years ago it would have been called witchcraft.'

'But how does that explain spirit sightings?' A middle-aged woman, plump and pleasant looking, had asked the question. 'There are so many cases of hauntings you hear about practically every day.'

'Perhaps not every day, but there are between two and three hundred sightings each year, and probably just as many not publicised. One of the many theories is that ghosts are caused by someone under stress, their minds giving out electrical impulses in the way the heart does, and these impulses are picked up later in particular circumstances.'

The puzzled frown on the woman's face and on the faces of several others in his audience told Bishop he wasn't making himself clear. 'It's rather like a mental picture being transmitted by one individual to be picked up later by someone else who acts as a kind of receiver. Like a television set. This could explain why apparitions are often misty, faded or why sometimes only faces or hands appear: the pictures, or transmissions, if you like, are wearing out, fading until there's nothing left.'

'What about places that have been haunted for centuries, then?' said a young, bearded man in the front row, who was leaning forward antagonistically. 'Why haven't they just faded away?'

'It could be explained by regeneration: the transmission, or apparition, draws on energy from electrical impulses that surround us all. This could account for the appearance of a ghost. A spirit can "live" on indefinitely as long as its image can be seen by others: the ghost is actually telepathic waves, the image created in the mind of a living person years, days, perhaps centuries before and transmitted into the mind or minds of others living today.'

Bishop sighed inwardly: he could see he was losing them. They hadn't expected him to explain ghosts as a scientific phenomenon. They wanted the subject romanticized, the mystic aspect heightened. Even the sceptics among them looked disappointed.

'You're putting it down to electricity, then?' The bearded man in the front row sat back and folded his arms, the slightest indication of smugness in his smile.

'No, not exactly. But an electrical charge given to the nerve tissues of the brain can make a subject see flashes or hear noises. It would seem that a charge given to the appropriate receptive area of the brain can create a phantom image. Remember, the brain functions through electrical impulses and we're also surrounded by them. Impulses picked out of the air by our senses – that's us acting as receivers – isn't a difficult concept to understand. You may have heard of crisis apparitions, where someone sees an image of a friend or relative who is going through some traumatic experience, perhaps dying, many miles away. A voice may even be heard at the same time.'

A few heads nodded appreciatively.

'This can be explained by the person who is undergoing that extreme moment of stress thinking of the person closest to him, perhaps calling out to them. At such times, brainwaves are extremely active – this has been proved by the use of electroencephalograph machines. When they reach a certain pitch a telepathic image can often be transmitted either to a recipient or into the atmosphere. New factors concerning our own brain power are being brought to light by science at an ever-increasing rate. My guess is that by the end of the century, mysticism and technology will be one. There really will be no such thing as "ghosts".'

A low murmur ran through the gathering as they looked around at each other with various expressions of bemusement, disappointment, or satisfaction.

'Mr Bishop?' The woman's voice came from the back row and Bishop squinted his eyes to see her more clearly. 'Mr Bishop, you term yourself as a ghost-hunter. Can you tell us, then, why you've spent so many years hunting electrical impulses?'

A small ripple of laughter ran through the audience and Bishop smiled with them. He decided to use his reply as a closing statement for the lecture.

'I'm involved in the investigation of hauntings because I believe they have special scientific significance. All phenomena have some rational explanation – it's just that we are not yet advanced enough to perceive that explanation. Any useful information we can gain towards those ends must have value. Mankind is at an exciting stage of development where science and the paranormal are heading towards a meeting point. We have reached the time where parapsychology has to be taken seriously and studied logically with all the advanced technology we have at hand. We can no longer afford to tolerate the fools, the romantics, the misguided; even less can we tolerate the charlatans, the professional ghost-seers, or the mediums who live off the ignorance and distress of others. The breakthrough is nearly here and cannot be allowed hindrance by these people.'

His last words induced a smattering of polite applause from the audience. He held up a hand to let them know he had not quite finished.

'There's one other point. Many people have been emotionally disturbed or frightened by evidence of the paranormal, by "ghostly" appearances: if I can help them understand such occurrences and not fear them, then that alone justifies my work. Now, I have a list of organizations dealing in psychical research, paraphysical studies, metaphysical and ESP research groups and plain old ghost-hunting organizations. There's also a couple of addresses where you can find your own ghost-hunting equipment. Please help yourself to a copy before you leave.'

He turned his back on them, shuffled his lecture notes together and placed them in his briefcase. As usual, his throat was dry after the two-hour talk, and his thoughts now were only of the tall glass of beer that would soothe it. He hardly knew this town, but he hoped the pubs were decent. First, though, he had the gauntlet to run, for there were always those eager to continue the debate on a more personal level long after the allotted time was up. The chief librarian, who had arranged the series of talks in the town library's lecture hall, was the first to come forward.

'Most interesting, Mr Bishop. I'm sure next week's attendance figure will be even higher once word gets around.'

Bishop smiled cynically. He wondered if there would be half as many judging by the disappointment on some of the faces.

'I'm afraid they didn't hear quite what they expected to,' he said without apology.

'Oh no, on the contrary, I think many now realize just what a serious subject the whole matter is.' The librarian rubbed his hands together as if in glee. 'I must say, you've certainly whet my appetite. Let me tell you of the strange experience I had just a few years ago . . .'

Bishop listened politely, knowing he would have to hear several 'strange experiences' from the others in the hall before he could take his leave. As an authority on the subject, he was constantly used as a kind of father confessor by the many who had witnessed real or imaginary phenomena. A small group had soon gathered round and he answered their questions, encouraging them to make a serious study of the paranormal themselves. He also reminded them to keep an open mind and to maintain a careful balance between belief and scepticism. One or two expressed their surprise at his own reservations and he informed them his researches had always been more clinical than biased. The fact that a few years ago an American university had offered £80,000 to anyone who could prove conclusively that there was life after death and as yet the amount was still unclaimed had to have some significance. There was much evidence but still no substantial proof and, although he believed in the continuance of life after death *in some form*, he was still unsure there was a spirit world in the sense of latter- and present-day concepts. While he spoke, he saw the woman who had asked the final question of the lecture period sitting alone at the back of the hall. He wondered why she hadn't joined the group. Eventually, Bishop was able to disengage himself from his inquisitors, mumbling that he had some distance to travel that night and further questions could be asked during the course of the following lectures. Briefcase in hand, he strode briskly down the centre aisle towards the exit. The woman's eyes gazed at him fixedly and when he drew near, she rose from her seat. 'Could I talk to you for just a moment, Mr Bishop?'

He glanced down at his watch as though worried about a pending appointment. 'I really haven't the time now. Perhaps next week . . .?'

'My name is Jessica Kulek. My father, Jacob Kulek, is . . .'

'Is founder and president of the Research Institute of Parapsychological Study.' Bishop had stopped and was looking at the woman curiously as she made her way from her seat towards him.

'You've heard of him?' she said.

'Who in the field of psychical research hasn't? He was one of the men who helped Professor Dean to persuade the American Association for the Advancement of Science to finally accept parapsychologists as members. It was a giant step in forcing scientists throughout the world to take the paranormal seriously. It gave the whole business credibility.'

She gave him the briefest of smiles and he realized she was younger and more attractive than he had at first thought from a distance. Her hair, neither dark nor fair, was short and tucked in closely to the nape of her neck, her fringe cropped high and neatly across her forehead. The tweed suit she wore was stylishly cut and emphasized her slim figure, perhaps too much so – she seemed too slender, frail even. Her eyes were made to look larger by the thinness of her face and her lips were small but finely drawn, like a child's. She seemed hesitant, almost nervous now, yet he felt there was a determination about her that was belied by her appearance.

'I hope my comment didn't offend you,' she said, an earnestness in her expression.

'Hunting electrical impulses? No, I'm not offended. In a way you're right: I am hunting electrical impulses half the time. The other half is spent searching for draughts, land subsidence and water seepages.'

'Could we talk privately for a few moments? Are you staying here tonight? Perhaps your hotel?'

He grinned. 'I'm afraid my talks don't pay well enough for me to stay overnight in hotels. I'd have nothing left over from the evening's work if I did. No, I'll have to drive back home tonight.'

'It's really very important. My father asked me to see you.'

Bishop paused before answering. Finally, he said, 'Can you tell me what it's about?'

'Not here.'

He made up his mind. 'Okay. I'd intended to have a drink before I hit the road, so why not join me? We'd better make our exit fast, though, before the throng back there catches us up.' He pointed over his shoulder at the remaining group of chattering people who were gradually edging their way down the aisle. Bishop took her arm and guided her towards the door.

'You're a little cynical about your profession, aren't you?' she said as they descended the library steps, the cold night drizzle dampening their faces.

'Yes,' he answered brusquely.

'Can you tell me why?'

'Look, let's find a pub and get out of the rain. Then I'll answer your question.'

They walked for five minutes in silence before finding a welcoming pub sign. He led her inside and found a quiet corner table.

'What would you like?' he asked.

'Just orange juice, please.' There was a slight hostility in her tone.

He returned with the drinks, placing the orange juice on the table before her, sinking into the chair opposite with a grateful sigh. He took a long, satisfying swallow of beer before looking across at her.

'Are you involved in your father's research?' he asked.

'Yes, I work with him. You were going to answer my question.'

He was irritated by her persistence. 'Is it important? Has it anything to do with your father asking you to see me?'

'No, I'm just curious, that's all.'

'I'm not cynical about my job – I'm just cynical about the people I come in contact with. Most of them are either fools or publicity seekers. I don't know who are the worst.'

'But you have a good reputation as a psychic investigator. Your two books on the subject are standard reading for any student of the paranormal. How can you deride others who follow the same pursuits as yourself?'

'I don't. It's the fanatics, the idiots steeped in mumbo-jumbo mysticism, and the fools who turn the whole thing into a religion that I despise. The people they prey on, I just feel sorry for. If you've read my books you'll know they're directed towards realism and away from mysticism. For Christ's sake, I've just spent two hours talking about that very thing!'

She flinched at his raised voice and he immediately regretted his impatience. But she came back at him, her lips tight with her own suppressed anger.

'Then why don't you do something more constructive about it? The Society for Psychical Research and other organizations wanted you as a member. Your work could have been invaluable to them. As a ghost-hunter, as you like to call yourself, you're one of the foremost in your field, your services are in great demand. So why do you disassociate yourself from others in your profession, others who could help you?'

Bishop leaned back in his seat. 'You've been checking up on me,' he said simply.

'Yes, my father asked me to. I'm sorry, Mr Bishop, we didn't mean to pry. We just wanted to find out more about your background.'

'Isn't it time you told me why you came here tonight? What does Jacob Kulek want with me?'

'Your help.'

'My help? Jacob Kulek wants *my* help?'

The girl nodded and Bishop laughed aloud.

'I'm truly flattered, Miss Kulek, but I don't think there's much about psychic phenomena that I could tell your father.'

'He doesn't expect you to. It's a different kind of information he wants. I promise you, it's important.'

'Not important enough for him to come himself.'

She looked down into her glass. 'It's not easy for him nowadays. He would have come, but I convinced him I could persuade you to see him.'

'It's all right,' Bishop conceded. 'I realize he must be a busy man . . .'

'Oh no, it isn't that. He's blind, you see. I don't like him to travel unless it's absolutely necessary.'

'I didn't know. I'm sorry, Miss Kulek. I didn't mean to be so blunt. How long . . .?'

'Six years. Chronic glaucoma. The nerve structure was already severely damaged before they diagnosed the disease. He'd left it too late before consulting a specialist – he put his blurred vision down to old age and hard work. By the time they realized the real cause, the optic nerves were too far gone.' She sipped her orange juice, then looked at him defiantly. 'He still goes on lecture tours both here and in America and, as head of the Institute, with its growing membership, his days are even more active than before.'

'But if he knows I want nothing to do with organizations such as yours, what makes him think I'd want to help?'

'Because your thinking is not that much different from his. He was once an important member of the Society for Psychical Research until he felt their ideas were at variance with his own. He rejected them too, Mr Bishop, to form his own organization, the Research Institute of Parapsychological Study. He wanted to research phenomena such as telepathy and clairvoyance to find out if the mind can gain knowledge by means other than the normal perceptual processes. It has nothing to do with ghosts and goblins.'

'All right, so what information does he want from me?'

'He wants you to tell him exactly what you found in Beechwood.'

Bishop's face paled and he quickly reached for his beer. The girl watched him as he drained the glass.

'That was nearly a year ago,' he said, carefully placing the empty glass back on the table. 'I thought it had been forgotten by now.'

'The memory has been revived, Mr Bishop. Have you seen today's papers?'

'No, I've been travelling most of the day. I haven't had a chance to.'

She reached for her shoulder-bag which was propped up against a table leg and drew out a folded newspaper. Opening it, she pointed to the main news item on an inside page. He quickly scanned the bold headline: TRIPLE TRAGEDY IN HORROR ROAD.

He looked enquiringly at the girl.

'Willow Road, Mr Bishop. Where the Beechwood house is.' His eyes returned to the open newspaper, but she told him the details of the story herself.

'Two teenage brothers were blasted by a shotgun last

night while they slept. One died instantly, the other is now in hospital in a critical condition. His father is there with him, half his face blown away when he attacked the assailant. He is not expected to live. The madman who did it is in police custody but as yet no statement has been released.

'A fire, which started in the kitchen of a house nearby, burnt through the floor of the bedroom above. The two sleeping people, presumably husband and wife, fell through when the floor collapsed and were burnt to death. Firemen found a little girl in the garden outside watching the flames, petrified with shock. It's not yet known how the fire started.

'In another house, near the end of Willow Road, a woman knifed her common-law husband to death. She then cut her own throat. Their milkman apparently saw the bodies lying on the hall stairs through the glass front door. The report says the woman was in her nightclothes and the man was fully dressed as though he had just come home when she attacked him.'

She paused as if to let the related events sink in. 'All this in one night, Mr Bishop, and all in Willow Road.'

'But it can't have anything to do with the other business. Christ, that was a year ago!'

'Nine months to be exact.'

'So how can there be any connection?'

'My father believes there is. That's why he wants you to tell him everything about the day you went to Beechwood.'

Just the name made him feel uncomfortable. The memory was still too fresh in his mind, the terrible sight he'd witnessed inside the old house still firing his vision like a suddenly projected film slide. 'I told the police everything that happened that day, why I was there, who had hired me. Everything I saw. There's nothing new I can tell your father.'

'He thinks there might be. There has to be something,

some explanation. There has to be a reason for thirty-seven people committing mass suicide in one house. And *why* that house, Mr Bishop.'

He could only look down at his empty glass, suddenly feeling the need for something much stronger than beer.

3

Jacob Kulek was tall even though stooped, his head thrust forward as if in a constantly enquiring gesture. The ill-fitting suit he wore seemed to hang from his thin frame in draped folds, his shirt collar and tie joining loosely at the very base of his neck. He rose when his daughter showed Bishop into the small room he used as a private study at the Research Institute, the building itself almost anonymous in the medical and financial ghetto of Wimpole Street.

'Thank you for coming to see me, Mr Bishop,' he said, extending a hand.

Bishop was surprised at the firmness of his grip. A muted voice – he realized it was Jessica Kulek's – came from a pocket-size cassette-recorder lying on a low coffee table beside Kulek's easychair. The tall man reached down and switched off the machine, his fingers finding the stop button without fumbling.

'Jessica spends an hour each evening recording for me,' he explained, looking directly into Bishop's eyes as if scrutinizing him. It was hard to believe he could not see. 'New research information, business correspondence – general matters that fail to receive my attention during the day. Jessica unselfishly shares her vision with me.' He smiled at his daughter, instinctively knowing where she stood.

'Please seat yourself, Mr Bishop,' Jessica said, motioning

towards another easychair facing her father's across the coffee table. 'Would you like some coffee – tea?'

He shook his head. 'No, I'm fine, thanks.' As he sat, Bishop glanced around the room; nearly every inch of space on the walls was taken up by volumes of books. It seemed ironic that a man with a mind like Kulek's should surround himself with what must have been the greatest source of frustration imposed by his infirmity.

As if reading his thoughts, Kulek waved a hand generally towards the book-covered walls. 'I know every work in this room, Mr Bishop. Even its position on the shelves. *Masonic, Hermetic, Quabbalistic and Rosicrucian Symbolic Philosophy* – middle bookcase of right-hand wall, third shelf up, seventh or eighth book along. *The Golden Bough* – end bookcase by the door, top shelf, somewhere in the centre. Every book here is important to me, every one taken from those shelves many times before my blindness. It seems that without vision, the mind is more free to turn inwards, to examine more closely one's memory. There are compensations for everything.'

'Your blindness doesn't seem to have affected your work,' Bishop said.

Kulek gave a short laugh. 'I'm afraid it is a hindrance. There are so many new concepts, so many old theories abandoned – Jessica and our little machine have to keep me aware of the changes in thought. My legs are not as strong as they used to be, either. My trusty cane serves both as a guide and a crutch.' He patted the stout walking-stick leaning against the chair almost as though it were a pet animal. 'I have reluctantly cut down on my lecture tours at my daughter's insistence. She likes to have me where she can keep an eye on me.' He smiled reprovingly at his daughter and Bishop felt the closeness between them. The girl had seated herself in a high-backed chair near one of the two windows in the small study as if she were to be an observer only of the conversation about to take place.

'My father would work twenty-two hours a day if I allowed him,' she said. 'The other two he would spend talking about the next day's work.'

Kulek chuckled. 'She is probably right. However, Mr Bishop, to the matter at hand.' His forehead creased into deep lines of concern and his shoulders became even more stooped as he leaned forward. Again, Bishop had to remind himself of Kulek's blindness as his eyes bore into him.

'I believe Jessica showed you the news item on Willow Road last night.'

Bishop nodded, then remembered to voice his affirmation.

'And have you seen this morning's papers?'

'Yes. The man who shot the boys and their father apparently refuses to speak to anyone. The little girl whose parents – no, it turned out to be the mother and her boyfriend – died in the fire is still in a state of shock. The woman who knifed her lover committed suicide, of course, so it can only be assumed that the motive was jealousy or a dispute between them.'

'Ah yes, motive,' said Kulek. 'So it would seem the police have not established a clear motive for each case.'

'There wouldn't be one for all of them. Don't forget, the mother and her boyfriend were killed in the fire. The girl was lucky to get out alive. There's no mention of arson.'

Kulek was silent for a few moments, then he said, 'Don't you think it's rather strange for these three bizarre events to happen on the same night and in the same road?'

'Of course it is. It would be strange if two murders happened over the course of several years in the same road, let alone on the same night. But how could there possibly be a connection between them?'

'On the surface, I agree, there seems to be none other than the time and location. And, of course, the fact that mass self-destruction took place in that same place only months ago. Why were you asked to investigate Beechwood?'

The abruptness of the question startled Bishop. 'Mr Kulek, don't you think you should tell me why you're so interested in the events of Willow Road?'

Kulek smiled disarmingly. 'You're quite right, I have no right to question you without giving you some explanation. Let me just say I have reason to believe the incidents in Willow Road and the suicides of nine months ago have some connection. Have you heard of the name Boris Pryszlak?'

'Pryszlak? Yes, he was one of the men who killed himself in Beechwood. Wasn't he a scientist?'

'Scientist, industrialist – he was an unusual combination of both. He had two main interests in life: making money and the study of energy. A dedicated man in both pursuits. He was an innovator, Mr Bishop, and a man who could turn his scientific achievements into hard cash. A rare man indeed.'

Kulek paused, a curious, hard smile on his lips as if he had a mental picture of the man he spoke of and the memory was unpleasant. 'We met in England in 1946, just before the Communist regime was established in Poland, our homeland. We were refugees: we had realized what was about to happen to our ravaged country. Even then, I could not say he was the kind of man I would choose as a friend, but . . .' he shrugged his shoulders '. . . we were fellow countrymen and homeless. The situation itself formed our relationship.'

Bishop found it difficult to return Kulek's stare, for the sightless eyes were unwavering. He felt a little unnerved by them. He glanced across at the girl, and she smiled encouragingly, understanding his discomfort.

'One of the other factors that drew us together was our shared interest in the occult.'

Bishop's eyes quickly went back to Kulek. 'Pryszlak, a scientist, believed in the occult?'

'As I said, Mr Bishop, he was a most unusual man. We were friends for a few years – no, perhaps acquaintances would be a better word – then, because our ideas on so many matters differed, we went our separate ways. I settled in this country for a while, married Jessica's late mother, and eventually went to the United States where I joined the Philosophical Research Society under the leadership of Manly Palmer Hall. I heard nothing from or of Pryszlak during those years. Nothing, in fact, until after I returned to England ten years ago. He came to me with a man called Kirkhope and invited me to join their very private organization. I'm afraid I neither agreed with the direction in which their research was taking them, nor had any sympathy for it.'

'You said the other man's name was Kirkhope. Would that be Dominic Kirkhope?'

Kulek nodded. 'Yes, Mr Bishop. The man who used Beechwood for his occult activities.'

'You know Kirkhope was indirectly one of the reasons I went to the house?'

'I suspected it. His family hired you?'

'No, it was done entirely through the estate agents. Apparently Beechwood has been in the Kirkhope family for years, but never used by them. It was always rented out along with other properties they owned. It seems in the 1930s some strange practices went on there – the estate agents were not allowed to disclose exactly what kind of practices to me – and Dominic Kirkhope became involved. The goings-on were so bad that the Kirkhopes – Dominic's parents, that is – had the tenants forcibly removed. New families moved in but they never stayed long – they complained the house "wasn't right". Naturally, over the years the house gained a reputation for being haunted and eventually it just remained unoccupied. Because of Dominic Kirkhope's past association with Beechwood, it became a kind of bugbear to the family, a blemish on their good name. It was neglected for a long time, until just over a year ago they decided to try and rid themselves of the place once and for all. It was modernized, cleaned up, made presentable. But still it didn't sell. There were continuous reports of an "atmosphere". I think sheer desperation made them decide to hire a psychic investigator to try and root out the problem. That's where I came in.'

Kulek and his daughter were silent, waiting for Bishop to continue. They suddenly realized his reluctance to do so.

'I'm sorry,' Kulek said, 'I know the memory is unpleasant for you . . .'

'Unpleasant? My God, if you'd seen what they had done to each other in that house. The mutilation . . .'

'Perhaps we shouldn't have asked Mr Bishop to relive his terrible experience, Father,' Jessica said quietly from her position near the window.

'We must. It's important.'

Bishop was surprised at the sharpness in the old man's voice.

'I'm sorry, Mr Bishop, but it's vital that I know exactly what you found.'

'Dead bodies, that's *all* I found! Torn, cut, dismembered. They'd done things to each other that were sickening!'

'Yes, yes, but what else was there? What did you *feel*?'

'I felt bloody sick. What the hell do you think?'

'No, not within yourself. I meant what did you feel in the house? *Was there anything else there, Mr Bishop?*'

Bishop's mouth opened as if he were about to say something more, then it closed and he slumped back in his chair. Jessica rose and went to him; the old man leaned further forward in his seat, puzzlement on his face, not sure what had happened.

'Are you all right?' There was concern in Jessica's eyes as she touched Bishop's shoulder.

He looked at her, his face blank for a few moments, then recognition came filtering through. 'I'm sorry. I was trying to think back to that day, but my mind just seemed to close down. I don't remember what happened, how I got out.'

'You were found in the road outside the house,' Kulek said gently. 'You were lying half-collapsed against your car. Residents reported you to the police and when they arrived, you couldn't speak, you could only stare at Beechwood. That much I found in the official police report. At first they thought you were involved in some way, then your story checked out with the estate agent's. Have you no memory at all of what else happened in that house?'

'I got out, that's all I know.' Bishop pressed his fingers against his eyes as if to squeeze the memory from them. 'I've tried to think back over these past few months, but nothing happens; I see those grotesque corpses, nothing more. I don't even remember leaving the house.' He let out a deep breath, his face becoming more composed. Kulek seemed disappointed.

'Can you tell me now why this is of so much interest to you?' Bishop asked. 'Apart from Pryszlak being involved, I can't see why this business should involve you.'

'I'm not sure that I can be specific.' Kulek rose from his seat and surprised Bishop by walking to the window and gazing out as if he could see into the street beyond. He inclined his head towards the investigator and smiled. 'I'm sorry, my behaviour as a blind man must seem idiosyncratic to you. It's the rectangle of light from the window, you see. It's all my eyes can perceive. I'm afraid it attracts me rather like a moth to a flame.'

'Father, we do owe him an explanation of some kind,' the girl prompted.

'Yes, we do. But what can I really tell our friend? Would he understand my fears? Would he understand, or would he sneer?'

'I'd like the chance to do either,' Bishop said firmly.

'Very well.' Kulek's thin frame swung round to face Bishop. 'I mentioned earlier that Pryszlak wanted me to join his own organization, but that I did not approve of the direction in which his research was leading. I even tried to dissuade him and this man, Kirkhope, from continuing their dubious pursuits. They knew of my own beliefs relating to the psychic linkage between man and the collective unconscious; they thought I would ally myself with their particular cause.'

'But what were they looking for? What were their beliefs?'

'Evil, Mr Bishop. They believed in evil as a power in itself, a power derived from man alone.'

4

The two policemen began to wonder why they both felt so tense. Their night shift should have been an easy number for them; boring, but easy. The main duty that night was to keep an eye on the road, to report anything suspicious and let their presence be known to the residents by occasionally cruising the road's length in the Panda. Two hours so far, two hours of tedium. Yet their nervousness had grown by the minute.

'This is fucking ridiculous,' the slightly heavier of the two men finally said.

His companion looked across at him. 'What's that?' he asked.

'Sitting here all night just to keep the bleedin' neighbours happy.'

'S'pect they're a bit worried, Les.'

'Worried? Murder, manslaughter, bloody house burning down – all in one night? It'll be another hundred years before anything else happens down this road, mate. They've had their lot all in one night.'

'You can't blame them, though. I mean, it's not Coronation Street, is it?'

Les looked out of his side window in disgust. 'Bleedin' right it isn't.'

'We'll have another ride down there in a minute. Let's have a smoke first.'

They lit their cigarettes, hands curled round the match flame to cover the sudden flare. Les wound down his window a little to toss the match out, leaving the gap open so the smoke could escape. 'I dunno, Bob. What do you put it down to, then?' He drew in deeply on the cigarette.

'One of them things. Normal road, normal people – on the surface, anyway. Just happens sometimes. Something snaps.'

'Yeah, well it fuckin' snapped last year, didn't it? Thirty-seven people bumpin' themselves off? Nah, there's something wrong with this road, mate.'

Bob grinned at him in the dark. 'What, touch of the old supernatural? Leave it out, Les.'

'You can laugh,' Les said indignantly. 'Stands to reason something's not right down here, though. I mean, did you see the nutter who blasted those two kids and their old man? Right round the twist, he is. I had a look at him down the cells. Sittin' there like a fuckin' zombie. Won't do nothin' unless somebody makes him. He's an old poof, you know.'

'Eh?'

'Yeah, got a record. Been done a couple of times.'

'Well how come he had a gun, then? There's no way he'd have a licence, so where would he get a gun from?'

'Wasn't his gun, was it? It was the old man's, the bleedin' kids' father. That's the joke of it. This nutter, Burton, broke into the house and found the gun. I reckon he knew they had it. He found the cartridges, the lot. Even reloaded it to do the old man in after he'd got the boys. Then, so the sarge was sayin', he tried to turn it on himself. Barrel's too fuckin' long on a shotgun, though. Couldn't even part his hair with it. Bloody funny, tryin' to get it up his nose and he can't even get it past his forehead.'

'Yeah, bloody hilarious.' Bob sometimes wondered if his partner would have been happier as a villain.

There was a silence between them for a few moments and once again the feeling of unease began to build up.

'Come on,' said Bob abruptly, reaching forward to switch on the ignition, 'let's take a ride.'

'Hold it a minute.' Les had raised a hand and was peering intently through the windscreen.

'What's up?' Bob tried to see what his companion was looking at.

'Over there.' The bigger policeman pointed and Bob frowned in irritation.

'Where, Les? You're pointing at the whole bloody road.'

'No, it's nothing. I thought I saw something moving along the pavement, but it's only the street-lights flickering.'

'Must be, I can't see anyone. They should all be tucked up in bed, anyway, this time of night. Come on, we'll have a closer look just to be sure.'

The police car slowly crept away from the kerb and crawled quietly down the road. Bob flicked on his headlights. 'Might as well let anyone who's interested know we're here,' he said. 'They'll sleep more easily.'

They had travelled the length of the road three times before Les pointed again. 'Over there, Bob. There's somethin' movin' around in there.'

Bob brought the Panda to a smooth halt. 'But that's the house that had the fire the other night,' he said.

'Yeah, so why should anyone be in there now? I'm goin' to have a look.'

The burly policeman clambered from the car while his companion radioed in a brief message to their station. He reached back inside and grabbed the torch in the glove compartment. 'Bloody dark in there,' he muttered.

The gate was already open, but Les gave it a brisk kick as he went by; he sometimes liked to warn anyone who might be lurking in the shadows of his approach and give them the chance to get away – confrontations with villains wasn't one of his bigger joys in life. He stopped for a moment, giving Bob a chance to catch up, and shone the powerful torch towards the house. Although the damage to the front, apart from the empty, hollow-eyed windows, was not too bad, the building had a shattered, humbled look, no longer a home. He knew the worst of the damage was at the back, for the fire had started in the kitchen. He swung the light to the attached next-door house. They were bloody lucky, he thought. They could have gone up with this one.

'See anything, Les?' He glanced angrily towards Bob who had crept stealthily up the front path.

'Don't creep about like that, will you?' he whispered. 'Frightened the fuckin' life out of me.'

Bob grinned. 'Sorry,' he said in a pleased way.

'I thought I saw someone climbin' through a window when we were in the car. Might just have been a shadow from the headlights.'

'Let's have a look while we're here. Bloody stinks still, don't it? Is there anyone still next door?' Bob was moving towards the house and Les hurried to keep up with him.

'Yeah, I think so. Their place wasn't touched.'

Bob left the path and crossed the tiny front garden to reach the glassless downstairs window. 'Bring the torch over, Les. Shine it in.'

Les complied and they both peered into the shattered room beyond the window-frame. 'Bit of a mess,' Les observed.

Bob did not bother to agree. 'Come on, let's have a look inside.'

They walked back to the open front door and the bigger policeman shone the torch along the length of the hall.

'After you, Les.'

'It might not be safe. Those floorboards might have been burned through.'

'No, the carpet's only been scorched. The firemen got here before there was too much damage done to this part of the house. Go on, get in there.'

Les entered the house, gingerly testing each footstep as though expecting to go crashing through the floorboards at any moment. He was halfway down the corridor when a strange thing happened.

The broad, undefined circle of light at the end of the torch beam began to dim as though it had run into a thick blanket of smoke. Except there were no swirling eddies, no grey reflected light. It was as if the beam had met something solid, something that was devouring its brightness. Something dark.

Bob blinked rapidly. It had to be his imagination. There was a movement coming towards them, but there was no shape, no substance. The end wall seemed to be closing in on them. No, it had to be the torch batteries; they were dying, the light becoming dim. But there was still a bright beam along its length, only fading towards the very end.

Les was backing away into him, forcing him to go backwards too. Almost as one, they retreated down the narrow corridor towards the open front door, the torch beam growing shorter as they went until it reached no more than twelve feet ahead of them. Inexplicably, they were afraid to turn their backs on the approaching darkness, fearing that to do so would leave them vulnerable, unprotected.

They had reached the doorway when the torch beam grew strong again and began to force back the gloom. They felt as if an oppression had left them, a fear had been abruptly removed.

'What was it?' Bob said, his voice as well as his legs trembling.

'I don't know.' Les was leaning against the door-frame holding the torch in both hands to control the shaky beam. 'I couldn't make anything out. It was just like a bloody great black wall coming at us. I'll tell you something – I'm not going back in. Let's get some back-up down here.'

'Oh yeah. And tell them what? We got chased out by a shadow?'

The sudden scream made both men jump. Les dropped the torch and it clattered on to the doorstep, its beam dying instantly.

'Oh my Gawd, what was that?' the big policeman said, his legs growing even weaker.

The scream came again and this time both men realized it wasn't human.

'It's coming from next door,' Bob said, a brittleness in his voice. 'Come on!' He ran across the small garden and leapt over the low fence dividing the two properties. Les trundled after him. Bob was pounding on the door by the time the bigger policeman reached him. Inside they could hear a terrible, agonized howling, then another sharp scream sent a coldness running through them.

'Kick it in, Bob! Kick the door in.' Les was already standing back, bringing his foot up high and crashing it against the door lock. The small frosted-glass panel above the letterbox became illuminated and both men stood back in surprise. A faint buzzing noise came to their ears.

Bob thrust his face up to the letterbox and pushed open the flap. His body went rigid and Les could see his eyes widening in shock in the light shining through the letterbox.

'What is it, Bob? What's going on in there?' He had to push his partner aside when he got no reply. He bent down and stared through the rectangular opening. His thumb released the flap as if his own body were rebelling against the sight and refusing to let his eyes see any more. But the sight was already ingrained in his mind. The howling dog pushing its way along the corridor towards him, its back legs slithering frantically in the trail of blood it left behind. Its progress was slow, no more than a panic-stricken shuffle, for it had no front legs, just stumps oozing blood. Behind it, staring down and smiling, stood a man, in his hands a machine of some kind. A machine that whirred, its blades moving faster than the eye could see. He was walking towards the front door as the policeman's thumb had let the letterbox flap drop.

5

He was beneath the ocean, swimming downwards, deeper and deeper, away from the silvery light of the sea's calm surface, into the depths where it was dark, the blackness waiting for him, welcoming him. His lungs were bursting, the last bubble of air having escaped an eternity before, yet his body glowed in some strange ecstasy, the pain having no meaning as he reached for the sublimity waiting within that dark, cavernous womb. He entered and swiftly it closed around him, clawing at his limbs, clogging his orifices, choking him as he realized the deception. He gasped for air and the darkness filled him. He floated downwards, arms and legs no longer flailing, his body spinning in a tight circle, faster, faster. Deeper. Then the faint glow, the small shape growing larger, rising to meet him, black waters giving way to its progress. He recognized her face and tried to call her name, but the ocean smothered his cry. She smiled, eyes sparkling in her small, child's face, and reached for him, a plump little hand appearing from the gloom. She still smiled when the other face appeared by her side, her mother's face, the eyes wild, angry, the venom in them meant for him. They began to recede, to grow dim, and he called out for them not to leave him, to help him escape the terrible crushing darkness. They grew smaller, the girl still smiling, the woman's face becoming blank, her eyes lifeless; they disappeared, two tiny wavering flames extinguished, only the total blackness remaining. He screamed and the gurgling became a ringing sound which forced its way into the nightmare, drawing him out, dragging his bedraggled senses back to the surface and reality.

Bishop lay staring at the white ceiling, his body damp with perspiration. The telephone in the hall downstairs refused him time to think of the dream, its shrill cry insistent, demanding to be answered. He threw back the bedclothes and scooped up the dressing-gown lying on the floor by the bed. Slipping it on, he padded down the stairs to the hall, his mind still reeling from the nightmare. He had learned to control the memory, its harshness softened by constancy, but every so often it tore into him mercilessly, shattering the protective wall he had built around his emotions.

'Bishop,' he said into the receiver, his voice dull with fatigue.

'It's Jessica Kulek.'

'Hello, Jessica. Sorry I took so long . . .'

'There was another incident last night,' she interrupted.

His fingers curled tightly around the phone. 'Willow Road?'

'Yes. It's in the morning editions. Haven't you seen them yet?'

'What? Oh no. I've only just woken up. I had to drive back from Nottingham last night.'

'Can I come over and see you?'

'Look, I told you last week . . .'

'Please, Mr Bishop, we have to put a stop to this.'

'I don't see what we can do.'

'Just let me talk to you. Ten minutes of your time.'

'With your father?'

'He's at a conference this morning. I can come over right away.'

Bishop leaned against the wall and sighed. 'Okay. But I don't think I'll change my mind. Have you got my address?'

'Yes, I have. I'll be there in twenty minutes.'

He replaced the receiver and stared down at it, his hand still resting on the black surface. Snapping himself out of his brooding thoughts, he walked to the front door and pulled the newspaper from the letterbox. The headline sent the remaining nightmare fragments scurrying away.

He was washed, shaved, dressed and drinking coffee by the time he heard her car pull up outside.

'I'm sorry, it took a little longer than I thought,' she apologized when he opened the door. 'The traffic across the bridge was terrible.'

'That's the trouble with being south of the river. You wait till you try to get back.'

He showed her into the small sitting-room. 'Join me in breakfast – coffee?' he said.

'Black, one sugar.' She took off her fawn-coloured topcoat and draped it over the back of an armchair. The slim-legged jeans and loose crew-neck sweater she wore combined with her short hair and small breasts to make her look boyish.

'Take a seat. Be with you in a minute,' Bishop told her.

He went back into the kitchen and poured her a coffee, topping up his own. Her voice made him jump, for she had followed him out.

'You live here alone?'

He turned to see her in the doorway. 'Yes,' he answered.

'You're not married?' She seemed surprised.

'Yes, I'm married.'

'I'm sorry, I didn't mean to pry.'

'Lynn is ... away. Hospital.'

She seemed genuinely concerned. 'I hope she isn't ...'

'She's in a mental institution. Has been for three years.

Shall we go through into the sitting-room?' He picked up the two cups of coffee and waited for her to move from the door. She turned and led the way.

'I didn't know, Mr Bishop,' she said, seating herself and taking the coffee from him.

'It's all right, no reason why you should. And my name is Chris, by the way.'

She sipped her coffee and once again he was bemused by her. One minute she seemed tough, almost brittle, the next, young and timid. An unsettling mixture.

'Did you get a chance to see today's newspaper?' she asked.

'I read the headline, glanced at the story. "More Madness in Horror Road". I'm surprised the Residents Association doesn't take it up.'

'Please, Mr Bishop . . .'

'Chris.'

'Please, the situation is more serious than you think.'

'Okay, I shouldn't be flippant. I agree, a man cutting his sleeping wife's throat with an electric hedge-trimmer, then cutting the legs off his dog isn't a joke. Running out of cable before he could attack two policemen outside is mildly funny, though.'

'I'm glad you think so. You read he turned the machine on himself, didn't you? He severed the main artery in his thigh and died from loss of blood before they could get him to a hospital.'

Bishop nodded. 'Maybe that was his intention from the start, kill his wife, pet dog, then kill himself. He wanted to share his death wish with them.' Bishop held a hand up to ward off her protests. 'I'm not joking now. It's common enough for a suicide to take his loved ones with him.'

'Suicide or not, it was still an act of madness. And why did the other two kill themselves?'

'The other two?'

'The woman who killed her lover and the man who shot the two boys and their father.'

'But he didn't die.'

'He did, last night. My father and I went to the police station where he was being held – we hoped to be allowed to question him. He was dead when we arrived. He was left alone in a cell and he cracked his skull open against the wall. He ran at it, Mr Bishop. From one end to the other, a matter of only eight feet, but enough to split open his head. They said he must have run at the wall twice to cause such damage.'

Bishop winced at the thought. 'The girl. The little girl . . .?'

'They're keeping a very close watch on her. The police are now wondering about the cause of the fire; they seemed to think it may have been deliberately started.'

'Surely they don't imagine the kid set fire to her own home?'

'She has been under psychiatric care for some time.'

'You think that's the link? Everyone in Willow Road is going mad?'

'No, not at all. We've done some checking since we saw you last and discovered that the three people involved in last week's slayings . . .'

'There's no evidence against the child,' Bishop was quick to point out.

'I said the police think the fire may have been deliberately started. There were no electrical appliances switched on, no gas leaks, no fireplace in the kitchen, and they haven't as yet discovered any faulty wiring. What they are reasonably sure of is that the kitchen curtains went up first. A burned-out box of matches was found on the sill. They're now wondering just how the girl got out when the couple in the room next to hers couldn't. Maybe they're wrong in their suspicions, Mr Bishop ... Chris ... but the fact that she has needed psychiatric help in the past, that the fire was no accident, and that she got out completely unscathed – and unmarked by smoke – well, it all seems to point in her direction.'

Bishop sighed. 'Okay, so maybe she did cause the fire. What was your point?'

'The woman and the girl were mentally unstable. The woman tried to commit suicide six months ago. The man with the shotgun had been convicted for child molesting. He'd lost his job, had become a social outcast, and the neighbours say the two boys he shot had derided him. It could have been enough to tip him over the edge.'

'You're saying all three were mad?'

'Most people who kill have reached a point of madness. I'm saying something in Willow Road acted as a catalyst.'

'To make them insane?'

She shook her head. 'To direct their instability.'

'Towards murder.'

'Towards an evil act. I don't think it necessarily has to be murder.'

'And you think this is all tied up with the mass suicide last year?'

Jessica nodded. 'We believe there was a reason for the suicides. Pryszlak, Kirkhope and all those others had a motive.'

Bishop placed the coffee at his feet and stood up. Thrusting his hands deep into his pockets, he walked thoughtfully towards the fireplace. He gazed down at the empty grate for a few moments before turning to her again.

'It's all a bit fantastic, isn't it?' he said mildly. 'I mean, there can only ever be one basic reason for suicide. Escape. That's what it finally comes down to.'

'Release might be another word.'

'Well, yes, release. It's the same thing.'

'No, not quite. Escape means running away. Release is a freedom, something you can embrace. The thirty-seven people who killed themselves in Beechwood were not being persecuted in any way. Not one note was left from any of them to say why they were committing such an act and no individual reasons could be found. There had to be some point in their self-destruction.'

'And you and your father think the events of last week have something to do with it?'

'We're not certain. But we know of the ideals of Pryszlak and his sect. My father told you they wanted his help.'

'He told me they believed in the power of evil. I wasn't quite sure what he meant by "power".'

'He meant evil as a physical entity, a solid force. Something to be used as a weapon could be used. Pryszlak believed this not only as an occultist, but as a scientist, too. He endeavoured to use his knowledge of both to harness that power.'

'But he killed himself before he met with success.'

'I wish we could be sure of that.'

'Oh, come on. At least the man and his lunatic cronies are out of the way. If there is such a power – which I seriously doubt – none of them seems to be around to use it.'

'Unless their very deaths played some part in their search.'

Bishop looked at her in dismay. 'You're not being logical. What good would the knowledge be if they weren't around to use it?'

Jessica's face took on the determined look he had come to recognize. She reached down for her bag and drew out cigarettes. Her hand was trembling slightly when she lit one. She blew out a puff of smoke and regarded him coldly through the sudden haze. 'Then why these sudden acts of violence? Why this sudden madness, Mr Bishop?'

'Chris.'

'Why then?'

He shrugged. 'Who the hell knows? I'm not sure I even care.'

'You're a psychic researcher. You're supposed to have an interest in the paranormal.'

'Sure, but I like to keep my feet planted firmly on the ground. You're flying high.'

'When I first came to you, you seemed to express some respect for my father.'

'I respect his work and his opinions in many things.'

'Then why not in this?'

He turned away from her, resting an elbow on the mantelpiece, his other hand still tucked into a pocket. A small, framed face smiled up at him, the photograph taken when she was only four. A year before she died. Christ, he thought, the bitterness still strong enough to tighten the muscles in his chest, she would have been nearly thirteen now. Even then they could tell she would be the image of her mother.

'Chris?'

He shut the thoughts from his mind. 'It's too implausible, Jessica. And it's all speculation.'

'Isn't all investigation into the paranormal speculation to begin with? You said in your lecture the other night it was your belief that man's natural evolution was reaching the point of breakthrough, that science and parapsychology were converging to become one and the same thing. Is it beyond you to accept that a man like Pryszlak had already reached that point, had made the breakthrough? At least keep an open mind to it. Isn't that what you tell your students? Isn't that the whole point of your books – open-mindedness, with a little realistic scepticism?'

Jessica was on her feet now, her head jutting forward like her father's. 'Or are you too wrapped up in your own personal cynicism? Psychic research needs clear-minded people, Mr Bishop, not cynics, nor fanatics. People who are willing to accept facts and people who are willing to uncover those facts.'

She stabbed her cigarette towards him. 'You're a paid ghost-hunter. All right, we'll hire you. We'll pay for your services. We'll pay you to finish the job you started nine months ago. We want you to investigate that house in Willow Road. Maybe *you* can come up with an answer.'

6

Bishop brought the car to a halt, relishing the satisfying sound of crunching gravel. He looked out at the tall, red-bricked, Queen Anne building and said, 'Looks like she's worth a few bob.'

Jessica followed his gaze. 'The Kirkhopes are a great tradition in the shipping industry. At least, they were in the thirties and forties when Dominic Kirkhope's father was alive, but his offspring have had problems now that the shipping boom is over.'

'And she's all that's left?' He tucked his glasses into his breast pocket.

'Agnes Kirkhope is the last of the direct descendants. She and her brother took over when their father died, but, from what I can gather, Dominic played little part in the running of the business.'

'Do you think she'll talk about him? Families are generally reticent about their black sheep.'

'I suppose it depends on our questions. She may not like us digging too deep.'

'When the estate agents hired me to investigate Beechwood I asked to see the owners of the property, but they wouldn't let me. They felt it was unnecessary. In a strict sense they were right – but I usually like to know a house's history. I let it go then because it was just another routine job to me.

This time I want to know as much as possible before I set foot in there again.'

'First we have to get her permission to carry out another investigation.'

'Correction: an investigation. The last one wasn't even started.' He switched off the engine and reached for the door-handle on his side. Jessica placed a hand on his other arm.

'Chris,' she said. 'You really think this is for the best?'

He paused before opening the door wide. 'If we tell her the whole story she'll run a mile. Do you really think she'd want her brother's bizarre suicide dredged up again and, even worse, linked with these recent deaths? Let's stick to the story I told her over the phone. She was reluctant enough to see me anyway without giving her further cause for alarm.'

They walked across the drive towards the large main door which opened at their approach.

'Mr Bishop?' a plump, dark-skinned woman enquired.

'And Miss Kulek,' he replied. 'Miss Kirkhope is expecting us.'

The maid nodded, grinning in agreement. 'You come in, Miss Kirkhope is expecting you.'

She busily ushered them into a large, high-ceilinged room off the wide hallway. Pictures of sea-going vessels, from ancient clippers to modern liners, adorned the walls and several detailed models of ships were encased in glass cabi-nets at various points.

'You wait, please. Miss Kirkhope will be down. She is expecting you.'

The maid left the room, still grinning enthusiastically as though their presence had made her day worthwhile. Bishop ran his eyes around the room while Jessica took a seat on an old Chesterfield, its dark brown bulkiness enhancing the maritime surroundings.

'Business can't be that bad,' he mused.

'It isn't that bad, Mr Bishop, but it lacks the impetus of a few decades ago.'

Agnes Kirkhope's sudden appearance in the doorway startled them both.

'I'm sorry, I didn't mean to be rude,' Bishop apologized.

'That's quite all right, quite all right,' she said striding briskly into the room, her eyes alive with some private amusement. 'I must say this is my most impressive room, though. That's why I receive visitors here.'

She was a small woman, her body thin but ramrod straight, an alertness about her that defied the passage of years. Her hair was pure white but still had a wavy softness to it. She sat at the opposite end of the Chesterfield, her body at an angle so she could still face Jessica, and peered at them through tiny, gold-rimmed spectacles. There was still amusement in her eyes for the embarrassment she had caused Bishop when she spoke.

'I didn't expect two visitors.'

'No, I'm sorry, I should have said on the phone. This is Miss Kulek.'

The old lady smiled at Jessica. 'And *who* is Miss Kulek?'

'Jessica works for the Research Institute of Parapsychological Study.'

'Really.' Miss Kirkhope frowned. 'And what exactly is that?'

'We study the paranormal,' Jessica answered.

The old lady's frown increased. 'For any particular reason?'

Bishop grinned.

'To find out more about ourselves, Miss Kirkhope,' Jessica answered.

Miss Kirkhope sniffed as if to dismiss the subject. 'Can I offer you both a sherry? I like to indulge myself at least once a day. Anna! The sherry please!' The maid appeared as though she had been hovering outside the door waiting for the command. She beamed at them all.

'And I think the Cyprus,' Miss Kirkhope added, 'not the Spanish.'

Bishop and Jessica glanced at each other, sharing their own amusement at the slight. They restrained their smiles when the old lady turned her attention back to them.

'Now, Mr Bishop, you said on the telephone you would like to resume your investigation of Beechwood. Hasn't your dreadful experience last time put you off?'

'On the contrary,' Bishop lied, 'it's given me even more reason to investigate the property.'

'Why, exactly? And please do be seated.' She flapped a hand towards an armchair.

He sat on the edge of the seat, resting his forearms on his knees. 'There has to be some explanation as to why all those people killed themselves. There may well be some psychic forces at work in the house.'

'Really, Mr Bishop. The agents told me you were a most practical man despite your profession. You were hired originally to find more material reasons for Beechwood's disturbing atmosphere.'

'Yes, and I still hope to. But we can't just ignore what happened, we have to look for other . . . elements. That's why I'd like to take along Miss Kulek and her father, who is President of the Research Institute. They may discover more than I can on my own.'

The sherry arrived and was distributed by Anna who treated the amber liquid as if it was holy wine and left the room in a fluster of smiles.

'She's new,' Miss Kirkhope explained crisply. She raised her glass. 'Your very good health, my dears.'

They sipped their drinks, Bishop wincing at the sweetness.

'And what has suddenly encouraged you to resume your investigation, Mr Bishop? I wonder if the other recent happenings in Willow Road have rekindled your interest?'

He almost choked on his sherry.

'I ran my father's shipping business practically single-handed for years after his death with precious little help from dear brother Dominic.' She nodded towards a framed photograph standing on a nearby sideboard; the picture showed a pudgy-faced young man with curly black hair. The resemblance to Miss Kirkhope was minimal. 'True, we eventually went into decline, but that was the case of shipping in general, so please don't take me for a fool just because I'm an old woman. I follow the news and Willow Road is a name I'm hardly likely to forget.'

Jessica spoke up. 'We're very sorry, Miss Kirkhope, I hope we haven't offended you. Chris had no intention of going back to that house until I persuaded him.'

'If we're going to be frank, let's go all the way,' said Bishop. 'Jacob Kulek is hiring me to investigate Beechwood – that is, if I get your permission. We don't want to drag up old memories for you, but Jessica and her father feel there is a link between Beechwood and the recent deaths in Willow Road.'

'Do you feel there is?'

Bishop hesitated before he answered. 'No, I don't. But . . .' he looked across at Jessica '. . . I think it's worth looking into. Jacob Kulek is a renowned figure in his field of work, so any opinion he has on this subject has to be respected. He knew your brother, by the way, and a man named Pryszlak, who was a colleague of your brother's.' He saw the old woman flinch at the mention of Pryszlak's name.

'I warned Dominic about that man.' Her lips were a thin line. 'My brother was a fool, little more than a buffoon, but

Pryszlak was evil. I knew it as soon as I set eyes on him. A son of the Devil.'

Both Jessica and Bishop were astonished at the outburst. Just as suddenly, the tension left the old woman's body. She smiled at them, almost mischievously.

'I try not to let things bother me nowadays, my dears, but sometimes memories intrude. Now, assuming I gave you permission to enter Beechwood, what would your plan of action be?'

'You'd have no objections?' Bishop asked, surprised.

'I haven't said that yet,' came the curt reply.

'Well, first I'd like some background history on the house. I'd like to know about the activities that took place there in the 1930s. I'd like to know what your brother was involved in, Miss Kirkhope.'

'And if I decide not to give you any information?'

'Then as far as I'm concerned, the matter is ended. I won't investigate the house.'

Silence descended on the room. Bishop and Jessica studied Miss Kirkhope as she sipped her sherry thoughtfully. She stared down at the floor for a long time and there was a sadness in her voice when she finally spoke. 'Beechwood has been part of my family's history for many, many years. Dominic was born there, you know. An accident really. It was a country house for my parents, you see, built at a time when it really was open country in those parts, long, long before it became a residential area. My father sent my mother and me there for the weekend; he wanted her to rest. He was busy, so very busy, and Mother was seven months pregnant. He thought the change would be good for her.' She gave a bitter laugh. 'She had no rest that weekend. Dominic was premature; it was just like him to rush foolishly into the world before his time.'

Her eyes took on a faraway look as though she were studying an image in her mind. 'I was only seven at the time, and I was the one who found her at the foot of the cellar stairs. Why she went down there in the first place nobody ever found out. Mother certainly couldn't remember after the pain she suffered giving birth to Dominic. My God, how she screamed that night. I remember lying in bed listening, praying to God to let the baby die so it couldn't hurt Mother any more. She hadn't wanted to be moved, she would have had Dominic right there in the cellar if the servants hadn't ignored her pleas. I can still hear her screams of agony to this day as they dragged her up those steps. He came in the early hours of the following morning and I heard one of the servants say she wondered what all the earlier fuss was about because of the way he finally just plopped out on to the sheets.

'I don't think Mother ever really recovered from that dreadful night. She always seemed to be frail after that, always sickening for something or other. She loved Dominic, though. Oh how she doted on that boy! She would never go back to Beechwood after his birth, so Father began renting it out rather than let it go empty. It had become too modest for folk as grand as us, anyway! Our fortunes were rising rapidly, you see. I haven't seen the place myself since, had no wish to. But Dominic went back – he must have been twenty-five, twenty-six, I can't remember how old exactly. He was inspecting several properties we owned at that time, doing his duty as Father's son, you see. But Beechwood held some strange fascination for him; I suppose it was because he was born there.'

Miss Kirkhope paused to sip her sherry, then suddenly looked up at the other two occupants of the room as if remembering they were still present and that her reminiscences were for their benefit. 'That was the real turning-point for Dominic, I think. Up until then he had certainly been wayward, but that was only the robustness of youth. He returned many times to Beechwood and we naturally assumed he enjoyed the company of the people who occupied the house. There seemed to be no harm in it although my father did warn him it wasn't wise for landlords to become too friendly with their tenants. The area was becoming more populated then and Beechwood was soon surrounded by other properties; it was still an impressive house, perhaps not the most elegant, but firm, solid, a house that would last forever. Dominic became rather an elusive character – we never seemed to see much of him. It was only years later when the police informed my father that they had received complaints about the activities of Beechwood's occupants that we became alarmed. I think my father had already lost hope of Dominic following in his footsteps by that time and, in fact, I myself was fulfilling that role. I was, as they say, on the shelf – I don't know why, I don't think I was unattractive in those days; possibly the shipping business interested me more than men. I think it was a relief to my father that he had at least someone to rely on, someone he could trust to help him in his business ventures. I'm afraid Mother had become progressively more fragile over the years and, God bless her, she wasn't much use to anybody. She only seemed to come alive in Dominic's presence which, of course, wasn't very often. Mr Bishop, you've hardly touched your drink. Perhaps you'd like something stronger?'

'Uh, no, it's fine. Thanks.'

'Then perhaps you'd be kind enough to refill my glass. Miss Kulek, another for you?'

Jessica declined and Bishop took the thin glass from the old lady to the silver tray resting on a small, ornately carved table. As he poured he prompted Miss Kirkhope. 'What exactly was going on in Beechwood?'

Anxiety deepened the many lines already ingrained on the old woman's face. 'Some new kind of religious sect was using the house as their church – The Temple of the Golden Consciousness, I believe they called it. Something silly like that. There seemed to be so many ridiculous societies around in those days.' Her anxiety had given way to disdain.

'Unfortunately there still are,' Jessica said.

'Had your brother joined this religious sect, Miss Kirkhope?' Bishop asked as he handed her the sherry.

'Oh yes, he belonged to it. A full, practising member by that time. My father kept the more sordid details from my mother and me, but I gather sexual orgies played a large part in their worship. I suppose they could have got away with that but for the terrible row they made. The neighbours objected. Father cancelled the lease on Beechwood right away, of course, and ordered the tenants and their strange friends out. Dominic wouldn't come anywhere near us; he hid himself away somewhere. Suffering from shame, no doubt.'

'Who were these tenants?' Jessica asked gently.

'Oh, I can't remember their names, it was too long ago. A man and his wife or mistress – I can't be sure now. They must have been insane, anyway.'

'What makes you say that?' said Bishop.

'They refused to leave. Nothing odd in that, I know, but when they were informed they would be forcibly evicted, they took a rather extreme stand.'

'What did they do? Barricade themselves in?'

'No,' Miss Kirkhope replied mildly, 'they killed themselves.'

Bishop felt his muscles tense and he knew by the expression on Jessica's face she had been startled too.

'For some reason,' the old lady continued, 'nobody seemed to settle in Beechwood after that. Stories, silly rumours spread by neighbours, saw to it. People would move in, stay perhaps a few months, then leave. I think a year was the longest anyone ever stayed in that house. My mother died, my father's health became poor, and I became even more involved in his business activities, so Beechwood was rather lost in the background of things. We had agents who looked after our various properties and they rarely bothered us unless a specific problem arose. I must admit I didn't give much thought to Beechwood over the years.'

'What of your brother?' Jessica enquired. 'Did he ever return to the house? Apart from the . . . last time, that is.'

'I don't know. Possibly. Probably. As I said, Beechwood held a special fascination for him. The only time I had any real contact with Dominic after the earlier scandal was when Father died. Let me see, that would be . . . 1948. He came for his share of the inheritance. He gladly relinquished any rights in the family business, but was rather chagrined at being left out on the property. Father, rather wisely, left it all to me, you see. I remember my brother wanted to buy Beechwood from me, but I refused, having recalled what went on there in the past. Quite enraged, he was, like a naughty little boy who couldn't have his way.' She smiled but it was only a sad memory.

'I didn't see much of him after that, nor did I want to. I didn't like what he'd become.'

'What was that, Miss Kirkhope?'

She looked steadily at Bishop, the smile still on her face. 'That is my secret, Mr Bishop. I only heard stories from other people and I had no proof that they were true; but whether they were or not, I've no wish to discuss it.' Her thin, white hands curled around her glass, the fingers locking together. 'The house remained empty for many years, until I decided to put it on the market along with the other properties I owned. I was no longer able to carry on with the business in an efficient manner and I placed responsibility in more capable hands. I still have a nominal place on the board, but hardly any influence in how the company is run. I sold the properties at a time when the company needed a swift injection of ready cash, but the respite, I'm afraid, was only brief. Still, I'm comfortable enough. There's not much financially that can touch me in my last years. That's one of the nice things about old age – you have less of a future to worry about.'

'But you didn't sell Beechwood.'

'Couldn't, Mr Bishop, *couldn't*. That was the irony of it – the one property I wanted to be rid of, no one would buy!' She shook her head in amusement. 'The Kirkhope Folly you might call it. Or the Kirkhope Curse. I even went to the lengths of having it completely renovated, but still nobody wanted it. The agents blamed it on "bad atmosphere". Apparently it happens occasionally in the property market. That's why your services were called upon, Mr Bishop, to officially "cleanse" the house, if you like.'

'I told the agent at the time I was no exorcist.'

'Nor did you have any belief in ghosts as such. That was why they chose you in particular. The estate agents informed me that unexplained disturbances in a place could often be due to nothing more than an underground stream running beneath the house, land subsidence or even shrinkage.'

'A great many strange happenings can be explained by a detailed site examination, Miss Kirkhope. Rappings, doors opening for no reason, creaks, groans, sudden pools of water, cold spots – there's usually a logical explanation for them all.'

'Well, the agents felt sure you would uncover the cause.'

'Unfortunately, I didn't get the chance to.'

'No. But now you want another crack at it.'

He nodded. 'With your permission.'

'But your motives are not quite the same as Miss Kulek's and her father's.'

'No. Jacob Kulek and Jessica believe there is something sinister in Beechwood. I'd like to prove them wrong.'

'And I thought you were doing it for money,' Jessica said, the sarcasm heavy in her voice.

'There's that too.'

Agnes Kirkhope ignored the sudden antagonism between her visitors. 'Don't you think there has been enough publicity concerning Willow Road? Do you really think it's necessary to drag up the whole terrible affair of Beechwood again?'

'I told you earlier that Jacob Kulek's opinion is highly regarded in the field of psychical research. From what I know of him he's not a man to make rash judgements or speculate wildly. He thinks I may remember something more about the day I went to Beechwood. For my part, I'd just like to finish the job I started and, for reasons of my own, I'd like to prove him wrong about the house.'

'I promise you the investigation would be discreet,' Jessica said earnestly. 'We would report our findings to you before taking any other action.'

'And if you did, and I asked you not to take the matter any further, would you comply?'

'I can't say, Miss Kirkhope. That would depend.'

'On what you discovered?'

'Yes.'

With a loud sigh and a shrug of her shoulders, Agnes Kirkhope surprised them both again by saying, 'Very well. There's very little to interest an old woman like me nowadays. Perhaps this will throw some light into my rather dull life. I take it, then, that you will pay Mr Bishop's fee?'

'Yes, of course,' said Jessica.

'I think I would like to know why Dominic killed himself.'

'There's no way we'll find that out,' Bishop said quickly.

'Probably not. But perhaps I believe more in the mysteries of life than you do, Mr Bishop, despite your profession. We shall see.'

'Then we can go ahead?' asked Jessica.

'Yes, my dear, you can go ahead. There is just one thing.'

Bishop and Jessica leaned forward as one.

'You have a very short time in which to complete your investigation. In four days from now, Beechwood will be demolished.'

7

Night fell with little preamble and the residents of Willow Road nervously drew their curtains against it as if the darkness was a seeing thing. It was quiet out there now, the journalists and TV men having long since departed, their notebooks and cameras crammed with the opinions and fears of the road's inhabitants. Even the sightseers had left, finding nothing in the ordinary, rather drab, road to fuel their curiosity. Two constables strolled the pavements, up the left-hand side, down the right, conversing in low tones, their roving eyes studying each house they walked by. At the passing of every twenty minutes, one would speak into his small hand-radio, reporting back to their station that all was quiet. The street-lights were inadequate, the gloom between them somehow threatening, each entry the policemen made into the shadowed areas briefly and secretly considered first.

At No 9, Dennis Brewer switched on the television set, telling his wife to come away from the window where she stood peeking through the curtains. Their three children, a boy of six and a girl of seven sitting on the carpet in front of the television screen, an eleven-year-old boy struggling with his homework on the living-room table, stared curiously at their mother.

'Just checking to see if those policemen are still there,' she said, letting the curtains drop into their closed position.

'Nothing else is going to happen, Ellen,' her irritated husband said. 'Bloody hell, there's not much more that *can* happen.'

Ellen sat on the sofa beside him, her eyes on the over-colourful shapes on the screen. 'I don't know, it's not natural. I don't like this road any more, Dennis.'

'We've been through all that. There's nothing for us to worry about – all those other silly sods were round the twist. Thank God they've all been sorted out in one go, is what I say. Now we can have a bit of peace and quiet.'

'They can't all have been lunatics, Dennis. It doesn't make sense.'

'What does nowadays?' For a second his eyes flickered away from the screen to find the children watching them with rapt attention. 'Look what you've done,' he complained. 'You've frightened the kids.' Disguising his annoyance, he smiled reassuringly at them, then allowed his thoughts to return to the programme.

At No 18, Harry Skeates was just closing the front door behind him.

'Jill, I'm home!' he called out.

His wife came hurriedly from the kitchen. 'You're late,' she said and he was alarmed by her anxious tone.

'Yeah, had a drink with Geoff at the station. You all right?'

'Oh, I'm a bit nervous, I suppose.'

He kissed her on the cheek. 'There's nothing to be nervous about, silly. You've got the law walking up and down outside.'

She took his overcoat from him and hung it in a cupboard under the stairs. 'I'm okay when you're around. It's just when I'm on my own. This road's become a bit frightening.'

Harry laughed. 'Old Geoff was full of it. Wants to know who's going to be bumped off next.'

'It's not funny, Harry. I didn't know the others very well, but Mrs Rowlands was very nice the times I spoke to her.'

Harry shoved his dropped briefcase to the side of the hall with his foot and made his way into the kitchen. 'Yeah, what a way to go. Throat cut by a hedge-trimmer. He had to be potty, that bloke.'

Jill switched on the electric kettle. 'I didn't like him very much. I don't think she did either, the way she spoke about him. She said he hated her dog.'

'Well I don't like poodles much.'

'Yes, but to do that to the poor creature.'

'Forget about it now, love. It's all over and done with.'

'You said that last week.'

He shook his head. 'I know, but who'd have thought anything else would have happened after that? It's beyond all reason. Anyway, I'm sure that's the last of it. Let's have that cup of tea, eh?'

She turned away, reaching into the kitchen cabinet and wishing she felt as confident.

At No 27, the elderly man lay in his bed and spoke to the nurse in a quavery voice.

'Are they still there, Julie?'

The nurse re-drew the curtains and turned to look down at the old man. 'Yes, Benjamin, they've just passed by.'

'All the years I've lived here, we've never had to have police patrols before.'

She walked over to the bed, the table-lamp by its side casting her giant shadow against a corner of the room, creating a deep black void. 'Would you like some milk now?' she asked quietly.

He smiled up at her, his wizened old face parchment yellow in the poor light. 'Yes, I think so, just a little. You will sit with me tonight, won't you, Julie?'

She leaned over him, her full breasts pressing against the high-necked, starched dress she wore in place of a uniform, and straightened the bedclothes around his shoulders. 'Yes, of course I will. I promised, didn't I?'

'Yes, you promised.'

He reached for her plump, but firm hand. 'You're good to me, Julie,' he said.

She patted his hand, then tucked it back inside the blankets, rearranging them again around his frail old body.

'You will sit with me, won't you?' he said.

'I just told you I would,' she answered patiently.

He settled back into the bed, shuffling his shoulders more comfortably into the sheets. 'I think I'll have that hot milk now,' he sighed.

The nurse rose from the bed, tiny beads of perspiration glinting in the fine hairs above her upper lip. She crossed the room and quietly closed the door behind her.

At No 33, Felicity Kimble glared angrily at her father.

'But why can't I go out, Dad? It's not fair!'

'I told you, I don't want you out of the house tonight,' Jack Kimble said wearily. 'I don't want you stopping out late while all this business is going on.'

'But I'm fifteen, Dad. I'm old enough to look after myself.'

'Nobody's old enough to look after themselves these days. I'm not telling you again – you're not going out.'

'Mum!' she whined.

'Your dad's right, Felice,' her mother said in a softer voice than her husband's. 'You don't know what sort of people all these goings on have attracted to the neighbourhood.'

'But what could possibly happen? We've got the fuzz on the doorstep.'

'The police, Felice,' her mother corrected.

'Anyway, Jimmy can bring me home.'

'Yes,' her father said, rumpling his newspaper, 'and that's another reason for not going out.'

Felicity looked at them both, her mouth a tight line across her face. Without a further word, she marched from the room, 'accidentally' kicking over her younger brother's Lego tower as she went.

'Perhaps we should have let her go, Jack,' her mother said as she helped her wailing son reassemble the plastic bricks.

'Oh don't you start,' Jack said, dropping his newspaper on to his lap. 'She can go out as much as she likes when things quieten down a bit. Providing she comes home at a reasonable hour, that is.'

'It's not the same for kids today, Jack. They're more independent.'

'Too bloody independent, if you ask me.'

Upstairs in her room, Felicity flicked on the light and flounced on to her narrow bed. 'Silly old twits,' she said aloud. They treated her like a ten-year-old. She only wanted to go down the club for a couple of hours. Jimmy would be waiting. She'd had enough of it, treated like a kid at school, treated like a kid at home. She was a woman now! She looked down at her ample swellings to reassure herself she was. Satisfied, she turned over on the bed and thumped the pillow with a clenched fist. Bloody silly street, people bumping each other off all the time! She thought a little wistfully of the two brothers who had lived further down the road, both blasted by a shotgun; the younger of the two had been nice looking, she quite fancied him. Not that Dad had a good word to say about either of them. Still, they were both dead now, the younger one having died of his injuries only the day before. He and his father had died within minutes of each other. What a waste! Felicity jumped up from the bed and went to her portable cassette player. She rewound the tape already settled in its deck, then pressed the play button. A soft, slow number began, the kind she preferred, the rhythm emphasized rather than exaggerated. She moved in time with it, lost in the meaning of the words, her resentment towards her parents forgotten for the moment. Her movements led her unconsciously towards the window where her own reflection against the black backdrop made her stop. She pressed her face against the glass, cupping her hands between its surface and her eyes, providing a dark tunnel for her to see through. The two policemen passing below glanced up and continued walking. Felicity watched their progress for a few moments until they disappeared into shadow beyond the street-light. She drew the curtains, her expression thoughtful.

Across the road at No 32, Eric Channing grunted in disappointment. A rectangle of muted light was all he could see of the window opposite. The girl usually left her curtains half-drawn, seemingly unaware that she could be seen from the bedroom across the road. Eric had spent many lonely vigils in his bedroom over the past year, his wife downstairs imagining he was in the small room next door tinkering with his hand-built railway set. He knew Veronica felt his trains were a childish pastime for a man of thirty-eight but, as she often said in company, it kept him out of mischief. It had often been a tricky business, his eyes glued to the window, ears pinned to the stairs, listening for her footfalls. He would rush silently on to the landing as though he had just emerged from the loo when he heard the living-room door open. She would give him hell if she ever found out. He had often sat there for hours in the cold while the miniature train next door whirred round and round on its tireless journey, scrutinizing the ten to eighteen inches – depending on how wide she had left the curtains drawn – of bright light across the road, tensing at the flicker of movement, heart almost stopping when she came into view. On a bonus night, she would suddenly appear wearing only a bra and panties. Once, and only once, on a super-bonus night, she had taken off her bra in front of the window! Occasionally he wondered if she really was unconscious of the interest her lush young body caused, or whether she secretly knew he was crouching in the dark as she flaunted herself.

Eric sat there for another ten minutes, his face only inches away from the parted curtains, where the light from the street could not shine directly on to him. He knew from experience that tonight was a minus night: there would be nothing more to see. He would pop up now and again to make sure a gap hadn't appeared in his absence, but he felt certain the evening's performance was over. He had jumped back further into the shadows when she had suddenly appeared at the window. His heart pounding wildly, he realized she was only watching the two policemen below. They must have been the reason for her closing the curtains. Interfering bastards! He reluctantly tore his eyes from the window and slunk dolefully from the room. Sometimes he wished he was Clark Kent and had X-ray vision. Or the Invisible Man and then he could actually be in the room with her.

His wife looked away from the television screen and her knitting stopped momentarily when he opened the door. 'Not playing with your trains tonight, darling?' she said.

'No,' he replied mournfully, 'I'm not very interested tonight, dearest.'

In the street outside, the two policemen strolled in step with each other.

'Bleedin' cold tonight, Del,' one said, blowing into his gloved hands.

'Yeah, don't know why they didn't put another Panda on.'

'Can't waste a car on one street every night, can they? We haven't got enough to cover the whole patch anyway.'

'Plenny of helmets, though.'

'Eh?'

'Not enough patrol cars but plenny of helmets. I've had three new ones this year. Keep getting them dented at the matches.'

'Go on.'

'Every time I'm on duty. It's about time they slung those little bastards inside for a couple of weeks instead of lettin' them off with piddlin' fines.'

'Yeah, I used to enjoy the old football duty. So you've had three helmets then?'

'And a new radio. One of the bastards ran off with the last one. Crowd opened up in front of him like the partin' of the Red Sea. Soon came tumblin' down on top of me when I went after him, though.'

They walked on in silence for a few moments, their own unisoned footsteps a comfort to them in the quietness of the road.

'Yeah, plenny of 'em,' Del observed.

'What, helmets?'

'Yeah. Not enough recruits coming into the force, you see. Lots of helmets to go round. And radios.'

'Not enough patrol cars.'

'No. Not enough of them. Beats the old whistles.'

'What does?'

'Radios.'

'Oh yeah. Bit before my time, whistles, Del.'

'Yeah, s'pose it would be. Still handy to have them on us though. You never know when your radio's going to pack in.'

They walked in silence for a few steps. 'Too many, you know.'

'What, helmets?'

'No, you silly bastard. Soccer hooligans. Too many of them, not enough of us. We can't control 'em any more. There used to be just a few troublemakers at a match, now it's most of 'em. Too many for us to handle.'

'Yeah, nutters, the lot of 'em.'

'No, most just go along with the ringleaders. They get carried away with the atmosphere.'

'I know what I'd like to do with 'em.'

Del tutted. 'You're not allowed to, son. They're only victims of their environment.'

'Environment? I've never seen one of 'em with rickets yet. A bloody good hidin' would do 'em a lot of good.'

'Now, now, that's not the attitude. Mustn't upset our friendly neighbourhood social worker.'

The younger policeman's sneer of derision was hidden in the shadows as they passed beyond the feeble circle of light. He glanced to his left, squinting at the huge, detached building looming up from the general gloom.

'Gives me the creeps, that place,' he remarked.

'Yeah, I don't care for it much, either.'

'Another bunch of lunatics.'

Del nodded in agreement. 'This road seems to have its share.'

The younger policeman looked back down the road. 'I wonder whose turn it is tonight?'

Del grinned. 'No, it's due for a bit of peace and quiet, this road. It's had its share of troubles. I don't think there's any more murderers left in those houses.'

'Let's hope you're right,' the younger one said as they continued their watchful journey, the sound of their footsteps fading as they strolled beyond the house called Beechwood.

*

Julie poured the lukewarm milk into the cup, then drank a little to test it. She wouldn't mind if it burnt the old bastard's throat except it would mean a night of whining. And she wasn't sure she could stand much more of that.

Six years she had been with him: six years of fetching and carrying, nursing, placating, cleaning up his filth, and ... the other thing. How much longer could he last? When she had first arrived from the private nursing agency, she had expected him to survive for two or three more years at the most. But he had fooled her. Six years! The temptation to slip something into his soup or milk was almost irresistible, but she knew she had to be careful. The circumstances would be too suspicious. His Will would immediately point the finger of suspicion directly at her; there was no one else it could be pointed at. And no one else he could leave his money to. He wasn't wealthy, she knew, but he had enough to pay her salary all these years without any visible means of income, and he owned the property they lived in. Christ, when he went, she would turn it into a glorious house. Perhaps a small residential nursing-home for the elderly. It was certainly big enough. There were a few other similar properties in Willow Road – old Victorian houses that had seen better, grander days, but they, too, had become immersed in the general drabness around them. Yes, it would make a fine nursing-home. Just five or six old people, none with complicated illnesses – that would be too much trouble. And a small staff to do the work. No more skivvying for her! She would merely supervise the running of the place. How much money did the old man have? Her eyes glinted greedily in the dim kitchen light. He'd hinted often enough about his 'little nest egg' that he was saving just for her. She had tried to find out – surreptitiously, of course – just how much that 'little nest egg' amounted to, but the old fool would only grin slyly at her and touch a withered finger to his nose. Cunning old bastard.

She placed the mug of milk on a tray that already held his medicine bottle, spoon, and an assortment of pills. God, he would rattle if she ever picked him up and shook him – and that wouldn't be difficult to do with her size and him being nothing more than skin and bones. Half the pills he didn't really need, but they gave him the impression he was being looked after. They were harmless enough. How much longer, though? How much longer would the stubborn old fool live, and how much longer could she stand being around him? Patience, Julie, she told herself. It will be worth waiting for. Christ, she'd dance on his fucking grave, all right. Maybe the winter would finish him off. The mean old skinflint didn't believe in central heating and the single-bar electric fire he had in his room just about heated the piece of carpet in front of it. She had left his bedroom window open often enough when she went out shopping as well as creeping in to open it in the middle of the night when he was asleep, always closing it first thing the following morning before he woke. If he didn't catch pneumonia before this winter was out, then he was never going to die, he would go on forever. But she had to be careful: sometimes she thought he wasn't as senile as he pretended.

She carried the tray from the kitchen and began to climb the stairs to the bedroom. She almost missed her footing on the gloomy stairway, the milk slurping over on to the tray, and she silently cursed his meanness. The whole house was dismally lit because of his insistence on low wattage light bulbs. Even when one expired it was difficult to get his permission to buy a new one. He scrutinized every bill she presented him with, his whole body suddenly becoming alert, helplessness mysteriously disappearing; it was as though he suspected her of swindling him, that the weekly shopping bill was a concoction of her own making. Crafty old bugger! The only thing he didn't mind paying for was the medicines and pills she fed into him. He regarded this as the mortgage on his life.

Benjamin's rheumy old eyes watched her from over the top of the bedclothes as she entered the room. He pulled the blankets down under his chin and smiled toothlessly at her.

'Bless you, Julie,' he said as she used her broad rump to close the door behind her. 'You're a good girl.'

She brought the tray over to the bed and moved the lamp on the small bedside table back against the wall to make room for it. The shadows in the room adjusted themselves to the change.

'There now,' she said, sitting heavily on the side of the bed. 'Medicine first, then your pills. You can take them with your milk.'

'Help me sit up, Julie,' he said, putting on his weak voice.

Julie groaned inwardly, knowing full well he was capable of propping himself up. She stood and reached under his armpits, heaving his light frame into a sitting position, fluffing up the pillows behind him. He sat grinning at her, yellow, wrinkled and gummy. She turned her head away.

'Medicine,' he said.

She shook the bottle then poured some of its contents on to the spoon. Benjamin opened his mouth wide and she was reminded of a baby gannet waiting to have a worm dropped into its beak. Julie pushed the spoon in, resisting the urge to shove the whole thing down his scrawny throat, and he sucked noisily at the sticky liquid.

'One more, there's a good boy,' she forced herself to say.

He put on a childish mock grimace, then dropped open his lower jaw.

When he had swallowed the second dose, she scraped the spoon up his grizzled chin, shovelling the dribbles back into his mouth. The pills came next, delivered on to his glistening, wavering tongue like communion wafers, and washed down with the warm milk. She patted his mouth with a Kleenex tissue and he sank back down into the bed, his head still propped up by the pillows, a smile of contentment on his face.

'You promised to sit with me,' he said slyly.

She nodded, knowing what he meant. It was a small price to pay for the old bastard's money, she supposed wearily.

'You're good to me, Julie. All these years, you're the only one who's cared for me. You're all I've got in my last years, dear. But you won't be sorry, I promise you that, you won't be sorry. You'll be well taken care of when I pass on.'

She patted his hand. 'Now you mustn't talk like that. You've years ahead of you. You'll probably last me out.' She was only thirty-nine, so there was no bloody chance of that, she thought.

'You'll be well taken care of, Julie,' he repeated. 'Untie your hair, dear. You know how I love to see it.'

Julie reached up behind her head and with a few swift tugs, her lush, dark brown hair cascaded down on to her broad shoulders. It was long and when she tossed her head it fell beyond her shoulders to settle almost to the bottom of her back.

He reached up a trembling hand. 'Let me feel it, dear, I love to touch it.'

She leaned forward so her glistening mane was within reach. He ran a gnarled hand through it, relishing its rich texture. 'Beautiful,' he murmured. 'So thick, so strong. You really have been blessed, Julie.'

She smiled despite herself. Yes, her hair was her greatest attribute. She knew her body was heavy, although her well-rounded curves were not unattractive – Rubensesque would be a way to describe them; and her face, too, was a little plump, but then again, not unattractive. Her hair, though – as her drunken old father in Ireland used to tell her – was a 'gift from the gods'. She became coy, playing the game the way he liked it.

'Come on, Julie dear,' he said in mock pleading, 'let me see you.'

'You know I shouldn't, Benjamin.'

'There's no harm in it. Come on now,' he coaxed.

'It might overexcite your heart, Benjamin.' She hoped one day it would.

'My heart is already excited, dear. Won't you give me some reward for the reward I'll be leaving you.'

'I told you not to talk like that. Besides, my reward is taking care of you.'

'Then take care of me now, Julie dear.'

She stood, knowing he would become impatient if the game went on too long. Reaching behind her back, Julie unhooked the clasp at her neck, popping the descending buttons open so the stiff dress hung loose around her shoulders. She shrugged herself free of the top and stood there before him in a fake pose of modesty, her breasts hanging heavily inside her bra.

His mouth opened as he gazed up at her, the corners wet with saliva. He nodded his head in quick jerky movements, encouragement for her to go on. Julie undid the bow that secured her white nurse's apron to her waist, letting it fall to the floor. The rest of the dress was pushed, not without effort, over her hips, and the starched material crackled as she slid it down her legs. The elastic in her dark tights was tucked inside a deep crease around her middle and she dug her thumbs into her flesh to find it. Benjamin groaned when these were pulled from her firm legs and she stood over him, a mountain of white flesh contained only by bra and panties.

'Lovely,' he said, 'so very lovely.' His hands disappeared beneath the covers to scurry around in search of his shrunken member. 'The rest, Julie dear. Now the rest.'

She unhooked the bra, her great mounds spilling free and resting sullenly on the rise of her belly. The bra was dropped on to the pile of clothes at her feet and she ran her big hands over her breasts, squashing them flat and teasing the two pink buttons at their centres until they rose like blunted antennae. She allowed her fingers to run down her large expanse of tummy, hooking her thumbs into the top of her panties and slowly drawing them down over her thighs. He moaned aloud and craned his neck forward off the pillow to see her dark, bushy triangle more clearly.

Completely naked, she placed her hands on her hips and stood before him.

'Yes, yes, Julie. You know what to do now.'

She did. She danced.

Her gross shadow matched her movements around the room, sometimes stretching over the ceiling as she drew near to the lamp, hovering darkly over them both. She weaved and turned, crouched and leapt, flinging her arms high in the air, giving him the chance to see every inch of her fleshy body. She finished with a pirouette, crudely performed and grotesque to see, but he cried, 'Encore!' his eyes alight with the thrill.

Julie slumped breathlessly into a wicker chair standing in one shadowy corner of the room, the wooden struts uncomfortable under her bare skin. But this was where he liked her to sit for stage two of the game.

He watched her expectantly, waiting for her to catch her

breath, his own breathing sharp and fast with excitement. If only she knew the money was nearly all gone. Paying her for her services all these years had drained it; there was just enough to last another year, a year-and-a-half at the most, then there would be nothing left. But she had been worth it! By God, she had! He knew as soon as Julie had walked in the door that she would be the one. Everything about her had been sensual: her robust figure, the way she moved, those starchy, high-buttoned nursing frocks she wore. Even her voice with its bare traces of an Irish lilt. And when he had first seen the full glory of her wonderful hair flowing over her shoulders like a soft, umber waterfall! Bliss! She was the one! The others had done their job well enough, but they cared little for him and his needs. It hadn't taken long to convince Julie her future was with him and not with the nursing agency. Of course, a little deception had been necessary. But after all he had provided for her all these years. It was a shame it had to end, but the money he would get for the house would pay for his last years in a comfortable nursing-home. He would give her a couple of hundred pounds from the proceeds, maybe even three hundred; she had been very obliging. That should keep her happy! Oh yes, Julie, now, do it now!

Julie's legs were stretched wide and her hand was travelling down between her thighs. Her fingers cut a path through her triangle of hair and found the fleshy lips lurking beneath. She moaned, not just for his pleasure, but because her own passion was beginning to awaken. Self-abuse was her greatest pleasure nowadays. Men, on the rare occasions she had found one to smuggle in, were seldom strong enough for her demands. Her teeth bit down on to her lower lip and her face became moist with perspiration as her middle finger forced entry. Her hand moved in a soft, languid motion, but gradually the strokes increased in both speed and firmness as the muscles in her stomach tautened.

Benjamin's hand movements beneath the bedclothes had increased also, but to no avail. 'Julie,' he called out, 'over here now, please, over here.'

He blinked his eyes as her white, mountainous shape seemed to dim in the poor light. The bulb in the lamp must be dying, he thought, unless his vision was failing along with certain other parts of his tired old body. The shadows in the room became darker and he could hardly see her now, just the ends of her legs from the knees down sticking out of the black patch in the corner, her large feet jerking spasmodically.

'Julie! Please come into bed now,' he pleaded. 'I need you, my dear.'

Her great flabby shape emerged from the shadows and she padded over to the bed. He grinned in welcome as she threw the covers back, and held his limp member upright for her to see. She climbed in next to him and he shivered as her cold feet touched his legs.

'Good girl, Julie. That's my girl,' he murmured as she smothered his thin body with her own oozing flesh.

'Careful now,' he gasped as her weight bore down on him, forcing the air from his lungs. She rolled off and her hand grabbed down at him, brushing his own hands away. He winced at the rough treatment she gave his half-erect penis, pulling and kneading it as though to mould it into a firmer shape.

'Do be careful, Julie,' he complained, 'you're being rather rough.' He could feel her hot breath panting in his ear and his skinny old hands grabbed her wobbling breasts, squashing the two points together, holding them out for his gummy lips to close in on. He sucked at the nipples making baby-like gurgling sounds, then yelped as her arm went beneath him and pulled his body on top of hers with a great heave.

'Come on, you old bastard, give it to me,' she whispered.

'Julie, what . . .'

His words were cut off as she spread her legs and tried to put him into her. She had to stuff his flaccid organ in with her fingers and it was like dough being forced into an open purse. Her great hands clasped around his fleshless buttocks and she heaved him in, her own hips rising up from the bed to meet him.

'Julie!' he screamed. 'Stop this at once!' He felt as if his lower body was being crushed, his bones ground to powder.

'Come on, you old bastard! Fuck me!' Tears of frustration ran from the corners of Julie's eyes, running into her ears, filling the wells. She rose and pulled, writhed and jerked, but there was nothing of substance inside her. 'Fuck me!' she screamed, and the shadows closed in around them until there was a barely audible fizzing sound as the light bulb splattered into lifelessness and the darkness engulfed them like a black tide.

He was wailing now, hurt in the struggle, desperate to be free. But she would not release him. She held him against her with one hand, her knees rising up on either side of him, her ankles hooked over his reedlike legs. Locking him there. Her hand reached behind her lifted head, gathering up the hair that billowed out on to the pillow. She worked it into one long, thick length and wound it round his scrawny neck.

'Julie, what are you doing? Please stop this! I don't want to play any . . .'

His words were choked off as she began to pull on the hair, tightening it, using her other hand to hold the roots firmly against her head. She pulled harder, tighter, his face twisted to one side, his eyes wide in terror, his mouth spitting small white specks.

'All these years,' she hissed between clenched teeth. 'All these years . . .' Her tears were now because of her own pain, the roots screaming against her scalp. But still she pulled, his gurgling sounds music in her ears. 'All these years . . .'

The darkness in the room became even denser until there was not even light shining through the cracks of the curtains. She could not see anything at all in the blackness. She could only hear his gurgling chokes. And that was enough.

8

He sat in the car, watching the house, afraid. Although the engine was switched off, his hands were gripped tightly around the steering-wheel as though whether to stay or drive off was still unresolved in his mind. The sun was hidden behind troubled clouds this time and the windows were black and secretive. Beechwood was no longer an ordinary house.

Bishop drew in a deep breath and released the wheel, one hand whipping off his glasses and tossing them on to the passenger seat, then reaching back for his case. He strode briskly across the paved area, knowing if he hesitated any longer he would never enter the house. He knew his fear was irrational, but that did not make it any less real. The door opened as he mounted the steps and Jessica smiled down at him. As he drew nearer, he saw the smile was restrained; a nervousness was in her eyes. He understood that nervousness.

'We thought you might not come,' she said.

'You're paying me, remember?' he replied and instantly regretted his harshness.

Jessica looked away and closed the door behind him. 'They're waiting for you.' She pointed to the first door on his left, the one opposite the stairs. For a moment he couldn't move, almost expecting to see the legs still dangling over the stairway, the fallen shoe lying on its side beneath them. They were gone, of course, but the scuff marks on the wall remained.

He felt the gentle pressure of Jessica's hand on his arm and shook the thoughts from his mind. Almost. He walked down the gloomy corridor and entered the room she had indicated. A woman was waiting with Kulek and she rose as Bishop walked in.

'I'm glad you came, Chris,' Kulek said from the armchair he occupied, one hand curled around the top of his walking-stick. 'This is Mrs Edith Metlock. She is here to help.'

Bishop shook her hand and tried to remember where he had heard the name before. She was short and stout, almost matronly in appearance. Grey streaks broke up the blackness of her tightly curled hair and her cheeks bulged ruddily when she smiled. He realized she must have been rather beautiful in her younger days, but plumpness and time had concealed most of that beauty now. Like Jessica, her pale eyes held a nervousness in them. Her grip was firm but, despite the coldness of the room, the palm of her hand was moist.

'Please call me Edith,' she told Bishop, curiosity now mingled with her unease.

'In what way are you going to help . . .?' He stopped in mid-sentence. 'Edith Metlock. Yes, I thought I knew the name. You're a medium, aren't you?' He felt his anger rising.

'I'm a sensitive, yes.' She let go of his hand, recognizing the aggression, knowing the scepticism that would follow.

Bishop turned to Kulek. 'You didn't tell me. There's no need for this.'

'It was only decided at the last moment, Chris,' Kulek said placatingly. 'If the house is soon to be demolished, then we do not have too much time. Edith is here to observe. She will assist only if necessary.'

'How? By calling up the ghosts of the people who died here?'

'No, nothing like that. Edith will tell us of the atmosphere of the house, the feelings she receives. She will help you remember.'

'I thought we were going to investigate this house by more scientific means.'

'And so we shall. Edith will be an extra method of investigation if we fail with your, shall we say, more material approach.'

'But you still think there's something I've forgotten from my last visit here. What the hell makes you so sure?'

'I am not sure. But several moments have been lost to you. You found yourself outside the house without knowing how you got there.'

'It's not unusual when someone panics.'

'No, but we *are* talking of an unusual event.'

'May I interrupt?' Edith Metlock said, looking from one to the other. Without waiting for a reply, she asked Bishop: 'Why are you so afraid?'

'Afraid? What makes you say that?'

'Your whole manner, Mr Bishop. The uneasy way you entered this room . . .'

'My God, if you'd seen . . .'

'Your resistance to Jacob Kulek's efforts to discover the secret of this house . . .'

'That's nonsense . . .'

Bishop's protests faded and he stared down at the medium, his face grim. 'Yes, I object to your presence. I've heard you have an excellent reputation as a medium; unfortunately I can't have the same high regard for your kind.'

'My kind?' She smiled at him. 'I have heard of you also,

Mr Bishop. You have a reputation for taking great delight in exposing the mistakes of my "kind".'

'Not the mistakes, Mrs Metlock. I'd rather call them the deceptions.'

There was concern on Jacob Kulek's face. 'Chris, please. Edith is here at my invitation.'

She walked over to Kulek and patted his hand. 'That's all right, Jacob. Mr Bishop is entitled to his views. I'm sure he has his own reasons for his attitude. Perhaps he will tell us?'

'I think we've wasted enough time,' Bishop said angrily. 'By all means stay. But please don't try to interfere with my work here.'

Jessica came forward and stood beside the investigator. 'Chris is right. We *are* wasting time. Let's get on with this business, Father.'

'I'll stay out of your way, Mr Bishop,' Edith Metlock said. 'I'll keep to this room while you go about your investigation. If you should need me . . .'

'I won't. But maybe you can help me, Jessica?'

'Of course.'

'What do you intend to do, Chris?' enquired Kulek.

'First I want to take the temperature of each room. I don't know if any of you have noticed, but it's freezing in here, much colder than it is outside.'

'Yes,' said Jessica, 'it was the first thing I noticed when I came in. I thought it was just the fact that the house had been unoccupied for so long.'

'It probably is the reason. It'll be interesting to see if every room is the same, though.' He ignored the faint smile on the face of the medium. 'Miss Kirkhope's agent has managed to supply me with a geological map of the area as well as a two-and-a-half-inch scale survey map. One will tell us the type of soil the house is standing on and the general structure of the land around it; the other will show if there are any streams or wells near the property. Tunnels or underground streams beneath the house could cause the chill – or perhaps you would call it "atmosphere", Mrs Metlock.'

'I most certainly would,' the medium said, still smiling. 'I felt it immediately I entered. But I hope you do find some physical reason for it, Mr Bishop.'

'Then I want to test the structure of the house itself. No plans of the building are in existence, unfortunately, but I'll do my own survey. I want to know the materials used in its construction, test the walls for damp, look for shrinkage of any kind.'

'It seems you need a more practical knowledge for your work than just experience of the paranormal,' Kulek remarked.

'Practical knowledge outweighs any other as far as I'm concerned. I used to be a planning surveyor before I took up chasing ghosts, and I needed to know just how houses got themselves built for that.'

'And when you have done all this?' Kulek asked.

'Then I want to set up some equipment to be left here overnight.'

'Equipment?'

'I want to know if there's any activity in this place when it's supposedly empty. I intend to set up a camera connected to a tape-recorder, linked up to photo-electric cells and a sound and vibration detector. If anything moves or makes a noise in this house tonight, we'll know.'

'But you can only set this up in one room,' said Jessica.

Bishop nodded. 'This will be the room. For the others I'll have to rely on powder and black cotton. If we find traces of disturbance in any other room, we'll move the electrical equipment into there for the following night.'

'Have you considered staying overnight in Beechwood yourself?' It was the medium who posed the question.

'Sure. And my considered reply to myself was "no".'

'But I thought you didn't believe in ghosts.'

'I don't believe in being uncomfortable.' He turned to the girl. 'Jessica, I've brought along two thermometers, the greenhouse kind. It would save time if you tested one room while I did the same in another.'

'All right, shall we start down here?'

'No, upstairs. I want to get an idea of the general layout first. Jacob, do you want to come with us?'

'I'll stay and keep Edith company. I'm afraid I wouldn't be much help to you.' He smiled encouragingly at his daughter and Bishop.

Bishop picked up his case and told Jessica to follow him. He paused at the foot of the stairway, looking up into the sombre greyness of the landing above.

'I suppose there's no electricity?'

'No, we tested the lights when we came in,' Jessica said.

Bishop shrugged. 'I didn't really think there would be.'

He climbed the stairs, taking two at a time, his strides swift, leaving the girl hurrying to keep up. He stopped at the top and waited for her.

'That's where I found the first body,' he said, nodding towards the balustrade. 'It was hanging from there.' He saw her shiver.

'Did you come up here, to any of these rooms?'

'No. Just into the main room downstairs. That was enough.' He walked to the end of the landing and drew back the curtains. Light sprang in but made little progress along the hallway.

'Come on,' he called to her and she joined him at the foot of another staircase.

'Two upper floors,' he commented, reaching into his case and producing a torch. 'The principal bedrooms will be on this floor and upstairs will probably be what was once the servants' quarters. There's enough light to see by, but we'll need the torch for looking into cupboards and suchlike.'

His progress up the second staircase was slower and Jessica was able to keep close behind him. There were four doors on the landing above, all closed. Once again he walked to the window and drew back the curtains, a strong musty smell from the material irritating his nasal passages. The daylight revealed the hatchway in the ceiling and he flicked on the torch, shining its beam upwards.

'I'll have a look in the loft later,' he said.

Jessica tried the handle of the door nearest to her. It turned easily and she gave the door a gentle push. The small room was devoid of any furniture, the floorboards bare, dark with age. A tiny, iron-framed fireplace faced her. Bishop pushed past her and walked over to it, crouching and shining the torch up the chimney. He withdrew his head and said, 'Can't see too much. I can't tell if it's blocked or not.'

'Is it important?'

'I need to know where any draughts come from. Or if there are any birds nesting in the chimneys. Our feathered friends are often the cause of "ghostly flutterings".' He took a thermometer mounted on a thin block of wood from his case and looked around for a suitable peg to hang it on. He settled for resting it on top of the small mantelshelf above the fireplace, placing it in an upright position, top resting against the wall. Then he produced a ten-by-eight sketchbook and a felt-tipped pen. There were no curtains at the window, so the light was adequate for his purposes.

'I'm going to make a plan of each room,' he explained, 'then an overall plan of the house. I'll mark on it any draught points, holes that shouldn't be there, rotted floorboards and any structural alterations from the original building. You can help by looking for any signs of dampness.'

'Shall I start in here?'

'No, take this other thermometer into the next room. It'll save time if we move them on when we get a stable reading.'

Jessica took the instrument from him and left the room, stopping for a moment outside. Somehow there seemed to be less light in the hall than before. It was almost as if dusk were falling. That was silly, she told herself. It was still mid-morning. The clouds outside had become heavier, that was all. She moved along to the next door and twisted the handle.

It turned easily enough, but when she pushed against it, the door barely moved before meeting resistance. Jessica pushed harder and the door seemed to sink into something soft yet resilient. This time she put her shoulder to the door and gave it a short, sharp shove. It moved inwards about an inch. She put her eye to the gap, but it was too dark in the room to see anything clearly. Her gaze travelled down the crack and she could just make out the shape of something bulky lying across the bottom of the door. She dared not admit to herself what it might be.

'Chris,' she called out, keeping her voice steady. 'Could you come here for a minute, please?'

He came from the room and frowned when he saw the anxiety on her face. She pointed to the door.

'There's something blocking it.'

He tested the door, pulling it back then pushing against the unseen object. He felt the wood sink into something before meeting firm resistance. Jessica's features were not clear in the poor light, but he could see her eyes were wide.

'It feels like . . .' she said.

'A body? Don't let your imagination run away with you. It

could be anything.' Nevertheless, there was a prickling sensation around his scalp.

He gave the door a hard push using the weight of his whole body and it swung inwards six inches. 'Get the torch,' he told her and she quickly disappeared into the other room. He pushed again, keeping up the momentum of the swing, and the door opened wide, one foot, two, a slithering noise accompanying its movement. He took the torch from the girl and stepped halfway into the room, keeping the beam low. Jessica watched his back as he leaned forward and peered around the door. It seemed so dark beyond him.

He looked back at her, a broad grin on his face. A curled finger beckoned her, then he disappeared from view. As she slowly crept forward she could hear his footsteps crossing the floor, then the sound of material being swished back. Dull grey light filled the room.

Jessica stepped sideways through the gap and breathed out when she saw the rolled carpet lying at an angle across the floor, one end resting against the open door.

'This kind of house can make you imagine all sorts of things, Jessica,' Bishop said, one hand still on the heavy drapes he had just pulled back from the window. There was a softness in his voice that she didn't expect from him.

'I'm sorry, Chris. You're right about the house, though: it does stir the imagination. It's so gloomy in here.'

He drew nearer to her. 'The carpet must have been standing in the corner over there. Some disturbance – perhaps when the police were here last – made it topple and block the doorway.'

She managed a weak smile. 'I'll try not to be so shaky from now on.'

'Don't worry about it. It's happened to me in the past. I've come to learn there's generally a rational explanation.'

'And the times when there isn't?'

'That means I haven't been clever enough to discover it.'

Before he could snap up the barrier between them again, she reached for his arm. 'Tell me, Chris, why were you so angry when you found Edith Metlock here?' She saw the coldness flicker behind his eyes.

'It was a surprise to me. I think you're well aware of my feelings towards such people, yet you asked her here.'

'But she's a genuine sensitive. Her reputation is beyond reproach.'

'Is there such a thing as a genuine sensitive? I've no doubt she thinks she is and her belief in the spiritual world is quite sincere. But how much of it is real and how much comes from her own subconscious? I'm sure she is clairvoyant, but then again, couldn't that just be the power of her own mind?'

'It could be, I'll admit that. Whatever it is, it seems to work.'

He smiled at her and some of the antagonism between them melted.

'Look,' he said, 'I've been pretty rude to you and your father – not to mention Mrs Metlock. I'll try to keep my opinions to myself while this investigation is going on and I promise to keep an open mind to whatever we find providing you and your father do the same.'

'But we have.'

'No. Your father seems to be obsessed with this Pryszlak and his view could be clouded by what he knows of the man and his work.'

'My father is totally objective.'

'If he was, he would have brought in a headshrinker to help me remember those forgotten minutes, not a spiritualist.'

She realized he had a point and kept quiet.

His voice was gentle when he spoke. 'I'm sorry, I didn't

mean to bark at you again. I'm only trying to make it clear that there are two sides to this and I happen to be in a minority of one. If there is a connection between this house and all the recent killings in the road, then I'd like to find out what it is, too.'

'Let's work together, then, not against each other.'

'Agreed.'

She looked away from him and, for a moment, he felt she was flustered.

'Okay,' he said, 'set the thermometer up over there then let me know the reading on the other one before you move it on to the next room.'

They worked their way systematically through the upper floor of the house, recording the temperature of each room, checking for draughts and damp, Bishop making detailed drawings. They descended the stairs to the main bedrooms and followed the same routine. The rooms on that floor were much larger than those at the top of the house, but the low temperature seemed constant throughout: five degrees centigrade. The rooms themselves, although in good repair, had the musty smell of emptiness, the creeping decay of walls without the echoes of life.

Jessica stood alone in one room waiting to take an accurate reading from the thermometer she had placed in there moments before. She looked at the solitary bed, its bare springs somehow heightening the loneliness of the room. She wondered why they hadn't taken away the few remaining pieces of furniture and decided they probably meant nothing to Miss Kirkhope neither financially nor for sentimental reasons. When the house came down, then the contents would undoubtedly be crushed along with it. She moved to the window and watched the road below. An old woman shuffled by, not even giving Beechwood a passing glance. A cyclist came into view, his head down, scarf tight around his neck, pedalling steadily, vapour breaths dissolving fast in the cold air. An ordinary suburban street. Like millions of others. But behind certain walls, a difference.

Jessica turned from the window and crossed the room. She stooped to pick up the thermometer propped against a wall and her face creased into a look of consternation. The temperature had dropped from five degrees centigrade to below zero. Even as she watched, the mercury crept down, the movement slow but visible. When it had reached ten degrees below and was still sinking she placed it back in position and hastily went to the door.

'Chris!' she called out.

'In here.'

Jessica ran to the next room. He had his back to her, scribbling notes on to the sketch he had just made.

'Chris, the temperature next door is dropping rapidly. It's unbelievable. I can actually see it going down.' She was suddenly aware how cold she felt physically.

He turned in surprise, then strode towards the thermometer in that room. 'Christ, you're right,' she heard him say. 'It's below twelve in here.'

The scream made them both jump. It came from the rooms below, screeching its way up the staircase and echoing around the landing walls.

For a frozen instant, Jessica and Bishop stared at each other, then, as one, they raced towards the stairs. Bishop reached them first and as he descended he sensed a blurring before his eyes, shadows hanging like cobwebs in front of him. Jessica saw him sweep a hand before his face as though brushing aside invisible curtains. She followed close behind, but could see no obstruction.

Bishop almost stumbled halfway down, missing a step as

though avoiding something lying there. Jessica could see nothing.

He swung round the banister at the bottom of the stairs, then staggered against the opposite wall, a look of bewilderment on his face. Jessica reached him and held him steady. They ran onwards as another scream pierced through the suddenly cloying air and reached the room in which they had left Jacob and the woman. Bishop stopped in the doorway and collapsed on to his knees, his face draining of blood.

The room was filled with people. Their bodies, many naked, writhed and twisted in agony, features contorted as if they were screaming their pain, but no sounds coming from their lips. A woman, near enough to Bishop for him to reach out and touch, swayed unsteadily, her head swung back, beseeching the ceiling. Her blouse was open, the buttons torn away, heavy breasts thrusting the material apart. She wore no clothes from the waist down and her fleshy thighs trembled in some strange paroxysm. Her fingers were curled around a small glass and he could see the whiteness of her knuckles as she strained against it. The glass shattered and its few drops of liquid mingled with the sudden gush of blood from her cut hand. Bishop flinched as spots of blood spurted against his face and he pulled back when the woman fell. She landed in front of him, her back still heaving.

His eyes darted around the room, widening with each individual scene of horror. On the floor, not five feet away from him, three figures were locked in tight embrace, one on top of the other. Their naked bodies shook, but he could not tell whether it was from pain or ecstasy. He realized it was a woman underneath, her legs spread wide, arms scratching at the arms and backs of the two men above her. One had entered her and was moving his hips in unison with the man who clung to his back and who had entered him. The woman's face was pointed towards Bishop, but he could see her eyes were glazed as though heavily drugged. A heavy-set man lumbered towards them, his clothes open to display his genitals. Wild hair and beard almost obscured his face, but Bishop could see this one's eyes were sharp, obsessed. In his hand he held a long, pike-like object, its length black and tapering gradually to a fine point. He held the point against the back of the man uppermost in the tangled heap, pressing it slowly down until it punctured the skin and a tiny drop of blood oozed out. The naked man paid no heed to his injury, continuing to press into the man beneath him. The man with the pike reached upwards and closed both hands against the flat base of the weapon. Bishop opened his mouth to scream as he realized what was about to happen, but the cry stayed locked deep inside his chest. The bearded man plunged downwards and the long, black point sank from view, the pike descending into a fountain of red liquid, its length smoothly disappearing until the man's blood-stained hands were only inches away from his victim's flesh. All three bodies went rigid with shock, then continued trembling, this time the movements jerky, spasmodic, reaching separate crescendos before falling limp, unmoving. Bishop could see the bearded man laughing, but still no sound came to him.

A young girl, probably in her early twenties, struggled with two men on the room's worn settee which stood beneath the high, bow window. They held her wrists and legs. Her skirt was pulled up around her waist and a woman knelt before her, pushing something bulky between the girl's thighs. The girl looked down at the object, her eyes wide with pleading and Bishop saw the tape sealing her lips. She arched her body and the trapped end of the object rose with her. Bishop raised a hand towards them, but it was as though he was engulfed in a sticky fluid that hindered his movements, bearing down on him with a debilitating force. He saw the woman squeeze the twin triggers of the shotgun and closed his eyes when parts of the girl's body ruptured through her clothes. Even the shotgun blast was silent.

A hand touched his shoulder and he opened his eyes again. Jessica was standing over him, her lips moving.

A man stood behind the door, an insane grin on his face. Liquid drooled from the corner of his mouth and the glass he held slipped from his fingers, landing on the floor without breaking, rolling away from him, then back in a semi-circle. The man slid down the wall, still grinning, his lips only curling down in an expression of painful horror when he reached the floor. His back was stiff against the wall when he slowly toppled sideways, the action like the movement of a second hand against a clockface. His legs kicked out, once, twice, and his chin receded into his neck as his jaw opened to its fullest extent, not even relaxing when he was dead.

A group of men and women sat around the table at the far end of the room, their hands joined across its surface. They waited patiently while one man walked around behind them carefully slitting their throats with a butcher's knife as he went, each member holding on tightly to the hand of the dying man or woman next to them until forced to let go because of their own dying. Soon none of the hands was joined as the bodies lay slumped across the table or had slipped from their chairs. The man who had done the slaying calmly ran the knife across his own up-stretched throat, his chest becoming sodden and red as he sank back to his knees; he fell forward on to his face.

Bishop tried to rise, the girl, Jessica, tugging at his arm to help. A man was watching him from the armchair in which Jacob Kulek had been sitting. His face was thin, cheeks hollow, shadowy, and his eyes seemed to protrude

unnaturally from his skull as though he suffered from menin-
gitis. The lips were thin, unformed, the line of the mouth
curled at one end in an expression that could have been a
smile or a sneer. His hair was black but sparse, swept back
from his forehead, making the distance between his scant
eyebrows and hairline seem extraordinarily long. His elbows
rested on either arm of the chair, his hands raised steeple-
shaped before him, a small glass of clear liquid held at their
apex. His lips parted as though speaking, then he looked
away from Bishop towards a man and woman nearby. They
were coupled together, the woman holding the man's head
down between her thighs while he thrust himself into her
throat. They were frail with age, the skin hanging loosely
over prominent bones; their hair was white and brittle.

The mallet was wielded by the bearded man, who laughed
when the old man's skull cracked under the blow, his head
becoming wedged between his partner's skinny legs. The
bearded man knelt beside the aged couple and brought the
mallet down hard on the man's buttocks, the woman beneath
him suddenly struggling to free herself from his choking
member. She twisted her head to one side, but the force of
the blows pushed the man's pelvis against her, smothering
her, pinning her neck at an awkward angle. It was impossible
to know if she died from suffocation, a broken neck, or just
shock.

The bearded man was laughing gleefully as he rained
blows on the now still bodies. He stopped abruptly and looked
towards the man sitting in the armchair. The man was
speaking to him, but Bishop could not hear the words. The
bearded man shuffled on his knees towards the seated figure,
the mallet still grasped tightly in his hand. The glass of clear
liquid was offered to him and he took it, hesitated, looked
deep into the contents. Then he drank.

The sneer – or was it a grin? – on the seated man's face deepened and he looked towards Bishop once more. He picked up something that had been lying in his lap unnoticed by Bishop. It was heavy, black. A gun. The man took a long, sweeping look around the room, his bulging eyes finally coming back to rest on Bishop. His lips moved, then his mouth opened wide; the muzzle of the gun was pushed in, pointing high into the roof of his mouth. Everything around Bishop seemed to slow down, all movements losing speed, the struggles becoming graceful, a ballet of death. It took a lifetime for the man's finger to slide around the trigger and pull it back tight against the guard, the recoil blurred but still slow, the flame lighting up the inside of his mouth so that Bishop saw the hole appear, could almost follow the bullet's path as it travelled through the man's head, erupting on the other side, carrying bits of brain, mucus, blood, into the air to shatter high against the wall behind leaving a red smear of dripping substance.

Bishop stared at the running pattern and traced a trail of slow-moving blood back to the man below. But it was not the same man. The eyes still bulged, still stood out from their sockets, but it was fear that made them so. Fear of the unseen, sensed only, for the eyes were sightless. It was Kulek who now sat in the chair.

He was calling out and the sounds came creeping through to Bishop. It was as though Kulek was at the end of a long, winding tunnel and was drawing near, his voice becoming louder and louder at his approach. The figures around Bishop became misty, ethereal, their twisting and writhing becoming even slower until they were still; and as they faded, so another body became clearer, more defined. Edith Metlock lay slumped against the wall, eyes closed, head hanging limply sideways. Kulek's cries came fully to Bishop's ears and with them he found the strength to raise himself, staggering back against Jessica who tried to support him.

He whirled around and she fell to one side, gasping sharply as she went down on one knee. Bishop had to get out, had to get away from the house and the terrible thing that had happened there. That was still happening.

He fell against the door-frame, his body swinging round at the impact so his eyes were looking down into the far end of the hall. There were more moving shapes, fading, slowly dissolving, their bodies grey in the dim light. He pulled himself upright and cried out, 'No!' when he saw the legs hanging above the stairway. They kicked out wildly, scuffing the wall, a shoe falling loose and rolling down several stairs before coming to rest. Dismembered hands clutched at the fading legs, tugging at them, pulling them downwards till they no longer kicked. The hands faded away and only a dim twitching outline of the limbs remained.

Bishop had to get away from the house. He knew the slaughter was going on all over; in the bedrooms upstairs; in the rooms on the second floor. He had to get out. He began to run towards the front door, his legs leaden, his breath drawn in short, sharp gasps. The door beneath the stairway was ajar, a long, narrow gap beckoning to him.

He stopped running and pushed his back against the opposite wall as he had once before. And, like before, the door seemed to be moving outwards as if someone were pushing it from the other side. He found he was reaching forward in repeat motion, his fingers clutching the door's edge, afraid to look, but compelled to, something down in that cellar commanding him to. He pulled the small door back and it swung wide, the blackness lurking behind it shuddering and falling away at the sudden light, dim though it was.

He heard a movement. A shifting sound. Something on the stairs below. He had to see. Had to.

He approached the open doorway and looked down into the bowels of the house. The darkness at the bottom of the stairs seemed solid, a brooding night that invited him below, a living blackness that waited to devour. And from the blackness a shape began to emerge.

Bishop could not move. Even when the shape grew larger as it mounted the steps and the strange murmuring came to his ears he stood mesmerized. Even when he could see the wild-staring eyes, the long, dark hair hanging forward almost to her waist, the flow broken by huge bare breasts like boulders in a fast-flowing stream. Even when she was near the top step and curling her hair in big hands, stretching it taut across her chest like a thick rope, the words becoming clearer now as she repeated over and over again, 'All these years . . . all these years . . .'

The woman was real, not a spectral shape like the others. As she emerged from the shadows he saw her body had substance and seemed to grow in its firmness rather than fade. And her murmuring, almost an incantation, told him she was not one of those already dead. He backed away, the deranged look on her face as frightening as the visions he had just witnessed. She stopped before him, her hands constantly twisting and turning the thick cord of hair stretched between them. Her big body was shivering, her plumpness no protection against the seeping coldness of the house. Her eyes rolled away from him, searching for something, and she suddenly wheeled away, shuffling down the corridor towards the room he had just left. Bishop slumped against the wall, his forehead beaded with perspiration that turned icy as soon as it escaped from his pores.

Jessica stood in the doorway of the room and held up her arms to ward off the lumbering woman, but she was grabbed roughly and pushed aside, the woman screaming in rage at the feeble obstruction. Jessica fell heavily and for a moment appeared dazed. Bishop could only watch helplessly as the big woman disappeared into the room and he felt a new dread when Jessica uttered a cry of alarm.

She turned her face towards him, pleading in her eyes. 'Help him, please help him!'

He wanted to run in the opposite direction, wanted to be free of the terrible house, away from the horrors that dwelt inside; but her pleas held him there and would not release him from the madness. He stumbled towards her.

Bishop tried to pull the girl to her feet, but she pushed his hands away and pointed into the room. 'Stop her! Help him, Chris!'

The woman was standing behind Jessica's father, leaning over him, her long dark hair curled around his neck. Her knuckles were white as she pulled in opposite directions.

Kulek's face was flushed red, his sightless eyes straining at their sockets, his tongue unwillingly beginning to protrude from his gaping mouth. A rasping, hissing sound came from his throat as the walls of his trachea were squeezed together. His thin hands were wrapped around the woman's wrists in an effort to pull them apart. Bishop ran forward and grabbed her arms.

It was hopeless; she was too strong, her grip too secure.

The old man's body was arched in the seat and he began to slide forward on to the floor, but the woman maintained her hold on him, keeping him from collapsing completely. Bishop knew he was failing, that Kulek would not survive much longer. His grip on the woman's arms was only relieving the pressure slightly, only prolonging the blind man's agony. Jessica had joined in the struggle now and was tugging at the naked woman, trying to pull her away from her father. But the woman had the strength of the obsessed.

In desperation, Bishop released his hold on the woman, stepped swiftly around to the back of the armchair and kicked her sturdy legs away from under her. She fell almost to her knees, supported by the grip she had on Kulek's throat. Bishop kicked out again, the tip of his shoe sinking into the fleshy side of the woman's stomach. She screamed with the sudden pain, her head swivelling towards Bishop, still keeping the pressure on the blind man's neck. Bishop drew a clenched fist back, then swung it with as much force as possible at the round, upturned face. He felt the small bones of her nose shatter under the impact and her lower face was instantly covered in running blood. Still she would not let go.

He hit her again, again, again. And finally her fingers uncurled, releasing the thick rope of hair. She sank to the floor, swaying there on hands and knees, groaning, shaking her gross body as if to shrug off the pain. Jessica ran to her father who was now lying on the floor on the other side of the chair, gasping for air. The injured woman began crawling forward around the armchair and, for a moment, Bishop thought she was trying to reach Kulek again. But she went by, heading for the open doorway, her movements slow, yet determined. He tried to stop her, grabbing her flowing hair and yanking backwards. She half-turned, sweeping a sturdy arm back and knocking him sideways. Her strength frightened him: from her build, he guessed she was a powerful woman, and now her insanity was increasing that strength. She was halfway out the door when he lunged for her ankle, grabbing it and pulling her back. He was in an awkward position, his body stretched out on the floor, elbows supporting him, face exposed to the sudden kick she dealt him with her free foot.

The blow stunned him and he rolled on to his side, his hand releasing her and going to his head. She began crawling forward again and was soon completely through the doorway and disappearing down the hall. Suddenly he knew where she was making for. And he knew he had to stop her.

But before he could move, a figure had dashed past him into the hall. He pushed himself up and staggered through just in time to see Jessica raise Jacob Kulek's stout walking-stick above her head and bring it crashing down against the crawling woman's head. The sharp crack made Bishop wince, but he was relieved to see the woman collapse into a motionless heap, one arm stretched out towards the open cellar doorway. The darkness there was suddenly obliterated as the door was kicked shut. Jessica leaned against the stairway, the weapon she had used against the woman falling from limp fingers and clattering to the floor. Her eyes met Bishop's and for several moments they could only stare at each other.

9

All three looked up expectantly when Bishop entered Kulek's private study at the Research Institute.

'Is it Chris?' the old man asked, his head craning forward.

'Yes, Father,' Jessica answered, smiling hesitantly at Bishop, unsure of his grim expression.

'What happened? Are the police still at the house?' Kulek asked.

'They've left a guard outside, that's all.' Bishop sank wearily into a hard-backed chair and rubbed his face with both hands as if to relieve the tension there. He looked across at Edith Metlock. 'Are you all right?'

'Yes, Mr Bishop,' she replied. 'Exhausted but not harmed in any way.'

'You, Jacob?'

'Yes, yes, Chris,' the blind man said a little impatiently. 'My neck feels somewhat tender, but my doctor says nothing was damaged. Some bruising, that's all. Do they know who the woman was?'

The memory of her being carried from the house on a stretcher, her body covered by a thick red blanket, only her face showing, the wide, blank eyes, the constantly moving lips, made Bishop shudder inwardly. Her hair had cascaded over the side of the stretcher, enhancing the madness in her features. Beneath the blanket, heavy straps kept her pinned down.

'A neighbour recognized her when she was taken to the ambulance,' he said. 'She was a nurse or housekeeper to an old man who lived further down the road.'

'But how did she get into Beechwood?'

'The police found a broken window at the back. She must have got in that way. A couple of them went off to see the old man while I was being questioned. Apparently the front door was wide open – it didn't take them long to find the old man's body.'

'He was dead?'

'Strangled.'

'With her hair?'

Bishop shook his head. 'They don't know yet. And from the look of her, it'll be a long time before she answers any questions.'

'If she killed the old man in the same manner she tried to kill me, they'll find strands of hair embedded in his throat.'

'Lilith,' Edith Metlock said quietly.

Kulek turned towards her and smiled kindly. 'I don't think so, Edith, not in this case. Just a demented woman.'

Bishop looked at Kulek in puzzlement. 'Who the hell is Lilith?'

'Lilith was an ancient demon,' Kulek said, the smile on his face implying that his words should not be taken too seriously. 'Some say she was the first woman, before Eve, joined back to back with Adam. They quarrelled constantly and, using a cabbalistic charm, she acquired wings and separation from Adam. She flew away.'

Bishop's voice was cold. 'And what has that got to do with this madwoman?'

'Nothing. Nothing at all. Edith was merely comparing their method of slaying. Lilith also used her long hair to strangle her victims, you see.'

Bishop shook his head in exasperation. 'I think this whole business is bizarre enough without dragging mythical demons into it.'

'I quite agree,' Kulek said. 'It was only an observation on Edith's part. Now please tell us what happened back at the house.'

'They ran me through the mill after they let you go. They were very curious to know exactly what we were doing there.'

'No, all that is not important. I had already informed the local police station that we would be there today with Miss Kirkhope's permission. All they needed to do was check.'

'They did that, all right. But they still wanted to know what a naked madwoman was doing in Beechwood. Finding the dead man in the other house didn't improve their disposition towards me.'

'I'm sure you explained everything adequately . . .'

'I tried to, but they'll be calling on you later. It was only because you – and Mrs Metlock – obviously needed medical attention that they let Jessica take you both away.'

'Chris, the house . . . what did you see?' Kulek's impatience was growing.

Bishop looked around in wonder at the other occupants of the study. 'I saw the same as Jessica and Mrs Metlock,' he said to Kulek.

'I saw nothing, Chris,' Jessica said. She was standing by the window behind her father's desk.

'Nor I, Mr Bishop,' said the medium. 'I . . . blacked out.'

'But that's crazy! You were both there in the room.'

Jessica spoke. 'I heard Edith scream, and I followed you downstairs. I tried to help you when you collapsed in the room. I knew you were seeing something – you were terrified – but, believe me, I couldn't see anything. I wish to God I had. All I know is that you seemed to be having some kind of fit, then you rushed from the room and made for the cellar. I saw the woman come from there – she was real enough.'

Bishop's head swung towards the medium. 'As a sensitive you must have had the same vision.'

'I think I may have caused the vision,' Edith Metlock said calmly. 'You see, I believe I was used by them.'

'You called up the dead?'

'No, I was receptive to them, that's all. They manifested themselves through me.'

Bishop shook his head. 'That's fine if you believe in ghosts.'

'What would you call them?'

'Vibrations. Electro-magnetic images. Jacob knows my theory on such phenomena. An electro-cardiograph shows the heart giving off electrical impulses; I believe someone under stress does the same. And those impulses are picked up later by someone like you, someone sensitive to such impulses.'

'But you saw them, not me.'

'Telepathy. You were the receiver; you transmitted those visions to me.'

Jessica cut in. 'Then why weren't Edith's thoughts transmitted to me? Why didn't I see them?'

'And why not me?' Kulek said. 'If they were only telepathic thoughts from Edith, then why didn't I see them in my mind's eye?'

'And why were you so afraid?' Jessica put in.

'Maybe I didn't actually see anything at all.' They all looked quizzically at Bishop. 'It could be that I just remembered what I'd seen before in that house. Mrs Metlock may have triggered off something in my subconscious, something so horrible I'd been trying to keep it from myself. And if any of you had experienced it, you'd have been afraid.'

'And the woman?' said Jessica. 'Why was she in the house?'

'She was hiding, for God's sake! She'd killed the old man. She knew Beechwood was empty, so she hid there.'

'But why did she try to kill my father? Why not you? Me?'

'Perhaps she just hates men of your father's age,' Bishop said in frustration. 'Men like her own employer.'

'She went straight to him. She hadn't even seen Jacob, but she went past us both to get to him.'

'She could have heard his voice from the cellar.'

'Yes, the cellar, Chris. You felt it too, didn't you?'

'Felt what?'

'Felt there was something evil in that cellar.'

Bishop rubbed a hand across his eyes. 'I just don't know. It all seems so insane now.'

'Chris, you still haven't told us what you saw or what, as you would have it, you remembered,' Kulek said quietly.

Angry though she was over the investigator's refusal to accept the reality of what had happened inside Beechwood, Jessica wanted to comfort him when his face became pale.

It was seconds before he spoke, and the words came out dull and flat as if he were deliberately holding back his emotions, afraid he would lose control of them. He described the scene at Beechwood, the mad, perverted suicides, the cruel slayings. Jessica felt the muscles inside her stomach knot into a tight ball. When he had finished, there was a heavy silence in the room. Jacob Kulek's sightless eyes were closed, Edith Metlock's could not look away from Bishop's face. At last, the blind man opened his eyes and said, 'They tried to die in the foulest way possible. They had to.'

Bishop frowned. 'You think there was a motive behind all this?'

Kulek nodded. 'There is always a motive for suicide and murder. Even the insane have their reasons.'

'Suicides usually want to free themselves from the troubles of life.'

'Or the restrictions.'

Bishop was puzzled by Kulek's remark – Jessica had talked of death as some kind of release before – but he felt too drained to pursue it. 'Whatever the motives were, it won't matter after tomorrow. The house will no longer be there.'

They were startled. 'What do you mean?' Kulek asked apprehensively.

'I rang Miss Kirkhope before coming here,' Bishop replied. 'I told her there was nothing in the house except a cold atmosphere and recommended she carry out her plan for demolition as soon as possible. She said, that being the case, she would bring the date forward to tomorrow.'

'How could you . . .?' Jessica said, furious.

'Chris, you don't know what you have done!' Kulek was on his feet.

'Perhaps he is right.' Jessica and her father turned to Edith Metlock in surprise. 'Perhaps the demolition of Beechwood will free their poor souls. I believe the house and everything that has happened there is holding them to this world. Now they may be free to go on.'

Jacob Kulek sank back into his chair and slowly shook his head. 'If only that were so,' was all he could say.

10

'Lucy died three days after her fifth birthday.'

The words were spoken without emotion, as though Bishop had cut himself off from the sadness that went with them. But below, somewhere inside where only he could touch, the pain fed upon itself, weaker now, yet still a living thing, a slow-dying disease of grief. Jessica, walking by his side through the cold London park, remained silent. The physical gap between them somehow symbolized their mutual antagonism, an antagonism that had frequently abated then reared into bitter life again in the few days she had known him. Now, hearing him speak of his daughter, she wanted that gap closed, yet she could not find it in herself to move closer.

Bishop paused to stare into the grey lake, the ducks tucked in close to its edges as if even they found its sombre expanse unwelcoming. 'Laryngotracheo-bronchitis was the indirect cause,' he said, still not looking at Jessica. 'When I was a kid, we called it croup. Her throat closed up, she couldn't breathe. It took us a long time to convince the doctor to leave his warm bed to come and see her that night – even in those days there were many who were unwilling to make house calls. It took three phone calls, the second threatening, the third begging, for him to come. Maybe it would have been better if he hadn't.'

Jessica stood beside him, watching his profile. The heavy cloth of her overcoat brushed against his arm.

'It was a bitterly cold night. The panic rush to hospital may have made it worse for her. Two hours we waited: an hour waiting for the hospital doctor to look at her, another hour waiting for them to decide what to do. They gave Lucy a tracheostomy, but by then she had pneumonia. Whether it was the shock of the operation in her weakened state, or the illness itself that killed her, we never found out. We blamed ourselves, the doctor who refused at first to come, the hospital – but most of all, we blamed God.' He gave a short, bitter laugh. 'Of course, Lynn and I believed in God then.'

'You don't any more?' She seemed surprised and Bishop turned his head towards her.

'Can you believe any Supreme Being would allow all this misery?' He nodded towards the tall buildings as though the city were the container for mankind's torments. 'Lynn was a Catholic, but I think her rejection of God was even stronger than mine. Maybe that's the way it works: the more you believe in something, the more you go against it when that belief is shattered. In that first year, I had to watch Lynn day and night. I thought she'd kill herself. My caring for her may have been the thing that pulled me through – I don't know. Then she seemed to accept it. She became calm, but it was a brooding kind of calmness, almost as if she'd given up, lost interest. In a way, it was unnerving, but at least it gave me something to work on. I could plan our lives again without the hysterics. I planned, she listened. It was something. A few weeks later she perked up, seemed to come alive again. I discovered she had been going to a spiritualist.'

Bishop looked around and indicated a bench on the opposite side of the path behind them. 'Shall we sit for a while? Is it too cold?'

Jessica shook her head. 'No, it's not too cold.'

They sat, and she pressed closer to him. He seemed distracted, almost unaware of her presence.

'Did you believe in spiritualism then?' she prompted.

'What? Oh, no, not really. I'd never thought about it before. But it was like a new religion to Lynn; it replaced her God.'

'How did she find this spiritualist?'

'A friend, probably well-meaning, told her of him. The friend had lost her husband years before and had supposedly made contact with him again through this man. Lynn swore to me he had found Lucy for her. She told me she had spoken to her. I was angry at first, but I could see the change it had made in Lynn. Suddenly she had a reason for living again. It went on for a long time and I admit my arguments against her seeing the spiritualist were only half-hearted. She was paying him for each session, of course, but not enough for me to suspect he was making a lot of money out of her.' Bishop smiled cynically. 'But isn't that how they operate? Build up a large clientele, accept small, individual "gifts"? It soon mounts up.'

'They're not all like that, Chris. There are very few that practise spiritualism just for money.' Jessica stemmed her irritation, not wanting to become involved in another argument with him.

'I'm sure they have all sorts of reasons, Jessica.' The implication was that any other reason was just as bad as that of financial gain, but she refused to rise to the bait.

'Anyway,' Bishop continued, 'Lynn finally persuaded me to go along to one of her meetings. Maybe I wanted to see or hear Lucy again. I missed her so much I was ready to grasp at anything. And for the first five minutes, the man almost had me fooled.

'He was middle-aged, spoke with a soft, Irish accent. His

whole manner was soft, in fact; soft but persuasive. Like Edith Metlock, he looked like any other ordinary member of the public. He made no exaggerated claims to me, didn't even try to convince me he was genuine. It was all up to me, he said. The choice whether to believe or not was mine. It was his very casualness that almost convinced me of his sincerity.

'With few preliminaries, the seance began. It was in a darkened room, holding hands around a table – the sort of thing I expected. He asked us to join him in a short prayer to start the proceedings and, surprisingly, Lynn readily did so. There were others at the seance, Lynn's friend who had introduced her to the medium among them, and one by one, their dead friends or relatives were contacted. Frankly, I was a little scared. The atmosphere of the room seemed to be – I don't know – heavy, charged? I had to keep telling myself it was only created by the living people in the room itself.

'When Lucy's voice came through I was shocked rigid. Lynn was grasping my hand tightly, and without looking at her I knew she was crying. I also knew those tears were because she was happy. The voice was small, distant; it seemed to come from the air itself. A child's, but it could have been any child's. It was the things she said that made me believe. She was glad I'd finally come. She had missed me, but she was happy now. She'd felt no pain when she died, only a sadness, then a great joy. She had many new friends in the world she was now in and her only concern was that we, her mother and father, were unhappy. I felt my own tears coming, but suddenly, things didn't quite ring true. Lucy was only five when she died and here she was speaking in the manner of someone much older. If you really wanted to believe, you could convince yourself that that was how things were on the other side: you gained a wisdom beyond your mortal years. I wasn't quite that ready to accept, though. I was perplexed when she spoke of things that only we three, myself, Lucy and her mother, knew of. But then they made their first mistake. The voice was reminding me of how once, when Lynn was out shopping, Lucy and I were having a rough-and-tumble in the sitting-room. In the scramble, a favourite ornament of Lynn's got broken. It was a figurine – an 18th Century courtesan, I think – but only reproduction, not valuable. Lynn loved it though, so we knew we were in trouble. Only the head had come off and I spent the next half-hour gluing it back on. It fooled Lynn until she tried to dust it. The head just toppled off again. Unfortunately, Lucy and I were both in the room at the time and we couldn't help going into hysterics at the look on Lynn's face. Anyway, I owned up to it, and that was the last of the matter. Until the giggling voice in the room reminded me of it.

'Okay, seances are full of these trivial incidents related by departed loved ones. It's what makes them seem so genuine, isn't it? Little moments that no one else could possibly know of. That was fine, except they'd got it wrong. It was Lucy who had broken the statuette, not me. I had accepted the blame because Lucy thought she might have been spanked. She wouldn't have, of course, it was an accident. But that's how kids are.

'So now I was even more suspicious. The medium had heard the story second-hand from someone. Who? Lynn? Maybe she had told the story in one of her visits. Or her friend, the woman who had brought her along in the first place. If it was her, there was probably no bad intent. As I said, the Irishman was a soft, persuasive talker. He could have learned many things about us.

'I played along with them for a while, pretending to be convinced, waiting for another mistake. And they made it, all right. A stupid, almost farcical mistake. I suppose they had been lulled into a false sense of security by my act, imagining that here was another punter to be bled. A smoky substance came from somewhere behind the medium. It was near the back of the room, over his left shoulder, where Lynn and I had a clear view of it. An image began to appear in the smoke, hazy, not clearly defined. It was a face, fluctuating between sharpness and a blur. After a few seconds we recognized it as Lucy. The features were hers, the expression was hers; but there was something not quite right. I realized what it was and it was so silly I could have laughed out loud had I not been so angry. Her hair was parted on the wrong side, you see. They were projecting a photograph of Lucy on to a small screen from behind. The screen's edges were well camouflaged, and the smoke helped conceal it even more.

'I lost control when I realized how it was being done and rushed towards the smoke which was coming from a small tube in the wall. I pounded my fist against the screen. It was inside a small alcove that was covered by a panel when the lights were on and made of some kind of black Perspex. I managed to crack it with my fist.'

Bishop leaned forward, resting his elbows on his knees, studying the gravel path. 'Sometimes I wonder what would have happened if I had let it ride. Maybe Lynn wouldn't have had her breakdown.' His bitter smile returned as he remembered the immediate consequences of his action. 'As you can imagine, the seance ended in uproar. The medium was screaming at me, his brogue a little sharp by then. Lynn's friend was in hysterics, while Lynn herself was white-faced and quiet. The others were in various stages of shock and anger. I'm still not sure who their anger was directed at – me or the Irishman.

'I didn't even bother to look for the hidden microphone the child's voice had come from; I'd seen enough. The medium was coming at me looking as if his red face was about to burst open. A good hard shove took care of him, then I grabbed Lynn and got out of there. She didn't say a word for three days after. Then she cracked.

'Her last hope had been shattered, you see. It was as though Lucy had died twice.'

'Oh, God, it must have been terrible for her, Chris. For you both.' Jessica, too, was leaning forward.

'Lynn just seemed to sink further and further into herself over the next few months. I just couldn't reach her. She seemed to be blaming me. I finally got her to a psychiatrist and he explained that, to Lynn, I had almost become Lucy's murderer. In her confused mind, I had taken Lucy away from her again. I didn't believe him, I couldn't. Lynn and I had always been so close. When she suffered, I suffered; when I was happy, she was happy. To us, Lucy had somehow represented that closeness, had been a product of it. It was as if with her gone, our ties had been snapped. Lynn tried to kill herself twice before I was forced to have her committed. Once, she tried to kill me.'

Jessica shivered, not from the cold, and impulsively placed a hand on his arm. He sat back against the bench as if to shrug her hand off and she quickly withdrew it.

'She took sleeping pills the first time, tried to slash her wrists the second. I managed to get her to hospital before it was too late on both occasions; but I knew there would come a time when we wouldn't make it. After the second attempt, she really hated me. She wanted to be with Lucy and I was preventing her. I woke up one night and she was standing over me with a knife. Why she hadn't struck while I was still asleep, I don't know. Perhaps deep inside the old Lynn didn't want to kill me. When I woke, it must have acted as a trigger. I just managed to move out of the way in time. The knife went into the pillow and I had to hit her hard to make her let it go. After that, I had no choice: I had to have her taken into care. There was no way I could watch her all the time.'

He was silent for a few moments and from the way he avoided looking directly at her, Jessica wondered if he now regretted telling her all this. She wondered if he had ever told anyone else before.

'That happened six, seven years ago,' he finally said.

'And Lynn is still...?' she hesitated, unwilling to use a title, afraid it might give offence.

'In the mental institution? She's in a private one – not the best, but one I can afford. The people who run it like to call it a rest home for the mentally disorientated. Kind of takes the sting out of it. Yes, she's still there, and as far as I can see, there's been little progress. The reverse, in fact. I visit her as much as I can, but now she doesn't even recognize me. She's built a protective barrier around herself, I'm told. I'm her biggest threat, so she's cutting me out.'

'It seems such an inadequate thing to say, Chris, but I'm sorry. These past years must have seemed like hell to you. Now I can understand why you hate spiritualists so much.'

Bishop surprised her by taking her hand. 'I don't hate them, Jessica. The real phoneys I detest, but I've learned that many are completely sincere, if misguided.' He shrugged and let go of her hand. 'That first one, the Irishman, was a complete amateur compared to some I've investigated. They've got it down to a fine art. Did you know there's a shop in America where you can buy spiritualistic miracles. A couple of dollars for the Mystery of the Gyrating Tables, a few more for the Joe Spook Spirit Rapper. It even has an Ectoplasm Kit. Spiritualism has become big business with the wave of interest in the occult. People are looking beyond the materialistic side of life and there are plenty of shysters around to cater for their needs. Don't get me wrong – I'm not on any crusade against them. At first I was ready to expose any group or individual I believed was operating fraudulently and I was pretty lucky most times. Their tricks were so obvious when you went along as a complete unbeliever. But other times I was stumped, impressed even. I began to develop a deeper interest in the whole topic of mysticism, keeping my acceptance at a realistic level. I found there was so much that could be explained by down-to-earth investigation. By practical, scientific reasoning, if you like. Of course, there's an awful lot that can't be explained, but we're slowly finding the answers, gradually moving towards the truth.'

'That's what my father's Institute is all about.'

'I know, Jessica. That's why I wanted to speak to you. I've been pretty rough on you, Jacob and Edith Metlock. It seemed to me that events were being exaggerated, moulded into a shape that complied with your way of thinking. It was a kind of hysteria. I've seen it so many times in my investigations.'

He put a finger to her lips to still her protests. 'I believe what you said about this man Pryszlak. Perhaps he *was* on to something. Perhaps he *had* discovered that evil was a physical force in itself and was searching for a way of harnessing that force. But it all ended with his death and the deaths of his crazy henchmen. Don't you see that?'

Jessica gave a deep sigh. 'I just don't know any more. It could be that my father's conviction is swaying my own judgement. He knew the man so well. Their mental capabilities were so alike, so extraordinary. If anything, my father's blindness has enhanced his extrasensory faculties, although it's become a very private thing for him, not one he shares with others.'

'Not even with you?'

She shook her head. 'He will one day, when the time is right.' She smiled, almost whimsically. 'He likens himself to an explorer who cannot lead others until he has found the right path himself. His concern is that Pryszlak was way ahead of him on that path.'

'I've met many like Pryszlak in my investigations. Obviously not as extreme, but all with that same fanaticism that you tell me the man had. It's like a disease, Jessica, it spreads. I've almost caught small doses of it myself when I've been baffled by certain cases.'

'But you've always been content to label them as "unexplained phenomena" and put them aside.' There was no sarcasm in her voice, just a hopelessness.

'For the moment, yes. It's like UFOs: it's just a matter of time before we find the explanation for them.'

She nodded her understanding. 'All right, Chris. Perhaps it's good to have a cynic like you nosing around in this field; we may all be too dedicated to our own causes. I think your experience in that house has shaken you more than you're letting on, though. Your recommendation that it be destroyed immediately could be your way of chasing away your own ghosts.'

He had no answer for her; the truth wasn't clear even to himself. Instead, he tried to make light of it. 'It might destroy a reasonable living if I became a believer.'

She smiled and said, 'Thanks for telling me all this, Chris. I know it wasn't easy.'

Bishop grinned. 'It wasn't, but it helped. It's been good to talk to someone after all this time.' He rose from the bench and looked down at her. 'Tell your father I'm sorry, will you? I didn't enjoy bringing everything to such a sudden halt. I thought it was for the best, though. Really.'

'We owe you your fee.'

'For half a day's work? Forget it.'

He turned to go, but she stopped him by saying, 'Will I see you again?'

His confusion showed before he replied, 'I hope so.'

Jessica watched as he made his way towards the park exit that would take him in the direction of Baker Street. She reached into her shoulder-bag and took out a cigarette. She lit it and inhaled deeply. He was a strange man; intense. But now that she understood his cynicism, all her resentment towards him had evaporated. She wished she could help him in some way. She wished she could help rid her father of his obsession with Pryszlak. She wished it really was all over but, like Jacob, she somehow knew it wasn't.

A screech from one of the ducks startled her and she saw two of them were fighting greedily over a lake-sodden piece of bread thrown by an elderly woman. Jessica rose from the bench, drawing her coat tight around her to keep out the dampness of the air. She stopped to stub out the scarcely-smoked cigarette on the gravel path, then tossed the broken remains into a nearby bin. Hands tucked deep into her coat pockets, she walked slowly from the park.

The demolition company moved in, their machines battering the walls of Beechwood, the men swinging their sledge-hammers with relish. The neighbours gawped, surprised at the sudden attack on the property and some, those who knew the history of the house, were pleased at the destruction. Within two days the building was reduced to rubble, an unsightly scar between the houses of Willow Road, an empti-ness that was only filled when nightfall came. A rough wooden barrier was erected to prevent the curious, especially children, from entering the site, for the debris was dangerous, the ground floor not having collapsed completely into the basement area. There were small openings through which someone could fall.

The shadows beneath the rubble welcomed the night, merging with it, becoming more substantial, and the darkness in the cellar seemed to creep from the openings like a living, breathing thing.

Part Two

Have regard for thy covenant;
for the dark places of the land are
full of the habitations of violence.

Psalms 74:20
(R.S.V.)

Part Two

11

Detective Chief Inspector Peck groaned inwardly as the Granada slid to a smooth halt.

'Looks like Armageddon,' he remarked to his driver, who chuckled in response. Peck climbed from the car and surveyed the scene. The smell of smoke still clung to the air and large puddles filled the hollows of Willow Road, forming small shiny ponds. Water tenders were dampening the ashes of the three fire-ravaged houses, their bright red bodywork a bulky intrusion on the drab greyness of the street. An ambulance stood by, its back doors open wide as though expecting a fresh delivery at any moment. A blue-clad figure disengaged itself from an agitated throng and strode briskly towards Peck.

'Chief Inspector Peck? I was informed you were on your way.'

Peck acknowledged the uniformed man's curt salute with a casual nod of his head. 'You'd be Inspector Ross from the local shop.'

'Yes, sir. We've got a right bloody mess here.' He indicated the general background scene with a flick of his head.

'Well, I think the first thing you'd better do is clear the street of anyone not directly involved in last night's business.'

'Just about to do that. Trouble is, half of them *were* involved.'

Peck's eyebrows rose in an arch, but he said nothing.

Ross called his sergeant over. 'Get them all inside their houses, Tom. We'll take door-to-door statements from everyone. And get the Press back to the end of the road; we'll issue a statement later. I thought you posted men at each end to stop anyone getting through?'

'We did. It didn't work.'

'Okay, get on to HQ and have some barriers sent down. Tell them we need more men, too. Right, all civilians off the street. Now.'

The sergeant wheeled away and began barking orders at his men and bystanders alike. Ross turned back to Peck, who said, 'Okay, Inspector, let's get in the car and talk quietly for a few moments.'

Once inside, Peck lit a cigarette and opened a side window just enough for the smoke to escape. 'So tell me,' he said, looking distractedly at the activity outside.

The inspector placed his cap on one knee. 'The first sign of trouble was a radio message from one of our constables patrolling this road. Constable Posgate, it was, on surveillance duty with Constable Hicks.'

'Surveillance?'

'Well, not exactly. But it was more than the normal patrol. You've heard about the funny goings-on here recently?'

Peck grunted and Ross took it as affirmation.

'The residents demanded some protection. We gave them the patrol to let them know we were keeping an eye on things, but frankly, we didn't really expect anything else to happen.'

'Seems you were wrong. Go on.'

The inspector shifted uncomfortably in his seat. 'Our man reported what he thought was a scuffle or a mugging going on at the end of the road.'

'What time was this?'

'About half-eleven. They went down to sort things out and got pretty well sorted out themselves.'

'How many involved?'

'Three. Youths. Two white, one black.'

'And they gave your coppers a seeing-to?'

'They were vicious bastards, sir.'

Peck hid his smile by cupping the cigarette against his mouth.

'And it wasn't a mugging,' Ross said seriously.

'No?'

'No. It was a rape.'

'In the street?'

'Yes, sir, in the street. No attempt to drag the victim off into cover. But that's not the worst of it.'

'Surprise me.'

'The victim was a man.'

Peck looked incredulously at the inspector. 'I'm surprised,' he said.

Ross felt a grim satisfaction at shocking his superior. By the end of his report, Peck would be even more shocked.

'Skeates was the name of the man. He lives in the road – a young exec type. Apparently he was just returning home late from the pub.'

'He'll get a cab next time. What about your officers? How badly were they hurt?'

'Hicks has a broken jaw. Not too many teeth left, either. By the time the backup got there, those three bastards had broken both Posgate's arms and were trying to do the same with his legs.'

Smoke escaped between Peck's clenched teeth in a thin, forceful stream. 'Spiteful bitches,' he commented.

Ross failed to appreciate the senior officer's sarcasm.

'There was nothing effeminate about those three. I know, I interviewed them when they were brought in.'

'Was there anything left of them?'

'They'd had a going over. They resisted arrest.'

'I'll bet.' Peck grinned at the inspector's rising indignation. 'All right, Ross, I'm not having a go. I don't blame your lads dealing out some punishment of their own. Did you get anything out of the bastards?'

'No. Like zombies, all three. Haven't spoken a word all night.'

'The victim?'

'My men found him crawling down the street trying to get home. He claims the three youths were just sitting on the pavement as if they were waiting for someone to come along. They don't live in this road, apparently. At least, he's never seen them before.'

'All right, Inspector, I'm already impressed. What else happened here last night?' Peck nodded towards the still smouldering house. 'Apart from the obvious, that is.'

'About half-past one this morning we received a report of an intruder on the premises of number . . .' Ross produced a notebook from his breast pocket and flicked it open '. . . thirty-three. The call came from a Mrs Jack Kimble. By the time my lads got there, her husband had dealt with the trouble himself.'

'Don't keep me guessing.'

'The Kimbles have a fifteen-year-old daughter. She sleeps in a room that looks on to the road itself. A man had forced himself into her bedroom.'

'Not another rape,' Peck said in disgust.

'Yes, sir. The intruder lived opposite the Kimbles. Eric Channing was his name.'

'Was?'

'Was. He no longer is.'

'This . . . what's his name – Kimble? . . . took the law into his own hands?'

'Channing had used a ladder to reach the girl's bedroom window. He didn't even bother to open it, just jumped head first through the glass and attacked the girl. While Mrs Kimble was phoning us, Mr Kimble was busy throwing the would-be rapist back out the way he had come. The fall broke Channing's neck.'

'Love thy neighbour, eh? Is there anything dodgy about this Kimble? Is he known?'

'No record. He just over-reacted, that's all.'

'Let's hope the judge doesn't. What else have you got?'

'Well, as if these two incidents weren't enough, all hell broke loose around three o'clock. That's when the fires started.'

'Cause?'

'It started in one semi and took the adjoining house with it. We think flying sparks probably started the fire in the nearest house to them.'

'Yes, but *how* did it start?'

Ross took a deep breath and consulted his notebook again to check on the correct name. 'A Mr Ronald Clarkson, a retired businessman, raised the alarm. He'd been woken up by the smell of burning. It was his wife sitting in the middle of the bedroom floor. She'd used paraffin from one of those oil burners and doused herself with it. He was lucky: she'd doused the bed too. He only just got out in time.'

Peck's eyes were wide now, all complacency gone.

Ross continued, taking some enjoyment from the sight. 'By the time the fire engines got here, the whole house had gone up and there was no saving the one next door. The house opposite was well under way, but they managed to bring it under control before it destroyed the place completely. Eight engines they had here last night; it was like the blitz all over again.'

'Anyone else killed – apart from Clarkson's wife?'

'No. Fortunately, they got out in time thanks to Clarkson giving the warning.'

'Did he give any indication why she'd done it? Burnt herself?'

'He said she'd been depressed lately.'

Peck snorted his disgust. 'Depressed! Jesus Christ!'

'One other thing.'

'Oh, you're kidding.'

'No. This one's not so bad, though. Just as daybreak came, when the firemen were still fighting the blaze and I was running around like a lunatic trying to find out what the hell was going on, a man approached one of my officers and asked to be arrested.'

'It must have made a nice change. Who was it – another nutter?'

'He doesn't seem to be. His name is Brewer. He lives at number nine.'

'And?'

'He was afraid of what he might do to his family. The officer went back to the house with him and found Brewer's wife and three kids all tied up and locked inside a wardrobe.'

'And you say he's not a crackpot?'

'I've spoken with him. He appears to be a nice, ordinary bloke, thoroughly scared of what he did. He can't explain, doesn't know why he did it. But he wanted to be put away so he can't harm them. That's what he's afraid of.'

'I hope you obliged him.'

'Of course we did. He's in a cell now, but later on, when all this is straightened out, we'll get him to a hospital.'

'Do that, but after I've spoken with him. Is that the lot?'

'As far as we know. As I said, we're checking all the houses.'

'Just what kind of crazy road is this, Inspector? Suburbia's crackpot ghetto?'

'Until recently it was just another quiet residential area. We had all that business a year ago, of course.'

'The mass suicide you mean?'

'Yes, sir. The house – Beechwood it was called – was demolished only yesterday.'

'Why was that?'

'From what I can gather, the owner was fed up with the place. It hadn't been lived in for ages and apparently the agents couldn't sell it.'

'Maybe its ghosts have been taking their revenge for the destruction.'

Ross glanced sharply at Peck. 'Strangely enough, some funny business went on in there the other day. Someone called Kulek informed us he was holding a seance or something in the house. We checked that he'd got permission from the owner.'

'So it really was supposed to be haunted?' Peck shook his head, bemused.

'I don't know about that. But they found a naked woman hiding in the cellar. She was a private nurse who, it turned out, had done in her employer, an old man she'd been nursing for years in his house further down the street.'

'Yes, I heard about that. I didn't know about this seance going on, though.'

'I'm not sure it was a seance exactly. I know there was some kind of ghost expert present.'

'All right, I want to speak to this Kulek and anyone else who was with him at the house.'

'You don't think it's got anything to do with ghosts, do you?' There was a curious expression on Ross's face.

'Do me a favour, Inspector. On the other hand, I don't think it's got anything to do with the drinking water. I just think it's about time we collected all the pieces and started putting them together, don't you? Otherwise, before long there'll be nobody left to talk to; they'll either be dead or in the nuthouse.'

A sharp rap on the window at Peck's side made both men look in that direction. A gnarled old face squinted in at them. The woman knocked again, even though she had the attention of both men.

'Are you in charge here?' she rasped, looking directly at Peck.

'What can I do for you, madam?' Peck asked, winding down the window a little more.

'Where's me bleedin' dog?' the old woman asked, and Peck was relieved to see the sergeant whom Ross had spoken to earlier hastily making his way towards her.

'Sorry, madam, but if . . .' Peck began to say.

'He's bleedin' gone. Been away all night. Why don't you find 'im instead of sittin' there on your arse?'

'Give the details to the sergeant; I'm sure he'll help you find your dog,' Peck said patiently. He gave a sigh of relief when the officer led the grumbling woman away by the arm. 'All this mayhem and she's worried about a bloody dog!'

Inspector Ross shook his head in wonder.

'Excuse me, sir.' The sergeant had returned to the car window.

'What is it, Tom?' Ross asked.

'Just thought you'd like to know. About the dog.'

Peck's eyes looked heavenwards.

'Er, it's probably nothing, but that old lady's complaint was the fifth one we've had this morning. It's the fifth family pet that's been reported missing. Seems like they've all run away.'

Ross could only shrug his shoulders when Peck looked blankly at him.

12

The drive through the peaceful Weald of Kent helped settle Bishop's troubled mind. A sudden, welcoming spring-like change in the weather had taken the dullness from the countryside and, although there was still a definite bite in the air, it could easily be imagined that the seasons had changed order. He had chosen to keep to the minor roads, avoiding the busy main routes that led more directly to his destination, but which would be crammed with other vehicles. He needed time to think.

The madness in Willow Road had persisted, had increased, in fact. The day before, two CID men had paid him a visit at his house in Barnes and had questioned him for almost two hours on his knowledge of Beechwood and the reasons for his investigation of the property. He had told them all he knew of Jacob Kulek's concerns, of his own determination to prove the house was not haunted, of discovering the naked woman hiding in the cellar. He did not tell them of the hallucination he had had there. When they left they hardly seemed satisfied and gruffly informed him that he would probably be asked for a formal statement within the next day or so; a Detective Chief Inspector Peck would be most interested in his story.

Bishop had later considered contacting Jacob Kulek and Jessica, but something stopped him. He realized he was sick of the whole business, that he wanted to keep away from it. Yet he felt the need to speak to Jessica again and he was confused by that need. The animosity that existed between them had faded with the conclusion of the investigation. The day before, in the park, all his resentment towards her beliefs had dissipated and he was able to look upon her as she really was: an attractive woman. But he resisted the attraction; he had to.

As Bishop kept a watchful eye out for road signs, he felt the pricking of tiny needles in his stomach. Time for something to eat. He glanced at his watch, knowing he wasn't far from his destination. Good, plenty of time to grab a bite. He wasn't due at the house until three-ish. The phone call had come after the two detectives had left, and the man at the other end had identified himself as Richard Braverman. Bishop had been recommended to him by a friend and he wished to engage his services as a psychic investigator to examine his home in Robertsbridge, Sussex. The new client seemed pleased that he was able to proceed with the investigation the following day. Apart from directions to the property itself, Bishop asked for no information concerning the alleged haunting; he preferred to be on the spot when he asked such questions. He was pleased with the job, wanting to be busy again. That night he had visited Lynn in the mental home and, as usual, had come away disappointed, depressed. If anything, she was becoming even more withdrawn. This time she had refused to even look at him. Her hands were still covering her eyes when he left.

The brightness of the following day had eased the pressure a little and anticipation of the work ahead had kept his mind occupied. He pulled in at the welcoming pub that had suddenly appeared on his left.

An hour later he was back on the road, his mood considerably brightened by a full stomach. When he reached the village of Robertsbridge he had to ask directions for the Braverman house and was guided to a small side road that crossed a railway line and led up a steep hill. At the top a discreet weathered sign, almost hidden in a hedge, reluctantly admitted that 'Two Circles' could be found down the small lane leading off from the main road. 'Two Circles' was the name Braverman had given him. He swung the car into the lane, no more than a rutted track, and almost enjoyed the bumpy ride down to the house; it made driving something to be worked at.

The house came into view and he suddenly understood its unusual title, for it was a converted oast-house, or oast-houses to be more accurate. There were two circular buildings joined together by a more conventional shaped structure which must have been at one time an enormous barn. The conversion was modern and solid, its unique shape pleasing to the eye. Beyond it stretched green fields, their lustre muted by winter, their boundaries marked by fringes of darker green. Bishop drove the car into a wide courtyard that ran the length of the square-shaped building, the adjoining oasts themselves seated in an area of lawn that ran downhill from the house towards the open fields, becoming coarse grass about halfway. Bishop already felt confident about exorcising any alleged ghosts as he strode towards the main door, for large-scale structural alterations like this were often prone to strange creaks and rappings, the owners more concerned that they had aroused a resentful spirit than with the effects of joining new materials to old. He rang the large brass doorbell and waited.

No one came. He rang again.

A movement inside? But still no answer. He rang once more.

Bishop rapped on the door with his knuckles, and called out, 'Hello, anybody there?'

Only us spooks, he told himself.

He tried the handle and pushed the door inwards. It swung smoothly open.

'Hello! Mr Braverman? Anyone about?' Bishop stepped into a long balconied hallway and nodded appreciatively at his surroundings. The wood flooring was stained a rich walnut, light from the many windows bouncing off its highly polished surface and reflecting on to the dark, hessian walls. The odd pieces of furniture scattered around the spacious hallway were interesting enough to be of antique value, and a few carefully scattered rugs managed to diffuse any bareness the flooring may have presented. To his right were two double-doors leading to the circular sections of the house. He walked over to the nearest, his footsteps ringing hollowly around the walls, avoiding a rug in case he dirtied its delicate pattern, and knocked once, then pushed the door open. A huge table imitated the round shape of the room, its surface of the darkest oak. A broad beam, recessed into the curved wall, acted as a mantel to the open, log-filled and unlit fireplace. A small portrait hung just above the mantelpiece and the image it represented seemed vaguely familiar. The floor was covered with a dark brown carpet, its pile deep and springy.

'Mr Braverman? Are you home?'

A noise from behind made Bishop turn. He glanced up towards the balcony. 'Mr Braverman?'

No sound, then a bump. *Someone* was up there.

'Mr Braverman, it's Chris Bishop. You rang me yesterday.'

No reply. He approached the stairs. Movement up there.

He placed a foot on the first step.

Jessica descended the stairs leading to the Institute's reception area.

'Mr Ferrier?' she said to the small bespectacled man waiting there. 'I'm Jessica Kulek.'

The man sprang to his feet and nervously turned the brim of the hat he was holding round in his hands like a steering-wheel. A smile briefly quivered on his face, then was gone. His raincoat was dotted with dark specks as if it had just started to rain before he'd entered the building.

'I'm afraid my father hasn't much time to spare today,' Jessica told him, not unused to nervousness in those visiting the Institute for the first time. 'We've been rather ... busy, lately, and have a backlog of work to catch up on. You said you were from the Metaphysical Research Group?'

Ferrier nodded. 'Yes, it's rather important that I see Jacob Kulek.' His voice was thin and reedy, like the man himself. 'If I could just have ten minutes of his time? No longer.'

'Can you tell me the nature of your business?'

'I'm afraid not,' the little man snapped. Then, realizing his brusqueness, he added apologetically, 'It's confidential.'

He saw a firmness stiffen her features and stepped quickly towards her, casting a nervous glance at the receptionist as he did so. The girl was speaking to someone on the phone, but still he kept his voice low.

'It concerns Boris Pryszlak,' he whispered.

Jessica was startled. 'What do you know of Pryszlak?'

'It's confidential,' Ferrier repeated. 'I can only speak to your father, Miss Kulek.'

She hesitated, uneasy. But it might be important.

'Very well. Ten minutes then, Mr Ferrier.'

Jessica led the little man up the staircase and along to her father's private study. They heard the muffled tones of Jacob Kulek's voice before they entered the room. The blind man switched off the dictating machine and looked up at them.

'Yes, Jessica?' Kulek said, knowing her knock, knowing her footsteps, knowing her presence.

'Mr Ferrier to see you. I mentioned his visit earlier.'

'Ah yes, from the Metaphysical Research Group, wasn't it?'

The little man was strangely silent and Jessica had to answer for him. 'Yes, Father. I've explained you're very busy, but Mr Ferrier says it's a matter concerning Boris Pryszlak. I thought it might be important.'

'Pryszlak? You have some information?'

Ferrier cleared his throat. 'Yes, as I explained to Miss Kulek, it's confidential.'

'My daughter is also my personal assistant, Mr Ferrier. As well as being my eyes.'

'All the same, I'd rather . . .'

'Jessica, perhaps Mr Ferrier would like some coffee. Would you mind?'

'Father, I think . . .'

'Black coffee would be fine, Miss Kulek.' Ferrier smiled anxiously at Jessica, his eyes suddenly hidden by the light reflecting off his spectacles. Her unease persisted.

'I'll take coffee, too, Jessica.' Her father's voice was quietly firm and she knew it would be pointless to argue. She left the study and hurried along the corridor, not wanting to leave Jacob alone with the nervous little man for a minute longer than necessary. She paused when she drew level with her own office, then changed direction and went in. She picked up the telephone.

Anna opened the door and beamed at the two women standing there, her smile as warm for strangers as it was for those she knew.

141

'Yes, please?' she asked, giving a little bow of her head.

'We'd like to see Miss Kirkhope,' the taller of the two said, returning Anna's smile.

A regretful frown creased the housekeeper's broad face. 'Oh, I don't tink . . .'

'Please tell her it's about her brother Dominic,' the other woman said, face unsmiling, her tone abrupt.

Anna was too polite to close the door fully on the two women and when she returned moments later she found them waiting in the hallway itself. If she was surprised, she did not show it.

'Miss Kirkhope will see you much soon. You will wait in here, please.' She beckoned them to follow and showed them into the visitors' room. They seated themselves on the Chesterfield, the taller one smiling sweetly at Anna, the shorter one studying her surroundings, her face impassive.

'One moment please. Miss Kirkhope will arrive shortly.' Anna bowed her way from the room.

It was a full five minutes before Agnes Kirkhope entered, insisting that she and Anna finish that particular round of rummy in the kitchen before she received her unexpected guests. The Filipino housekeeper had an uncanny knack of finding black deuces to bolster otherwise unpromising hands and Miss Kirkhope was determined to win back the five pounds she had already lost that afternoon. One card away from victory, she had groaned aloud when Anna had rapped the table and splayed her hand before her mistress, the inevitable black deuce substituting for the Queen of Hearts that Miss Kirkhope held. Why hadn't she plucked a couple of useful cards from the deck when Anna had been answering the door?

Miss Kirkhope looked down at the two women, her irritation plain on her face and in her voice.

'You had something to say about Dominic,' she said without preamble.

'Did you know he was a paraphiliac?' the shorter of the two replied with even less preamble.

'A what?' Miss Kirkhope was taken aback by the coldness in the woman's tone.

'A paraphiliac,' the taller one said, smiling sweetly. 'It's someone who indulges in abnormal sexual practices.'

Miss Kirkhope's hand went involuntarily to her throat. Recovering quickly, she strode stiffly to the centre of the room and glared down at them. 'I suppose this has something to do with blackmail.' She spat the words out.

The taller woman reached into her handbag and said pleasantly, 'Oh no, Miss Kirkhope. Much worse than that.'

13

Bishop paused on the top step and looked around. To his right were doors leading off to rooms in the square-shaped section of the house; to his left was the balcony rail overlooking the hall below and another staircase leading upwards.

'Mr Braverman?' Bishop called again. He swore under his breath. Was the house empty? Had the noises he had heard just been the house settling? Or the wandering ghosts the owner alleged inhabited the house? One more try, then forget it. Braverman should have been here to meet him.

Light rain began to patter against the windows.

'Is there anybody home?'

Bump. Bump. Bump, bump, bump. The red rubber ball bounced down the stairs, gathering speed, then struck the facing wall. It bounced back against the stairway and lost its impetus, skipping low then rolling towards the wall again where it trickled to a stop.

Bishop craned his neck to see the floor above. It had to be kids playing a prank. 'I've come to see Mr Braverman. Can you tell me where he is?'

Nothing, except a movement. A scuffle of feet?

Bishop had had enough. He mounted the stairs two at a time, annoyance reflected in his forceful stride.

Had they attempted to kill him right away they would have

succeeded; but they wanted to enjoy his dying, to relish it. So the blow to his head was too light.

The man appeared in the doorway, the double-barrel held shoulder high and pointed at Bishop's face. The man had enjoyed the game so far and grinned in anticipation at what was to follow. Bishop had stopped dead on the landing, his mouth open and alarm in his eyes; the woman stepped from another doorway, her raised arm which held the hammer already beginning its descent. Stun him, her husband had told her. Hit him just behind the ear, just hard enough to stun him. Then we can have some fun with him before he dies.

The blow knocked Bishop sideways, but he had turned to see the woman coming at him and had instinctively ducked when he saw the falling hammer, so the weapon had glanced across his scalp rather than striking solidly. He fell against the wall and felt himself spinning backwards down the stairs. The woman was too close: her legs became entangled with his and she went with him, the hammer clattering down the wooden steps ahead of them. She screamed as they tumbled and finally slid on to the landing below.

Stupid bitch! the man with the shotgun cursed silently. Trust her to do it wrong! He raised the gun again and aimed it at the struggling figures below. 'Get away from him, you silly cow! Let me get a clear shot!' he bellowed. Bishop would have to be killed outright.

The woman tried to free herself from the tangle of arms and legs and, though he was dazed, Bishop saw the twin-barrels pointing down at him. He pulled at the squirming woman just as one of the black holes exploded with light. Her chest took the full blast, tiny fragments of scattered lead tearing past her body and tugging at Bishop's clothes. She would not stop screaming as he tried to roll clear of her.

The man at the top of the stairs seemed hardly shocked,

merely angry, as he lowered the shotgun then raised it again. His aim was more careful this time. Bishop saw the hammer lying propped against the bottom stair and, now on his knees, scooped it up and hurled it towards the man above. It was a wild throw and missed completely, but the man automatically ducked, giving Bishop the chance to gain his feet and run. The second blast powdered the floor behind him. He ran through a doorway leading off from the balcony, sure he could not make it to the front door below before the man had reloaded, praying there would be another staircase leading down at the back of the house. At least this way there would be some cover. He found himself in a room that contained a small bed and ran across to a facing door. The next room also had a bed and little else. Another door, then he was in a dark, narrow corridor. Stairs led down to a closed door.

He could hear footsteps close behind, the man screaming abuse at him. He ran down the stairs, slipping near the bottom, crashing into the door. He scrabbled around in the gloom searching for the handle, found it, jerked downwards. It was locked. A shadow above blocked out what little light there was.

Bishop sat on the second step and kicked out with both feet. The door sprang open, slivers of wood bursting away from the frame. He staggered through, slamming it behind him to stop any gunshot blasted from above. He was in a kitchen and there was a back door.

Footsteps were pounding down the stairs. He ran across to the back door, almost crying out in frustration when he found this, too, was locked. He hurled himself back across the room just as the door leading from the stairs into the kitchen opened. The man was halfway in when the door slammed back on him, trapping the shotgun across his chest, his head jolted back against the door frame. Bishop grabbed the exposed section of gun barrel, pushing against the door with all his strength. The man tried to free himself, but he was in an awkward position, his head turned sideways, his chest crushed by the pressure of the door against the weapon.

The dizziness was beginning to clear from Bishop's head and he concentrated on exerting as much pressure on the door as possible, maintaining his advantage, but not knowing where it would get him. They could hardly stay like that all day. The man's face was beginning to go red as he pushed back against the door; his eyes were wide, turned towards Bishop, glaring their hate. His mouth was open and curved downwards in a snarl, the snarl itself a choking sound. Bishop felt the door moving towards him, slowly pushing him back. He redoubled his efforts, digging his feet into the tiled kitchen floor, his shoulder pressed flat against the woodwork.

The quivering hand that grabbed at his hair from behind made him shriek with fright. He whirled around and saw the woman, her face and chest oozing fresh blood, swaying before him. She had come into the kitchen through another door that must open out into the hallway. The door at his back burst open and he was propelled forward into the mutilated woman. She fell to her hands and knees, the blood flowing freely and forming a deep red puddle beneath her.

Bishop swept his arm round without taking time to look at the man rushing through the door. His elbow caught the man square against the bridge of his nose, abruptly stopping his advance. The decision whether to run or stay was made for Bishop as the gun barrels were raised towards him once more. He had no choice: he had to fight, to run would be suicidal.

He pushed the gun upwards and lunged into the man. They fell back through the doorway on to the stairs beyond, their hands locked around the weapon between them. Bishop heaved himself up and the man came with him using the momentum to push Bishop backwards. They staggered into the kitchen once more and Bishop's foot slipped in the spreading pool of blood. He fell to his knees and suddenly his assailant was standing over him, his contorted face only inches away. Bishop's body was arched backwards, his hold on the shotgun now being used against him. He went back on to the floor, his legs forced sideways and out, his shoulders sinking into the sticky redness beneath him. Still he refused to let go of the gun, but he could not prevent the weapon from being turned inwards towards him.

A hand flailed weakly at his face, trying to gouge out his eyes. The woman was still alive, trying to help the man destroy him. He suddenly allowed the gun to turn, bringing it towards him but twisting his body so the twin-barrels struck the floor. The man staggered forward, falling with the gun, and Bishop let go of the warm metal with one hand and struck out, hitting him below the left ear. The man fell sideways and Bishop grabbed at the gun again, but the woman dug painfully into his eyes, forcing him to wrench himself free, to roll his body away from the sharp claws. He realized his mistake when he was halfway across the kitchen floor. The man was free to raise the gun and take a shot at him.

He could only stare as the man grinned in triumph and began to rise to his feet, knowing his quarry was trapped. His fingers had already curled around the two triggers and he was stepping forward when his foot slid in the viscous mess on the kitchen floor. His leg shot out and he staggered to keep erect, but then both feet were in the blood and he fell, going forward, slightly sideways. The gun roared, taking off the top of his head with the double blast. The kitchen ceiling became a shocking canvas of red fluid.

The woman's moan was long and agonized as she stared at the twitching form of her husband and she did not look away nor did the moan die in her throat until his body was still. Then she turned to look at Bishop and held him there sprawled on the floor with her wild-eyed, mesmerizing gaze. It was only after the thick gob of blood oozed from her lips that he realized she was dead and her eyes saw nothing. Released, he rose weakly to his feet and stumbled towards the kitchen sink, his stomach heaving in juddering movements. He was still crouched over the metal sink ten minutes later when the pattering on the window panes increased its intensity as the rain became more fierce and the skies overhead darkened.

Jessica hurried along the corridor, her heart thudding. She had just called the Metaphysical Research Group at their headquarters in Sussex: they had never heard of Ferrier. She reached her father's study and pushed against the door, twisting the handle, prepared to feel foolish if the man and her father were merely engaged in conversation, but somehow knowing that would not be the case. She cried out in alarm when she saw the thin, leather belt around Jacob Kulek's throat, the little man behind him, his hands pulling the belt tight, his body shaking with the effort. Jacob had one hand against his own throat, fingers curled around the improvised garotte as though he had become aware of his assailant's intention just before the little man had struck. His face was a deep red, turning purplish, his tongue emerging from his open mouth, his sightless eyes bulging from their sockets as though a parasite growing inside his head was pushing everything else out. A tight asthmatic wheezing sound came from his throat as he tried to suck in air through his strangulated windpipe.

Jessica ran forward, afraid that she was already too late. The little man seemed almost oblivious of her as she grabbed at his wrists and tried to force them together again to relieve the pressure on the belt. But it was no use; his strength belied his frame. She struck out at his face when she realized that her father's gasps for breath had stopped. Ferrier turned his head away to avoid the worst of her wild blows, but still he maintained the pressure, still he pulled at the leather belt, still his whole body quivered with the effort.

Jessica screamed, knowing she was losing. She pulled at the man's hair, scratched at his eyes, but it had no effect: he was like a robot, unfeeling, governed by something outside his own body. She looked around desperately for something to use against him. The silver paperknife lay gleaming on the desktop.

Frantically, Jessica grabbed it, turning on the man, the weapon raised high. She hesitated before sweeping her arm down, the intent abhorrent to her, but knowing she had no choice. The narrow blade sank into the side of Ferrier's neck, just above the shoulder bone.

His body suddenly went rigid and, for a moment, his eyes stared unbelievingly at her. Then they seemed to cloud over and with horror she saw his hands resume their pressure. The knife protruded from his neck, only half of its length sunk into his flesh, and Jessica threw herself at him, screaming with frustrated fury, beating at his exposed face, thrusting down on the knife again to sink it in further, praying the blade would find a vital artery.

The little man's body shuddered, and his knees sagged. Then he straightened as if he had regathered his strength. He let go of one end of the belt to sweep his arm around and knock the girl to one side. Jessica staggered against the bookshelves, her eyes blurring at the pain and tears of helplessness that had formed.

'Stop!' she cried out. And then a moan: 'Please stop.'

But both hands pulled at the belt once more.

She heard the footsteps running along the hall and then suddenly, mercifully, there were figures in the doorway. The two men and the woman who peered over their shoulders were members of the Institute.

'Stop him!' she implored.

They were stunned by what was happening, but one, a tall grey-bearded man, generally timid, and usually slow in action, rushed forward, lifting a chair as he went. Without losing stride, he raised it over the desktop and half-threw, half-pushed it into Ferrier's face. The rungs of the chair caught the little man across the forehead, knocking him back, sending him against the window behind, the glass shattering outwards, his body hanging there, hands outstretched to grasp at the window-frame. He seemed to study them for a moment, their actions temporarily frozen, before his fingers uncurled and he let himself fall backwards, his legs rising upwards then slithering down out of sight over the sill.

Jessica wasn't sure whether or not she really heard the sickening squelch of his head bursting open on the pavement below, for the woman was screaming hysterically and she, herself, was stumbling towards her father, who had now collapsed on to the floor. But her mind had recorded the sound, imaginary or not.

Anna had packed away the playing cards and was on her way back to the visitors' room to see if her mistress would require tea for herself and the guests, when the smile disappeared from her face leaving an expression of total incomprehension. Miss Kirkhope had appeared in the hallway, crawling on hands and knees, something wrong with her face, something distorting her features. Her eyes looked beseechingly at Anna, a thin, heavily veined hand reaching towards her, a weak croaking noise coming from a face that was sizzling, the skin popping and tearing.

For Anna, confusion did not turn to terror until she saw Miss Kirkhope's two women guests stroll from the room behind her crawling mistress, each holding what seemed to be nothing more than small bottles of clear liquid. They could have contained water – the fluid looked harmless enough – but the old lady's head shook in horror when the taller woman smiled and raised her bottle. Miss Kirkhope tried to scramble away, but the woman jerked the bottle in her direction, the liquid splashing out and landing in heavy splats on the old woman's back and head. Anna's hands went to her mouth as she heard the faint sizzling sound and saw what looked like small trails of curling steam rise from the wetness.

Miss Kirkhope arched her back inwards, her agonized groans spurring the housekeeper onwards a few paces. But Anna's courage failed her when she saw the shorter of the two women step forward and kick the old lady over on to her back. Anna sank to her knees and joined her hands in supplication when she saw the woman stand astride Miss Kirkhope's slumped body and slowly pour the contents of her bottle in a steady stream into the open, upturned mouth.

The gargled screams filled Anna's head before they became a low rasping sound as vocal cords were burnt away. Anna found she could not rise, not even when she felt the trickle run down between her legs and the floor around her became wet with urine. Not even when the taller woman strode towards her, still smiling, sprinkling the contents of the bottle before her like holy water. Not even when the first splattering of acid touched her skin and began to burn.

14

Peck looked disbelievingly across his desk at Bishop. 'Do you know how incredible all this sounds?'

Bishop nodded without apology. 'I find it hard to believe myself.'

'But why should a total stranger try to murder you?'

'Braverman had to be a part of Pryszlak's sect. They didn't all commit suicide. Some were left to carry on his work.'

'Which was killing people?'

'I don't know, Inspector. Maybe we were getting too close.'

'Too close to what?'

Jessica spoke up, and there was repressed anger in her voice. 'The reason for the mass suicide. My father knew there had to be a reason for Pryszlak and his sect to kill themselves.'

Peck sat back in his chair and regarded the girl silently for a few moments, his thumb scratching an itch at the end of his nose. She looked pale and worried, on the surface the type who would crack when things got too rough. But Peck knew better; he had dealt with too many people for too many years to be deceived by appearances. The girl was stronger than she seemed.

'But you still have no idea what this is all about,' he said.

Jessica shook her head. 'I told you Pryszlak came to my

father to enlist his help a long time ago, and that my father refused.'

'You think this could be some kind of perverted revenge, then? Instructions carried out by Pryszlak's followers after his death?'

'No, it's not revenge. Why should they try to kill Chris? Why did they kill Miss Kirkhope?'

'And her housekeeper.'

'The housekeeper probably got in their way. Pryszlak's sect has no regard for human life, not even their own. This man, Ferrier, killed himself without hesitation when he saw he was trapped. The motive wasn't revenge. I think the idea was to kill anyone who had any knowledge at all of their organization.'

'There's been no attempt on your life?'

'Not yet, Inspector,' Bishop said. 'Maybe Ferrier would have turned on Jessica once he'd disposed of Jacob Kulek.'

Peck frowned and turned to Bishop. 'I still don't understand why I haven't booked you for the murder of Braverman and his wife.'

'I came to you, remember? I could easily have left that house without anyone ever knowing I'd been there. I could have wiped away any fingerprints. It would have been easy for the police to have believed that Braverman fought with his wife, shot her, then shot himself. It makes no sense for me to have murdered them and reported the crime myself.'

Peck still looked sceptical.

'And the others,' Bishop went on. 'The attempt on Jacob Kulek's life. The murder of Agnes Kirkhope and her maid. All connected with the Pryszlak business. Kulek, because he was investigating Pryszlak's activities. Agnes Kirkhope, because we had been to see her and told her of our suspicions. And, of course, her brother, Dominic, had been a sect member. It's logical, Inspector, that I should have been a victim too.'

'Nothing's logical about this business, Mr Bishop.'

'I agree. Even more illogical are the events in Willow Road. How do you explain them?'

'At the moment, I wouldn't even try. We've got people locked up and they're like zombies. Even the one man who didn't seem to be as bad as the others has deteriorated – he's now like the rest of them. A man named Brewer – he'd tied his family up and locked them in a wardrobe. But he gave himself up before he could do any harm.'

Bishop noticed the puzzled look on Jessica's face. He was concerned for her: the near-death of her father had left her in a brittle state. He had rung the Research Institute from the house in Robertsbridge, resisting the urge to flee from the blood-stained corpses lying there on the kitchen floor, worried that if an attempt had been made on his life, then the same could happen to Jacob Kulek. He had seen for himself how the madwoman in Beechwood had tried to get at Kulek. And he knew there was a connection: the portrait he had seen in the round room at Robertsbridge was of Dominic Kirkhope; he had remembered Agnes Kirkhope's photograph of her brother and although there was an age difference between the portrait and photograph, the resemblance was distinct. He had been surprised to find that Detective Chief Inspector Peck, the man who was apparently in charge of the investigation into Willow Road and its mishappenings, was at the Institute. It came as no surprise that an attempt on Jacob Kulek's life had already been made.

'Now all I've got,' Peck was saying, 'are murders, suicides, attempted rape – homosexual and otherwise – mutilation, arson and cells full of people who don't know what time of day it is. To help me with my report to the Commissioner – and which you seem to think explains everything – I've got your information on a nutcase named Boris Pryszlak and his crackpot organization who believed in evil as a powerful, physical force. How do you think he's going to take it, Miss Kulek? He'd order me to be locked up with the other nutters.'

'I've given you no explanations, just what I know. Your job is to do something about it.'

'Any ideas exactly what?'

'I'd start by trying to find the names of all Pryszlak's associates.'

'You mean the members of his sect?'

'Yes.'

'And then?'

Jessica shrugged. 'I don't know. Keep a watch on them?'

Peck snorted.

'At least you'd find out if Braverman and Ferrier were members,' Bishop said. 'It might even lead you to the murderers of Miss Kirkhope and her housekeeper.'

Peck wished he could make up his mind about Bishop, one way or the other. He had ordered him to stay at the house in Robertsbridge until the local police arrived, and then arranged to have him escorted back to London, to Peck's office in New Scotland Yard. He had questioned the ghost-hunter – what kind of profession was that? – for a solid hour before Kulek's daughter, again under escort, had arrived from her father's hospital bedside. It was getting on for ten now and still he wasn't any nearer to the truth. It would have been easier if he could believe Bishop was either lying or totally innocent.

Peck leaned forward on his desk. 'Okay, we're not going to find out much more tonight. I'm letting you go, Bishop. I'm not convinced, but your story might just be feasible. This

Pryszlak may have had friends who didn't like you and Jacob Kulek snooping around Beechwood. It could be that they regarded it as some kind of holy shrine after the mass suicide. The fact that poor old Miss Kirkhope ordered it to be demolished may have been her undoing. We'll put it down to a lunatic fringe for the moment. It still doesn't explain all the disasters in Willow Road, of course, but I can hardly blame you for that. Anyway, we'll be keeping a close eye on you.'

'Don't worry,' Bishop said wryly, 'I won't be running away.'

Peck stabbed a finger against the desktop. 'We'll be keeping an eye on you not just because I'm suspicious – and I bloody am – but for your own protection. That goes for your father, too, Miss Kulek. For protection, I mean. If his assailant was part of Pryszlak's mob, they might have another try.'

Alarm showed in Jessica's eyes.

'Sorry. Didn't mean to frighten you,' Peck said soothingly. 'It's better to be safe than sorry, that's all.' He turned to one of his officers, who had been leaning against the wall, arms folded, bemused by the whole exchange. 'Frank, get someone to show them down, will you?'

As Bishop and Jessica rose to leave, Peck looked up at them, his scowl still in evidence. 'Keep us informed of any more little trips, Mr Bishop. I'll probably want to speak to you again tomorrow. I hope your father recovers, Miss Kulek.'

Jessica nodded her thanks and they left the detective's office.

The officer returned a few seconds later, amusement on his face.

'What are you bloody grinning at?' Peck growled.

'You don't believe in all this bollocks about the power of evil, do you, guv?'

'That's not the point, Frank. *They* believe it, that's what matters. At least, the girl does. I think Bishop hasn't made his mind up yet. To tell you the truth, I don't think *I've* made my mind up, either.'

They drove away from the tall building, silent for a few moments as if Peck could still hear their conversation from his office high above them. The rain had finally stopped, leaving a dampness in the night air. Jessica pulled her coat collar tight around her neck.

'Will you take me back to the hospital, Chris?'

'I'm already headed in that direction,' he told her. 'How was he when you left?'

'Shocked, weak. He was still finding it difficult to breathe.'

'How much damage?'

'Physically, just bruising, as before. The doctor said his difficulty in breathing was more to do with the emotional shock than constriction of his windpipe. Oh God, if I'd have gone back to his study a few seconds later . . .' She left the sentence unfinished.

He wanted to reach out to her, to pat her hand, to touch her; but he felt awkward, a stranger.

'He'll be all right, Jessica. He's a strong-minded man.'

She tried to smile at him, but failed. His attention was on the road ahead, anyway. She studied his profile, noticing the lines of tension around his eyes. 'And you've been through so much, too,' she said eventually. 'It must have been a nightmare.'

'It was even more of a nightmare for Agnes Kirkhope and her housekeeper; one they didn't come out of. What manner of creature could do such a thing?' He shook his head in regret, disgust. 'I think Peck still believes I murdered Braverman and his wife.'

'He can't, Chris. It doesn't make any sense.'

'None of this does. You and I, in our different ways, deal with matters that defy logic all the time. Peck's a policeman: they like some kind of order to things. We can't blame him for his suspicion.'

'Nor his aggression.'

'Nor that.'

He pulled up at traffic lights, floodlights turning the square before them into a daylight scene. Tourists, thousands it seemed, watched the silvery fountains and craned their necks to see the sculptured naval man standing aloft on the huge rising column as though it were the crow's nest on one of his ships. As a brilliantly lit backdrop, the impressive structure of the National Gallery dominated the thriving square, while a constantly surging stream of traffic flowed round and out.

'It's so bright,' Jessica remarked. 'So alive. It could be daytime.'

The red light blinked off and the green appeared. Bishop edged the car forward into the metal throng, finding a niche and flowing with the tide. 'I wonder how many of Pryszlak's people stayed alive? And why?'

'Perhaps for a time like this.'

He had to concentrate on avoiding a taxi which was making a claim to a three-foot space just ahead of Bishop's car.

Jessica went on. 'If the police can locate them all, perhaps this can end now, before it's too late.'

He snatched a quick glimpse of her. 'What can end, Jessica? Do you and your father know what's happening?'

She hesitated before she spoke. 'We're not sure. We discussed it with Edith Metlock only yesterday – '

They both looked at each other at the same time.

'Christ!' Bishop said quietly.

*

Bishop turned the car into the wide tree-lined avenue, keeping in second gear and peering from left to right at the houses on either side.

'What number is it?' he asked Jessica.

'I'm sure it's sixty-four. I've never been to her home, but I've often contacted her there.'

'Even numbers on the right. Keep your eyes peeled.'

Once they had passed through London's West End they were able to make rapid progress to Edith Metlock's address in Woodford. Both were angry at themselves for having forgotten the medium, for they realized that she, as a part of the group investigating Beechwood, might also be in danger.

'Fifty-eight . . . sixty . . . sixty-two . . . There! Just ahead.' Bishop pointed towards a small bungalow, twenty feet of garden on either side separating it from its neighbours. He waited for an approaching car to pass, then drew over to that side of the road, stopping just in front of the bungalow.

'She's there,' Jessica said. 'All the lights are on.' Suddenly she felt afraid to leave the car.

Bishop slid his glasses into his top pocket and switched off the engine. 'We're probably over-reacting,' he said unconvincingly, then sensed Jessica's fear. 'Do you want to stay in the car?'

She shook her head and reached for the door-handle.

The garden gate squealed noisily as Bishop pushed it open. Light from the windows spilled on to the lawn on either side of the narrow path leading to the bungalow's porch, the clipped grass a flat green vignetting into total blackness. The porch itself was lit by an external light.

Bishop rang the doorbell and they waited for movement inside. Jessica bit down on her lower lip; her eyes were wide, almost vacant. He touched her arm, at the elbow, giving it a little shake as if to dispel her anxieties. He tried the doorbell again.

'Maybe she's asleep,' he said.

'With all the lights on?'

'She may have dozed off.'

He rattled the letterbox for added noise, then ducked to look through it.

'All the doors in the hallway are open. She must have heard us. Looks like every light is on, too.' He put his mouth to the opening and called out Edith Metlock's name. There was no reply.

'Chris, let's get the police,' Jessica said, slowly backing away from the front door.

'Not yet.' He caught her arm again and this time held it firmly. 'Let's be a little more sure there's something wrong first.'

'Can't you feel it?' Jessica looked around at the shadows surrounding the house. 'It's . . . I don't know . . . unearthly. As if . . . as if something is waiting.'

'Jessica.' His voice was soft. 'You've been through a bad time today – we both have. It's getting to you, eating away at your imagination.' And it was eating away at his, too. 'I'm going to take a look round the back. Why don't you go and sit in the car?'

Her alarm flared to a new level for a brief moment. 'I think I'll stick with you,' she said firmly.

Bishop smiled and moved off, stepping on to the lawn and glancing into a window as he passed. The curtains were drawn wide and lace netting diffused the image inside. He saw it was a small dining-room, the table bare except for a pot containing a leafy plant. There was no one in the room. They moved around the corner of the one-floor building and Bishop felt Jessica draw closer to his back as they found themselves in an area of darkness. The ground became softer beneath their feet as if they were walking through a dormant flower bed. More light shone ahead and they passed a reeded glass window which Bishop assumed would be the bungalow's bathroom. Beyond, the light was more brilliant, throwing back the night with unimpeded force. The blinds to the kitchen were drawn upwards and Bishop blinked against the harsh neon light.

'Empty,' he told Jessica. 'There's a door over there leading out to the back garden. Let's try it.'

More light flooded outwards from the back of the house and he wondered if it was only because of the natural nervousness of a woman living alone. But Edith Metlock had not struck him as the nervous type.

He tried the kitchen door and was not surprised to find it locked. He jiggled with the handle for a few moments, then rapped on the glass. Maybe she was out and had left the lights on to discourage any would-be burglars. But every light? And the curtains open?

'Chris!'

Bishop turned to see Jessica gazing into a window nearby. He hurried over to her.

'Look,' she said. 'Over there, in the armchair.'

He found himself looking into a bedroom, again the curtains drawn wide. Through the lace netting he could see an unoccupied bed, a bedside table, the lamp on it adding more brightness to the already well-lit room, a wardrobe, a chest of drawers. And in an armchair in the far corner sat the figure of a woman. His vision was hazy through the lace, but he was sure it was Edith Metlock.

'Mrs Metlock.' He tapped at the window. 'It's Chris Bishop and Jessica Kulek.' He used his knuckles against the glass.

He thought he saw a movement, a slight turning of the head, but couldn't be sure.

'Why doesn't she answer?' Jessica said. 'Why is she just sitting there, Chris?'

The thought flashed through his mind that Edith Metlock may have had a stroke; but her body sat erect, not slumped. Was she too afraid to answer?

'I'm going to break in,' he told Jessica. He walked back to the kitchen and angled his body to see through the small glass panels that ran the length of the door. He could just see the end of the key poking from the lock on that side. He half-turned away from the door, then brought his elbow swinging back at a pane alongside the lock. The glass fell inwards and clinked to the floor. He pushed his hand through the opening, carefully avoiding any remaining shards, and twisted the key, grunting with satisfaction as the lock clicked. Turning the handle, he pushed inwards. It wouldn't open. There was less resistance when he put pressure on the top, and solid defiance when he tried the bottom. Without hesitation he kicked in one of the bottom panes, then stooped and drew back the bolt inside. The door swung open.

Jessica followed him in, keeping close, trying to see over his shoulder. Edith Metlock's eyes were closed when they entered her bedroom and they remained so even when they called her name. Her back was stiff, her face pointed towards the ceiling light. Her hands clutched at the arms of the chair.

'She's breathing,' Bishop said and, as if his voice had triggered off something in the medium, her breathing became deeper, her breasts beginning to heave with the effort. Her lips parted and air was exhaled, then noisily sucked in. Her breathing became sharper, gasping, and Jessica knelt before her, touching the medium's shoulders, gently calling her name. The panting became frantic and Jessica looked anxiously at Bishop. He felt useless, tempted to slap the medium and bring her out of her trance-like state, but afraid of what the sudden shock might do to her. Then Edith Metlock jerked forward in the seat, her gasps brought to an abrupt halt. She sat that way for long seconds, then slowly sank back into the armchair, her breath released in a long, drawn-out sigh. The medium's eyelids flickered, opened; her pupils were tiny pinpoints. Her jaw was slack, lips moving, tongue lolling within its cavity as though its muscles were limp. A low murmuring came from somewhere at the back of her throat.

'She's trying to say something, Chris. Can you understand her?'

Bishop leaned his head closer to the medium's and listened. Slowly, the words began to take form, began to shape themselves into a meaning.

'Keep ... it away,' Edith Metlock said, her voice slurred but just coherent. 'Keep ... it ... away ... The dark ... keep it away ...'

15

The home crowd was angry, its wrath rolling around the stadium in a mighty roar. The ref was a wanker: even the minority away-fans, delighted though they were at his dubious decisions in their team's favour throughout the match, had to admit it. Now even the goalkeeper was going into his book for dissent and *he* had never received a booking in fifteen years of soccer. The overwhelming anger reached fever pitch when the tiny yellow card was raised into the air and the away-fans – except for the lunatic few whose brains were in the tips of their tongues – refrained from jeering. The hostility around them had made them nervous.

The home team had been playing well all season, and the smell of the First Division was in their fans' nostrils. They had completely dominated their rival clubs in the Second Division. Their new striker, imported from Italy for an incredible sum of money (to make up the loss, the club had had to sell two players, one mid-field, the other a popular left-back, and admission prices had been raised) had contributed remarkably to their success. But after only ten minutes, the Italian had been stretcher-carried off with a leg injury. The word spread around at half-time like an uncontrolled brush fire that his leg had been broken. In two places.

The away-team had played like non-league factory workers throughout the match, their studded boots scything opponents rather than playing the ball. It had been the same on Saturday when ugly brute force at their own ground had earned them the draw. Their fear of relegation next season had turned them into eleven crude defenders, only occasional bouts of real skill reminding the crowd they were playing football and not rugby. Tonight the match was a gruelling affair and already several fights had broken out among the crowd. The policemen seated on benches placed strategically around the pitch, helmets at their feet, glanced nervously over their shoulders at the ranting mob, the surge of faces merged into a dark swaying mass behind the brilliant glare of the floodlights. The mood was ugly.

Eddie Cossins pulled his girlfriend, Vicky, closer to him. He was beginning to wonder if it had been wise to bring her tonight. She didn't even like football as a rule and he suspected her insistence on coming with him was more to do with ingratiating herself with him than interest in football itself. Five weeks was a long time to be going out with a bird. Too long, really. They started getting ideas.

'What's he booked him for, Eddie?'

He barely heard her shrill voice above the uproar even though she had stood on tiptoe and bellowed into his ear.

'Ref don't like bleedin' arguments!' he yelled back.

'What's he arguing about?'

Eddie groaned. 'The ref's given the other side a penalty. Anyone could see the player took a dive. All the bleedin' fouls they've done and they get a penalty. What a tosser!'

Vicky sank back inside her heavy overcoat, pulling Eddie's club scarf tighter around her neck. Stupid game, she told herself. Grown-up men kicking a bag of wind around a field. And the crowd getting upset just because their team wasn't winning. Like a load of kids. Eddie too. Look at him shouting at the referee as if he could hear him. Poor little man was only doing his job. So this was what she had to compete against. Another girl might have been easier. Oh no. Now it's raining. Jostled, pushed, crushed, touched-up by invisible hands – and now a soaking! It wasn't worth it. He could have his bloody football! He was spotty, anyway.

The crowd hushed as the away-team's skipper placed the mud-smeared ball on the penalty spot. His left foot was renowned.

On the terraces, Jack Bettney held his breath, almost afraid to watch. Twenty-five years he'd supported the club, through the good years and the lean. After a long stretch in the Second Division they were on the way up again, back to their rightful place among the leaders of the game. They had won back their old days' glory last season and this one. Nothing would stop them now. Nothing except a team full of cowboys and a bent referee. He kept the anger tight within himself.

He blinked away rainspots from his eyes and watched the enemy pace himself away from the ball. The goalkeeper danced nervously from foot to foot and finally settled down on his line, heels raised from the muddy earth. To the right, son, he'd aim it at the bottom right-hand corner, Jack Bettney told him silently. He knew the opposing captain's favourite spot. Jack could feel the tenseness around him; the apprehension passed through the mass of tightly packed bodies like an electric current. The enemy began his run, pounding up to the glistening ball like an express train. To the right, son, to the right.

Animal, sometimes known as The Beast to his friends, whooped with glee when the ball shot into the bottom left-hand corner of the net, the goalkeeper left sprawled in the mud on the other side of his goal-mouth. Animal leapt in the air using the shoulders of a fellow supporter in front to hold himself aloft. His friend's knees buckled under the seventeen stone weight, but others grabbed his arms to keep him upright. It would have been difficult to get up again in that crowd.

'Fuckin' magic, fuckin' magic!' Animal screeched. Hostile eyes turned to look in his direction.

He chortled as the goalkeeper dejectedly retrieved the ball from the back of the net. 'What a load of wankers!' he chanted.

'Leave it out, Animal,' one of his companions said nervously, feeling the resentment around them. 'We're not bloody at home now.'

Animal didn't give a shit and he let the home supporters around him know it. Personally, he didn't care much about the game either. It was the excitement he liked, not the excitement of the competition but, although he couldn't have expressed it himself, the raw emotion the game produced, feelings that could be demonstrated without embarrassment.

He turned to face the crowd behind him, his thick, porky arms raised, middle and index fingers stiff and parted in his favourite up-yours gesture. The rain suddenly fell as though someone had pulled the plug from the clouds above and it spilled on to his fat cheeks and open-necked shirt. He laughed, catching the torrent in his mouth. Their faces were just a watery blur, but he could feel their hate and it cheered him.

He found another pair of shoulders to leap on and this time his companion went down, Animal collapsing with him. He giggled in the darkness, thrashing out at the jostling legs around him. It was like being underground, subdued light sinking down through cracks in the earth, the surrounding legs like moving tree roots. He giggled louder at his friend's muffled cursing, maliciously pushing his gross body on hands and knees further into the throng, causing those above him to lose their balance and spill over. He liked the darkness as much as he liked being in a crowd. It was almost the same thing: you couldn't be seen. For a moment it had become too black down there, as though the crowd had joined together to form a solid crust above him, and he felt a little afraid. The darkness somehow had a gooey thickness to it.

Animal burst to the surface like a whale from the sea, throwing those nearest to him backwards, laughing at their shouts of anger. The fact that their club scarves differed from the one he wore tied around his wrist didn't bother him at all: Animal was afraid of nothing and no one.

Fans at the back resented the crowd ripple that had thrust against them and several saw the cause of it, the fat grinning face turned away from the pitch in their direction, thick bare arms, despite the weather, raised in defiance against them, the opposition scarf tied to one wrist. The rain had drenched them, their team was losing – and this fucker was taking the piss. They surged forward as one, a ripple that grew into an onrushing wave, gathering momentum, gaining force, breaking over the fat man and pounding him like a rock on the sea-shore.

Eddie and Vicky had been standing halfway between the grinning monster and the fans at the back who had started the push. The girl screamed as they were carried forward, her feet swept off the ground, her body held tightly aloft, desperately clinging to Eddie who was powerless to resist the torrent. Eddie had been used to crushes like this before, but he had never had a girl to look after. He knew these sudden rushes could be dangerous, fights inevitably breaking out in the aftermath. The thing was not to go down – you'd be kicked to death beneath all those feet. It was the poor sods at the front who took the full weight of it: they'd be crushed against the barriers. He managed to get an arm around Vicky's waist, his other arm locked tight against his body. He shouted a warning to the girl when he saw what was happening ahead of him. Bodies were going over, *going down*!

Jack Bettney felt the swell reach him. Fortunately, he was away from the path of the main stream, but even so he and the other fans around him were pushed back then sucked in with the flow. He kept his balance, well experienced nowadays in the art of surviving a football match. Silly bastards! he thought. No wonder the armchair was the best place to watch a game these days. Those nearest to him managed to steady themselves and they jigged on tiptoe to see what was happening in the other part of the crowd. A great hole had appeared and they realized many of the people had gone down, more bodies toppling over them as the surge continued.

Jack winced. There'd be a few broken bones among that lot. His woolly cap was sodden now, and rain ran off the end of his nose. He blinked and saw the ball was in the centre of the pitch again, the players deliberately oblivious of the reaction in the crowd. They probably couldn't see too much against the glare of the floodlights anyway. Jack turned his attention away from his team's centre forward who was preparing to tap the ball towards a mid-field player, and tried to see what was happening to the fallen spectators. The atmosphere in the stadium was bad tonight and he was glad he was a home supporter. The hostility towards the away-fans had been growing since the beginning of the match and the commotion over there was just the start of the trouble to come. Needle matches always infected the fans and tonight the infection was going to run wild. He could feel it.

A flickering behind and high above distracted him. He looked up at the tall metal tower set into the concrete terraces towards the back of the stadium, sixteen blinding lights at the top helping three other similarly situated towers around the ground to turn night into day on the pitch. Fifteen lights. One was spluttering, going dim, reviving briefly, sparks flying into short-lived arcs, then fading completely. Bloody rain. That shouldn't be happening, though. When was the last time they were checked? A cheer rang out from the other side of the pitch as another light abruptly popped off, then another. More sparks began to fly and soon the whole array of lights was fizzing and smoking. The section of the crowd beneath the tower began to grow anxious and started backing away from the area beneath it, pushing at those around them for room. All the lights suddenly exploded at once, glass and sparks falling with the rain on to the people below and a sharp, tangy smell was carried into the air. The gloom on that side of the stadium suddenly became denser and Jack felt the panic as a crowd wave started again, this time rippling outwards, the movement resembling a pond's surface disturbed by a stone.

Animal was on the ground kicking out with heavy boots, trying to clear a space for himself. It had become darker now, almost black and, strangely, rather than fearing the blackness, he welcomed it. Someone was on top of him and he managed to get one beefy hand beneath the man's chin. He pushed up sharply and was delighted to hear above the clamour of the spectators – or had he only felt it? – something snap. The body fell limply against him and Animal felt good. He had enjoyed that. Something chuckled in the blackness of his mind and it wasn't him.

A foot came down on his cheek and he twisted his head to dislodge it. He heaved the body on top of him away, but there were others, alive and thrashing, to take the man's place. Animal managed to get an elbow beneath himself and raised his shoulders from the ground. A figure crashed down beside him – man or youth, he couldn't tell – and this time he definitely heard the crack of skull on concrete. He lifted the fan's head by the hair and shoved it down to hear the sound again. Nice one.

Eddie tried to pull Vicky closer to him, but he was pinned to someone else's back. The body beneath him squirmed to free itself, but there were others on top of Eddie. Vicky's screams could be heard clearly over the predominantly male cries of alarm and anger and he tightened his grip around her waist, determined not to let her go. He felt a blow behind his ear, then another. For fuck's sake, someone was hitting him! Twisting himself around, he spilled the two on top of him over, using his elbow to help them on their way. He rolled on to someone else and he realized it was Vicky.

Pushing himself up, not caring if he was treading on anybody, he pulled at the girl, drawing her halfway out of the scrambling heap.

Hysteria was in her eyes as she grabbed wildly at him.

'Take it easy, Vicky!' he shouted. 'You'll have me over!'

Something thudded into him from behind, causing him to lose his precarious balance. Then someone had him by the throat and was pounding a fist into his face to the accompaniment of Vicky's screams. Rage replaced the fear inside him as he struck back at his aggressor. No one was going to belt him and get away with it! And as he fought, a blackness seemed to fill him.

The girl felt the mob violence. It wasn't just the physical aggression of the crowd; it was something else, something that slowly, stealthily, smothered them all. Her head snapped upwards when she felt icy, black fingers tapping on the surface of her mind, fingers that wanted to scratch their way through and explore inside. She screamed again, fearing the dark hand more than the madness around her. Someone was pulling her up and she opened her eyes, grateful for the firm grip beneath her arms. The face was smiling, she could just make that out in the gloom. But she sensed there was no humour in the smile. It was a huge bloated face, the hair closely cropped and plastered to his scalp by the rain. His body was big, his arms bare, and he held her upright against the frenzied tide surrounding them. She knew the evil that was in the air was also in him. The cold black fingers had found easy access into this man.

Animal's smile became a grin as the voices inside told him what to do.

Something was tugging at Jack Bettney and it had nothing to do with the spectators who were clawing at each other to get clear of the crush. It was something nipping away at his thoughts. No – it was something nipping away at his will, he was sure of it. He had read somewhere about mass-hysteria, how panic or even adulation could pass through a crowd, hopping from mind to mind, touching every person present until they were enveloped in a binding cocoon of emotion. That was what was happening here! But it was something more than panic. There was a savagery about these struggling, heaving people. Not all of them, for many were under attack from others; but the earlier hostility had somehow manifested itself into an overwhelming madness. It was the madness that was tugging at him!

He began to hit out, not caring whom he struck, knowing he had to get away from them, sensing he was different – *he was not with them*. They would sense it too!

Hands reached out to him, grabbing at his clothes, pulling the woolly cap from his head, reaching for his eyes. He went down and as he lay underneath the trampling feet, the darkness all around, he began to give in to the silent, pounding voices, wanting to join them if it would give him peace, agreeing to be part of them, whatever their intent. Realizing too late they were not offering him peace.

Animal was finished with the girl. Others wanted her even though her body was limp, no life left in it. He let her fall and pushed a way through the mob, making slow but firm progress, eyes fixed on the metal structure protruding from the mass of human flesh and towering over them like a soulless sentinel.

All activity on the field below had stopped, the players, linesmen and referee staring in bewilderment at the crowd on that side of the pitch. Policemen had left their benches and were hurrying around to gather just below the section where the trouble had started. But there was no longer one place of activity, for the skirmishes had spread, joined, merged into one massive battle, everyone on that side of the stadium involved. None of the constables felt inclined to wade into the thick of it, nor did the officer in charge encourage them to do so. Suicide was not part of their duty.

Animal finally reached the base of the floodlight tower, the short journey through the press of bodies taxing even his great strength. But adrenaline was coursing through him, for he knew what he had to do and it excited him. He was pushed up against the metal, its surface slimy wet with rain; he reached inside for the junction box from which heavily protected cables emerged, soaring their way up towards the rows of burst lights above. The cover to the box would not budge, for it had been built to resist the attention of destructive fans. Animal climbed the first two cross-struts of the tower and poked his foot inside. He kicked at the box, his heavy boot scarring and denting its surface. It took long minutes for the cover to work itself loose but, for perhaps the first time in his life, Animal had patience. He kept doggedly at his task and whooped with glee when the cover finally fell away. Then he reached inside and curled his huge hand around two of the heavy cables. He began to tug, the crowd pressed tight around him, the rain drenching everyone and everything.

The cables finally came away, for Animal was strong, and the power passed through him into the wet, tightly-packed crowd, sweeping outwards with paralysing swiftness, spreading like a deadly germ. Hundreds had been touched before the current finally blew itself out and plunged the entire stadium into total, screaming darkness.

16

Bishop studied Lucy's tiny face, holding the framed photograph in one hand, his other hand resting on top of the mantelpiece. His thoughts of her had become frozen moments, still-life images like the photograph he held, single frames his memory had captured. He could still hear her squeaky giggles, her panting sobs, but they were echoes, not attached to Lucy herself. He missed her and, with a slight feeling of guilt, realized he missed her more than Lynn. Perhaps it was because in reality his wife was still there: only her mind was dead. Did it amount to the same thing? Could you still love a person when they had become someone else? Something else? You could, but it wasn't easy; and he wasn't sure he was capable any more.

He replaced the photograph and sat in an armchair facing the empty grate. A new guilt was rising in him, compounding the old, and it was to do with Jessica. Perhaps it was because she was the only woman he'd had any real association with for a long, long time. Since Lynn's illness he hadn't sought female company, nor missed it. So much had been drained from him after Lucy's death and Lynn's breakdown; only resentment had been left, the remnants of his own sorrow. The resentment had become a fierce anger which had been channelled into the new work he had found for himself. But even that had begun to die, leaving only the bitterness that clung like a withered vine to a crumbling wall. Now some-thing inside that had lain dormant for many years had begun to breathe again, lightly at first, stirring gently, unfurling, becoming steady. The old feeling had moved aside a little, making room for the new. Was it because of Jessica or because of the passage of pain-healing time? Could any attractive woman coming into his life at that point have had the same effect? He didn't have the answer, nor did he want to ponder the question. One day, Lynn might become whole again. And if she didn't . . . she was still his wife.

Restless, he heaved himself from the chair and went into the kitchen, taking a can of beer from the fridge. He pulled the tab and drank straight from the can, half its contents gone before he took it from his lips again. He returned to the armchair, his thoughts dark and brooding.

It was crazy. Everything that was happening was crazy. The madness was growing, a virulence that was spreading like an ancient, uncontrolled plague. An exaggeration? The suicides at Beechwood had been the beginning. Then the insanity that developed a year later, a madness that had soon enveloped most of those living in Willow Road. An attempted murder on himself and Jacob Kulek. The slaying of Agnes Kirkhope and her housekeeper. And then the riot at the football stadium last night. *Nearly six hundred people dead!* Hundreds electrocuted, floodlight wiring torn loose and the current directed into the rain-soaked crowd. Hundreds of others beaten, kicked to death by the mob. The rest – mass suicide. Any way they could find. Climbing then leaping from the floodlight towers or the girders supporting the covered stand area. Or hanging themselves with their club scarves. Belt buckles, metal combs – other concealed weapons that troublemakers always managed to smuggle in – anything that was sharp used to sever arteries. There had been a record gate for a midweek match in the small Second Division ground: twenty-eight thousand. Nearly *six hundred dead!* What kind of nightmare must it have been inside that darkened stadium? Bishop was unable to control the shudder that ran through him. The beer spilled on to his chin when he raised the can again and he realized his hand was shaking.

Others had run into the streets, most to escape the bedlam, many seeking alternative means of destroying themselves. Hands had been smashed through shop-front windows, the jagged shards used to slash wrists. Twenty youths had run into the nearby railway station and jumped as one from the platform when an express hurtled through. The nearby canal was still being dredged for the bodies of those who had chosen drowning. Tall buildings had been used to leap from, lorries or buses to leap under. Cars as weapons. The destruction had gone on through the night. *Six hundred!*

When daylight finally came, scores of them had been found wandering the streets, their faces blank, their minds seemingly empty. The word *zombie* flashed through Bishop's head, a word that had always held humorous connotations for him in the past; but now the description had a true, sinister meaning. That was what these people had become. Zombies. The walking dead.

Just how many had been found in this state was not yet known, but according to the news media, there were more still not accounted for. Still wandering mindlessly? Dead but not discovered? Or had they found a place to hide? The horror of it had been with Bishop throughout the day, for he had made the connection, the obvious connection. And so had Jacob Kulek, who was now out of hospital, and Jessica – Bishop had spoken to her earlier that day. The insanity was not confined to Willow Road: it had travelled a distance of nearly a mile to the football ground.

He wondered if Edith Metlock had been touched by the same madness. When he and Jessica had found her in her home two nights before, she had mumbled something about the dark over and over again as though she were afraid that the night outside might enter the house and somehow consume her. Bishop had wanted to get her to a hospital, but Jessica had told him she had often seen mediums in this state, that Edith had become lost within herself and could only find her way back on her own. The trance would wear off; all she needed was protection until it did. They had put the medium on to her bed, Jessica covering her with a quilt, propping her head up with a pillow. While Bishop had checked every room in the house and relocked the kitchen door, Jessica had rung the hospital where her father was being kept for observation. He was fine, sleeping under mild sedation and there was no point in her coming over that late; unless there were any unforeseen developments overnight, she could come and collect him in the morning.

They had sat with Edith Metlock all night, and they had talked, occasionally breaking off to listen to the medium's sudden disturbed murmurings. It was well past three before the tension drained from Edith's face and she seemed to drift off into a deeper, peaceful sleep. By that time, Jessica's eyes were closing and he finally persuaded her to lie down on the end of Edith's bed. He found a blanket to cover her with and, half-asleep, she had smiled when he touched a hand to her cheek; then she was gone, her breathing becoming deep and regular to match Edith Metlock's.

Bishop had sat in the chair previously occupied by the medium, uneasy at being left alone with the oppression that seemed to surround the house. It was just his imagination, he told himself. There was nothing out there. It was just the result of everything that had happened catching up.

Eventually the oppression seemed to lift. His eyelids grew too heavy and he slept.

Gentle prodding had woken him the following morning and he had found Jessica kneeling before him, her smile a welcome sight. Edith Metlock was propped up on the bed and, although she appeared to be exhausted, she thanked them both for staying with her through the night. She seemed nervous and constantly glanced around the room as though expecting someone else to be there hiding in the shadows. She was too confused to tell them what had happened the night before – Bishop suspected she wasn't sure herself. Fortunately, because of her unsettled state, it had not occurred to Edith to ask them what had brought them to her house, and they deemed it wise not to tell her.

After a light breakfast cooked by Jessica, they had persuaded the medium to stay at Jacob Kulek's house for a few days. Edith had declined at first, but when Jessica mentioned that her father had had a slight 'accident' – she would explain later – and that it would be enormously helpful if Edith could take care of him for a few days until he was better while Jessica organized the day-to-day running of the Institute, she readily agreed. There was much she and Jacob could discuss over the next few days, Edith told them, a distant look in her eyes.

By the time they were ready to leave the house, some of the colour had returned to the medium's cheeks, although they still found her occasionally glancing around the room in a perplexed manner.

Bishop was surprised when he saw the home in which Jacob Kulek and his daughter lived. It was in a small, secluded lane just off Highgate Village and, as they turned into the narrow driveway almost hidden by trees, it was as if they were approaching a building constructed entirely of broad sheets of shining bronze, the sun reflecting from their surfaces, a dazzling contrast to the surrounding sombre winter greens.

'It's iodized glass,' Jessica had explained, amused by his reaction. 'You can see out, but you can't see in. At night, when it's lit inside, vertical blinds give us our privacy. My father can see shadows, you see. With daylight all around he can see any movement inside the house. It's the only vision he can enjoy.'

Jessica had rung the hospital again from the house and was relieved to hear Jacob was well and would be allowed home later that morning after one or two tests had been carried out. Bishop left and before he turned from the driveway into the small lane, he glanced in his rearview mirror and saw Jessica standing at the door of the house, watching him. He almost raised a hand to wave back, but stopped himself.

Once home, the drive through the rush-hour-filled city having wearied him even further, he had undressed and thrown himself into bed, not waking until five that evening. A phone call to Jessica's had disappointed him, for Edith Metlock had answered. Jacob Kulek was resting, she herself was fine although still not quite clear on what had happened the previous night, and Jessica was at the Institute. He put down the receiver and stood by it for a few moments, debating whether or not to ring Jessica's office. He decided not to.

He cooked and ate a lonely dinner, then settled down to work for the rest of the evening. A publisher was interested in a new book he had planned and had already agreed on a small advance on production of a synopsis. Bishop's idea was to write a detailed study on the many occult associations that were now thriving in different parts of the world, organizations as varied as the Institute of Parapsychology and Cybernetics Inc., in Texas, to the Foundation for Research on the

Nature of Man, in North Carolina. A list of all these associations and societies had been drawn up by him, but he would have to sift through and choose those he would major on, for there was no possibility of visiting every place in person and, indeed, some were behind the Iron Curtain and access to them might prove difficult. Several of these, however, sounded intriguing: the Czechoslovak Coordination Committee for Research in Telepathy, Telegnosis and Psychokinesis, and the Bioelectronics Section of the Polish Copernicus Society of Naturalists were just two he was determined to see for himself. His publisher had agreed to pay his travelling expenses as part of the advance, this later to go against royalties, and Bishop hoped that many of the associations would receive and accommodate him as a guest; most were eager to have their work recognized. He planned an objective study on these foundations, societies, associations, institutes – whatever they termed themselves – keeping his own attitudes carefully in check until the conclusion of the book. It was only then that he would know himself what those attitudes would be. In a way, the exercise was almost self-indulgent: he wanted to discover more about the paranormal. When he had begun his strange career as a psychic investigator, he had had an intransigent prejudice against mysticism in any form and had quickly come to learn that there was a great difference in what was commonly termed the supernatural and the paranormal: one had mystical connotations while the other was an unknown science, perhaps – and, as yet, no one was *really* certain – the science of the mind. He felt sure that by studying the activities of these various groups he would have a clearer picture of the overall progress this relatively new field of science had made. The growth in public interest was incredible. The young were shying away from materialism and seeking their own higher levels, their elders seeking a refuge from the chaos around them. It seemed that for many, conventional religion had failed to provide that comfort, for prayers and paying homage did not always work. In fact, for most, it rarely worked. Where was justice, where was right? The more communications improved throughout the world, the more the injustice could be seen. When the new generations looked at religion they could only see manmade ritual, manmade hypocrisy. Even history told them the pursuit of God had meant the slaughter and suffering of millions. Many turned to new cults, fringe religions such as the Scientologists, the Moonies, the People's Temple (what was the real reason for *their* mass suicide?). Gurus had replaced messiahs. Psychiatrists had replaced priests. Parapsychologists might eventually replace both.

There was a growing belief that man's soul was hidden deep in some dark recess of his mind, not an invisible entity filling his whole being. If it was there, it could be found; the scientists needed only to know where to look and produce the instrument to trace it. And science in its study of the paranormal, was slowly, very slowly, homing in. Bishop had to smile at his own uncomplicated logic; Jacob Kulek could probably improve on the substance of his reasoning, but he felt their separate conclusions would not be that far apart. He made a mental note: Kulek's Research Institute would be a good place to start with for his book.

Bishop worked late into the night, outlining the structure of his thesis, drawing up a shortlist of associations he would include, making a note of their locations and any specific field of the paranormal they were involved in. It was well past one when he went to bed and sleep quickly claimed him. The nightmare returned and he was once again sinking into the black, brooding depths of the ocean, his lungs crushed by the pressure, his limbs stiff and useless, his body's leaden weight dragging him below. A face was waiting for him down there, a greyish blur that grew clearer as he plunged. This time it was not Lucy's. It was a man he recognized, yet did not know. The man was grinning, and withered lips called Bishop's name. His eyes seemed to bulge unnaturally from their sockets and Bishop saw there was nothing but evil in them, a cold, mesmerizing darkness that sucked him in, that drew him into a blackness that was even deeper than the ocean. The grin was a sneer and Bishop suddenly knew it was the same man he had seen in Beechwood, the man who had watched his followers kill each other and themselves before putting a gun into his own mouth. The lips parted, yellow, ill-formed teeth guarding the glistening cavern inside, the fleshy, quivering tongue resting on the entrance floor like a huge slug waiting to curl around and engulf any intruder. Bishop floated through, the jaws closing behind him with a thunderous steely clang, and he was totally blind and screaming, the soft enveloping surface of the tongue reaching up for him and moulding itself around his feet. He tried to tug himself free but only sank further into the gripping slime and in the darkness he sensed the tongue curling round, rearing over him to descend upon his shoulders. His own panic-stricken screams deafened him as white, floating shapes came into view, rising from the tunnel that was the man's throat, their faces familiar, the images of those who had died in Beechwood. Dominic Kirkhope was with them. And so was Lynn.

Her eyes were wild, both terror and beseeching in them. Her lips formed words that were cries for help. She begged him. She pleaded. Help me.

And he couldn't; the tongue was pressing down on him, smothering his head and shoulders, choking him with its sticky juices, forcing him to fall, crushing him in a cushion of softness. Until everything exploded. And he was the bullet smashing its way through the man's brain. The man he suddenly knew was Boris Pryszlak.

He awoke still screaming, but no sounds came from his lips. It was light outside and he almost wept with relief.

The beer can was empty and Bishop placed it on the floor at his feet, then slumped back into the armchair, one elbow resting on the arm of the chair, hand across his brow as though shielding his eyes from the lamp-light. His head ached and every muscle in his body felt lifeless. He had spoken with Jessica that morning, ringing her as soon as he'd heard the news on the radio. She had been at home and told him she would stay there today to look after her father. Jacob had also heard the news of the bizarre tragedy at the football stadium and he, too, felt sure it was related to the incidents in Willow Road. He was still weak from the attack, but had made her promise to arrange a meeting for all of them later that evening, a meeting that would include Detective Chief Inspector Peck. Even if the policeman thought they were all insane, they had to try to convince him there was a connection between the Pryszlak sect and the recent events. Bishop had agreed to keep himself available that evening; she would ring him when she had fixed a suitable time.

He still hadn't heard from her and he was becoming concerned. That concern finally drove him out of the armchair into the hall. He was just reaching for the phone when it rang.

'Jessica?'

'Uh, no. Mr Bishop? Crouchley here. From Fairfield.'

Fairfield. The mental home.

'Has something happened to my wife?' Dread hit Bishop's stomach like a lead weight.

'It's important that you come over right away, Mr Bishop,' said the metallic voice.

'Is Lynn all right?'

There was a slight pause at the other end. 'We've had what you might call a slight breakthrough. I think we rather need you here. I'll explain when you arrive.'

'It'll take me twenty minutes. Can't you tell me a little more now?'

'It's better that you see for yourself.'

'Okay. On my way.'

Bishop's heart was thumping as he raced upstairs to grab his jacket. What did a 'slight breakthrough' mean? Was Lynn at last beginning to emerge from the shell she had retreated into? Would there be some warmth, no matter how faint, in her eyes when she saw him? He tugged on his jacket and raced back down the stairs, a new hope urging him on.

When the phone rang again only moments later, the house was already empty.

17

Bishop had to force himself to concentrate on driving as he sped towards Twickenham, the rain splatting off the road like tiny cannon shots. Fortunately, the traffic was light and he was able to make good progress. He was filled with apprehension; there had to be good reason for Crouchley to call him out at that time of evening. If Lynn had finally ... he refused himself the thought. Better not to expect too much.

It was not long before he reached the quiet cul-de-sac at the end of which stood the Fairfield Rest Home. He drove straight through the tall entrance gates into the wide drive. Slamming the car door, he hurried up the steps leading to the building's main door, rain speckling the driving glasses he had forgotten to remove. He whisked them off into his top pocket, ringing the doorbell with his other hand as he did so. The home was a large redbrick building which in appearance could have been anything from a small, private school to a residence for geriatrics. Only when the discreetly lettered sign mounted on the front railings had been read did the building take on a faintly daunting atmosphere. The fact that most of the interior lights seemed to be off, made it look even more grim.

Bishop heard the lock click, then the door opened slightly.

'I'm Chris Bishop. Dr Crouchley asked me to come over.'

The door opened wider and he saw the silhouette of a

short, plumpish woman standing there. 'Oh, yes, we were expecting you, Mr Bishop. Won't you come in?'

He stepped into the home's reception area and turned anxiously towards the small woman as she carefully locked the door again.

'Is my wife . . .?'

'We'll take you straight up to see her, Mr Bishop,' a voice said from behind and he turned to see another woman sitting at the reception desk to one side of the hall. Her face was turned away from the small desk-lamp that did its feeble best to light up the gloomy surroundings. The figure rose and came around the desk towards him.

'I'm sorry about the poor light,' she said as if reading his mind. 'We always keep the lighting subdued after eight o'clock. We find it's restful for our patients.'

She was taller than the woman who had let him in and Bishop realized he had seen neither of them before. Perhaps they were new, the tall one certainly, for patients were never referred to as such in Fairfield – they were always 'residents'.

'What's happened to Lynn?' he asked. 'Dr Crouchley wouldn't tell me over the phone.'

The two women eyed each other and a pleased look passed between them. 'I think you'll find a marked improvement, Mr Bishop,' the taller one said. 'Would you like to follow me?'

They walked towards the broad staircase that led to the first floor of the home, the smaller woman falling in behind Bishop, hands thrust into her white medical coat. The taller woman kept up a flow of conversation as they climbed the stairs, but he hardly listened; his mind was on Lynn. The corridor on the first floor was also lit only by a small lamp on a table at the far end and he found the dimness disconcerting. He hadn't realized they kept the lights to a minimum after visiting hours; it was more depressing than subduing. A door opened as they passed, the room beyond in total darkness; the smaller woman hurried over and stretched out an arm as if to gently push someone back towards their bed. The taller woman smiled sweetly at him as though nothing had happened.

Bishop had always found the mental home slightly unnerving, which was natural enough; but at this time of night, without the usual bustle of visitors and staff, it was more than that. His mouth felt dry and he wondered if the tension was because of Lynn or because he had become a little afraid of the place. They passed more doors and he wondered what lay behind them, what was going on inside those damaged minds.

'Here we are.' The tall woman had stopped outside a room he knew Lynn shared with three other residents. The wards were kept small at Fairfield, the doctors reluctant to separate their charges from each other, although they believed in keeping the numbers to a minimum.

'Won't we disturb the others?' Bishop asked.

'They're sleeping soundly – I checked just before you arrived. Please go in, your wife is waiting for you.'

'Is Dr Crouchley with her?'

'He'll be along shortly. He wants you two to be alone for a few moments.'

Bishop's face lit up, the tension beginning to leave him. 'She's . . .?'

The white-coated woman put a finger to her lips, then smiled pleasantly, her eyes sparkling at his anticipation. She pushed open the door and motioned him to enter. He said a quiet 'Thank you' and went into the room. The door closed behind him.

Lynn's bed was in a corner by the window and a small night-light had been placed on her bedside cabinet. She was propped up on pillows, her head turned to one side as if she had dozed off while waiting for him. He tiptoed towards her, conscious of the grey, sleeping forms in the shadows around him, his eyes moist, throat still dry.

'Lynn?' he said gently when he reached her side. 'Lynn, are you awake?'

He touched her hand lying on top of the bedsheets and softly shook it. Her head slowly came round towards him and in the poor light he saw the grin on her face. His body went rigid and all the openings in his body seemed to curl inwards.

'Lynn?'

Her eyes still bore the look of insanity. Her grin reflected the madness. She began to sit up and he was aware that the others in the shadowy beds around the ward were rising also. Someone snickered.

Lynn's lips were glistening wet as she pushed back the bedclothes and began to reach for him. He had to stop himself from backing away.

'Don't get out of bed, Lynn.'

Her grin widened.

One leg slipped from the covers.

Her hand touched his shoulder.

'Lynn!' he screeched as her other hand whipped up and clawed at his face.

She was laughing and it wasn't Lynn at all: the features were the same – same mouth, same nose, same eyes – but they were distorted, twisted into an ugly grimace, someone else, something else, behind those wild eyes.

He grabbed her wrists and held her away from him, her body exploding into violent motion. Screams were mixed with her laughter as she kicked out at him, snapping her teeth like a rabid dog. He pushed her back towards the bed, unnerved by her strength, frightened by her condition. The bloody fools! Why had they dragged him here to see this? Had she fooled them, made them believe she was changing for the better? Or had just the sight of him broken down what good had been done?

She was on the bed now, her head thrashing around on the pillows, her flimsy nightdress kicked high over her thighs. She hissed and spat at him, the bubbled saliva smearing his face. He was dimly aware that other shapes were moving towards him from out of the darkness, but he was afraid to let go of his wife's wrists, afraid of those claw-like nails.

His head was jerked back as a hand grabbed his hair from behind; he twisted his neck, trying to pull himself free. But the hand grasped him tightly and another reached around and across his throat. Bishop was forced to let go of Lynn and clutch at the arm that was squeezing his neck. She was off the bed immediately, coming at him, hands flailing, her mouth snapping at him once more. They went down in a heap, the woman behind losing her grip on his throat, but still gripping his hair at the roots. He blinked away the blur in his eyes and rolled over, taking Lynn with him, the other woman scrabbling at him with her free arm.

He managed to get a foot up and kicked out at Lynn, her cry of pain a terrible sound, but knowing he had no choice. She scudded away from him and he turned on the woman still clinging. A fierce backslap of his hand stunned her and she shrieked with the shock. Even in the darkness he could see she was an old woman, her hair white and frizzed out as though filled with static.

A bare foot kicked him, striking his cheek and knocking him sideways. Two other nightgowned women were standing over him, their faces masks of grinning hate. They ran forward, kicking out, crying their triumph. A body landed on him and teeth sank into his neck. In the nightmarish confusion he knew it was Lynn. He broke her grip, but felt skin tear away and a spurt of blood run into his collar. He grabbed a foot that was pushing at his chest and twisted it forcefully, the woman above him falling back with a scream. He got a knee beneath him and pushed himself upwards, taking Lynn with him, a figure in front pounding his face with clenched fists. He struck out, hitting the woman on the forehead, sending her hurtling backwards into the shadows. He held Lynn to him, pinning her close to his body, trapping her arms. The white-haired woman was slowly creeping towards him like a ghost from the mists, arms stretched out before her holding what looked like a rolled-up bedsheet, a twisted shroud he knew was to go around his neck. He almost collapsed with relief when he saw the door behind her begin to open, the dim light from the hallway casting dark shadows into the room.

The silhouettes of the two women who had shown him in, the tall one and the short one, stood there.

'Thank God,' Bishop said, the moans, the giggles, the screams – Lynn's squirming – suddenly coming to a stop. Even the old woman bearing the twisted bedsheet paused and looked back over her shoulder.

The tall woman stepped into the room and the other one followed. The two women moved to the side, opening the door wide, and he heard the tall one say: 'Bring him along.'

They poured into the room, demented, arm-waving creatures from hell, the women dressed in plain, shapeless smocks that served as nightgowns, the men in similar garments. Bishop backed away, almost believing he had walked into a terrible dream.

Lynn broke free and suddenly the twisted bedsheet was thrown around his shoulders, then jerked tight. He was pulled forward and a screaming mass of bodies enveloped him, hands tearing at his clothes, darkened manic faces appearing before him, disappearing as others brushed them aside to see their victim. Bishop blindly hit out, their screams deafening him, his fists sinking into fleshy parts of bodies and sometimes striking hard bone. Those that fell back were immediately replaced by others and he began to go down, clutching at their robes to stop himself. A knee came up into his face and for a second he felt only white-hot shock, the numbing pain reaching him split seconds later. He went down on to his knees and a hard slap rocked his head backwards. His hands spread themselves on the floor before him and he felt the sheet around his neck tightening. Bruising feet toppled him over.

They used the sheet to drag him towards the door.

The tall woman looked down at him, the gloomy light from the hallway throwing her face into half-shadow; the pleasant smile was still there. He lay on his back staring up at her and she and her short companion took delight in his horror. She held up a hand and for a moment the clamour died, just a sigh, a moan, a giggle, coming occasionally from the shadows.

All she said was: 'It's too late, Mr Bishop. It's already begun.'

Then they were on him again and he was half-carried, half-dragged into the hall. He thought he heard Lynn laughing with them.

He managed to get his feet beneath him and forced himself erect, digging his heels into the tough cord carpet, pressing himself back against the mob, unwilling to go wherever it was they wanted to take him. He groaned aloud when he saw what lay ahead of him in the corridor.

The bodies of the mental home's staff had been tumbled out from the rooms on either side of the long corridor. Very little white showed through their bloodstained uniforms. With revulsion, he saw they had not just been murdered; mutilation had taken place. Whether or not they had been dead before ... He shook the thoughts from his mind.

He was shoved forward and the fury inside him broke. He did not know what had happened to them all, why or how their unbalanced minds had turned to such appalling violence, but he hated them for it. Events of the past weeks told him they were not responsible – their enfeebled minds had been taken over by a greater madness. It was *that* madness he felt hate for, but they were its hosts, they were its perpetrators. They had allowed themselves to be used. They were no longer human.

The short woman stepped in front of him, her face pinched and malicious, ready to taunt. His foot came up and caught her just below her plump belly, and her ducking face met his swiftly lifted knee, choking off her piercing shriek.

Those holding him were momentarily stunned and a dagger of fear found its way through their insanity. Bishop tore an arm free and twisted himself to strike the madman holding his other arm. He felt a fleeting satisfaction as the man's nose squelched beneath his knuckles. The sheet around his neck loosened and he quickly pulled it over his head, already jumping away from the mob crowding into the corridor. The cries reached a new pitch as he shoved the man who had been holding on to his other arm back into the mob. Hands were clutching at him, trying to drag him back into their midst.

He was backing away, slapping at their hands as though they were naughty children grabbing for sweets. He almost stumbled over the outstretched legs of a male nurse and then he had turned and was running for the stairs, the sight of the dead man looking up at him, deep red holes where his eyes should have been, completely unnerving him. The residents chased after him, stumbling and giggling over the bodies of those they had already slain.

Bishop reached the top of the stairs and fell against the banister. Two figures, clad in the white starched trousers and jackets that were the Fairfield uniform, were mounting the steps, their faces hidden in the shadows. One held a long iron bar that he was rattling along the uprights of the banister and, when their heads and shoulders came into view, Bishop saw the same wild-eyed glee in their eyes that belonged to the mad men and women behind him. He staggered up the staircase leading to the second floor.

A hand curled round his ankle, bringing him down, and he grasped at the banister to stop himself from sliding to the bottom. He twisted and found it was Lynn holding on to him, a chuckling, drooling Lynn, a Lynn he no longer knew, who was enjoying the game, who wanted him dead. He had to close his eyes when he brought his foot down into the upturned face.

The metal bar crashed against the rails his fingers clung to, only inches away, and the grinning face of the male nurse peered up at him from the other side. The mob at the foot of the stairs were tripping over the fallen body of Lynn as Bishop lumbered onwards, taking the stairs three at a time, the terrible fear that his legs would turn to lead fuelling his panic. He used the rail to pivot himself around the bend in the stairs, the mob now trampling over Lynn to reach him. He reached the second floor corridor and it was dark. But not so dark that he couldn't see the white clad figures drifting down the corridor towards him, doors opening on either side and others stepping out, dim spectres in a world of blackness and screams.

He was trapped.

Except for a door on his left that had not yet opened.

He burst through and slammed it behind him, leaning back against it to prevent them from following, sucking in huge swallows of air. Keeping a shoulder against the door, he scrabbled around for a key in the lock. There was no key. Not even a bolt.

He could hear them gathering outside.

And his feet were wet.

He reached for a light switch, found nothing, but felt something brush against the back of his hand. A cord. A light. He pulled. He was in a bathroom, the white tiles stark and blinding. That was why there was no lock on the door: mad people were not allowed to lock themselves in rooms. The floor was covered in puddles and the deep, claw-footed bathtub was filled to overflowing, the water smooth and placid, its highest level reached.

A chair with two carelessly dropped towels draped over its back stood in a corner next to him. He reached for it gratefully and jammed it against the door at an angle, its back beneath the handle. It might hold them for a precious few moments, time enough to reach the high window opposite. He saw the frosted glass was reinforced with metal wire and prayed he would be able to break through, already sure the frame was set in its surround, unable to be opened naturally. He splashed across the bathroom floor, ignoring the shrill laughter from outside. And as he passed by the huge bath, he realized it had all been an evil game for them, that they meant to let him escape to the second floor, that they had directed him to this particular room. They had wanted him to see what lay beneath the unstirring water in the bath.

18

The house surprised Peck. Not the kind of place he expected Jacob Kulek to live in; somehow he thought the old man would have preferred oak beams, roses running up the outside walls, or maybe something Georgian, tall and elegant. Still, his kind was unpredictable; something a little cranky about most of them. Seemed well-balanced enough until you started listening to what he was saying.

'Some shack, eh, guv?' Frank Roper, his DI said as Peck pressed the doorbell. 'All glass and chrome. I'd hate to be their window cleaner.'

Peck grunted, his thoughts now distracted. He was wondering why Kulek had insisted on seeing him, especially at this time of night. The insanity of the night before had meant an overload – and that was an understatement – for everybody: how the hell do you deal with mass murders by a mass of murderers? And what was the connection between the incidents at the football ground and Willow Road? Or, to be more specific, the house that had once been there: Beechwood. Because there was a definite link now. If Kulek hadn't asked for the meeting, then Peck, himself, would have wasted no time in interviewing the old man. It seemed he was the only person who could give some clue as to what was going on.

The door opened and Jessica Kulek's white nervous face peered out at him.

'Come in,' she said, opening the door wide.

'Sorry we're a little late,' Peck apologized. 'As you can imagine, we've been pretty busy today.'

'That's why my father wanted to see you, Inspector. It's about what happened last night.'

'You're going to tell me there's a link. And you'd be right.'

Jessica's eyebrows arched in surprise. 'You think there is, too?'

'Let's say it's a strong possibility.'

Kulek was waiting for them in a large L-shaped lounge, the room itself, like the house, of modern design, although the furniture seemed old, possibly antique; surprisingly, the combination worked. Peck noticed everything was set out in straight lines or at right-angles to each other and he realized a blind man wouldn't want odd bits of furniture scattered at random around the room. The vertical blinds were drawn against the night.

'Good of you to come, Inspector,' Kulek said. He was standing by an armchair, one hand resting on its back, whether for support or merely guidance, Peck wasn't sure. He looked older than when the policeman had first met him, but infinitely better than when he had seen him in the hospital two days ago. His skin had taken on a dry, pale yellow cast and his stoop had become more pronounced. A silk scarf peeping over the top of his shirt-collar hid his bruised neck.

'You've met Detective Inspector Roper,' Peck said without looking at his colleague.

'Yes, indeed. And this is Edith Metlock.'

The medium smiled briefly at the two policemen.

'Won't you sit down? Can we offer you something to drink? Something stronger than tea or coffee?'

Peck relaxed his body into a sofa while Roper chose an

uncomfortable hardbacked chair. 'Whisky, a little water, for me,' Peck said. 'I believe Inspector Roper will have the same.'

Roper nodded and Jessica made herself busy at the drinks cabinet.

'I thought you said Chris Bishop would be here tonight?' Peck said.

Kulek seated himself in the armchair he had been standing behind. 'My daughter has been trying to contact him for the past half-hour. He must have left his house.'

Jessica came over with the drinks. 'Chris may have decided to come over anyway. I said I would ring him as soon as I fixed the time for the meeting with you. I'm afraid you weren't easy to reach today.'

'Well, we can soon find out where he is. I've had two men watching him all day. Frank, tell Dave to radio through, will you?'

Roper placed his glass on the deep red carpet and left the room.

Kulek spoke. 'Jessica tells me there has been a man in a car parked near this house for the last two days.'

'For your protection, sir. There's been one attempt, no sense in risking another.'

An awkward silence followed Peck's statement before the detective cleared his throat and said: 'I had planned to see you first thing in the morning, Mr Kulek. I think there's a lot we have to discuss.'

'Yes, Inspector, indeed there is. But I gave you all the facts concerning Beechwood and Boris Pryszlak at our first meeting. Tonight I wanted to talk theory with you.'

'I'm always interested in theories. Provided they're sound, that is.'

'I can't promise you that. What may be sound to me might be completely irrational to you.'

'I'm prepared to listen.' Peck turned to Edith Metlock. 'Mrs Metlock, one of my detectives spoke to you the other day, after the madwoman was found in Beechwood. You were there at the seance.'

'It wasn't a seance, Inspector,' the medium said. 'At least, it wasn't planned as such.'

'You said you saw nothing yourself of this, uh, vision or hallucination – whatever you might call it – that Bishop claims to have seen.'

'No. As a medium, I seldom see or remember such things. My body is used as a receiver by the spirit world. They speak to others through me.'

'And you think this is what happened at Beechwood? The spirits of Pryszlak and his people used you to speak to Chris Bishop? He was the only one who saw them, wasn't he?' Peck shifted uncomfortably in his seat, glad that Roper wasn't in the room to hear his line of questioning.

'They didn't speak to him,' Edith replied. 'He was shown what had happened there.'

'Why not you, Mr Kulek? Or your daughter, Jessica?'

'We don't know,' the old man answered. 'Perhaps it was because Chris Bishop discovered the bodies originally. Perhaps Pryszlak was mocking him with the truth of what had happened.'

'Pryszlak's dead.'

This time there was no reply.

'There could be another, more reasonable, explanation,' Peck said finally. 'Bishop had a mental block on what he stumbled across in Beechwood for nearly a year. It could be that going back into the house shocked him into seeing it all over again.'

'But he only discovered them when they were all dead,'

said Jessica. 'The other day he actually saw them killing themselves and each other.'

'We only have his word that they were already dead.'

Jessica looked at her father, who said: 'Wasn't there a witness who saw him go into the house? A woman with a child who was passing by at the time?'

'Yes, I've read the report. But how do we know he hadn't already been to the house, hadn't actually been present when the suicides and executions took place. From what I've learned of this Bishop, he believes in a more scientific approach to the supernatural. Didn't you tell me Boris Pryszlak also had a scientific interest in these matters?'

'Yes, but . . .'

Peck went on. 'You see, it could be that our Mr Bishop is part of Pryszlak's secret sect himself. It could be that he was a member chosen to stay behind to carry on whatever fanatical cause they were all involved in.'

'That's nonsense!' Jessica's face was flushed red. 'Chris was also attacked two days ago!'

'He says.'

Kulek's voice was calm. 'I think you're wrong, Inspector.' His sightless eyes looked towards his daughter and Edith Metlock. 'We all think you're wrong.'

'I also got the impression that he wasn't entirely in favour of your investigations into Beechwood.'

'That's true,' said Jessica, 'but only in the beginning. His opinion is different now. He's trying to help us.'

'Is he?' Peck's tone was flat.

Roper came back into the room and sat in his chair again, retrieving the whisky glass from the floor with an undisguised look of relish. He glanced over at Peck before he drank.

'Bishop went out just after eight. Our obo followed him to

a place near Twickenham, er, Fairview . . . no, Fairfield Rest Home.'

Jessica said, 'It must be the home where his wife is a patient.'

'A mental home?'

She nodded and couldn't read the expression on Peck's face.

'Get back on the radio, Frank. Tell them to bring Bishop here. I think he could be useful to this little gathering.'

'Now?' Roper's lips were poised over the edge of his glass.

'Right away.'

The policeman replaced his glass and left the room once more.

Peck sipped at his own whisky and water and regarded Jacob Kulek over the rim of his glass. 'Okay, sir, you said you wanted to talk theory.'

The blind man's mind was still on Bishop. No, it wasn't possible. Chris Bishop was a good man, he was sure. Confused. Angry. But not of Pryszlak's kind. Jessica had finally come to like the man and she was the best judge of character he knew. Sometimes he felt her judgement was a little too good, a little too critical . . . The few men in her life had never come up to her expectations.

'Mr Kulek?' There was a note of impatience in Peck's voice.

'Sorry, Inspector. My mind was wandering.'

'You have a theory?' Peck prompted. Kulek's eyes seemed to be boring into him and he could have sworn he felt the back of his mind being searched.

'It's difficult, Inspector. You are a practical man, a down-to-earth person who does not believe in ghosts. But, I think you are probably very good at your job and therefore, you may have some imagination.'

'Thank you,' Peck said drily.

'Let me start by telling you of the strange experience Edith had two nights ago. Or perhaps she will tell you herself?' He turned to the medium.

'As a sensitive – medium, spiritualist, are words you are probably more familiar with, Inspector – as a sensitive I am more susceptible to forces, influences, that are outside our daily lives. Forces from a world that is not of our own.'

'The spirit world.'

'If it can be called that. I'm not sure any more. It may be that we have a misconception about what we term "the spirit world". There are others in my profession who are beginning to have the same doubts.'

'Are you saying there are no such things as, er, ghosts?'

Roper had re-entered the room and he gave Peck a bemused look. He nodded at his superior to indicate that his instructions were being carried out, then took his place in the chair and reached for the glass at his feet.

'Perhaps not as we have always considered them,' the medium replied. 'We have always thought of them as individual spirits, existing in another world not unlike our own, but on a higher lever. Closer to God, if you like.'

'And that's all wrong?'

'I'm not saying that.' There was a trace of irritation in her voice. 'We just don't know. We have doubts. It may be that this spirit world is not as far removed from our own as we thought. And it may be that they do not exist as individuals but as a whole. As a force.'

Peck frowned and Roper gulped his drink noisily.

'Inspector, I will try and explain later,' Kulek interrupted. 'I think Edith should just tell you what happened two nights ago.'

Peck nodded his agreement.

'I live alone in a small house in Woodford,' Edith told him. 'On Tuesday evening – it was late, some time between ten and eleven, I think – I was listening to the radio. I like those phone-in programmes, you know. It's good to hear what ordinary people think of the state of the world occasionally. But the set kept crackling as if someone nearby was operating a machine without a suppressor. I tried twiddling the knobs, but the interference kept coming back. Short bursts of it, then longer. In the end it was one continuous buzz so I turned the radio off. It was then, sitting there in the silence, that I noticed the change in the atmosphere. I suppose my attention had been too fixed on that blessed radio interference for me to have noticed it before. There was nothing alarming about it – presences have often made themselves known to me in the past without invitation – so I settled back in my armchair to allow it through. It took me only a few seconds to realize it was unwelcome.'

'Hang on,' Peck interrupted. 'You've just been telling me you aren't sure there are such things as ghosts.'

'Not as we think of them, Inspector. That doesn't mean something other than what we see or feel does not exist. You can't ignore the incredible number of psychic experiences that have been recorded. I must stress that at the moment I'm confused as to just what it is that communicates through me.'

'Please go on.'

'I felt my house was being surrounded by a ... a ...' she searched for the word '... a dark shroud. Yes, as though a blackness were creeping around my home, pressing itself up against the windows. And part of it had already reached me. Part of it was already in my mind, waiting to spread itself, waiting to absorb me. But it needed to smother me physically and something was holding it at bay.'

'Your will power?' Peck said, ignoring Roper's grin.

'Partly that, yes. But something else. I felt darkness was its ally, its travelling companion, if you like. I don't know what made me do it, but I switched on every light in the house.'

Nothing unusual in that, thought Peck. He didn't personally know of any woman living alone who wasn't afraid of the dark. Plenty of men, too, although they wouldn't admit it.

'I felt as though a pressure had been taken off me,' the medium said, and Peck could see by her expression she was reliving the experience. 'But it was still outside . . . waiting. I had to block my mind, resist the urge to let it flow through me. It was as though something were trying to devour me.' She shivered and Peck himself felt a certain coldness at the base of his neck.

'I must have gone into a trance – I can't remember any more. Except for the voices. They were calling me. Mocking me. But enticing me, also.'

'What were these voices saying? Can you remember that?'

'No. No, not the words. But I felt they wanted me to turn off all the lights. Somehow, a part of me knew if I did I would be lost to them. I think in the end I just retreated into myself, fled to a corner of my mind where they couldn't reach me.'

That would be a nice trick for me to use when the Commissioner asks me what I've uncovered so far, thought Peck, holding back a weary smile.

They sensed his cynicism, but understood it. 'Edith was in that state when Chris and I found her,' Jessica said. 'When we left you that evening, Inspector, we were suddenly afraid that something might happen to her. Chris, my father, and Mrs Kirkhope had been attacked; we'd forgotten about Edith.'

'And what did you find at Mrs Metlock's house? Apart from the good lady herself.'

'We didn't *find* anything. We sensed an atmosphere. A cold, oppressive atmosphere. I was afraid.'

Peck sighed heavily. 'Is this really getting us anywhere, Mr Kulek?'

'It might help you to understand my . . . theory.'

'Perhaps we can get on to that now?'

The blind man smiled patiently. 'Believe me, we understand how difficult this is for you. We cannot give you solid evidence, no hard facts. However, you must not dismiss us as cranks. It's vital that you seriously consider whatever we tell you.'

'I'm trying, Mr Kulek. You've told me very little so far.'

Kulek bowed his head in acknowledgement. 'My daughter and Chris Bishop brought Edith here – they thought she would be safer. As you know, I was in hospital but returned home later that day. It wasn't until yesterday evening that Edith began to talk of what had happened. When she had been found she was in an extreme state of shock, you see, and it took some time for her to emerge from that state. The only words she had said before then were, "Keep the dark away." It seems the darkness was somehow symbolizing whatever it was she feared. Now I'm sure it hasn't escaped your notice that everything that has happened in Willow Road recently has taken place at night.'

'The woman who attacked you in Beechwood. That was in the daytime.'

'She had killed her employer the night before. I believe that was when the madness hit her. Remember she was hiding in the cellar of Beechwood; in the dark.'

'The murder of Agnes Kirkhope and her housekeeper? The further attack on you? Bishop's alleged attack? These were all during the day.'

'It's my belief that the perpetrators were disciples of Boris

Pryszlak. Theirs was a different kind of madness. I think they were a physical guard left behind by Pryszlak to carry out certain duties. Protectors, if you like.'

'Why should he need protection if he's dead?'

'Not for *his* protection. They were left as a safeguard to his plan. Perhaps a tangible force to support his ethereal force.'

Peck and Roper exchanged uncomfortable glances. 'Could you explain exactly what you mean by "ethereal force"?'

'A force not of this world, Inspector.'

'I see.'

Kulek smiled. 'Bear with me; you might see some sense to it by the time I've finished.'

Peck hoped so, but he wouldn't have laid odds on it.

'When Boris Pryszlak came to enlist my assistance some years ago, he told me he was a man who did not believe in the existence of God. For him, science was the key to mankind's salvation, not religion. Disease and deprivation were being overcome by technology, not by prayer. Our economic and social advances were achieved by science. The decision to create new life was now our own; even the gender of the newborn would one day be decided by ourselves. Death itself, if not entirely thwarted, could at least be delayed. Our superstitions, our prejudices and our fears were steadily becoming obsolescent in the face of new scientific discoveries. World wars had been virtually eradicated not because of Divine Intervention, but because we, ourselves, had created weapons too fearsome to use. Old barriers had been broken down, new barriers smashed through – by mankind's own ingenuity, not by some superior being in the heavens.

'Pryszlak claimed that one day we would even discover scientifically how we gained that ingenuity, how, in fact, we were not created by a mystical Someone, but created ourselves. We would prove by science that there was no God.'

Kulek's words were said calmly, his voice soft and even, but Peck could feel Pryszlak's madness in them. It was the cold logic of a fanatic and Peck knew these were the most dangerous kind.

The blind man went on: 'So, if there was no God, there could be no Devil. Yet, as a pragmatist, Pryszlak could not deny the existence of evil.

'Through the centuries, religious and mystical leaders had always played on the superstitions and the ignorance of their fellow men. The Church had always insisted that Satan was a reality: for them it helped to prove the existence of God. Freud had confounded the Church and demonologists alike by explaining that each of us had been through a phase of individual development corresponding to that animistic stage in primitive man, that none of us has traversed it without preserving certain traces of it which can be re-activated. Everything which now strikes us as "uncanny" fulfils those vestiges of animistic mental activity within us.'

'You're saying that somewhere in here –' Peck tapped his temple '– is a part of us that still wants to believe in all this "evil spirits" nonsense.'

'Freud said this and, in many respects, I believe he was right. In thousands of cases where ecclesiastical exorcists have tried to rid disturbed men and women of so-called diabolic possessions, rational examination has revealed a varied range of psychoses in those same people. Philosophers such as Schopenhauer advocated that evil sprang from man's fear of death, his fear of the unknown. It was man's will to survive that brought conflict to the world, and within himself. But his own iniquity had to be blamed on something – *someone* – else: Satan provided the ideal psychological scape-goat. In the same way, because of the adversities inflicted on man throughout life, and because he knew his own inadequacies, man needed a god, a superior, someone who would help him, someone who, in the end, would provide the answers. Someone who would pull him through.

'Unfortunately for the Church, the age of rationality is here; perhaps one could say that education has been the greatest enemy of religion. The edges have become blurred, questions are being asked: How could atrocities be committed to achieve right? Wars, killing, executions – how could "bad" acts achieve "good"? How could men the world knew to be evil claim God was on their side? Would a civilized country ever fight a religious war again? In the late seventies, who had been the more evil, the dictatorial Shah of Persia or the religious fanatic, Ayatollah Khomeini who overthrew him? Idi Amin claimed to have conversed with God several times. Hitler claimed God was on his side. The persecution of so-called heretics throughout the centuries by the Church itself has still not been answered. This dichotomy has been challenged and Pryszlak saw it as man's recognition of his own powers, a predetermination over his own destiny. He had discovered his own Original Sin and decided it wasn't as evil as the Church had always taught him. Satan has now become a source of ridicule, of entertainment, even. A comical myth. A bogeyman. And evil came from man alone.

'Pryszlak believed it was a physical energy field within our mind and, just as we were learning to use our psi faculties – energies such as telekinesis, extrasensory perception, telepathy, telergy – so we could learn to use physically this other power.'

Kulek paused as if to allow the two policemen's thoughts to catch up on all he had said. 'I think Pryszlak developed his concept into a proven fact: he located this source of energy and used it. I believe he is using it now.'

'That's impossible,' said Peck.

'Many things in your own lifetime that you once thought impossible have been achieved by science, and knowledge in every field of technology is in escalation. Man has accomplished more in the last hundred years than in the previous thousand.'

'But for Christ's sake, Pryszlak is dead!'

'I think he had to die, Inspector. It's my belief that Boris Pryszlak and his followers have become that energy.'

Peck shook his head. 'I'm sorry, you know I can't buy all this.'

Kulek nodded. 'I didn't expect you to. I just wanted you to hear a theory I'm convinced is true. You may have cause to reflect upon it over the next few weeks.'

'What do you mean by that?'

'The madness will get worse, Inspector. It will spread like a disease. Every night there will be more who will succumb to its influence, and the more minds it takes the stronger it will grow. It will be like the raindrops on a windowpane: one small drop will run into the one below, then both into the one below that, growing in size and weight until it is a fast-flowing rivulet.'

'Why night-time? Why do you say these things only happen when it's dark?'

'I'm not sure why it should be so. If you read your Bible you'll see evil is constantly referred to as darkness. Perhaps that terminology has more significance than we thought. Death is darkness, Hell is in the dark, fearful underworld. The Devil has always been known as the Prince of Darkness. And isn't evil expressed as the darkness in one's soul?

'It could be that darkness is the physical ally to the manifestation of this energy. Perhaps the biblical concept of the constant battle between Light and Darkness is a true, scientific concept. Whatever energy light rays contain, be they from the sun or artificial, it may be that they counteract or negate the catalystic qualities of darkness.

'Pryszlak implied much of this at our last meeting and I must admit that although I often found his ideas fascinating, this time I thought there was some madness in his thinking. Now I'm not so sure.'

Kulek's frame seemed to relax imperceptibly in his chair and Peck realized the blind man's disquieting statement was over. He looked at each individual in the room and noticed even Roper's secretive smirk had disappeared.

'You realize everything you've just told me is totally useless to my investigations, don't you?' he said bluntly to Kulek.

'Yes. It is at this moment. Soon I think you will change your mind.'

'Because more is going to happen?'

'Yes.'

'But even if what you say is true, what would be the point for Pryszlak?'

Kulek shrugged, then said, 'Power. More power than he had when he was alive. A larger following, one that will grow.'

'You mean he can still go on recruiting?'

Kulek was puzzled to find no trace of sarcasm in Peck's question. In fact, he was surprised the policeman had listened so patiently. 'Yes, others will join him. Many others.'

Peck and Roper exchanged sharp glances which were not lost on Jessica.

'Is there something you haven't told us, Inspector?' she asked.

Peck looked uncomfortable again. 'The crowd that ran amok last night – those that got away, that is – dispersed into the surrounding area. We've been picking them up throughout the day. Many have been dead when we've found them, mostly killed by their own hand. Others have been ... mindless, wandering around lost.'

His face was grim, as though he did not like what he had to say next. 'Quite a few made straight for Willow Road. They smashed the barrier surrounding the Beechwood property. We found them standing there in the debris, just waiting like bloody vultures.'

19

Bishop stared at the still body lying in the bath. The white, contorted features stared back.

He had spoken to Crouchley many times over the past few years, their conversations confined to Lynn's mental progress – or regress, as it turned out – and always on a professional basis. He couldn't say he ever got to like the man, his approach was a little too impersonal for Bishop; but he had respected him as a doctor and he had soon realized the man's dedication to his patients' welfare went beyond professional bounds. In the end they had turned on him.

The two women who had let Bishop in: had they been patients? He thought not; there seemed to be no insanity in them. Were they tools of Pryszlak as Braverman and his wife had been? Probably. They had taken over the home, the patients becoming their allies, and murdered those of the staff who had not succumbed to this new, deadly madness. Then they had forced Crouchley to ring him. After that, they had dragged him up here and drowned him.

Crouchley's mouth was open, the last bubbles of life-giving air having long exploded from his lungs to fight their way to the surface. His fair hair had turned dark beneath the water and now floated softly around his head like pondweed. Even though he was dead, fear still showed on his face.

They were banging on the door now, laughing and

screaming Bishop's name, taunting him with the terror to come. The small wire-toughened window was on a level with his face and he saw, as he had expected, the frame was fixed into its surround. He looked around desperately for something to smash it with, but the bathroom was bare of implements. The chair may have helped, but that was the only thing keeping his pursuers out. The blows on the door had become harder, their rhythm more definite, as though the crowd had stood back to allow someone to use his boot against it. The angled chair shuddered.

A faint hope fluttered inside him when he saw the towel rail hooked over the bathroom's radiator. It was made of chrome and felt heavy enough to have some effect when he lifted it clear. The large towel that had been draped over it slid to the floor when he raised the rail to shoulder level. With one hand behind the triangular shaped hook and the other around the long metal rail itself, Bishop ran at the window and thrust it at the frosted glass, his feet almost slipping in the puddles beneath him.

The glass fractured, a jagged hole appeared; the wire reinforcing the glass held it together. Bishop drew the rail back and thrust again. Still the wire held.

The chair shook.

He thrust again.

The chair legs moved a fraction.

Again.

Another fraction.

This time the hook at the other end of the towel rail became entangled with the wire mesh and Bishop pulled inwards, twisting the hook to entangle it more, drawing the wire with its clinging fragments into the room, stretching it until it snapped, dropping the rail and pushing his fingers through the tiny holes, ignoring the sharp pain as the wire bit into his flesh, tugging frantically, hearing the sound of the chair scraping on the damp bathroom floor, feeling the cool night air breathing on his face through the opening that was growing wider, the wire and glass coming loose from its frame, feeling the draught grow stronger, sucked through as the door behind him burst open, tearing and twisting the wire and glass free, seeing there was enough room for him to squeeze through . . .

. . . feeling the hands on his shoulders . . .

They clawed at his body, dragging him to the floor, their screams shrilling in his head as they bounced from the tiled walls. He kicked out, his own cries joining theirs. They bore down on him, smothering his thrashing limbs with their own. A hand reached into his open mouth in an effort to pull his tongue from its roots and he bit hard, tasting blood before the scrabbling fingers jerked themselves free. He screamed when excruciating pain stabbed up from his groin area, manic hands squeezing him in a merciless grip. His shirt was ripped open and sharp fingernails dug into his chest, sinking into his skin and drawing short jagged lines of blood.

His wrists were being held and even through the confusion he could feel someone bending the fingers of one hand back trying to snap them. Before they could succeed, he was lifted, his squirming body held in eager grips. Wild deranged faces were around him and, as he twisted his head to and fro, he caught a glimpse of the two women, the tall one and the short one, standing in the doorway. Their smiles were not sinister, merely pleasant.

He arched his body upwards, the circular light set in the ceiling a huge sun filling his vision, almost blinding him. Shock hit him as he was plunged downwards and water engulfed his body. He choked as it rushed into the canals of his nose and throat, forcing out air in huge explosive bubbles.

The light above was broken into frantic patterns as the water's surface scattered into stormy motion and he could see the blurred silhouettes of those who leaned over the bath and held him down. The body of the dead man stirred beneath him.

The illogical thought that Crouchley was suddenly waking from the dead threw yet more panic into him even though whatever reason was left inside told him it was only the water's disturbance that made the body move. He pushed himself upwards, resisting the hands that held him back, forcing his head above the surface. He coughed water from his lungs, retching and gasping in air at the same time. His head was gripped and he was forced down again, hands tugging at his legs to jerk him back. The water splashed at his face, covering his chin, nose, eyes. Then he was below the surface again, the world suddenly going quiet, the screaming an imaginary sound in his head. His hands reached upwards for the side of the bath and fierce pain told him they were being battered, prised away from the slippery, enamel surface. A shadow loomed over him and he felt a crushing weight on his chest. Another sudden weight on his hips pinned him helplessly to the body beneath him. They were standing on him.

His breath was beginning to go, the weight on his chest forcing it out. He closed his eyes and the darkness was tinged red. His lips were closed tight but the air bubbles steadily forced their way from them. Like his body, his mind began to drown and he felt it plummet downwards. There was no redness any more, only the deep sucking blackness and now he was living his constant nightmare, his body sinking down into the depths, small white blobs that he knew were faces waiting for him below. Pryszlak wanted him. But Pryszlak was dead. Yet Pryszlak wanted him.

He was fathoms beneath the ocean now and his body was still, struggling no more, resigned to its death. The last silvery pearl of air fled his lips and began its hasty mile-long journey to the ocean's surface above. There were many, many faces waiting below for him and they grinned and called his name. Pryszlak was among them, silent, watching. Dominic Kirkhope, gloating. The man who had tried to shoot him, Braverman, and his wife, were laughing. Others, some of whom he recognized from his vision in Beechwood, were reaching up with shrivelled, water-crinkled hands.

Then there was anger in Pryszlak's face and the others were no longer grinning. Now they were howling.

Bishop felt himself rising, rushing to the surface. He was suddenly worried about the rapid change of pressure, that nitrogen bubbles would be trapped in the tissues of his body and he would suffer what every deep-sea diver dreads: decompression sickness – 'the bends'.

Then he was above the surface, spilling bath water from his mouth, wheezing in air when he could, choking as uncleared water rushed back down his throat. Strong hands held the lapels of his jacket collar and above the roaring in his ears he heard a distant voice shout, 'There's another one underneath him!'

He was dragged from the bath and allowed to fall on to the wet, tiled floor. He sucked in air, his senses spinning. Crouchley's staring face appeared before him, his limp body hanging over the side of the bath, water flowing from his mouth as though it were the end of a drainpipe.

'This one's dead,' the distant voice said.

Bishop was pounded on the back and he retched up the rest of the water inside him. He was pulled to his feet.

'Lean against me, but try and stand, mate. We'll get you out!'

Bishop tried to see who was helping him, but the room spun dizzily. He wanted to be sick.

'Get back!' A cannon roared and he saw splinters of wood fly from the wooden frame around the open doorway. White shapes scurried back into the shadows.

'Come on, Bishop, you'll have to help me. I can't carry you on my own.'

The voice was coming nearer, the words becoming more clear. The man had slid a shoulder beneath Bishop's arm and was holding him up. Bishop tried to push himself away, thinking the man was one of the maniacs, but the grip tightened.

'Hold up, pal, we're on your side. Try to walk will you? Move your legs.'

They staggered forward and Bishop felt the strength willingly flow back into his body.

'Good man,' the voice said. 'Okay, Mike, I think he's going to be all right. Keep that bloody mob back.'

They lurched into the dark hallway and began a slow, stumbling march towards the stairs. Something moved in the shadows ahead and the man in front of Bishop and his helper fired a shot into the air. The hallway was lit up for a split-second by the gunflash and he saw the mad creatures crouching there, afraid but ready to pounce.

Bishop and his two men had reached the bend in the stairs when the mob decided to attack.

They came tumbling out of the darkness like screaming banshees, pouring down the stairs in an unbroken, human stream.

Bishop fell back into the corner as his support was taken away and he saw both his helper and the other man raise their guns and fire into the crowd.

Cries of pain and fear rang through the corridors of the

large house and he heard bodies falling, those behind toppling over the injured in front. Something slumped across his
outstretched leg and began to writhe there. Bishop kicked
the body away.

A hand tugged at his arm and he pushed himself upright,
ready to fight.

'Come on, Bishop, let's keep moving.' With relief he
realized the hand belonged to his helper.

'Who the hell are you?' he managed to say as they
descended the next flight of stairs. It was lighter down there,
but the man leading them improved matters by flicking on a
switch. The hall and stairs were flooded with light.

'Never mind that now,' the man helping him said. 'Let's
just get away from here first.'

A sudden thump on the stairs behind made them whirl.
The male nurse who had tried earlier to attack Bishop with
an iron bar stood above them. He still held the iron bar.

A blast from the gun and his white uniform became a
shredded mass of red just above the knee. His leg buckled
and he fell back on to the stairs, the bar clattering down
noisily. He clutched his leg and burbled his pain. Others were
creeping round the bend in the stairs behind him, their eyes
wide and fearful.

Bishop and the two men backed away to the next flight of
stairs which would lead them to the ground floor. His clothes
felt heavy with water, but noradrenaline was coursing through
him once more, giving him the strength he needed.

The two women were waiting below. The short one was
splashing liquid from a can on to the wide stairway. She stood
back, placing the can at her feet, and smiled up at her
companion. The taller woman struck a match and flicked it at
the stairway.

The petrol ignited in a brilliant *whoosh* and the three men at the top of the stairs raised their arms against the fierce heat. The flames hungrily climbed the wooden staircase towards them and beyond they could see the two women backing away, grinning delightedly.

'We can't get down,' one of the men shouted. 'There must be another way out. They've got to have a fire escape.'

Bishop's head was still reeling, but through the confusion he heard the other man say, 'Can you make it, Bishop? We're going to try the back way.'

He nodded and all three men turned as one, ready to run towards the back of the building. A ring of white-robed people blocked their way.

The patients shuffled forward, their nightclothes tinged red from the rising flames, and Bishop saw Lynn was among them.

'Lynn! It's me, Chris!' he cried, moving ahead of the two men to plead with her. 'Come with us, Lynn, before the whole building goes up.'

For a brief moment, Bishop thought he saw a tiny flicker of recognition in Lynn's eyes, but if she had realized who he was, the memory only renewed her hatred. She tore herself away from the crowd and ran at him, arms flailing, hands outstretched, claw-like. In his weakened state he could not hold her; he fell and she toppled over him. Her hands clutched at the stairs as she slithered down towards the flames and Bishop desperately tried to grab her ankle. He touched her heel but the limb was gone before he could gain a hold. Her screams pierced all other sounds as she slid into the fire and her nightdress and hair became a blaze. Her tumbling body was lost in the inferno and her screams stopped abruptly. Something fell half out of the flames into the hallway below, a blackened, charred shape that bore no resemblance to a human body. It was quickly covered as the flames spread.

'No! No!' Bishop's cry descended into a low moan.

He was pulled away from the raging heat by the two men, his body totally limp now, his senses numbed with shock. The patients had cowered back, the full horror of their companion's death striking fear into their disordered minds. The men with Bishop saw that whatever extreme madness had driven them to this, it had been overcome by their own natural terror of the fire. The patients began to whimper as the heat grew in strength, and smoke filled the hallway.

'Let's get going while we can, Mike,' one of the men holding Bishop said just loud enough to be heard.

'Right,' his colleague agreed, his back beginning to feel singed by the heat.

With Bishop between them, their Webley .38s pointed at the figures in the crowded hallway, they cautiously moved forward.

'This way, Ted,' the man called Mike said, indicating to the right with the muzzle of his gun. 'There's a window down at the end of the corridor. Oh shit!'

The lights in the hallway had suddenly gone off. Had the fire burned through the wiring or had someone pulled the master switch? Both men thought of the two women who had started the fire.

'Let's move,' Mike said grimly.

The hallway was bathed in a red, weaving glow, dark shadows rising and dancing against the walls. The whimpering patients glared at the men who were retreating down the hall and carefully stepping over the sprawled bodies lying there. The white-gowned figures edged forward and doors on either side of the three men began to open.

The man called Ted glanced nervously from left to right. The only sound that could be heard now was the crackle and roar of the spreading fire. 'They're going to rush us again,' he said.

Figures were stepping into the hallway, hemming them in, watching silently, not yet raising their hands against them.

But the tension was rising, a huge bubble of hysteria that was swelling to breaking-point, and when it broke the retreating men knew they would be easily overwhelmed. As they backed further down into the blackness at the end of the hall, each of the three men felt something else nudging against the walls of their mind, something that seemed to be seeking access.

The fresh attack was started by one old woman who stood in the centre of the hall near the burning staircase. Her brittle legs were wide apart, her hands clenched and arms held rigidly to her sides; flames licked up at the ceiling above her. The cry started somewhere low in her abdomen and began to build, rising to her chest then up through her throat until it came out as a shrilling scream. The others had joined in with her mounting cry and when it broke, so they broke and came running towards the men.

The ceiling above the staircase and the next flight of stairs had become potent with heat; the flames below billowed upwards, old timbers eagerly giving themselves to the fire. A huge bag of flame spilled into the hallway, enveloping the white-robed figures who stood in its way, searing others who were too near.

Black smoke swirled towards the three men and they began to choke, their eyes already stung by the heat of the fireflash.

Bishop was dragged to the window, his body heaving as his lungs tried to eject swallowed smoke. He was pushed into a corner while the two men struggled to open their only means of escape. The fire spread rapidly and patients were running into open doors on either side of the hallway, many of them with nightclothes on fire.

'It's fucking locked!' Bishop heard one of the men shout.

'Shoot the bloody glass out!' his companion told him.

Both men stood back from the large single-framed window, raised one arm each to shield their eyes, and pumped bullets through the glass. The window shattered and a cold blast of air sucked in towards the flames.

Bishop was yanked away from the corner and steered towards the window. He drew in a deep breath of air and felt some reason returning as he leaned out into the night.

'There's – there's no fire escape,' he managed to gasp.

'Jump! It's only one floor up!'

He climbed on to the sill and let himself go. It seemed a long time before he hit the soft earth below.

20

Peck gazed down at the slow-moving traffic and filled his lungs with cigarette smoke. He wondered if the people scuttling around below in their tiny Dinky-toy cars had any real idea of what was going on in their city. It was impossible to keep an absolute clampdown on the bizarre events of the past few weeks; the media had made the connection between the events at the stadium and Willow Road days ago, but had reluctantly agreed to contain the full story until the authorities had come up with some rational answer to quell the mounting anxiety of the general public. It was an uncomfortable collaboration between the authorities and the media and one that would undoubtedly fail when the next major incident occurred. The newsmen could only be suppressed for so long.

He took the half-smoked cigarette from his mouth using his index finger and thumb, the palm of his hand curved around the butt. Janice was always telling him he'd never make Commissioner if he continued to smoke cigarettes with such mannerisms. Sometimes he thought his wife was serious.

Peck turned away from the window and slumped into the chair at the desk, stubbing the cigarette out against the side of his waste-paper bin and dropping the butt inside. Mannerisms? It had taken her ten years to stop him rolling his own. The knot of his tie was hanging loose over his chest, shirtsleeves rolled up to the elbows. He rubbed a hand across his face, conscious of the scratching sound his chin made, and studied the last page of the report he had just completed. *Better grab a quick shave before I show this to the Deputy,* he told himself. *It wouldn't matter to that pompous bastard if you'd just arrested Jack the Ripper if you hadn't shaved beforehand.*

As he reread the last lines in his report his hand unconsciously travelled towards the back of his head, cold fingers breaking through his concentration to tell him no new hair had miraculously grown overnight. In fact, he thought, his attention now fully with his probing fingers, a few more had said their last farewells. He quickly dropped his hand lest any of his new men saw him through the glass panelling of his office. He'd rather be caught playing with himself than caught checking to see how his baldness was coming along. *Getting old and feeling it,* he silently grumbled. Still, they said baldness meant virility. He couldn't say he'd noticed lately.

He closed the report and sat back in his chair, taking another cigarette from the pack on the desk as he did so. He flicked the Zippo and stared through the billow of smoke as it escaped his lips.

What the fuck is going on? he asked himself.

The football incident had been the biggest so far, but there had been others just as alarming. The burning down of the Fairfield Rest Home, for one. The riot in the boys' Remand Home, for another – the little bastards had turned on their wardens and then on themselves. Sixteen dead, twenty-four terribly injured. The rest? Where were the rest? The inmates of another mental home, this one run by the National Health, therefore known more accurately as a hospital for the insane, had turned on the staff first and then, as with the boys' home, themselves. Fortunately, the alarm had been raised before too much damage was done, but five were dead – two nurses, three patients – before the police had arrived in force. The mystery was why several of the staff had joined in the riot.

There had been many smaller incidents and if anything some of these were even more disquieting than the major events. Perhaps it was because they had involved perfectly normal people – at least considered to be normal before they had committed their individual acts of madness. A man had slaughtered every animal in the pet shop he owned, afterwards taking to his bed with the one fortunate creature he had spared, the show-piece of his collection: a ten-foot-long South American boa constrictor. He had been found dead with the snake wrapped around his throat like a muffler. Three nuns had gone berserk in their convent, creeping through the corridors one night and attempting to smother several sleeping sisters with pillows: they had succeeded twice before they were discovered. A doctor on night duty – the inquiry discovered he had worked non-stop for two days and nights – had toured the wards of his hospital injecting patients with a lethal dose of insulin. Only the intervention of a duty-nurse had prevented more than a dozen deaths – she herself had been injected and killed when she had struggled with the doctor. A labourer, working late to finish an urgent job on a block of offices that was undergoing modernization, had knocked his foreman semi-conscious, then pinned him to the wall with a nail-gun. The gun individually shot six-inch nails with a force strong enough to pierce concrete and by the time the other workmen got to the unfortunate foreman, his arms and legs were firmly pinned. The crazed workman managed to fire a nail through his own head before they could get to him and another labourer had narrowly missed being punctured when the nail had emerged from the other side without losing any impetus. Perhaps the most bizarre of all was the butcher who had served his chopped-up wife to his customers – Today's Special, regular customers only. A section of thigh was still missing and the police were desperately trying to trace the unlucky housewife who had made the 'bargain' purchase.

There had been other crimes, other suicides, but it was not yet known if these were connected with the more bizarre incidents. And what exactly could the connection be other than the fact that each horrendous act had seemingly been carried out at night? Could the dark really have something to do with this madness as Jacob Kulek had suggested?

Peck had included the blind man's theory in the report, but had left it as a separate section, adding no personal comment himself. He had been tempted to leave it out completely and if he could have offered any reasonable theories himself, then perhaps he would have done so. What the Commissioner would make of it all he dreaded to think but he, Peck, was only a small cog in the operation now; the big boys had taken over. All he could do was provide them with every scrap of information he had. A couple of weeks ago Peck had considered Kulek to be a little crazy; now too much had happened for him to dismiss the man as such. If only they could find out more about Boris Pryszlak. His home had been a flat in a huge apartment block near Marylebone although, according to his neighbours, he was hardly ever there. The flat itself offered no information whatsoever; it was a spacious accommodation which held little comfort in the way of furniture. There were no pictures on the walls, no bookshelves, few ornaments of any kind. What items of furniture there were were expensive but functional and bore little sign of wear. It was obvious the man used the apartment only as a base, his activities – whatever they may have been – keeping him away most of the time. Even the information gathered at the time of the mass suicides in Beechwood had revealed little. If Pryszlak was head of some kind of crazy religious sect, then his organization kept an extremely low profile. They seemed to have had no specific meeting place, and there was no indication of how they gained recruits. Also there was no record of the work – scientific or otherwise – Pryszlak had become involved in. Several of the people in the house had been wealthy, Dominic Kirkhope being a prime example, and Peck felt it reasonable to assume they were sponsoring Pryszlak with his project in some way. Did they have genuine aspirations or were they just a bunch of deviates who enjoyed getting together on odd occasions for orgies? The information gathered so far on Kirkhope and some of the others indicated that their sexual preferences were somewhat bizarre. Dominic Kirkhope had once owned a farm in Hampshire which, acting on complaints from neighbouring properties, the police had investigated. It seemed the animals kept there were not being used for natural purposes. The scandal had been hushed up, for the indignant landowners in the surrounding properties did not want their tranquil existence shattered by such adverse publicity. No charges had been brought against Kirkhope and his guests, but the farm itself had changed hands soon after the police raid. Kirkhope had been watched for a while after that, but if he indulged further in such sexual malpractices, then he did so very discreetly.

The backgrounds of Braverman, his wife and Ferrier, the man who had fallen from the window at Kulek's Institute, were being checked: so far, nothing unusual had been unearthed about any of them. Braverman had been a creative director of an advertising agency, a leading figure in his field. Ferrier had been a librarian. There seemed to be no obvious social connection between either party. Could they have been followers of Pryszlak?

There was only one lead on the murders of Agnes Kirk-hope and her housekeeper. Two women had been spotted strolling past the Kirkhope property by neighbours on the day of the murders. Had it not been a quiet residential area, then they probably would not have been noticed; as it was, they had been observed walking by Miss Kirkhope's house two or three times by different people. It could be that they were waiting for the right moment to strike. One woman had been tall, the other short.

Chris Bishop had said that two women, one tall, the other short, had let him into the Fairfield Rest Home. Were they the same two? It was possible. Probable in fact. Peck had almost lost all suspicions regarding the psychic investigator now. He was involved all right, but only as a potential victim, of that the detective was sure. Whoever – whatever – was behind all this was trying to get at Bishop. Why? Who the hell knew? None of it made any sense.

It had been fortunate for Bishop that Peck had ordered an obo on him. The two officers on observation duty that night had followed him to the mental home, then gone in to bring him to Kulek's house as instructed over the car radio. They had found the patients trying to drown Bishop in a bathtub. It was a good thing that the two detectives had been armed – Peck had suspected Bishop of murder at that time and was taking no chances with the lives of his own men. Without firearms, they would never have fought off the berserk residents. His men had also seen the two women at the mental home who had set light to the staircase. The home had been razed to the ground, burning almost half the patients to death and Bishop – poor bastard – had lost his wife in the fire.

All the nursing staff had been killed, whether in the fire or before it, no one would ever know – Bishop and the two detectives had seen several staff members already dead before the fire had struck. Some of the patients had leapt from the same window Bishop and Peck's men had escaped through, and had run off into the night to be picked up later by patrol cars; others had managed to use the fire escape on the other side of the building and these, too, had been found wandering the streets later that night. But a few had disappeared completely, the body count of those living and dead carried out the following day failing to tally with the known number of residents and staff.

Peck scratched the bottom of his nose with his thumb. He briefly wondered if he should recommend that a general alert be put out, to warn the public of the menace that was roaming the streets, then discarded the thought. Why be accused of over-reacting when it was up to the boys upstairs to make such drastic decisions? Besides, the trouble was still confined to an area south of the river. No point in causing panic in the rest of the city. No, he would just hand in his report and let his superiors get on with it. The only thing was, he thought, studying green pins on the large map of London he had stuck to his office wall board, the trouble was growing outwards, the pins spreading from the centre like a green starburst. Each pin indicated a fresh incident, the common denominator being that they had happened at night and that there was some kind of evil lunacy involved. What was it Kulek had said about rainspots on a window? It did seem to be gathering momentum.

The police cells and hospital wards were full of people who had had to be taken into custody for their own protection. Not all had committed acts of violence, but every one of them had that same brainless appearance. There had to be several hundred people being held at that moment, most of them part of the football crowd. The football match incident had been put down to crowd hysteria. Crowd hysteria! Jesus, the understatement of all time. Fortunately, it had been regarded as a single major phenomenon by the public and the authorities had played down the other comparatively 'minor' incidents, never once suggesting and always refuting any connection between them. The condition of those held seemed to be deteriorating rapidly, the first ones taken into custody having become nothing more than empty shells. Dozens, particularly those from Willow Road, had somehow managed to take their own lives, for there was no way such vast numbers could be watched all the time. Many were being fed intravenously, all will to live seemingly gone. Zombies, that was the word Bishop had used when he had spoken with him earlier that week. It was a good word. Apt. That's just what they were. Many shuffled around all day, some murmuring, others silent and immobile, lost within themselves. The medics were baffled. They said it was as if part of their brains had decided to close down, the part that controlled motivation. They had a fancy name for it, but however it was termed it amounted to the same thing: they were zombies. Only one thing seemed to stir them, one thing that had them all staring at the windows of their wards, rooms or cells: the coming of night. They all welcomed the darkness. And that worried Peck more than anything, because it gave substance to Kulek's theory.

The other matter that concerned Peck almost as much was the fact that over seven hundred people had been reported missing, most of them part of the crowd that had run amok at the football match. His chair scraped noisily against the floor as he pushed it back. He straightened his tie and began to roll down his sleeves as he walked to the window once more. He dragged on the cigarette, deep, sharp breaths, wanting to finish it before he went to see the Deputy

Commissioner. *Seven hundred!* He gazed down at the slow-moving traffic once more. Where the hell could seven hundred people disappear to?

'Gorn, out of it!' Duff aimed part of a crumbled brick at the creature caught in the beam from the lamp fastened to his safety helmet. The rat scuttled from the narrow ledge running alongside the sewer channel and plopped into the foul-smelling water. It vanished into the darkness ahead.

Duff turned to his companions and said, 'Watch yourselves along here. It's part of the old network – bit dodgy.'

The man immediately behind him wrinkled his nose against the heavy nitrous smell in the sewer, cursing the bright spark at the GLC who had thought up this unpleasant little assignment for him. There was a growing concern over the decaying state of the major cities' sewer networks and inspections were being hurriedly carried out to see if what was happening in Manchester could happen elsewhere. Huge holes had appeared in the busy roads in the northern town, holes big enough for a bus to drop through, caused by the collapse of the underground walls. The danger had been coming for years, but it was something out of the public eye and therefore something that could be put off to a later date. Now the worry was that it would soon be very much in the eyes of the public as cracks and holes appeared in the streets; in their noses too, as the stench wafted upwards. Berkeley, the lucky man in his department chosen to study this section of London's sewer network, shivered in the damp air and had visions of the whole city collapsing inwards into the slimy catacombs beneath. So long as he wasn't down here when it happened he didn't give a damn.

'All right, Mr Berkeley?'

He shielded his eyes against the glare of Duff's headlamp. 'Yes, let's get on with it. You say there's a section ahead that's particularly bad?'

'Last time I had a look at it. That was about two years ago.'

Wonderful, Berkeley thought. 'Lead on,' he said.

There were three men in the inspection team: Charlie Duff, senior repairs foreman for the water authority, Geoffrey Berkeley from the ministry, Terry Colt, assistant to the foreman. They were forced to stoop as they moved along the old tunnel and Berkeley tried to touch the fungus-covered walls as little as possible. His foot slipped at one stage and his leg disappeared up to the knee into the murky waters flowing beside them.

Terry Colt grinned and reached down to grasp the man's elbow, saying jovially, 'Slippery, innit?'

'Be all right in a minute, Mr Berkeley,' Duff said, also grinning. 'Tunnel widens out up ahead. Just have a look at this brickwork.'

He reached up and prodded the ceiling with a spiked metal bar he always carried when inspecting the sewers. Loose cement and brickwork crumbled away and plopped down into the centre channel.

'I see what you mean,' said Berkeley, shining his torch upwards. 'Doesn't look too good, does it?'

Duff grunted his reply and moved further along, poking the ceiling as he went. Suddenly a small section of brickwork came away completely causing Berkeley to cry out in alarm.

Duff merely stared up at the damage, shaking his head and mumbling to himself at the same time.

'I suggest you are less forceful with your probing, Duff,' Berkeley said, his heart pounding wildly. This job was unpleasant enough without adding danger to it. 'We don't want the whole roof down on top of us, do we?'

Duff was still grumbling to himself, his torch beam weaving from side to side as he shook his head. 'All these old tunnels are the same, you know,' he finally said to Berkeley. 'It's gonna cost millions to put them right. Solid enough when they were built, but all that traffic up there over the years, all those bleedin' juggernauts, all those buildings goin' up ... People who built these never dreamed they'd have to bear such a load. Never thought they'd have to carry so much shit, either.'

Berkeley wiped his slime-covered hands on his overalls. 'Fortunately, that's not my problem. I only have to submit a report.'

'Oh yeah?' said Terry from behind. 'An' who d'you think pays for it, then? Only comes out of our pockets, dunnit?'

'Shall we move on? It's rather uncomfortable crouching like this.' Berkeley was anxious to get the inspection over with.

Duff turned and made his way further down the tunnel, keeping his experienced eye on the ceiling, looking for breaks and signs of sagging. He saw plenty.

His assistant's voice came from the rear. 'D'you know what? If you got lost down here on your own, Mr Berkeley, you could wander around for years and never find your way out.'

Silly sod, Duff thought, but grinned to himself all the same.

'There's miles and miles of tunnels,' Terry went on. 'You could get from one end of London to the other.'

'Surely you would have to stop at the Thames?' came Berkeley's acid-toned comment.

'Oh yeah, if you could find it,' Terry answered, unabashed. 'You could drown before you did, though. You should see some of these tunnels after heavy rainfall. Some of 'em fill right up. Just think of it, wandering around down here, your lamp battery runnin' down, things scuttlin' around in the dark. I think the rats'd get you in the end. Some big bleeders down here.'

'All right, Terry, leave it out,' said Duff, still grinning. 'It's gettin' wider up here, Mr Berkeley. We'll be able to stand up soon.'

Berkeley wasn't bothered about Terry's remarks – he knew the idiot was only trying to intimidate him – but he could not help being afraid of the tunnels themselves. He felt a huge pressure bearing down on him, as though the city above were slowly sinking, pressing down on the tunnel roofs, compressing them, squeezing them flat, inch by inch. He would be forced into the slime flowing beneath him, the ceiling pushing him underneath, holding him there until he had to swallow, the filthy waters gushing down his throat, filling him . . .

'There you go!' Terry had spotted the opening ahead where their tunnel joined another.

Berkeley was grateful to step through into it and stand erect. This branch of the sewer network must have measured at least twelve feet across and the domed ceiling was high at its apex. The causeways on each side of the channel were wide enough to walk along comfortably.

'This looks fairly sound,' he commented, his voice ringing out hollowly against the damp curved walls.

'Should be all right along this stretch,' said Duff. 'It's the pipes and small conduits that give us the most problems – you'd never believe just what they get blocked up with.'

'No, I meant the brickwork here. It seems solid enough.'

Duff took the lamp from his helmet and flashed it down

the tunnel, searching walls and ceiling for breaks. 'Looks okay. There's a storm weir further down. Let's just have a look at it.'

By now, Berkeley had lost all sense of direction, not knowing whether they were heading north, south, east or west. The foreman's assistant was right: it would be easy to get lost in the maze of tunnels. He heard Duff poking at the walls with his metal pike and briefly wondered what would make a man take up this kind of work for a career. Career? Wrong word. His kind didn't have careers – they had jobs. And the young man behind – surely working in a garage or a factory was better than creeping around in the dark among the city's filth. Still, Berkeley reflected, thank God someone was stupid enough to do it. He peered into smaller openings leading into the main channel as he passed, shuddering at the total blackness they presented, his beam seeming to penetrate very little of their length. He imagined one of the huge rats the foreman's assistant had spoken of lurking there, waiting to pounce on any unfortunate who would unknowingly wander into its lair. Or a giant spider, huge and malformed, glutted on the slithering dark life all around, never before seen by human eyes, its web strung completely across a tunnel, waiting for an unsuspecting victim . . . Or a giant slug, blind and slimy, sucking itself to the lichen-covered walls, living in perpetual darkness, greedy for the next human feast . . .

'Oh my God!'

Duff swung around at the sound of Berkeley's shriek. 'What is it?' he asked, his voice a little higher-pitched than he'd intended.

The ministry man was pointing into a tunnel. 'Something moved in there!' His hand was trembling uncontrollably.

Duff lumbered back to him thinking, *silly sod*, and peered into the opening.

'You probably saw a rat,' he said reassuringly. 'Lots of 'em down here.'

'No, no, it was much bigger.'

'Trick of the light, probably all it was. It's the imagination that does it, every time. Takes a while to get used to things down here.'

Terry was peering over Berkeley's shoulder into the opening, a big smile on his face. 'They say the sewers are haunted by murder victims whose bodies've been dropped into them to get rid of the evidence,' he brightly informed the ministry man.

'Hold your noise, Terry,' Duff told him. 'You'll be givin' me the bleeding creeps next. Look, Mr Berkeley, there's nothing down there.' The combined lights from their lamps forced back the darkness in the tunnel revealing nothing but green-and-yellow-streaked walls. 'It must have just been your light throwin' a shadow as you passed. Nothin' to worry about.'

'I'm sorry. I'm sure . . .'

Duff had already turned away and was marching onwards, whistling tunelessly to himself. With a last look into the tunnel Berkeley followed, feeling foolish, but nonetheless, still nervous. Stinking bloody job to send him on!

As Terry moved away from the opening he thought – just thought – he heard a sound from its depths. 'Frightened me bloody self now,' he muttered under his breath.

Berkeley was hurrying to catch up with Duff, finding a small comfort in the man's no-nonsense, down-to-earth attitude, when the foreman came to an abrupt stop, causing the ministry man to bump into him. Duff was pointing his lamp down into the channel at their feet.

'There's something in the water,' he said.

Berkeley looked towards the centre of the wide torch beam. Something was floating lazily along, drifting with the slow-moving current, its progress hindered as it bumped against the raised side of the causeway. It looked like a large sack in the inadequate light.

'What on earth is it?' Berkeley asked curiously.

'It's a body,' said Terry, who had now joined them.

This time Duff knew his assistant wasn't joking. He knelt down on the edge of the causeway and caught the drifting shape with his metal bar as it came close. He pulled and the body turned languidly over in the water. All three men gasped when they saw the white bloated face and wide, staring eyes.

Berkeley found himself bent double against the moist wall, his stomach heaving up and down like a berserk lift. Through his dizziness, he heard Terry say, 'Christ Almighty, there's another one!'

He forced himself to look when he heard a splash. Terry had dropped into the sewer, his thigh-high boots giving him adequate protection against the foul-smelling stream that reached a point just above his knees. He was wading to another floating form on the other side of the channel.

'This one's a woman, I think!' he called back over his shoulder.

'Okay, Terry. Try and lift it on to the causeway,' Duff told him. 'We'll go back and get a team to come down and collect 'em. Mr Berkeley, give us a hand to pull this one out, will you?'

Berkeley shrank back against the wall. 'I ... I don't think ...'

'Would you believe it?' It was Terry's voice again. 'There's another one comin' down.'

Duff and Berkeley followed his gaze and saw the shape floating towards them. As it approached they saw it was the body of another woman, a white shape that could have been a nightdress billowing out around her. She was on her back, glazed eyes staring up at the dripping ceiling. Fortunately for Berkeley's stomach, her features did not have the puffiness of the first person they had found.

'Grab her, Terry,' Duff ordered.

The assistant heaved the body he was holding on to the causeway, then waded towards the new one. They watched him as he caught a leg, Duff with his hand grasped around the lapel of the dead man below him, Berkeley wondering at the assistant's lack of nerves. Perhaps the boy was too thick to be bothered.

Terry leaned over the floating woman, his arms going around her waist and reaching to grip her beneath the armpits. What happened next caused the same reaction in both men watching but with different results.

As Terry's head came close to the woman's, two pale-fleshed arms slid from the water and encircled his neck. He screamed as he was pulled down, the scream broken off by a choking gurgling sound as he plunged beneath the water. The oozing fluid became a white-foamed eruption as he struggled to free himself from the deathly grip, but the creature held on to him, dragging him down in her embrace.

Berkeley's mouth dropped open in a soundless scream and he was only dimly aware of the hot excreta that had been jettisoned down his sagging legs. He staggered back against the wall again, the knuckles of both hands filling his open mouth.

Duff's initial shock was instantly followed by a paralysing pain that began in his chest and swiftly travelled up to his neck and arms. A red, blinding mist closed the vision before him and he toppled forward into the water, his heart already given up before he could be drowned.

Berkeley watched as Terry rose from the water just once and he saw the assistant's eyes were staring into the face before him as if in disbelief. The woman hugged him tight, a lover's embrace, and her cracked and bitten lips were smiling. The boy stumbled backwards and the creature fell with him. Berkeley could see the dim glow of his lamp beneath the churning, green slime, but it grew weaker as he watched, the disturbance becoming no more than ripples, the ripples themselves fading after the last confusion of bubbles shot to the surface. Finally the light shrank to nothing.

The water was still.

Until she slowly emerged.

Green slime running from her body.

Looking at him.

Smiling.

Berkeley's shrieks echoed around the dingy caverns, the sound multiplied into a hundred screaming voices. There was more movement further down the tunnel. Figures were stepping from black openings into the main sewer. Others were in the water, wading towards him from the direction in which he and the two workmen had come. He didn't want to look, but he couldn't help himself, the headlamp swinging in a frantic arc towards the approaching figures. A cold, wet hand closed around his ankle.

The woman was standing close to him and he jerked his foot away from the edge of the causeway. Her long damp hair hung like the tails of rats over her face and the white gown she wore was ripped almost down to her pubic area, revealing sagging breasts and a stomach that was strangely distended as though she had not eaten for a long time. He cowered before her in the darkness and wondered if she was dead.

The woman reached for him again and began to clamber on to the causeway.

'No!' He kicked out at her and scrambled away on all fours. 'Leave me alone!'

He staggered to his feet and pushed himself against the wall, scraping lichen off with his back as he moved away. She began to crawl towards him. The others were moving closer.

He fell into an opening behind him and, as he looked for a means of escape, white, shaking hands reached for him from within. He tumbled back into the main tunnel, gasping, whimpering sounds burbling from his lips. He slipped from the causeway and fell headlong into the slow-moving fluid, emerging spluttering and crying, but still running. The water, thick with soilage, clung to his legs as though mud creatures at the bottom were gripping his feet and holding him back. Lifting his knees high, he splashed down the channel, away from the dark figures that followed, away from the woman who held her arms out to hug him. He was conscious of more and more objects bumping into his legs and was afraid to look down, knowing what they were, knowing arms would reach up to drag him down if he did look. The sewer opened up into a huge chamber, the ceiling some thirty or forty feet above him and supported by sturdy iron pillars. The massive weir controlling the flow of water through the sewers stood opposite. But he did not see it. For this was where they were all waiting.

They stood around the edges of the chamber, others in the water itself. More were crammed into the many openings in the circular wall. The water at the bottom of the chamber was full of bodies, several drifting away into various outlets as he watched. His headlamp swung round from face to face and he had the eerie sensation of being in a dark underground cathedral, the black-smeared people choristers awaiting the arrival of the choirmaster. The lamp beam seemed to be growing weaker, the surrounding darkness closing in around it, slowly stifling its brightness. Hundreds of eyes watched him from the shadows and the gaseous fumes from the chamber assailed his nostrils with added force. The stench here was somehow more acrid.

He began to back away from the crowded chamber. But a damp, white hand on his shoulder told him there was nowhere to run.

21

The cat kept to the shadows, its progress along the rain-freshened street silent and unseen. The rain had stopped, otherwise the cat would still be skulking somewhere under cover. It was an animal that had no owner, one that needed no permanent home; it lived on its own cunning, its own stealth, its own speed. Humans would never pet its kind, nor welcome it into their homes, for it was a scavenger and had the looks of a scavenger. The black fur on its back was sparse, almost bare in places where the cat had come off worse in fights with others of its breed. One ear was just a mangled shape, a stub protruding from its head; the dog that had inflicted the wound could now see only from one eye. Its claws were stunted from too much running on concrete, but were still lethal when fully extended. Its pads were hard, like tough leather. The cat sniffed the damp night air and its eyes, caught in the dull glow of an overhead street-light, were glassy yellow.

It turned into an alleyway and padded towards the dustbins hidden there in the dark doorways. The scent of other night creatures was strong in its nose. The cat recognized most of the individual smells, some friendly, others producing a new sharpness to its already acute senses. The furtive, sharp-nosed, long-tailed creatures had been here, a cowardly enemy that would always choose to run rather than fight. They were gone now. Its own kind had been there earlier, but they, too were gone.

The cat sniffed its way through the litter on the ground, then leapt on top of a dustbin, disappointed that its lid was sealed tight. The lid of the next dustbin was at a slight angle and the smell of corrupting food wafted through the narrow, new-moon gap. The cat poked its nose inquisitively into the opening, poking a paw through to tug at the loose paper and rubble at the top. The lid moved a little under the cat's insistent probing, then even more when the creature pushed first its head then its shoulders through the widening gap. The metal lid finally slid gratingly across the rim of the dustbin and landed with a loud clatter on the ground. The cat fled, alarmed by the noise of its own making.

It paused at the entrance to the alley, its one good ear pricked for unfriendly sounds, nose held high and twitching for hostile scents. The animal stiffened when it detected the slight acrid smell in the air and the sparse hairs on its back began to bristle. As its fellow creatures had been only minutes before, the cat became aware of a strange presence that somehow belonged to man, yet wasn't man. It crept over the paralysed cat like a crawling thing, a shadow that mixed with the other shadows. The terrified creature bared its teeth and hissed. Something was moving in the middle of the glistening wet road.

The cat arched its back, every hair on its body stiff and erect, mouth wide in a hissing snarl. It spat its defiance, afraid though it was, and its eyes narrowed, full of venom. The street-lights had dimmed as though a mist had drifted across them and the pavements no longer offered any reflections in their wetness. A heavy, metallic sound came from the road's centre as the manhole cover shuddered, then began to rise. It was pushed higher, one side resting on its base, and something black began to emerge. The cat recognized the shape that came over the edge of the hole. It knew it was a human hand. Yet instinctively, it knew the hand did not belong to a human.

The cat hissed once more, then fled, for some reason heading for the lights rather than the shadows.

The three youths waited in the weather-battered shelter on the common. Two were white, one was black. They puffed on cigarettes and jiggled their knees to keep out the cold.

'I ain't stayin' much longer,' the coloured boy said. 'It's too fuckin' cold.' His name was Wesley and he was on probation for purse snatching.

'Shut up an' wait a minute. Won't be much longer,' said one of his companions. His name was Vincent and he was on probation for half-killing his stepfather.

'I dunno, it's gettin' late, Vin,' said the third youth. 'Don't think there'll be no one about.' His name was Ed – his friends thought it was short for Edward but, in fact, it was short for Edgar – and he had recently finished his villain's apprenticeship in an approved school.

'What you wanna do, then, go 'ome?' asked Vince of his two friends. 'Got any money for tomorrow night?'

'No, but, I'm fuckin' cold,' Wesley told him again.

'You're always fuckin' cold. Miss the old Caribbean, eh?'

'Ain't never been there. Born in bloody Brixton, weren't I?'

'Get out of it. In your bloody blood. You all miss your bleeding sunshine. It's what makes your hair curly.'

'Leave 'im alone, Vin,' said Ed, peering around the edge of the shelter into the gloom. 'He's joinin' the Front, 'inne?'

'Do me a favour! They won't have 'im! He's a nig-nog 'imself.'

'Yeah, but I don't want no more of them comin' over 'ere. Specially those Pakis,' Wesley protested. 'Too bloody many.'

The other two youths shrieked with glee. The thought of Wesley marching along with the National Front holding a banner saying 'KEEP BRITAIN WHITE' was too much. Wesley was too puzzled by their laughter to feel aggrieved. Soon he was laughing with them.

''Ang on, 'ang on,' Ed said suddenly. 'I think there's someone comin'.'

'Right. Down to you Ed,' said Vin, springing to his feet. 'Me an' Wes'll be over there in the bushes.'

'Why always me?' Ed protested. 'You 'av a go.'

Vince patted him on the cheek, the last pat a little more forceful than the rest. 'You're so pretty, that's why. They like you more than us. Think you're one of them, don't they?'

Not for the first time, Ed cursed his own blond good looks. He would much rather have had Vince's tough, pock-marked features and short ginger hair than his own almost girlish looks. 'What about Wes, then?'

'Nah, they don't trust coloureds, do they? Think they're all fuckin' muggers.' He gave his black friend a playful shove. 'Right, innit, Wes?'

Wes grinned in the dark. 'They's fockin' right, man,' he said, mimicking his own father's accent.

Vince and Wesley ran quietly from the shelter, both sniggering and prodding each other as they went. Ed waited silently, taking a last drag from his cigarette and listening for the approaching footsteps. The common was a favourite haunt for clandestine lovers of all varieties, that variety having increased since the surrounding working class area had been infiltrated by middle-class residents. The cost of travelling every day from the surrounding suburbs to their jobs in London had become too much for the *nouveaux pauvres*. The area that had become multi-racial over the years was now fast-becoming multi-class. Ed threw the half-inch butt on to the ground, then took another loose cigarette from the pocket of his denim jacket. He was about to step from the shelter into view when he realized there were two sets of footfalls. He slunk back into the shadows.

The couple walked past the shelter, arms tight around each other's waists; Ed was worried that they were going to make use of his hideaway for their own purposes, but when they moved on he realized the stink of stale urine in the shelter would put any lovers off, no matter how desperate. He cursed under his breath and dug his hands deep into his pockets. There'll be no gingers about now, not this late, he told himself. Yet he knew from previous experience that the lateness of the hour meant nothing to certain lonely men, nor did the remoteness of the locations they wandered through. Sometimes Ed wondered if they went out of their way to be attacked. Maybe they enjoyed it. Or maybe it was their own subconscious way of punishing themselves for what they were. The last, deeper thought was immediately dismissed by one more obvious to Ed's way of thinking; maybe they just got more horny at night.

He looked out into the darkness towards the spot where Vince and Wes had disappeared. The feeble glow from a nearby lamp-post did little to pierce the shadows. He was about to call out to them, imagining them both giggling and playing around in the dark, when he heard more footsteps. Ed listened, making sure they belonged to one person. They did. The man came into view seconds later.

He was slightly built, about Ed's size. A heavy belted overcoat hung loosely on him, emphasizing his narrow shoulders rather than compensating for them. Definite poof, Ed told himself, not sure if he was pleased or displeased with their luck. He knew these men were easy pickings, that there was little danger from them; but something inside always made him scared of them. Perhaps that was why in the end he always used more violence against them than his companions did. The memory of when he had decided to tackle one on his own was still fresh in his mind for, instead of attacking his intended victim and relieving him of his wallet, he had let himself be used, then run off sobbing before he could even be paid. The shame of it still stung his face, and he knew his skin had become bright red in the darkness. If Vince and Wes ever found out . . .

'Got a light, John?' Ed had pushed all further thoughts away and stepped on to the pathway leading across the common.

The man came to an abrupt halt and glanced around nervously. The boy looked all right, but was he really alone? Should he walk on or . . . should he take a chance?

He took out his own cigarettes. 'Would you like one of mine?' he asked. 'They're tipped.'

'Oh, yeah. Thanks.' Ed stuck his battered cigarette back into his pocket and reached towards the proffered pack, hoping the man hadn't noticed his hand was shaking slightly.

'You can have the pack, if you like,' the man said, his face serious.

My Gawd, a right one 'ere, Ed thought. 'Oh, great, thanks a lot.' He pushed the pack into another pocket.

The man studied the boy's face in the glow from the cigarette-lighter. It became indistinct when he drew back, his cigarette lit. The man snapped out the small flame.

'It's rather cold tonight, isn't it,' he said cautiously. The boy was attractive in a rough sort of way. Was he genuine or just a tart? Either way, he'd want money.

'Yeah, bit nippy. Just out for a walk?'

'Yes, it's nicer when it's quiet. I hate crowds. I feel I can breathe at night.'

'It'll cost you a fiver.'

The man was slightly taken aback by the boy's sudden bluntness. He *was* a tart.

'Back at my place?' he asked, the excitement that had been triggered off at the boy's approach now accelerating.

Ed shook his head. 'No, no, it'll 'ave to be 'ere.'

'I'll pay you more.'

'No, I ain't got time. Got to be 'ome soon.'

The boy seemed a little afraid and the man decided not to push his luck.

'All right. Let's find somewhere nice.'

'Over there'll do.' The boy pointed towards a clump of bushes and trees and this time it was the man's turn to become a little nervous. It was so dark over there: the boy could have friends waiting.

'Let's go behind the shelter,' he suggested quickly.

'No, I don't think . . .'

But the man now had a surprisingly firm grip around Ed's shoulders. The boy allowed himself to be propelled towards the back of the wooden shelter, hoping his friends were watching. It would be just like those two bastards to leave it till the last minute.

They squelched through the mud at the side of the hut, the man warding off bushes that threatened to scratch their faces. They turned a corner and Ed found himself pressed up against the back of the hut. The man's face was looming larger in front of him, his lips only inches away, and Ed felt the revulsion rising in him. Fumbling fingers pulled at the zip of his jeans.

'No,' he said, turning his head to one side.

'Come on. Don't be coy. You want it as much as me.'

'Fuck off!' Ed screamed and pushed at the man's chest. His face had grown red-hot again and his vision had become blurred with sudden tears of rage.

The man was startled. He staggered back and stared at the youth. He began to say something but the boy rushed at him, lashing out wildly with his fists.

'Stop it, stop it!' the man screamed, falling backwards. Ed began to kick him.

'You dirty fuckin' queer!'

The man tried to rise, whimpering with fright now. He had to get away, the boy was going to hurt him. And the police might hear the disturbance.

'Leave me alone! Take my money!' The man managed to reach his inside pocket. He threw his wallet at his attacker. 'Take it, take it, you bastard! Just leave me alone!'

Ed ignored the wallet and continued to rain punches and kicks down at the curled form at his feet until his arms and legs grew heavy and his anger began to subside. He stumbled back against the shelter's wall and stood there leaning on it, chest heaving and legs weak. He could hear the injured man crying out but, for some reason, he could no longer see him lying there on the ground. The night darkness had somehow become more dense.

'Vin! Wes!' he called out when he had recovered enough breath. 'Where are you, for fuck's sake?'

''Ere we are, Ed.'

The youth jumped at the close proximity of their voices. It was almost as if they were inside his head. He could just see their dark outlines as they stood at the corner of the shelter.

'You took your time, you bastards. I 'ad to deck 'im on me own. Let's get 'is money and split.'

'Nah, I don't think so, Ed.' It was Vince's voice. 'Let's 'av some fun first.' He heard Wesley giggle.

This is stupid, Ed thought. It'd be better to get away . . . but it would be nice to do something to this cunt . . . something nasty . . . he was helpless . . . there was no one around . . . something that would hurt him . . . something . . .

There were other voices inside his head now, not just his own. Something was creeping along corridors in his mind, cold fingers that probed and searched, fingers that spoke to him and laughed with him. And he was leading them on, guiding them. The coldness was all-enveloping as it suddenly lunged and caught him in its icy grip, and he was pleased to receive it, the shock turning into pleasure like the swift effects of an anaesthetizing injection. He wasn't alone any more. The voices were with him and they told him what to do.

Vince and Wes had already begun and the damp earth that was being pushed into the struggling man's mouth stifled any screams.

The filling station stood at the edge of the common, an oasis of light in the surrounding darkness. The yellow Ford Escort pulled into the forecourt and came to a smooth halt before a petrol pump. The driver turned off the engine and settled back to wait for the attendant to emerge from his office. The car's occupants did not know that the man on duty, who was, in fact, the garage manager, had popped round to the back of the building twenty minutes earlier to lock up the toilets there; he didn't want any lingering customers at that time of night. Regretfully, he had had to let his usual attendant leave earlier; the man was obviously coming down with a bad attack of flu and the manager wasn't taking the risk of catching it himself. His profit margin was small enough without his being off sick and leaving the staff to run the garage. He'd go broke within a week with their fiddles. It was normally bad policy to man a garage alone at night, for it made the station an easy mark for villains; but tonight he had no choice. He kept the door of the office overlooking the forecourt permanently locked and scrutinized every customer that came in for petrol before unlocking it. If he didn't like the look of them, he turned the OPEN sign around to CLOSED and ignored their muffled curses. It had been well after twelve when he remembered the toilets were still unlocked.

'You sure it's open, George?' the woman next to the driver said testily. 'There doesn't seem to be anyone around.'

'It says "open" at the entrance,' her husband replied. 'And look, on the cashier's door. There's another "open" sign.'

'I should give him a toot, George,' said the driver's father-in-law from the back seat.

'I'll give him a minute. He might be round the back.' There was nothing pushy about George.

His wife, Olwen, pulled the hem of her flouncy, sequined dress into a tight bunch over her knees, afraid the chiffon and layers of netting would pick up dirt from the car's interior. A large polythene bag was draped over the passenger seat to protect her meticulously made ballroom frock and fur shouldercape from any hidden grime. Her high coiffured hair brushed against the car roof as she stared through the windscreen, her mouth set in a firm straight line.

'We should have won,' she announced grimly.

'Now, Olwen,' George said patiently, 'Nigel and Barbara were very good.'

'That's right, defend them. I suppose it doesn't matter that they bumped us twice on the dance floor. Never even apologized afterwards. You'd have thought there was no one else in the ballroom the way they pranced around. We should have objected. Bloody judges should have spotted it.'

'Well, we were runners-up, dear.'

'Runners-up! That's the story of your life, isn't it, George? That's all you'll ever be.'

'There's no call for that kind of talk,' Olwen's father rebuked.

'Shut up, Huw,' said Olwen's mother who sat cramped in the back with her husband. 'Olwen's quite right. She could have been ballroom champion by now, that girl.' She did not add, 'with a different partner'. There was no need to.

'Take no notice, George,' Huw said. 'Neither of them are ever satisfied.'

'Satisfied? What have I got to be satisfied with? What have you ever given me?'

'I'll give you the back of my hand in a minute.'

'Dad, don't speak to Mother like that.'

'I'll speak to her however I . . .'

'You certainly won't. You see what he's like, Olwen? You see what I've had to put up with all these years?'

'Put up with? I've had your nagging . . .'

'Nagging?'

'Mum doesn't nag.'

'She nags all the time. Same way you nag poor old George.'

'Me nag George? I never nag George. Do I ever nag you, George?'

'The attendant's a long time,' said George.

'Well bib him.' Exasperated, Olwen reached across George and thumped the car's horn. 'Lazy bleeder's probably sleeping under the counter.'

George ran his finger and thumb along his thin pencil-line moustache, smoothing down the Brylcreemed hairs, and briefly wondered what would happen if he punched Olwen on the nose. She'd punch him back, that's what would happen. And she could punch harder.

'Ah, here he comes,' he said, pointing to the figure that had emerged from the darkness at the rear of the garage.

'It's about bloody time,' said Olwen.

'Don't swear, dear, it's not very nice.'

'I'll swear if I like.'

'George is right, Olwen,' said her father. 'It's not very ladylike.'

'Leave her alone, Huw,' said her mother. 'She's had a lot of stress this evening. George didn't help by letting her fall on her bottom in the *pas redoublé*.'

'Best part of the bloody evening,' her father remarked, smiling at the memory.

'Dad!'

'Take no notice, Olwen. It's just like him to enjoy seeing his own daughter make a fool of herself.'

'Mum!'

'Oh, I didn't mean ...'

'Five of 3-star, please.' George had wound down his window and was calling out to the approaching figure.

The man came to a halt, smiled at the occupants of the car, and looked over towards the petrol pumps. He made towards them.

'He's slow enough, isn't he?' remarked Olwen's mother. 'And what's he got that silly grin on his face for?'

'Look at the state of him,' said Olwen. 'You'd think he'd been down the mines. I wonder if the manager knows his staff walk around like that?'

'Perhaps he is the manager,' said her father, chuckling in the back, not knowing that the manager lay dead on the floor of the toilets, his skull cracked open like an egg from the repeated blows of a brick.

They watched the man as he lifted the dispensing nozzle from the rack set in the pumping unit. He came towards the car holding the hosecock alongside his head like a duelling pistol. His eyes were half-closed as though they had not yet adjusted to the contrast between the harsh overhead lighting and the darkness from which he had just emerged. He grinned at the four people watching him from the car.

'Silly bugger,' Olwen remarked.

George poked his head out of the window. 'Er, no, old chap. I did say 3-star. You've still got it switched to 4-star.' He drew back quickly when he found himself staring into the black hole of the dispensing nozzle.

In the back of the Escort, Olwen's father had a puzzled frown on his face. He had seen movement in the fringes of darkness around the service area. There were shapes moving closer. They were stepping into the lighted area, then stopping. They were waiting. Watching. Others stood behind them, still in the shadows. What the hell was going on? Why were they staring at the car? He turned to say something but stopped himself when he saw the metal nozzle from the petrol pump stretching into the car window and George, a startled expression on his face, leaning away from it. Olwen's father could only watch in dumbstruck amazement as the index finger on the hand holding the nozzle began to tighten.

The petrol gushed out, covering George's head and shoulders in a filmy fluid. Olwen began to scream when the nozzle was aimed down into her husband's lap. Her father tried to push forward and grab the long barrel of the hosecock, but it was turned in his direction and he fell back, choking on the petrol that had poured into his open mouth. Olwen's mother was screaming now, knowing she and her husband were trapped and helpless in the back of the two-door vehicle.

Olwen's screams became even louder as her dress was suddenly splashed by the foul-smelling liquid. She tried to reach for the door-handle on her side, but her fingers slid from the petrol-soaked metal.

Her father, still choking on the fuel he had swallowed, could only watch in horror as the nozzle waved around, the petrol pouring out in a solid stream and filling the car with its noxious fumes and deadly liquid. George was striking out blindly, his eyes stinging and useless. Olwen's hands were covering her face as she cried out and beat her feet against the car's floor. Her mother was trying to burrow her way down into the gap between the back of the driver's seat and her own. The flow of petrol abruptly stopped and the nozzle was withdrawn.

Olwen's father could only observe the middle portion of the man through the windows; it was enough to see him drop the nozzle and reach into his jacket pocket for something. Huw began to moan when he saw the box of matches, the sudden bright flare as one was lit, the small arc of smoke as the match was tossed into the car.

The man stood back as the Escort's interior burst into a blinding cauldron of flame, his face peeling instantly as the fire licked out at him. He did not seem to feel the pain as he reached down for the hose at his feet and drew the dispensing nozzle towards himself. His fingers curled around the trigger and squeezed.

He walked around the forecourt as far as the hose could allow, splashing petrol everywhere, becoming saturated himself, but seeming not to care. Then he turned back towards the little yellow car that had by now become a raging inferno, the sounds of its occupants no longer heard, and he aimed the jet of fuel at it. The flames rushed towards him and he stood there and screamed as he became a black charred shape. His companions turned away from the heat and light, sinking into the darkness that was itself forced back when the filling station exploded into a huge ball of fire that rose hundreds of feet into the air and lit the night sky.

The Dark drifted on, an evil, creeping blackness that had no substance, yet was full of invisible energy, an expanding shadow that existed only in other shadows, an incorporeal thing that sucked at human minds, invading and searching for the hidden repressed impulses that were of itself. There were solid, dark shapes within it and these were the forms of men and women whose will it did not just govern, but who embodied the material part of it, those who physically enacted the evil that it was, its earthly force. It had a smell, a faint acridity that tainted the air it filled, a bitter aroma that men were aware of when lightning struck the ground, or when electric cables discharged sparks into the air. It was a dark stain on the night.

The blaze was left far behind with the wailing sirens and distant shouts, and the Dark relished the blackness it crept into, its edges probing like tentacles at the shadows before it, sensing a fresh force that was somewhere near, a huge source of energy that was as yet untapped, a chained gathering of dark minds that was the very substance it needed.

It seeped across the grassland on to an open road, shying away from the orange-glowing street-lights, surging around them like a stream around rocks projecting from its bed. The shadowy figures drifted with it, several collapsing, their bodies drained, lack of food or water finally bringing them down like machines not fuelled or oiled. Some died – the others would follow later – and as they did, a part of them was released: the darkness within them was welcomed by the mass.

The long wall loomed up high and the darkness flowed

over it, leaving the men and women who walked with it below, helpless and suddenly afraid. It rushed towards the sleeping inmates of Wandsworth Prison, creeping into the openings, pouncing and absorbing, the recumbent minds receptive and eager. Not all though. But these did not last long.

22

The ringing phone woke Bishop from a deep sleep. It was strange, but since Lynn's death two weeks before, his recurrent drowning nightmare had left him. Perhaps it had been purged from him by the experience in the mental home that night, living out the dream, almost taking it to death's conclusion. He pushed back the covers and switched on the bedside lamp. The small alarm clock told him it was just after two o'clock. Alertness spread through him as he heaved himself from the bed and padded down the carpeted stairs to the hall. He grabbed the phone.

'Bishop? Detective Chief Inspector Peck here.'

'What's wrong?' All drowsiness had completely left Bishop now.

Peck's voice was urgent. 'I haven't got long, so just listen and do as I tell you.'

Something knotted inside Bishop's stomach.

'I want you to lock your doors, front and back,' Peck went on. 'Check all your windows, make sure they're locked, too.'

'What's going on, Peck?'

'Have you got a room you can lock yourself into?'

'Yes, but . . .'

'Then do it. Barricade yourself in.'

'What the hell are you talking about?'

'Look, I haven't got time to explain. All I can tell you is

259

that something is going on near your part of London. Our Information Room is being flooded with emergency calls. Our biggest problem is a riot in Wandsworth Prison.'

'Jesus. Can they break out?'

'It looks like they already have.' There was a short pause at the other end of the line. 'It seems some of the prison warders themselves may have been involved. To make matters more confused, a garage on the other side of the Common has been blown up.'

'Peck, has all this got something to do with the Pryszlak business?'

'God only knows. If it has, some of these maniacs may come after you. That's why I want you to lock yourself in. I'm afraid I haven't got enough men available to send you any protection. I could be wrong anyway.'

'Thanks for the warning. Have you told Kulek and Jessica?'

'I still have a man watching their house. I've sent a radio message telling him to inform Kulek of what's happening. I've let the guard stay there, even though we can't really spare him. Unfortunately, the officer keeping an eye on you had to be called in – that's why I'm ringing you. You'll be okay if you do as I say.'

'All right. Just tell me one thing. Do you now believe Jacob Kulek's theory?'

'Do you?'

'I'm beginning to more and more.'

'Well, maybe I am too. I don't *understand* it, but there's nothing else to explain what's going on. The thing is to convince my governors. I've got to get back now. You just sit tight, understand?'

The receiver was replaced before Bishop could answer. He quickly checked the front door to make sure it was bolted as well as locked, then went out to the back. The kitchen door leading to his tiny rear garden was also locked. Next, check the windows, he thought, but instead he decided to first ring Jessica; even with police protection she was probably scared to death. He had seen her only twice since Lynn's death: once when she had come to his house after learning about the tragedy in the mental home, and then a couple of days later, at a meeting held by Peck and several of his superiors, including the Deputy Commissioner. Since then she had left him alone and he was grateful that she realized he needed time to get over the shock of losing Lynn, this time permanently. It disturbed him that rather than feel remorse, he felt anger at his wife's death. To him, she had begun to die years before, a long, lingering illness of the mind from which he somehow knew she would never recover; it was the manner of her death that angered him. She had been used, controlled by an unknown power along with the others at the home. Her death had been horrible, although mercifully quick, and he wanted it avenged. If Pryszlak was in some bizarre way involved, then he, Bishop, would find a way to strike back. There had to be a way.

He dialled Jessica's number, hoping she would still be awake after the policeman's message. It was several long moments before the receiver was lifted and Jessica's voice came through.

'Jessica, it's me, Chris.'

Her tone became alert as had his only minutes before when Peck had called him.

'Chris, what is it? Are you all right?'

'Didn't you get Peck's message?'

'No, what message? It's the middle of the night, Chris. We've been asleep.'

'But there's a policeman on guard outside. Hasn't he told you?'

'Nobody's told us anything. What on earth's going on? Tell me what's happened.'

Bishop was puzzled. 'Peck rang me a few moments ago. He said he'd got a message to you. There are more incidents being reported, Jessica. All on this side of the river, it seems.'

'What kind of incidents?' Her voice was calm, but it had an edge to it.

'A riot in Wandsworth Prison. Something else about an explosion in a garage nearby. Others that he didn't have time to tell me about.'

'And he thinks there's a connection . . .?'

'With Pryszlak and his sect? He's not sure, but he felt he ought to warn us, anyway. Jessica, he said they might come after us again if there is a connection.'

'Oh, Chris.'

'Don't worry, you'll be all right. So far, all the trouble is over here. You've got a man outside who will contact his headquarters if anything begins to happen there.'

'But what will you do?'

'I'll barricade myself in, don't worry. We're all probably going to feel embarrassed later when we learn these are entirely separate incidents that have nothing to do with us.'

'I hope . . .' Jessica's voice broke off. 'There's someone at the door now. Our guardian policeman, no doubt. I'd better let him in before he wakes my father – if he isn't already awake, that is.'

'I'm sorry, Jessica. I just wanted to make sure . . .'

'Don't be silly, Chris. I'm glad you rang. Just hold on for a minute while I open the door.'

Bishop heard the clunk of the receiver being placed on the small table he remembered the phone rested on in the long hallway. There was silence for a few moments save for the strangely hollow sounding atmospherics in his own ear-piece, then he thought he heard the distant noise of the front door being unlocked. For some reason he began to feel uneasy. Why had the detective been so slow in delivering his message? Perhaps he had taken it into his own head not to disturb the sleeping household – what they didn't know couldn't hurt them. After all, the policeman was keeping a watch on the place. The hall light being switched on by Jessica as she answered the phone could have prompted him to change his mind and inform them there and then. Yet Bishop could not imagine any of Peck's men not carrying out his instructions to the letter. He had said he'd told the officer to inform Kulek immediately.

Bishop's hand tightened around the receiver, his knuckles becoming white. 'Jessica, can you hear me?'

He listened and thought he heard approaching footsteps at the other end.

'Jessica?'

A click, then a burring noise as the receiver was dropped on to its cradle at the other end.

Bishop slowed the car as he turned from the main Highgate High Street into the village itself. The drive across London had been swift, for there was little traffic around at that hour, although there had been much activity in the Westminster area as police vehicles and minibus 'pixies' were deployed to deal with the emergencies across the river. Bishop had tried to ring Jessica back, but this time only got an engaged tone. He had also attempted to contact Peck again, but the detective had already left his office. Not sure if he wasn't exaggerating the situation, Bishop left a message and set off for Jacob

Kulek's house himself, a little wary as he stepped outside his front door, almost expecting to be attacked. The street was deserted.

He found the narrow lane leading to Kulek's house and headed into it, the car's headlights casting their twin beams far ahead, pushing back the darkness. Small, elegant houses sped by and, because the lane was downhill, he could see the bright glow of the city in the distance. He applied the brakes gently and changed down to a lower gear, sure that Kulek's house lay just ahead in a turn-off to the right. He brought the car to a halt when he saw the vehicle parked opposite the entrance to the house. It was tucked well into the side of the lane, the passenger doors no more than six inches away from a high brick wall that gave privacy to a residence beyond. Bishop pulled in behind and saw that the car appeared to be empty; he wondered if the policeman might be slumped down in the driver's seat – asleep or perhaps dead. He switched off his engine, but left the headlights on. Discarding his driving glasses, he stepped from the car.

The night was cold, but he wondered if the sudden chill he felt was due to something more. He cautiously approached the other vehicle and bent down to peer into a window. It was empty.

Bishop tried the handle and, finding it unlocked, pulled the door open. The radio equipment inside told him he hadn't been mistaken – it was a police car. Where was the policeman himself, though? He must have gone into the house. Bishop felt somewhat foolish for having panicked so easily. Yet, with all that had happened recently, he had reason to be a little jumpy. Peck may have told his man to stay inside Kulek's house – it seemed to make sense if Peck's concern for Jessica and her father's safety had suddenly been heightened by that night's events. Why had the phone been put down on him, though? Then he cursed himself, feeling even more foolish. The line had been engaged when he had tried to ring Jessica back – she must have realized she had cut him off, then tried to reach him again! He was behaving like a frightened old woman.

He went back to his own car, switched off the headlights, and strode across the lane towards the driveway leading to Kulek's house. From the entrance he could see a light shining ahead, a long rectangular glow that had to be the glass side-panel that ran the length of the front door. At least, if Jessica and her father were asleep, the policeman would be awake and could let him in. Yet, despite all the rationalization, his anxiety still persisted. Somewhere inside him he knew things were wrong. If he could have seen the corpse of the policeman, his throat slit from ear to ear, lying in the darkness of the undergrowth only two feet away, Bishop might have turned away from the house.

His feet crunched on the gravel drive as he approached the glass-structured building, its smooth exterior as black as the night around it. The light from the side panel guided him towards the door and he hesitated when he had stepped on to the wide porch area. He was afraid to ring the doorbell.

He did not need to – the door was already opening. The light from behind threw her shape in silhouette, but her voice was strangely familiar to him.

'Welcome again, Mr Bishop. We've been waiting for you,' the tall woman said.

Jacob Kulek and Jessica were in the living-room. Both were seated and dressed in nightclothes. The short woman was holding a knife at the blind man's throat, a long butcher's knife that had dark, reddish stains on its blade. She smiled at Bishop.

'Are you all right, Jessica? Jacob?' asked Bishop, standing in the doorway.

Jessica could barely tear her eyes away from the blade at her father's throat.

'We are all right for the moment, Chris,' the blind man answered. 'Unfortunately, our guard, we are told, has been murdered.'

A gentle push from behind with the small Beretta the tall woman held urged Bishop further into the room.

'Yes, Mr Bishop,' she said. 'You passed the poor policeman on your way in. I must say he was very easy to kill. But then would you suspect Miss Turner there would cut your throat if you didn't know better?'

The smile on the small woman's face broadened. 'The silly man thought I was a helpless old bag who'd had too much to drink.'

'We knew he was there, you see. We, also, have been watching this house all week. Would you please sit down, Mr Bishop? We don't want any more deaths just at the moment, do we? Later, of course, but not just yet.' The tall woman pointed to a place on the settee next to Jessica.

Bishop sat and saw the terror in Jessica's eyes. He took her hand and held it.

'Yes, very touching, Christopher. May I call you Christopher?' It was hard to imagine the tall woman was anything more than a member of the Women's Guild, the type who sold paper flowers on Poppy Day. The small gun in her hand and her next words reminded Bishop just how evil she really was. 'Have you forgotten your wife already, Christopher? Did she mean so little to you?'

He began to push himself from the seat, his rage smothering any fear, but Jessica caught his arm.

'No, Chris!' she cried out.

The pleasantness had suddenly left the tall woman's manner. 'Take notice of her, Christopher. She has been told her father will die instantly if there is any trouble from you.'

He sank back, the anger making him tremble.

'That's right,' the tall woman said soothingly, her pleasantness returned. She sat down in a straight-backed chair which stood against the wall, keeping the gun pointed in Bishop's direction. 'You're an interesting man, Christopher. We have been finding out more about you over the past few weeks. I've even read one of your books. In a strange way, your theories are not too distant from Boris Pryszlak's. Nor Jacob Kulek's here, although I gather you care more for explainable science than the unexplainable.'

'May I ask what Pryszlak was to you?' Kulek asked. 'And may I also ask that this knife be taken away? It is rather uncomfortable. Surely the gun that you hold is enough.'

'Yes, Judith, I think you can relax a little now. Why don't you sit on the arm of the chair and keep the knife pressed against Kulek's heart?'

'I don't trust the old man,' the short woman replied. 'I don't trust any of them.'

'No, dear, nor I. But I don't imagine there is much they can do in the short time they have left. I'll keep my gun pointed straight at Mr Bishop's head.'

The short woman grudgingly changed her position and Kulek felt the tip of the knife pressed against his chest a little harder than was necessary to make him aware of its presence.

'Will you now tell us of your relationship with Pryszlak?' he asked, seemingly unaffected.

'Of course. There's no reason why you shouldn't know.

Judith and I – my name is Lillian, by the way, Lillian Huscroft – were introduced to Boris many years ago by Dominic Kirkhope. Dominic knew the sort of games Judith and I enjoyed – I could say his knowledge was intimate – and he knew we were reasonably wealthy. Boris needed money at that time for his experiments. He also needed people, people of his own kind. If there was an overall characteristic among the members of his specially chosen group, I suppose you could call it "moral wickedness". We were all evil, you see. But we regarded that as a virtue, not a weakness. A quality held by many, but repressed because of the distorted prejudices so-called civilized society had thrust upon us. We found our freedom with Boris. Every sinful act we committed was a step nearer to our ultimate goal.'

She gave a short laugh and looked mockingly at her three captives. 'The police in this country would be amazed how tidy their files on unsolved crimes would become if we revealed the part many of our members played in them. The hardest crime to solve is the one without apparent motive and I'm afraid our dear law enforcement officers find the concept of evil for the *sake* of evil hard to grasp.'

'I find it somewhat hard to grasp myself,' said Kulek calmly.

'That, if I may say so, is why Boris is a great innovator, while you are merely a mundane theorist. It was a pity you did not accept his offer – you may have become as great as he.'

'You said "is". Are you telling me that Pryszlak is not dead?'

'No one really dies, Jacob.'

'The policeman outside is dead,' Bishop said evenly. 'My wife is dead.'

'Their bodies are discarded shells, that's all. Your wife, I believe, is still very active. As for the policeman – it's up to him how he continues. It will depend on which were the stronger powers within him. I can assure you, the fact that he was a law enforcer does not mean his powers for "goodness" were necessarily the more dominant. Far from it.'

'What the hell are you talking about?'

'She means there are two invisible powers that control the destiny of mankind,' Kulek explained. 'If you were a religious man, you might label them the Powers of Light and the Powers of Darkness. The Bible refers to them often enough. What we've never realized or, if you like, what we've forgotten over the centuries is that they were scientific concepts, not merely religious imagery. It seems Pryszlak did find a way of tapping that power. He used his knowledge of psychism to find the key. Others have achieved it in the past, only we've never recognized the fact. They probably did not fully realize it themselves. Just think of the tyrants, the mass murderers, the *evil* geniuses of the past. How did ordinary men like Adolf Hitler gain such incredible power?'

'Excellent, Jacob,' said the tall woman. 'You really could have been helpful to Boris.'

'But what was that key?' Kulek had involuntarily leaned forward and the sharp pain from the knife prick made him move quickly back.

'Don't you know, Jacob? Ah, but of course, you are not a scientist. You know little of the powers of pure energy. Have you any idea of the immense energy in one person's brain? The electrical impulses created by chemical reaction that keeps our bodies functioning throughout our lifetimes? An energy that cannot disappear, cannot dissolve just because our bodies die? An electrical force, Jacob, that can be reached. Its potential is limitless. Have you any concept at all of its collective force?' She laughed again, enjoying the moment, and her companion smiled with her. 'Of course you haven't. None of us has! But we will. Soon!'

'Electrical energy.' Kulek's face had gone deathly white. 'It's not possible. We must be more than that.'

'We are, Jacob. But then energy itself is more than just that. It is a physical thing but, you see, we underestimate the term. The paranormal is perfectly normal. We just need to understand it. I believe that is one of your own doctrines.'

'Matters that today we believe are extraordinary will not be so in the future.'

'Yes, scientific progress will see to that. And the momentum of that progression is increasing. Boris was far ahead of us all, and he had the courage to take the final step to give proof of his discovery.'

'By killing himself?'

'By freeing himself.'

'There has to be more to it.'

'Oh there is, and it was very simple. For a man like Boris, that is.'

'Won't you tell us?'

'I think not. You'll find out yourselves soon enough.'

'Why are you holding us here?' said Bishop. 'What are you waiting for?'

'You'll see. It shouldn't be long now.'

'Is it anything to do with the trouble that's going on tonight on the other side of the river?'

'Yes, it is very much to do with it.'

Jessica spoke. 'What is happening there, Chris? You said on the phone there was a prison riot.'

'All I know for sure is that the police are being kept pretty busy – and not just with the riot.'

Kulek sighed heavily and said, 'It's the Dark, isn't it? It's growing more powerful.'

The two women only smiled more meaningfully. 'No more questions,' the tall one said.

Bishop was puzzled. Kulek had just referred to the Dark as if it were some special entity, a force on its own. The Powers of Darkness, he had said before. Was it possible that the night could harbour such adverse potency? Bishop was confused and he forced himself to push the thoughts away to concentrate on the immediate problem. He felt helpless. If he made a move towards the tall woman Kulek would be stabbed in the heart. If he tried for the short woman, he would himself be shot in the head. Their only chance would be the failure of the policeman to report in – surely he would have to report back to HQ every so often? But then with all the confusion going on over the other side of London it might go unnoticed. Beside him, Jessica trembled and he reached for her hand again.

'Stop,' the tall woman ordered. 'If you move again, I'll kill you.'

Bishop let his hand drop and tried to smile reassuringly at Jessica. 'I think the waiting is making them more nervous than us.'

'Shut your mouth,' the short woman hissed. 'Why don't we kill him now, Lillian? He's not important.'

'We'll wait. But I warn you, Christopher, if you move or speak again, I will shoot the girl.'

As the minutes ticked by, the tension in the room began to mount. Bishop noticed the short woman kept glancing over at the dome-covered clock resting on the sideboard and then at her companion, agitation plain on her face.

'There isn't much time,' she finally said.

'Just a little longer. Concentrate, Judith, help me bring it here.'

The tall woman's face became damp with perspiration and

occasionally her eyes would half-close, the hand holding the gun wavering slightly. The short woman seemed to be undergoing a similar stress. Bishop tensed his muscles, waiting for the right moment.

Suddenly, the one called Lillian took in a sharp breath and then she was smiling again. 'Can you feel it, Judith? It's coming. It knows.'

'Yes, yes.' The short one had her eyes closed as though in a trance, but the knife was still pressed into Kulek's nightclothes.

The tall woman's expression was almost orgasmic and Bishop shifted his weight forward when her eyelids began to flutter. She knew his intentions, though, for her eyes abruptly became sharply focused on him. 'I'm warning you not to move!' The words were almost spat out.

'No!' Jessica and Bishop looked across at Kulek who had cried out. The blind man's hands were like claws around the sides of the armchair and his neck was stretched upwards, tendons standing out like stiffened rods, eyes gazing sightlessly at the ceiling. 'It's so close.'

The short woman began to laugh, her plump, round shoulders heaving spasmodically. The tall woman rose from her chair and approached Bishop, the gun only inches away from his head.

'Now you'll see,' she said, her breathing jerky, sharp. 'Now you'll see the power.'

He shuddered, the tension in the room reaching a peak, but now a stifling oppression seeming to mingle with it. Short gasps were coming from Jessica and he knew she was terribly afraid. And he, too, felt the same fear.

The figure that appeared in the doorway caused the scream that had been building up inside Jessica to finally break free.

23

Bishop grabbed the tall woman's wrist and pushed the gun away from his exposed face, at the same time driving his clenched fist hard into her midriff. Her shout became a breathless gasp as she bent double and Bishop wrenched the Beretta from her grasp. He threw her away from him as he rose and turned to face the short woman, who was still staring at the figure in the doorway. She realized Bishop's intentions and drew the knife back to give it added thrust when she plunged it into the blind man's heart. But Kulek was faster: he thrust out and she toppled from the arm of the chair, not falling completely, but unbalanced enough to reach out wildly to save herself from going down. She grasped the back of the armchair and Bishop quickly stepped closer, bringing the pistol butt down on her forehead. She let out a yelp and collapsed on to the floor, helped by Bishop hooking a foot under her knee and jerking it from beneath her. He leaned forward and took the knife away, slapping her with fist and gun as she tried to resist.

Jessica ran to her father and held him. 'I'm all right,' he told her, then turned his face towards the door, knowing someone was there even though he could not see.

Edith Metlock looked pale and frightened. Her eyes went from one figure to the next, confused and unable to take in the situation. She slumped against the doorway, her head shaking from side to side. 'I came to warn you,' she managed to say.

'Edith?' asked Kulek.

'Yes, Father, it's Edith,' Jessica said.

Bishop went to the medium. 'You couldn't have arrived at a better moment.' He took her arm and drew her into the room.

'I came to warn you,' she repeated. 'The door was open.'

'They were expecting someone – or something else.'

From the floor, her mouth still open and desperately sucking in air, the tall woman stared at the medium. Bishop kept a cautious eye on her, ready to use the gun if necessary.

'Edith,' said Kulek, 'what brought you here? How did you know we were being held by those two?'

'I didn't. I came to warn you of the Dark. It's coming for you, Jacob.'

The blind man was on his feet and Jessica led him over to the medium and Bishop. His voice was full of interest rather than fear when he spoke. 'How do you know, Edith?'

Bishop let her down on to the settee and she slumped back as though exhausted. 'Voices, Jacob. There are hundreds of voices. I was at home, asleep. They invaded my dreams.'

'They spoke to you?'

'No, no. They are just there. I can hear them now, Jacob. They are becoming louder, clearer. You must get away from here before it's too late.'

'What are they saying, Edith? Please try to stay calm and tell me exactly what they are saying.'

She leaned forward and clutched at his arm. 'I can't tell you. I hear them, but there are so many. They're so confused. But I hear your name, over and over again. He wants his revenge, Jacob. He wants to show you just what he has achieved. And I think he fears you, too.'

'Ha!' The tall woman was on her knees now, wary of her own gun that was pointed in her direction. 'He fears nothing! He *has* nothing to fear!'

'Pryszlak? Do you mean Pryszlak, Edith?' The blind man spoke more sharply.

'Yes. He's nearly here.'

'I'm going to call the police,' said Bishop.

'They can't help you, fool!' The tall woman's face was twisted into a malicious sneer. 'They can't harm him.'

'She's right,' said the medium. 'Your only chance is to run. That's all anyone can do.'

'I'm calling the police anyway, even if it's only to take these two away.'

'It's too late, don't you see?' The tall woman was rising, her eyes gleaming. 'It's here. It's outside.'

The arm that encircled Bishop's throat from behind was plump and powerful. His body was arched back as the short woman brought her knee up against the base of his spine. One hand was reaching for the knife he held.

Jessica tried to force the little woman away from him, grabbing at her hair and pulling, but it had no other effect than to overbalance the two figures and send them crashing to the floor. Bishop tried to twist himself away from the tenacious woman, unable to break the grip around his throat. He raised his elbow, then swiftly drew it back, feeling it sink into her fatness. He repeated the action, using all his strength, and felt her legs flailing out beneath him. The tightness against his throat began to slacken and he renewed his efforts. He managed to turn his body and, because she would not let go of either his neck or hand, the knife sliced across her plump breasts and blood spurted from them. She screamed.

At last he was able to pull himself free and he turned his head, expecting to see her tall companion bearing down on him. But she was gone.

Hands clawed into his face and his attention was drawn back to the squirming woman beneath him. Her chest was now a mass of red stickiness, yet still she fought on, her lips bared to reveal stained, yellow teeth. The sounds she made were like those of an enraged dog and her eyes were becoming clouded. Her struggles began to weaken as the wound sapped her strength; only her will prevented her from collapsing. He pushed her hands away and staggered to his feet, feeling no pity as he looked down on her, her hands still scrabbling feebly at empty air.

'Chris.' Jessica clung to his arm. 'Let's get away. Let's call the police from somewhere else!'

'It's too late.' Edith Metlock was looking over her shoulder at the glass walls behind. 'It's already here,' she said tonelessly.

Bishop could see their own reflections against the darkness outside. 'What the hell are you talking about?' he found himself shouting. 'There's nothing out there!'

'Chris,' Kulek said quietly. 'Please go and make sure the front door is locked. Jessica, turn on every light in the house, outside lights, too.'

Bishop could only stare wordlessly at him.

'Do as he says, Chris,' Jessica urged.

She ran from the room and he followed. The front door was ajar and before he pushed it closed, Bishop peered out into the night. He could barely see the trees that lined the narrow drive leading to the house. After slamming the door, he pushed home the bolts and turned to see Jessica flicking down all the light switches in the hall. She pushed past him to climb the stairs leading to the rooms on the upper level; Bishop followed.

'In there, Chris!' Jessica pointed at one of the doors leading off the upstairs hall as she disappeared through another. Still puzzled, Bishop obeyed and found himself in a large, L-shaped bedroom. This side of the house overlooked the city and he realized that on any other night, the view would have provided a dazzling display of lights. On this night, though, there was something odd about the shimmering glow. It was as if he were watching it through a moving lacy veil, the lights twinkling and growing faint, then emerging brightly again. It wasn't like fog, for that would have shrouded everything in its rolling grey mist; it was a shifting inky darkness punctured by the brightest of the lights, smothering those more distant, dulling their luminosity.

'Chris?' Jessica had entered the room. 'You haven't turned on the lights.'

He pointed towards the glass wall. 'What is it, Jessica?'

Instead of answering, she flicked down the light switch, then hurried over to a bedside lamp and put that on also. She left the room and he heard other doors opening. Bishop went after her and caught her arm as she emerged from one of the rooms.

'Jessica, you've got to tell me what's going on.'

'Don't you understand? It's the darkness. It's a living entity, Chris. We've got to keep it away.'

'By turning on lights?'

'That's all we can do. Don't you remember how Edith had kept it away that night we found her? She knew by instinct that that was the only way.'

'But how can darkness harm us?'

'It's what it does to people. It seems to prey on weak or evil

277

minds, it somehow makes the badness in them dominant. Can't you see what's been happening? That night at the rest home – don't you see how it used their enfeebled minds?' She saw the pain in his eyes. 'I'm sorry, Chris, but don't you see how it affected Lynn? She wanted to kill you again, and so did all the others. They were being directed, don't you see? Their minds were being used. The same happened at the football match – in Willow Road itself. Pryszlak has found a way to use the evil lying in everybody's subconscious. The stronger that evil, or the weaker the person's mind, the easier it is for . . .'

'Jessica!' Jacob Kulek was calling from the foot of the stairs.

'I'm coming, Father!' She looked earnestly up at Bishop. 'Help us, Chris. We have to try and keep it out.'

He nodded, his mind a jumble of thoughts, everything he'd seen and heard in some crazy way confirming her statement. 'You go down to your father, I'll see to the rest of the lights up here.'

Bishop checked every room, even turning on the bathroom light for, though its two outside walls were part of the rare brick segments of the structure, it had a huge glass skylight in the ceiling. He also twisted a wall spotlight around and directed it towards the skylight. When he finally descended to the ground floor, Jessica had switched on the outside lamps, flooding the grounds with their brightness.

Bishop, Jessica and Kulek stood in the main lounge again, Edith Metlock trying to stem the flow of blood from the injured woman lying on the floor with a white linen towel Jessica had found for her. The wounded woman, Judith, lay still, her eyes staring up at the ceiling and occasionally flicking towards the huge window-wall.

'What now?' Bishop asked.

'We can only wait,' Kulek replied. 'And perhaps pray.'

Almost to himself he added, 'Although I'm not sure that will help any more.'

'I'm going to try and reach Peck again,' said Bishop, heading for the hallway. 'We'll need an ambulance too – for her.' He indicated the injured woman lying on the floor.

Jessica clung to her father, both of them feeling the oppression that now hung over the house. 'Is it really possible for this to happen? Could Pryszlak have really found a way of tapping this power, Father?'

'I think he has, Jessica. Those who have studied the subject have always known it existed. The question is: does Pryszlak control the power, or does it control Pryszlak? I think we shall soon find out if what the woman called Lillian said is true. Will you find my cane for me? Then you must help Edith with the injured woman.'

Jessica found Kulek's stout cane lying behind the armchair in which he had been sitting; she gave it to him then went to the medium who was still kneeling beside the recumbent figure.

'How is she?'

'I . . . I don't know. She seems to be in a state of shock. If she's in pain, she doesn't show it.'

The linen towel was no longer white. Edith held it against the long slash, her hands, along with the cloth, red from the woman's blood. 'I don't think it's too deep, but she's losing a lot of blood.'

'I'll get another towel. We'll have to open her blouse and try to cover the whole of her chest.' Jessica felt herself shudder as she gazed down. The still woman's pupils had retracted to small pinpoints and for some reason, there was a distant smile on her face. She seemed to be listening.

The medium looked up at the glass wall. She, too, could hear something.

'Edith, what is it?' Jessica shook her.

'They're all around us.'

Jessica looked towards the windows, but could only see the glow of the outside lights. They didn't seem as bright as they should have been.

Bishop returned to the room, a determined look on his face. 'Peck was still unavailable, but one of the men in his department told me the trouble seems to be shifting over to this side of the river. There's been a constant stream of emergency calls and they're pretty thin on the ground for reinforcements. His advice is to sit tight and he'll get someone out to us as soon as possible. Even telling him one of their own officers has been murdered didn't get me too far. It seems he's only one of many dead policemen tonight.' He took out the small gun that he had put into his jacket pocket earlier. 'If anyone tries to break in, I can try and hold them off with this. Have you any other guns in the house, Jacob?'

The blind man shook his head. 'I have no use for them. And I think weapons of that sort will not help us.'

'Jacob, the lights outside are dimming.' There was dread in Edith Metlock's voice.

'There must be a reduction in power somewhere,' Bishop said, walking towards the glass wall.

'No, Chris,' said Jessica. 'The lights inside the house haven't been affected.'

Kulek turned towards the sound of Bishop's voice. 'Chris, are you by the window? Please keep back from there.'

'There's nothing outside. No movement, except . . .'

'What is it? Jessica, tell me what is happening.'

'The shadows, Father. The shadows are drawing closer to the house.'

Bishop spoke. 'The lights are just a dull glow now. There's a . . . sort of . . . blackness creeping forward. It's only a few feet away from the windows. It's moving all the time.' He began to edge away from the glass wall, stopping only when he had reached the back of the settee. Suddenly, all they could see was their own reflections, the outside lamps hardly visible. The feeling of oppression had increased: it seemed to be bearing down on all of them, straining against the very house itself, pressing, crushing.

Edith Metlock slumped against the settee, her eyes closed. Jessica reached for her father but found she was too frightened to move towards him. Kulek stared out at the darkness as though he could see it and, in his mind, he could. Bishop raised the gun towards the glass wall, knowing he could not pull the trigger.

'It can't get in!' Kulek shouted, his voice raised even though there was total silence in the room. 'It has no material form!'

But the bulging inwards of the huge sheets of glass joined by thin metal strips belied his words.

'Jesus Christ, it's not possible.' Bishop couldn't believe what he was seeing. The glass was bending like the distorted mirrors in a funfair's crazy house. He put his other hand up to protect his eyes, sure that the windows would burst inwards at any moment.

The injured woman pushed herself into a sitting position, the stained linen towel falling away from her chest and blood flowing freely into her lap. She watched the windows and laughed. The cackling sound she made died when, without warning, the bulges in the glass subsided and the windows returned to their normal shape. For several moments, no one in the room dared to speak.

'Is it ov . . .?' Jessica began to say when an ear-splitting *crack* made them all jump back in alarm.

The middle section of the wall was split from top to bottom, jagged streaks running from the main crack like forked lightning. Again the sharp sound of splintering glass came to them and they watched in paralysed horror as the section next to it began to split. They saw the thin cracks travelling in different directions, patterning a jigsaw of sharp lines on the treated glass. Soon the lines resembled a spider's web. Another *crack*, and the section on the other side of the centre piece began to break, this time two lines travelling up from the base and joining near the top, etching out a jagged mountain shape.

With explosive force, all the sections shattered inwards, showering the occupants of the room with thousands of lethal glass shards. The sound was that of a hundred pistols being fired at once. Bishop fell back over the settee, his clothes and hair covered in silver fragments. Kulek instinctively turned his body and ducked, his dressing-gown instantly covered in tiny porcupine quills of glass. The shock had sent Jessica reeling back, the long settee between her and the windows protecting most of her body; she screamed when a section of glass the size of a dinner plate scythed along the side of her raised arm as she fell. The settee served to screen Edith Metlock and the short woman completely from flying glass.

Bishop had rolled on to the floor, tumbling over the injured woman. He lay still for a few moments, waiting for the ringing in his ears to clear, then forced himself to stand. He saw Kulek groping his way towards Jessica, calling out her name.

'I'm all right, Father.' She was pushing herself up on to one elbow and Bishop winced when he saw the long, red tear in her arm. He reached her just as Kulek was leaning forward to help her up, pieces of glass falling from their bodies like brushed snow. There were many tiny cuts on Jessica's forehead, neck and hands, but the rent along her arm was the worst damage she had suffered. He held her with Kulek and all three looked across at the broken wall, cold air flowing in unhindered and chilling them.

There was nothing outside now but blackness.

They kept still, scarcely daring to breathe, waiting for something to happen. The first figure appeared, standing just beyond the area of light so his body was ill-defined, shadowy. Bishop realized he had dropped the gun.

The figure stepped over the threshold, out of the darkness, into the light. He stood there, head turned slightly sideways, eyes blinking as though the light was hurting his eyes. The man was filthy, his clothes torn and covered with grime. Even in their dazed state, they could smell his corruption.

'Who is there?' asked Kulek softly, his question directed at Jessica and Bishop. Neither could answer.

The man's head was slowly turning towards them and, even under the dirt that covered him, they could see his face was drawn and emaciated. His eyes were still half-closed, and there were no whites to them, only a dull, greyish-yellow. His movements were sluggish as he walked towards them.

Jessica began to back away, dragging her father with her, but Bishop stood his ground. There was a hollow, vacant expression on the man's face and Bishop felt revulsion when he saw the dried mucus and spittle that covered the lower half of his face. His revulsion heightened when the man grinned at him.

Bishop ran forward, afraid yet repulsed enough to want to crush the thing before him as though it were a loathsome spider. He pushed the man and to his surprise felt no resistance; it was as if he had no strength left at all, that his body had wasted into a debilitated state, a withered frame that was hardly living. The man staggered back and Bishop followed through by lifting him and throwing him back out into the darkness. He stood there, panting from fear rather than exertion, and looked out into the night. There were many more standing in the shadows, watching the house.

He backed away and, as he did so, three figures came running forward from the blackness. They leapt into the room and came to an abrupt halt as the sudden glare blinded them. There were two men and one woman: the men wore grey denims, and one of them was shoeless; the woman was dressed normally. Bishop realized these three were not in the deteriorated state the first man had been in. He quickly looked around for the lost Beretta and gratefully lunged for the pistol when he saw it lying on the floor half-under the settee. He was on one knee retrieving the weapon when Jessica shouted; he turned to see one of the men rushing at him. His intention had been to try and warn them off, but without thinking he swung the gun in the advancing man's direction and squeezed the trigger. His would-be assailant spun around and fell to the floor as the bullet spat into his shoulder. The woman fell over the sprawled figure, but the other man skirted them both and came running towards Bishop, who was still crouched low. The next bullet punctured the second man's neck.

'Chris, there are more of them outside!' warned Jessica.

He saw them hovering just beyond the area of light. 'Quick, upstairs. We haven't got a chance down here!'

Leaping over the back of the settee, he pulled Edith Metlock to her feet. 'Take your father up, Jessica. We'll follow.' He did not allow his eyes to stray from the broad wall of darkness before him, the gun held up, trembling slightly, towards it. His first two shots had been lucky, for he was not at all familiar with guns, nor was he used to maiming or killing people; but he was aware that at such close range it would be virtually impossible to miss and he would not hesitate to fire at anyone entering the room. He pulled the medium along with him and she allowed herself to be led, her hands over her ears as though the sound of the breaking glass was still reverberating in them. She looked dazed and pale. Bishop felt perspiration trickling into his eyes and he hastily wiped the back of his hand over his forehead. He was surprised to see his hand smeared with blood when he brought it away; parts of his face must have been lacerated by flying glass.

'They're at the front door,' he heard Jessica call out. 'They're trying to force it open!'

He could hear the muffled thumps coming from the hall-way. 'Up the stairs, quickly,' he ordered. At least they would not be able to rush him up there and he might just be able to hold them off until the police arrived. *If* they arrived.

The hand that hooked itself behind his knee and brought him down belonged to the short woman. He fell heavily, taking the medium with him, and the injured woman threw herself on top of him, oblivious of the pain she suffered. Twisting his head to avoid the sharp-edged fingers, Bishop saw the woman who had leapt into the room with the two men crawling towards him, a long sliver of glass held in her hand like a knife blade. He brought a knee up and it sank viciously into the plump side of the woman above him, causing her to topple sideways. His back still against the floor, he pointed the gun straight into the advancing woman's face. She did not seem to notice; or she did not seem to care. Panic-stricken though he was, Bishop could not pull the trigger. He twisted away as the jagged glass came rushing down at him and heard it break against the floor. The woman stared at her bloody hand, then reached for him again. He swiped away the arm that supported her weight and brought the end of the pistol down on the back of her head as she collapsed. Kicking himself free of the short woman, whose legs were still tangled with his, he pulled himself clear. A well-aimed shove sent her crumpling back against the settee and he thought she would not be able to rise again. Incredibly, he was wrong.

She flew at him with a strength that was frightening for someone in her condition and her blows sent crystals of glass that had already pierced his face deeper into the skin, making him cry out. Others were in the room now, men and women who had stepped from the cover of darkness they seemed to favour, some of them shielding their eyes from the harsh glare, others squinting their eyes against the light. Bishop felt the plump woman's body shudder as the bullet entered her groin, but it took two more to stop her struggles. As she slid away, he saw there was no fear in her eyes, only a strange look of pleasure.

He fired into the crowd that had invaded the room and, for a brief moment, their disorganized rush was halted. It gave him just enough time to gain his feet and stagger towards the door. Roughly pushing Edith Metlock through, he pumped two bullets into the nearest man, this one also dressed in grey denims which Bishop suddenly recognized as prison clothes. The man fell forward just as Bishop pulled the door closed and the wood shook as his body crashed into it on the other side.

Jessica and her father were on the stairs, the girl looking down over the balustrade at him. Her face was streaked with tears that came from absolute terror. Bishop felt the handle twisting beneath his grip and he knew he would not be able to hold the door shut for long.

'Move yourselves!' he shouted. 'Take Edith with you!'

Jessica was galvanized into action by the harsh command. She reached down over the balustrade and guided the medium around to the stairs. Bishop waited until they were out of view before he released the door-handle. It flew open and he kept firing into the room beyond until the gun made only a sharp click. It was empty, empty and useless. He turned and fled.

As he passed the glass panel that ran the length of the heavy, wooden door, it broke and a hand reached in and grabbed his arm. Another hand shot forward and pulled at his hair. It was then that all the lights in the house went out.

Even as he struggled, he realized someone had broken into another part of the house and found the main power switch. He tore himself away from the grasping hands, feeling his jacket rip and some of the hair pulled from his scalp. He collapsed on to the stairs, hearing the rush of footsteps in the darkness, the shrieks of the possessed, their cries of triumph. Hands groped at him through the banister rails as he forced himself upwards. They tore at his face and hands, ripping his clothes, trying to pin him down. A steel-like grip closed around his ankle and he was pulled back down the stairs. He groaned aloud as he held on to the balustrade, desperately trying to halt his descent back into the mob. Wild screams and laughter filled his head, then a voice, a voice that barely pierced the babble, but a voice he knew to be Jessica's. But the words made no sense.

'Close your eyes, Chris, close your eyes!'

The brilliant flash that lit up the hallway stung his vision and silver and red images danced beneath his closed eyelids for long seconds after. He felt himself released and heard the howls of anguish.

'Come on, Chris!' It was Kulek's voice this time. 'Up, up! While they are blinded!'

Bishop moved fast, even though dazzled; he knew which

way was up. He reached the landing and fell against the facing wall, his vision still swimming with swirling lights. More hands grabbed him and he knew these were friendly.

'This way, into the bedroom,' he heard Kulek say.

Heavy footsteps came from the stairway as the blind man guided him into a nearby room and Jessica's fear-filled voice cried out, 'Close your eyes!' just before the brilliant flash froze everything into an eerie white stillness. Screams and the sounds of tumbling bodies came to them. Bishop felt rather than saw Jessica rush into the room and quickly close the door; he rubbed his eyes, trying to clear the dazzle from them.

'Quickly, we must barricade the door!' Kulek shook Bishop's arm.

Jessica locked the door, then hurried over to a heavy-looking dressing-table. 'Help me, Chris, Edith.' She began pulling it away from the wall it rested against.

Bishop blinked several times and gradually began to make out shapes in the room. Just enough light filtered through the long window-wall for him to see the two women struggling with the dressing-table. He joined them and soon the unit was up against the door.

'Let's get the bed!' Bishop shouted. They tipped it up and he was relieved to feel its heavy weight. It crashed against the dressing-table, reinforcing the barricade. Footsteps came running along the hallway and they heard movement in the room next to theirs. More running, then the footsteps stopped outside their door. The handle turned and Bishop leaned against the makeshift barricade, whispering to the others to do the same. The pounding that started made them all jump even though they were expecting it.

The door shook in its frame, but mercifully held.

'Who are they? Where have they come from?' Jessica was

next to Bishop and he could just make out the white blur of her face in the gloom.

'Some of them are from the prison, I'm sure. They must have escaped in the riot.'

'But there are women among them, and other men. They're in a terrible state.'

'The missing people! It must be them! God knows how they got into that condition.'

'What condition?' asked Kulek, who was also pushing against the upturned bed.

'They're filthy, their clothes in rags. They look starved, too. The first one I tackled was as weak as a kitten.'

The banging against the door became louder as though those outside had found heavy objects to beat at the wood with.

Kulek's voice was grim. 'They were the first victims. Whatever it is that possesses them has no regard for their lives. It uses them and destroys them.'

'And the stronger are the more recent victims? Like the convicts?'

'It would seem so.'

The whole barricade trembled a fraction and Bishop knew the door lock had been broken. He dug his feet more firmly into the carpeted floor and pushed harder against the bed, one hand reaching round to steady the dressing-table behind it. He was vaguely aware that Edith Metlock had sunk to the floor and was swaying on her knees, head in her hands.

A crash from behind made them all turn sharply towards the long windows. Jessica covered her face, expecting the glass to shower inwards again, but as they watched, a black object sailed into view and smacked against the window again.

'They're throwing things at the window,' Bishop said breathlessly and was suddenly aware that the banging against the door had ceased. 'Keep pushing against the bed,' he told Jessica and her father as he crossed the room. In the gloom, he kicked something lying on the floor and he almost smiled when he saw it was a camera, a rectangular attachment fitted. Jessica had used the flashgun against the mob chasing him, blinding and stopping them with its brief but powerful light.

He reached the window just as another object crashed against it and he pulled away in reflex action. Fortunately the treated glass was extremely strong and, although a whitish crack appeared, the glass did not break. Cautiously, Bishop crept forward again and looked down into the grounds below. The bedroom overlooked the rear garden and he could see figures standing in the shadows of the shrubbery and trees. As he watched, a man began pulling at the brickwork of a low garden wall, then stepped out on to the lawn and raised the object of his efforts, his body leaning backwards for the throw. But the brick never came towards the window; it dropped from the man's fingers and thudded to the grass.

The man moved back, his gaze still on the window from where Bishop was watching; he sank into the shrubbery behind him and Bishop noticed that the other figures had now disappeared. The man became part of the shadows and then, like the others, was gone.

A movement by his side made Bishop turn his head; Edith Metlock was staring over the treetops at the city beyond. 'They're leaving,' she said simply. 'The voices have gone.'

Jessica and Kulek joined them at the window.

Bishop shook his head. 'Why should they suddenly go? We had no chance against them.'

There was a tiredness in Jacob Kulek's voice when he spoke and, as Bishop turned to him, he saw the tiredness was in his deeply lined face too. And, even as the blind man said the words, it occurred to Bishop that there *was* enough light to see him.

'The dawn is here,' Kulek said. 'There is a greyness in my eyes where before there was only blackness. They have fled from the morning light.'

'Thank God,' Jessica said softly as she leaned against Bishop and held on to his arm. 'Thank God it's over.'

Kulek's sightless eyes were still directed towards the approaching light, the world outside grey, almost colourless, but no longer black. 'No, it is not over. I'm afraid it has only just begun,' he said.

Part Three

They will growl over it on that day,
   like the roaring of the sea,
And if one look to the land,
   behold, darkness and distress;
and the light is darkened by its clouds.

Isaiah 5:30
(R.S.V.)

Part Three

24

Many were found wandering aimlessly through the streets of the city, confused, their eyes half-closed, hands acting as shields against the glare of the sun. Others cowered in darkened rooms or hid in the basements of any building they could find access to. The London Underground system was brought to a halt when shocked motormen staggered from their trains, the sight of countless bodies they had ploughed through in the black tunnels a nightmare they would never forget. A search of the sewer network was ordered – three men on inspection duty the day before had been reported missing – and the searchers did not return. Corpses were found in the streets, many with bodies wasted, clothes bedraggled. Some had taken their own lives, others had died through self-neglect. Not all were in a helpless state: a large number were bewildered, remembering the violence they had committed during the night hours, but unable to explain it. Many of these, if they managed to find their way home, were hidden by their families. Once safely inside, they insisted that the curtains be drawn against the daylight; they listened apprehensively to the reports of the previous night's mass violence, aware they had been a part of it, but afraid to go to the police. Those close to them could only watch, frightened by what had happened, but reluctant to seek outside help, for they knew that anyone involved in the riots was being rounded up and taken away. It was midday before the wailing sirens of fire-engines ceased, but the sounds of ambulances rushing through the streets went on well into the afternoon. It was never truly estimated just how many lives had been lost or how many minds had been taken on that first night of terror, for events after that took on such major proportions and with such rapidity that it became hopeless to keep accurate accounts of human or material damage. The prime objective was to survive, not to record details.

It began all over again the following night.

And continued the night after that.

And the next.

The congregation inside the Temple of the Newly Ordained had gathered earlier that afternoon, for they knew the five o'clock curfew would not allow them to leave their homes and travel to the modern, white-painted building. They had been ordered to keep silent while they waited – Brother Martin did not want their presence inside the church to be known – but their minds were in a turmoil of excitement. They were afraid, but eager, too. Their leader had told them of what was to come and they had faith in his word. Brother Martin had the knowledge, for he had spoken with the Dark.

In a room at the far end of the church which was not really a church but rather an assembly hall with rows of benches, near the altar which was not really an altar but an elaborate lectern, sat a neatly dressed man, his features lit only by a solitary candle that stood on the table before him. The man's eyes were closed and his breathing was deep and rhythmic. He felt the tension emanating from the hall next door and smiled. It would help; the vibrations of the thought-flow would act as a guide. He was ready and they were ready. Nearly a hundred and fifty people. The Dark would make them welcome.

His eyes snapped open as a soft tap on the door roused him from his deep thoughts. One of his followers, a tall coloured man, entered the room. The coloured man was in his early thirties, his hair allowed to grow Afro-style, but his suit conservative. Brother Martin smiled at him.

'Is everything ready?' he asked.

The coloured man was too nervous to return the smile. 'Ready,' he affirmed.

'Are you afraid, Brother John?'

'Brother Martin, I'm shit-scared.'

Brother Martin laughed aloud and his follower managed to join in.

'There's nothing to fear any more, John. This moment has been a long time coming – we mustn't balk at it.'

Brother John seemed uncertain. 'I know that, I know that. But what if you're wrong?'

Brother Martin's hand snaked out and struck the coloured man across the cheek. No resistance was offered, even though Brother John was at least a foot taller than his aggressor.

'Never doubt me, Brother John! I have spoken with the Dark and I have been told what we must do.' His voice became softer and he reached out and touched the cheek that now bore the marks of his hand. 'We've enjoyed what we've gained from these people, Brother, but it's time for something more, something better. Their faith has given us wealth; now they can help us reach something that transcends material gain.' He went to the door and turned towards his companion. 'Is the potion ready?' he asked.

'Yes, Brother Martin.'

'Let your faith rest in me, Brother John.' He opened the door and stepped into the hall beyond.

'Faith, shit,' the coloured man muttered. It had been good for them once, convincing the people they would find their salvation with Brother Martin, accepting their donations, travelling the country looking for more. They had trust in their leader, the man who preached that love was the giving of one's-self, the giving of one's possessions. And Brother Martin was there to receive everything they gave. Especially the women. Brother Martin would never turn away even the ugliest. It could churn a man's insides to think of some of the dogs Brother Martin had bedded. He, Brother John, had been more choosy.

The followers were grateful to be told lust was just as much a part of love as was affection: lust meant procreation and that led to more offspring to follow God's way. They loved to hear that to sin was good, for sin meant repentance, and only by repenting could they know humility, and only by feeling true humility could they reach the Almighty. Sin today, regret tomorrow – what could be better? The only problem was that Brother Martin had come to believe his own preaching.

They had both been surprised eight years ago when what had started out as a small-time confidence trick to gain a little extra cash had turned into an ongoing, lucrative profession. Those early years had been one great merry piss-take, both of them cracking up after meetings, their eyes too filled with laughter tears to count the night's take. They had both soon learned that money was not the only pleasurable benefit from their operation: the weakness of the flesh had quickly been established as a worthy sin for remorse. The more remorse he could help them feel, the more he praised the Lord he had been given to them as an instrument of sin. Privately, he would wink at John and ask: 'Who could resist the concept that to fuck illicitly is good for the soul?' But since Brother Martin, alias Marty Randall, had caught the syph three times in two years, his attitude had changed. Wasn't it only gonorrhoea that was supposed to drive you nuts? Gon today, gone tomorrow? Maybe it was just the idolization they had thrust upon Brother Martin that had made him begin to believe it all himself. Up until founding the Temple of the Newly Ordained, Randall – Brother Martin – had been small-time: now he had become something to be worshipped. It was enough to turn any mother's head. He, Brother John alias Johnny Parker, had watched with awe as Randall had begun to change over the years: his sermons had become more emotional, each one always reaching a crescendo that would leave the whole congregation on its feet, clapping and yelling, 'Amen, Brother Martin!' There were still the odd occasions when the two of them would snigger at each other and congratulate themselves on their good fortune and their flock's gullibility, but these occasions were becoming less and less frequent. Now, tonight, Brother Martin seemed to have really flipped his lid. Would he go through with it or was it just to test them all, a megalomaniac's way of proving his command over them, an experiment to be halted at the last moment? Brother John, alias Parker, hoped it was the latter.

Brother Martin strode to the lectern, his eyes quickly becoming accustomed to the brightness of the hall after the gloom in the small room next to it. A bustle of excitement greeted his entrance and the people nervously glanced at each other, afraid of what was about to happen, yet eager for this new and far-from-final experience. There were a few in the crowd who still doubted, but these were not too concerned with living anyway. Everything that was happening in the city gave credence to what Brother Martin told them. The time had come and they desired to be among the first.

Brother Martin directed their attention towards the three punch bowls that stood on a table at the head of the centre aisle. 'You see there, my dear brothers and sisters, our elixir,' his voice boomed out. 'With just one sip you will be eternal. You have seen for yourselves the chaos outside, the people who are dead yet still refuse to give up their bodies. Will you allow the torturous degenerations of the shell you inhabit, or will you follow me, cleanly, without stress? With purity!'

He allowed his eyes to glance over the congregation so that each member felt the words were meant for him or her alone. 'There are some among you who are afraid. We will help you overcome that fear. There are some among you who still doubt: we will help you overcome that doubt. There are many among you who hate the world and the terrible hardship it has caused you: and I say that is good! It's good to hate, for the world is a vile, loathsome place! Detest it, brothers, revile it, sisters! Remember the words: "Is not the day of the LORD darkness, and not light, and gloom with no brightness in it?" This *is* the day of the LORD! The brightness has gone!'

Brother Martin waved a hand and, at the signal, all the lights in the hall were flicked off by Brother John, who stood by the main switches. A moan came from the crowd as the hall was plunged into darkness, except for the poor light cast from the flickering candles strategically placed around the walls.

'Open the doors, Brother Samuel,' their leader commanded and a man standing by the temple's double-doors swung them wide. The darkness outside became part of the darkness inside. 'Concentrate, my brothers and sisters, bring the Dark to us. We must hurry.' He could see the street-lights beyond the temple grounds, the houses with every light in them turned on. The order had been given for every possible light in the capital to be left on overnight: the authorities knew the Dark's strength. Night after night it had returned, the natural darkness its ally, and each time the chaos had become greater. No one could tell who would succumb to its influence – father, mother, brother, sister. Child. Friend. Neighbour. What evil lay tethered in each of these, waiting to be freed, yearning to be cut loose. The light was the only barrier. The Dark feared light. 'The light shines in the darkness, and the darkness has not overcome it.' Gospel according to John. But *man* can overcome the light. Brother Martin chuckled to himself, the sockets of his eyes dark shadows in the candlelight.

'Come forth, drink of the liquid that will make us whole.' Brother Martin held out his arms towards the congregation.

Despite the chill sweeping in through the open doors, beads of sweat broke out on Brother John's forehead. Oh man, oh man, he's really going through with it. He really wants to kill them all. Randall really believed all this shit the people upstairs were putting out about the Dark. Jesus, didn't he know it was just jive? The word was out on the street: it was a chemical gas that couldn't activate under sunlight or any other fucking light. Nobody knew who had released it – a foreign power, terrorists? The fucking British scientists themselves? Nobody on the street knew. But the motherfuckers in power did. Only they weren't saying. Stay inside at night, keep your lights on – that's *all* they were saying. Police and troops patrolled after curfew to make sure the rule was obeyed, using powerful searchlights themselves for their own protection. And this stupid fuck Randall was disobeying the law, turning all the lights out, ordering the doors opened. What the hell would happen when he discovered the mixture in those punch bowls had no cyanide in it? What would he do when the stupid fucking sheep who followed him didn't drop dead after they'd tasted Potion 99? He'd know who to blame: it was sweet Brother John who'd been given the order to get the poison. Where the fuck did Randall expect him to find enough cyanide to kill off a hundred and fifty mothers? Brother John began to edge his way down the side aisle, away from the three containers of harmless Sainsbury's own-brand wine towards the open doorway. Time to split. Should have done it a long time ago.

The congregation were filing forward, each holding a plastic beaker they had been issued with on entering the temple. Brother Martin smiled benignly as they passed him. A woman in her early forties threw herself at him, her face soaked with tears, nose running. Helpers broke her hold on Brother Martin and gently led her away, soothing her with words she hardly heard. A man in his sixties passed before him, eyes downcast.

'I'm afraid, Brother Martin,' he said.

Brother Martin reached out with both hands and touched his follower's shoulders. 'We all are, Brother . . .' what the shit was his name? '. . . dear friend, but our fear will soon be replaced by great joy. Have faith in me. I have spoken with the Dark.' Now move on, you silly bastard, before you frighten the others.

It was important not to allow the mood of euphoria, albeit a tense euphoria, to be broken: if one panicked, then others would follow. He needed them all, wanted their strength, for he really *had* spoken with the Dark. Or at least, he had dreamt he had spoken with it. It amounted to the same thing.

The Dark wanted him, but it also wanted his people. The more life that was given to it, the stronger it would become.

Brother Martin, alias Marty Randall, was happy to be the Dark's recruitment officer.

The people moved in an orderly flow to the punch bowls and then back to their seats, disguising Brother John's progress towards the doorway; the general dimness of the interior also offered concealment. However, he expected to hear Brother Martin calling him back at any moment, and the further he moved away from his leader the more nervous he became. He licked his lips, aware his throat had become very dry. Some of the flock looked at him enquiringly and he had to nod and smile at them reassuringly. He was thankful that the light was so poor, for it meant they could not see the perspiration he felt on his face. Brother Samuel was still standing near the open doors and Brother John approached him cautiously. This man was a devout follower, a mother who would lay down his life for their leader, a honky whose brain functioned only under the guidance of someone else. Just the kind of dogshit Randall needed to keep his followers in order. The big man cocked his head to one side like a curious labrador when Brother John drew near. He didn't like black men and he particularly didn't like Brother John. The nigger always seemed to have a smirk on his face, as if he were taking the piss all the time.

Brother John leaned forward and whispered into the big man's ear. 'Brother Martin wants you to go forward, Brother Samuel, and drink with the others. He feels they need your encouragement.'

Brother Samuel cast an anxious glance over the shadowy congregation. A deep moaning noise came from some of them, while several of the women were openly wailing. He tucked his hand into his jacket pocket and closed his fingers around the gun lying there. Brother Martin had warned him it might be necessary to persuade some of the followers to carry out what was required of them. But he had also told him that he was to wait until last, just in case any were not killed by the poison, or had only pretended to drink. A bullet in the head was to be the answer to that. Why had Brother Martin changed his mind?

'He told me to stay by the door.'

'I know, Brother Samuel,' the black man said patiently, aware that his legs were beginning to feel weak. He could hear Randall's voice from the front urging the people to concentrate, to draw the Dark to them. 'He's changed his mind. He needs you up there, Brother.'

'Who'd watch the door? Who'll see no one gets out?'

'No one's leaving. They want to follow Brother Martin.'

A crafty look came into the big man's face. The nigger wasn't wearing his usual smirk. And at this close range, he could see he was sweating. Brother John was afraid. 'Then why does he need me up there if they want to follow Brother Martin?'

Oh shit. 'One or two need help, Brother Samuel. They're not all as strong as you.'

'Are you as strong as me, Brother John? Do you need help?'

The coloured man tried to keep his hands from shaking. 'No, Brother Samuel. It's the others. Now you do what the man says, Brother, and get yourself up there. He's gonna get mad if you don't.'

The big man seemed uncertain. He looked towards Brother Martin, his hand leaving the weapon inside his jacket pocket.

Brother John was cursing himself for not having left sooner. He should have vanished as soon as Randall had begun his crazy suicide talk. It had become a fascination with him after the mass self-destruction of the People's Temple sect in Guyana several years before, and kindled even further by the other group suicide that had taken place in the suburbs of London just about a year ago. During the last few weeks it had become an obsession; it was as though he had discovered the ultimate truth. Oh Jesus, he should have scooted when Randall ordered him to get the cyanide. He couldn't believe the man intended to go through with it. It was no place to be when they all sat around gawking at each other, waiting to drop like flies. They wouldn't be amused and neither would Brother Martin.

'Come on, Brother Samuel, don't keep him waiting.'

Unfortunately for the coloured man, Brother Martin had been scanning the crowd for him. Brother John's faith had seemed a little shaky over the last few days. He needed help, perhaps coercion. Of late he had become a cause of concern, his enthusiasm for Brother Martin's way seemed to be waning. It might be a good idea to let him be the first to taste this nectar of the after-life.

'Brother John, I can't see you? Where are you?'

The coloured man groaned inwardly. 'Right here, Brother Martin,' he said aloud.

'Come to the front, Brother, where we can see you. Yours will be the honour of leading the way.'

'I, uh, I'm not worthy of that honour, Brother Martin. Only you can lead us.' Brother John licked his lips and glanced nervously towards the doorway.

Brother Martin laughed. 'We are all worthy! Come now, drink first.' He walked over to a punch bowl and dipped a white beaker into the dark red liquid, then proffered it towards the black man. Heads began to turn and look towards Brother John. As if guessing his intention, Brother Samuel moved his big frame into the entrance, blocking any escape.

Oooooh shit! Brother John's head screamed and he brought his knee up into the big man's groin area. Brother Samuel fell to his knees, his hands clutching at his genitals. Brother John jumped through the open doorway into the even greater darkness outside. And stopped.

It was around him like cold clammy hands, like icy treacle smearing itself over his skin. He shivered and looked around, but could see only blurred pinpoints of light in the distance. He backed away from it, but it came with him as though it were stuck to his body. He felt an eerie kind of probing going on inside his head and cried out when the cold fingers touched something inside his mind. No, I don't want this! something inside him screamed, but another voice answered, yes, yes, you do!

Other hands reached around his throat, and these were real hands, the big, strong hands of Brother Samuel. The grip began to tighten as the inky blackness enveloped both men, and Brother John's thoughts tumbled over themselves to run from the unreal dark fingers that touched and ravaged his mind. He sank to the hard paving stones leading up to the temple, the big man standing behind him, never letting go, and slowly he realized Brother Martin was right: this was the eternity they had been seeking. Although his body was trembling with the pain, something inside him was dancing with happiness. Oh, you *mother*, you were right, Brother Martin, Brother Marty Randall, you were *soooo* right. Even as his closed throat strained to suck in air through to his lungs, his lips were parted in a rapturous smile. His red-filled vision began to cloud into a deepening blackness and soon that was all there was – total, welcoming darkness. Amen to that.

Brother Samuel dragged the limp body back into the temple and the Dark followed, flowing in greedily, spreading and seeping, dimming the already faint light from the candles.

Brother Martin closed his eyes and spread his arms wide, ignoring the sudden cries of fear around him, welcoming the Dark into his church.

'We will drink the poison and join you,' he said aloud and wondered at the mocking laugh he thought he heard. It had sounded like Brother John. One by one, the candles sputtered and finally went out.

'Tell them to keep the noise down, Alex. If the law finds out you've got a meeting going on in the back, they'll have your licence.' Sheila Bryan held the glass up to make sure she had wiped away all the smears in the bottom of the pint glass. It wasn't often the pub's glasses received such close scrutiny, but then it wasn't often a curfew was imposed. She briefly wondered if there had been such restrictions during the war. She didn't think so, but couldn't be sure; it was before her time.

'They're all right. They're not disturbin' anybody.' Her husband, Alex, regarded Sheila with ill-disguised impatience. He was a hefty man, large of gut, loud of voice, and it needed a woman with similar attributes to handle him. He was just approaching forty, she had just said goodbye to her twenties; their mutual largeness somehow made them appear the same age.

'I don't know why you have anything to do with them, anyway,' Sheila said, placing the glass next to its dry companions on the bar. Ash from the cigarette dangling between her lips fell into the murky washing up water as she leaned forward and reached in for another glass.

'They've got the right idea, that's why,' Alex retorted as he dumped the tray of glasses on the draining-board next to the sink. 'They want another round.'

'Well they'll have to use those. I'm not using fresh glasses.'

'Of course they'll bleedin' use these. Who's askin' for new ones? I don't know what gets into you at times. We wouldn't be makin' a penny if we didn't 'av that lot tonight. Bloody filth keepin' everyone indoors.'

'The Law says it's dangerous to go out at night.'

'That's all bollocks. They've got somethin' goin' on, that's all, somethin' they don't want anybody to see.'

'Don't be bloody daft. You've seen what's going on on the telly. Riots, fires – all those murders.'

'Yeh, because somebody's used a nerve gas on us, that's why. Bastard Lefties, that's who's done it, brought it in for their friends abroad.'

Sheila stood up from the sink and took the cigarette from her mouth with damp fingers. 'What are you talking about now?' she said, looking at her husband with disdain.

'Everyone knows the Commies are behind it. They won't tell you on the news, but just you ask anyone. It'll be New York next, maybe Washington. You wait and see. Then Paris, then Rome. All over. Won't 'appen in Russia, though.'

'Oh you do talk wet, Alex. That mob next door been filling your head with ideas again?'

Alex ignored the question and began filling the glasses with their appropriate drinks. 'It makes sense when you think about it,' he said undeterred as he poured.

His wife raised her eyes towards the ceiling and resumed polishing the glasses. It *was* worrying, though, the whole town being placed under some kind of martial law. It was the sort of thing you expected to happen in foreign parts, but not England. Not London. Why should they have to keep all lights on as though they were afraid of the dark? The Dark: that was what everyone was calling it because it only happened at night-time. They said people were losing their minds with it, roaming around the streets setting fires, killing. There was no sense to it. She, herself, had seen the army trucks searching the streets in the early hours of the morning, picking up people who seemed to be wandering loose and taking them away somewhere. She'd watched them from the window upstairs one morning when she couldn't sleep. Some poor sod had been just lying in the road, covering his head with his hands. There had been blood on his fingers because he had been trying to pull up the manhole cover in the middle of the road, but it must have been too heavy, or he couldn't get a grip. He didn't say a word when they slung him into the truck, and his face had been deathly white, white as a ghost, and his eyes black and half-shut. She shivered. It was like one of those old horror films, like Quatermass.

'Where's all the fuckin' light ales?'

Her attention was abruptly drawn back to her husband. 'Don't swear in the bar, Alex, I've asked you before.'

He looked back at her, then around at the empty saloon bar. 'There's no one 'ere, you know.'

'That's not the point. You've got to get out of the habit. It's not necessary.'

Silly cow, he said to himself. Then aloud, 'We can't 'av used all the light, we've only 'ad lunchtime trade the past couple of weeks.'

'Alex, there's plenty in the cellar if you'd like to make the effort and go down and get it.'

Alex's sigh turned into a grunt when he leaned forward and pulled at the ring set into the trapdoor behind the bar. He heaved it open and stared down at the blackness below. 'I thought we were supposed to turn on all the lights,' he said.

'I did,' his wife replied, looking over his shoulder into the square of darkness.

'Well that one's not bleedin' on, is it?'

Sheila walked over to the set of light switches that lay near the doorway to a small back room they used mainly as an office, their living quarters being on the floor above. 'They're all on,' she called back to her husband. 'The bulb must have gone.'

'Oh fuck it,' her husband groaned.

'I'll get you another one, Alex. You can put it in.'

'Great,' Alex replied wearily. He wanted to get back to the meeting; he enjoyed listening to the boys and tonight, because there were no other customers, was the ideal opportunity to sit in on their discussions. Fortunately, his was a Free House, so no interfering nosey-parker could inform any brewery of the type of organizations he allowed to hold meetings in his pub. One of his mates, a publican in Shoreditch, had had to vacate when the brewery which owned the pub discovered he was letting his back rooms out for National Front meetings. That was the trouble with being a tenant-landlord – you had to dance to someone else's tune. 'Come on, Sheila,' he called out, 'let's 'av it!'

She returned, a cold look on her face, and handed him a torch and a new light bulb.

'Forty watt?' he said disgustedly. 'This ain't gonna be much cop, is it?'

'It's all we've got,' she replied patiently. 'And you can bring up some Babycham while you're down there.'

'Babycham? Who the 'ell's gonna be drinkin' that tonight?'

'It's for tomorrow lunchtime. You know we're packed during the day now.'

'Yeh, they're all making up for what they can't get in the evening.'

'Just as well they are, otherwise we'd soon go broke. Hurry up, or your mates will be screaming for their beer.'

'They're not me mates.'

'You could have fooled me. You spend enough time with them.'

'I just 'appen to agree with a lot of what they say. You've seen 'ow many blacks there is around 'ere. More of them than us.'

'Oh go on, get down there. You talk like a big kid at times.'

Alex hoisted his frame on to the ladder. 'You mark my words, they'll be comin' in 'ere to drink next.' His big round head disappeared from view.

'Heil Hitler,' Sheila commented drily and took another puff of her cigarette. With a resigned sigh she returned to polishing the glasses.

Below, Alex flashed the torch around the grimy, beer-smelling cellar. The beam soon found the naked light bulb hanging from the low ceiling. Better have a stock-take tomorrow, he told himself as he crossed the dusty stone floor. Running low on – oh *fuck*! He stepped out of the puddle and shook droplets of stale beer from his shoe. He shone the torch down and dazzled himself with the reflection off the thinly spread liquid. The cellar floor sloped towards its middle so that all spillage would run into a centre channel then into a drain. He followed the direction of the channel with the torchlight and saw rags or sacking were blocking the flow.

'That silly bastard Paddy,' he said under his breath, referring to his daytime barman. It was the little Irishman's job to stock up the bar each morning, using the dumb waiter to carry the drinks to the floor above. He must have dropped the rags or whatever it was. 'Bloody Irish twit,' he muttered, kicking the damp bundle aside. He'd been dipping into the till again, too. Christ, it was difficult to get honest bar staff. Alex watched the strong-smelling mixture of combined beers gurgle into the square, grille-covered drain. At least it wasn't blocked. If there was one job Alex could not abide it was unblocking drains. All that shit and slime. The drains had to be kept clear otherwise the basement would be ankle deep and stinking like a brewery within a week with all the breakages that went on down there. The delivery men didn't give a sod. Slung the crates down any old how. He thought he saw something scuttle away from the circle of light cast by the torch. 'Don't say we've got rats down 'ere now,' he groaned aloud.

He swung the beam around but found nothing, only retreating blackness.

Alex plodded over to the dangling light bulb, not sure if he had only imagined the dark thing scuttling away. He hadn't heard any movement. The light itself hung over the drain and the publican stretched upwards to reach it, torch held precariously with the fingers of one hand and pointing up at the ceiling. His feet were spread out on either side of the drain.

'Ouch!' Alex cried out when his fingers touched the hot glass. The bulb must have blown just before he opened up the cellar. He jerked his hands away and the torch fell from his grasp. 'Oh *fuck* it!' he shouted when it crashed to the floor and its light was extinguished. The open trapdoor at the far end of the cellar threw down a little light, but its range was not enough to reach where he stood. He dug into his pocket and pulled out a handkerchief, his other pocket bulging with the new light bulb. Alex reached up for the dead one, this time using his handkerchief for protection against the heat.

The gloom did not bother him, for he had never been afraid of the dark, not even as a kid. But the prickling at the back of his neck warned him that something was not quite right in the cellar.

Sheila rested her elbows on the bar top and stared reflectively at the locked door. A fresh cigarette dangled from her lips and her large breasts lay comfortably on the bar's wooden surface like full sacks of graded flour. She didn't know how many more nights like this she could stand. Dolling herself up, slipping into the mental gear necessary to sustain herself through the evening's jollifications or commiserations, whatever the individual customer's mood required, being nice to everybody, firm to those who took liberties. It was like showbiz in a way, only these nights there was no biz. Surely they were going to get rid of this gas, or whatever it was soon. The whole town would go to pot otherwise. Still, she supposed she should have been grateful for the small amount of evening trade she had in the back room, as much as she disliked their views. It was only because they had booked the room a month in advance that she had let Alex persuade her to allow the meeting to be held. He was one of them, even though he wouldn't admit it. They'd have to pay for the use of the room all night, of course; there was no chance of any of them leaving before tomorrow morning. They'd be nicked if they were caught out on the streets at night. Where was Alex? He was taking his time. Who was it who came on telly the other night? A cardinal or bishop, wasn't it? Told them all to pray. Hah, that was a laugh! She could just see old Alex going down on his knees to pray. Probably would if someone held a gun at his head. What were they supposed to pray for? What good were prayers against a nerve gas, as Alex said it was? It was the scientists who had to do the praying. It was down to them, all this mess. Let them come up with something. And not prayers.

'Sheila.'

She looked around. What was that?

'Sheila.'

She sighed and lumbered towards the open trapdoor. 'What're you up to, Alex? How long does it take you to send up a crate of light and Babycham?'

She peered down into the blackness.

'Haven't you put the bulb in yet?' she said, irritated.

'Sheila, come down.'

'Where are you, Alex? I can't see you.'

'Come down.'

'Do what? Me, come down there? Do me a favour, Alex.'

'Please, Sheila.'

'Are you sodding about, Alex? I'm not in the mood.'

'Come on, Sheila, come down. I've got something to show you.'

The publican's wife chortled. 'You can show me that later, in bed.'

'No, come on, Sheila, now. Come down.'

Alex's voice sounded strangely urgent.

'It's dangerous, Alex. I might fall.'

'You won't, Sheila. I'll help you. Come down.'

Oh my Gawd, Sheila said to herself. The things I do for love. 'All right, Alex,' she called down, a giggle escaping her. 'It had better be worth it!'

She gingerly lowered herself on to the metal-runged ladder, her hands firmly grasping the wooden sides. Sometimes she wondered if Alex was all there, the strokes he pulled. But he was good for a laugh, she had to give him that.

'Alex? Alex! Where are you?' She was halfway down the ladder and looking around, trying to pierce the gloom. 'I'm going up again if you don't stop hiding right this minute.'

'I'm right here, Sheila, waitin' for you.'

'Well what do you want?' Sheila had decided she didn't really like this game. The cellar stank – beer dregs and something else. What? Funny smell. It was cold and dark there too. 'I'm going up, Alex. You're acting stupid, true to form.'

She waited for a reply, but there was only silence.

Sheila came down two more rungs then stopped. 'Right, that's it. This is as far as I come unless you come over here into the light.'

Alex didn't make a sound. But she heard his breathing. She suddenly felt uneasy.

'Bye, Alex.' She began to climb back up the ladder.

Alex came out of the dark, a lumbering shape that held something high above his head. Sheila just turned her head in time to see the mallet used for opening kegs of beer descending. There was no time for her to scream and no time to wonder what had come over Alex.

She fell to the floor and lay still, but the heavy wooden mallet continued to batter her head and soon it was blood that flowed down the basement's centre into the dark, noxious drain.

Alex climbed through the trapdoor minutes later, a smile of pleasure on his face. He heaved his heavy body through the opening, the bloodied mallet still held in one hand. Reaching up to the bartop with his free hand, he pulled himself to his feet. He walked to the set of switches that controlled all the downstairs lights in the public house and ran his hand over every one until both bars and back rooms were plunged into darkness. He walked back the length of the bar, careful not to fall into the even blacker hole that was the open trapdoor. Confused voices coming from one of the back rooms guided him, although guidance wasn't really necessary, for he knew his pub like the back of his hand. He hurried to rejoin the meeting. They would be pleased to see him. They would be pleased to see what he had brought along with him.

He looked to the right, studying the wide road for several long seconds before directing his gaze to the left. All clear. No police, no patrolling army vehicles. It was now or never. He ran, heading for the road leading to the big park. To where it was empty. And dark.

His gait was awkward, more of a waddle than a run, his short legs treading the hard, smooth road's surface as though it were cobblestones. The thought of the jogging which several of his colleagues in the House had taken up when it had become fashionable a couple of years back made him wonder at their sanity. Moving at any speed faster than a brisk stroll *had* to be damaging to one's health. No wonder some of them had collapsed with heart attacks. He remembered the leaflets all the Members had received encouraging them to use the Parliament gym, telling them that by keeping a healthy body, they would have the stamina to serve their constituents better. Well, his stamina was in the mind, not in the body. As far as he was concerned, each leaflet should have been issued with a GOVERNMENT HEALTH WARNING. You couldn't serve your constituents very well from a wooden box six feet under the earth. And if his heart was going to collapse, he would rather it was due to the demands of a good whore than running through the park in plimsolls. He paused at the entrance, his rotund body heaving and sucking in huge, rasping lungfuls of air. He studied the broad expanse of darkness before him, afraid now, then forced himself on, the night swallowing him up as though he had never existed.

Once he was safely inside the black sanctuary, he slumped to the grass, heedless of its cold wetness, and endeavoured to recover a normal rate of breathing. The lights of the city blazed away in the distance, but they barely penetrated the fringes of the park. He was in the Kensington Gardens section, deeming it wise to keep well away from Hyde Park on the other side of the Serpentine where a police station operated. He would find it difficult to explain his presence. Even being a Labour MP for the past sixteen years would not prevent his immediate arrest. Any Member of Parliament on government business had to have an army escort after nightfall, otherwise they had to stay indoors like other citizens. The uproar over the restrictions still raged every day in the House, but the PM and the Home Secretary were adamant. Anyone who wished to leave the capital while the emergency was on was perfectly entitled to do so, but if they remained, then they came under the government edict. Until the solution was found to this madness, conditions for living in London were severe. Never mind the solutions, backbenchers on either side had cried out, what was the problem? Just what was happening each night? Why was there, as yet, no official statement? The public were entitled to know. *The Members of Parliament themselves were entitled to know!* They had been astonished, then disbelieving, when they were told of the ethereal mass of dark substance that had strange effects on the brain, a mass that had no defined shape nor, as far as anyone could tell, material form. It was neither a gas, nor a chemical. Autopsies on the brains of victims affected by it, and who had taken their own lives, revealed nothing unusual. Why those who could be found wandering the streets by day were docile and in almost trance-like states, no one knew. Paranormal connotations were still being denied, as could be expected.

He rose to his feet, brushing the dampness from his knees. His eyes had become accustomed to the gloom and he realized the patch he was in was considerably lighter than the heavy blackness ahead. He shuffled forward, eager to be completely enveloped by the darkness. The bloody fools didn't understand the significance of it all! This was a new entity – no, not new: it was as old as the world itself. It was a power that had existed even before human life, a dark power that man had allied himself with from the beginning. Now it dwelt in man. It had always been there, the darkness where evil lurked, the darkness that bestial things crept in, the darkness waiting for man to give himself up completely to it. And now was the time.

He froze. Something was moving in the shadows ahead. No sounds. No more movement. His eyes must have been playing tricks on him.

The Dark had called to him, told him what he must do. The power of politics was nothing to the power he had been offered. It was a giant step to take, but the rewards were infinite. No hesitating now, no second thoughts. He had been chosen.

It was difficult to see anything in front of him, for the moon was behind heavy clouds. He could see lights through the trees coming from the hotels that edged the opposite side of Park Lane, but they were far away and had nothing to do with the void of blackness he stood in. Was this *the* Dark around him? Was this the force he had come in search of? Let it happen, then. Absorb me, take me in ... He stumbled over a figure sitting on the ground.

The politician fell heavily and rolled on to his back.

'Who's there?' he asked querulously when he had recovered from his surprise.

He heard a mumbling sound, but could make no sense of it. He squinted his eyes, hoping to see better. 'Who's there?'

he repeated, then became a little bolder. 'Speak up!' His voice was still a whisper, though the words were spoken harshly.

He cautiously crawled forward, afraid yet curious. 'Come on, speak up. What are you doing there?'

'Waiting,' came the murmured reply. It was a man's voice.

The politician was taken aback, somehow not really expecting an answer. 'What do you mean "waiting"? Waiting for what?'

'Waiting like the others.'

'Others?' The politician looked around and suddenly became aware that what he had thought to be dark shapes of bushes and shrubs were, in fact, the figures of people, some squatting on the ground, others standing. All were silent. He grabbed the man by the shoulder.

'Do they – do you – know about the Dark?'

The man shrugged his shoulder away. 'Piss off,' he said quietly. 'Leave me alone.'

The politician stared at the shadowy figure for a while, still unable to make out his features. Finally, he crawled away and found a space of his own. He sat there for a long time, confused, then ultimately, resigned. It made sense that he would not have been the only one; others would have been chosen. At one point, when the quarter moon was able to free itself of clinging black clouds for a few seconds, he was able to look around and see how many others there were waiting with him. At least a hundred, he thought. Perhaps as many as a hundred and fifty. Why didn't they communicate? Why were they not speaking? He realized that, like him, their minds were too full of what was going to happen, opening themselves to receive the probing darkness. Willing it, demanding it. The clouds covered the moon and he was alone once more, waiting for the Dark to come.

When the first haziness of dawn edged its way over the tall buildings on the horizon, he rose wearily and stiffly to his feet. His overcoat was covered in a layer of morning dew and his body ached. He saw the others were rising, their movements slow and awkward as though the night's long wait had rusted their joints. Their white, early morning faces were expressionless, but he knew they felt the same bitter disappointment as he. One by one they drifted away, the low-flying dawn mist swirling around their feet.

He felt like weeping with frustration and shaking a fist at the vanishing shadows. Instead, he went home.

25

Bishop sipped his Scotch, then lit his third cigarette since he had been sitting in the hotel bar. He glanced at his watch. The conference had been running for over three hours already and when he had left just half an hour earlier, it seemed far away from any firm conclusions. With so many now involved he wondered if there would ever be any real agreement between them. The combination of scientists and parapsychologists, with government ministers trying to find a common ground between both factions, was hardly conducive to an ideal atmosphere. An American Research Society had expounded on Jung's collective unconscious theory – 'Just as the human body shows a common anatomy over and above all racial differences, so too the psyche possesses a common substratum transcending all differences in culture and consciousness' – and maintained that this collective unconsciousness consisted of latent dispositions towards identitical reaction, patterns of thought and behaviour that were a common heritage of psychological development. Different races and separate generations had common instincts – why else the similarity between various myths and symbols? And perhaps one of man's most shared instincts was that for evil. It was argued that surely good was the more predominant instinct throughout history, despite the terrible atrocities that had taken place, and the speaker had agreed, but had gone on to add that perhaps after centuries of enforced suppression, the evil instinct had broken free of the mind's confines. It had finally evolved into a material form.

Bishop, seated in the back row of the modern auditorium, had almost smiled at the perplexed looks that passed between the Police Commissioner and the Army Chief of Staff. If they hadn't had official reports as well as personal eyewitness evidence of the massive unexplained destruction taking place in the nation's capital each night, they would have dismissed such jargonized theories out of hand. However, when a member of the delegation from the Institute of Human Potential insisted that this new madness was the final breakthrough to sanity, their looks turned to mutual anger. It was the Home Secretary, himself, who delivered a severe rebuke to the man who went on to explain that what society considered to be the norm was not necessarily so, and that the condition of alienation, of being asleep or unconscious, of being out of one's mind, was the natural condition of man. The men and women who had been affected had all been in a trance-like state, an altered state of consciousness, an *enlightened* state. They had a mission that so-called normal people – which included everyone in the conference theatre – did not yet understand, nor appreciate. The Home Secretary warned the man and others of his group that they would be removed from the auditorium if they persisted in putting forward these non-productive and rather absurd arguments. The country was in a state of emergency and, while every opinion was valued at this juncture, frivolous speculation would not be tolerated.

Relief on the faces of the Home Secretary and several of his ministerial and law enforcement colleagues showed visibly when the general discussion took on a more medically scientific aspect, but they were soon disappointed by the statement of a prominent neurosurgeon seated in the front row of the audience. He explained how he and a special team of surgeons had performed craniotomies on several of the London victims, dead as well as the living, in an attempt to find out if their brains had been affected physically in any way. The results had proved negative: no inflammation of the membranes or nerves, no deterioration of tissue, no blockage of cerebrospinal fluid, no bacterial infection, no blood clots or restriction of blood flow to the brain. The surgeon went on to list further defects such as chemical deficiencies that could have damaged the brain's normal functioning, and assured everyone present that none of these had been present. Other tests had been carried out, more in desperation than in hope, and these, too, had proved negative. There had been no lack of enzyme in the victims' systems – without this there would have been an accumulation of amino-acids such as phenylalamine in the blood. Nor had there been any sudden imbalance of chromosomes in the body cells. A thorough examination had been made of the central region of the brain, particularly the regions grouped around the fluid-filled cavities called the ventricles. One of these regions, the hypothalamus, controlled hunger, thirst, temperature, sex drive and *aggression*, and a close study of the collection of structures around that area forming the limbic system – the septum, fornix, amygdala and hippocampus – which were believed to be particularly responsible for emotional responses such as fear and aggression – had revealed nothing unusual. That is, as far as they could *tell*; no matter how far science had come, the brain was still very much a mystery.

The participating audience, many of whom had become lost with the eminent doctor's medical terminology, stirred uncomfortably. The Home Secretary, anxious to have as many opinions as possible aired in the time available, asked for the view of the psychiatrist seated next to the neurosurgeon, and the two main psychoses of the emotionally disturbed were quickly and clearly explained in a voice that was loud, yet somehow soothing. In manic depressive psychosis, the patient's mood changed from deep depression to mania, which might possibly explain the victims' trance-like quietness during the day and the uncontrollable urges to commit acts of destruction at night. Yet treatment with drugs such as lithium had had no effect on these people. The other chief psychosis was schizophrenia, which generally occurred in those with a hereditary disorder in their metabolism. The symptoms were irrational thinking, disturbed emotions and a breakdown in communications with others, all of which applied to the recent victims. Phenothiazines, also used as tranquillizers, and other drugs such as fluphenazine, had been used unsuccessfully on the victims. As yet, shock treatment had not been tried, but the psychiatrist had also expressed his doubts as to the effectiveness of this method. An alternative which would undoubtedly succeed would be a lobotomy on each individual, but he did, of course, understand that this would be impractical with so many victims. He looked steadily up at the Home Secretary and his hastily appointed 'emergency' council seated on one side of a long, highly polished table on the small stage, remaining silent until the minister realized the psychiatrist had nothing more to say. It was then that a member of an organization called the Spiritual Frontiers Fellowship Rescue Group rose to his feet and informed those present that the phenomenon being witnessed in London was no more than a large gathering of discarnate beings who did not know they were dead and were possessing others in their confusion. The destructive acts of violence that the possessed were committing were caused because the lost spirits were frightened. He asked that mediums be allowed to guide the tormented souls onwards, to leave their earthly ties behind.

Bishop had decided he needed a drink at that point in the proceedings.

He had crept from the conference theatre as unobtrusively as possible, pushing his way through the throng of journalists cramming the back of the auditorium. The hotel bar was empty and the lone barman seemed relieved to have some company. Bishop, however, was in no mood for conversation. He swallowed the first Scotch fast, then nursed the second.

The meeting was being held in an hotel at the Birmingham Conference Centre, a huge complex of exhibition halls and conference rooms. The complex was, in fact, some miles from the town itself, in a position easily accessible from the M1 motorway. The authorities considered it too risky to use a more convenient London venue for, although the danger only presented itself at nightfall, the situation in the capital was unpredictable. It was feared that many of the various organizations invited to take part in the general debate might have declined the offer if it were held in the danger zone. And anyway, as the Army Chief of Staff had said: 'A general doesn't hold his war council on the field of battle!' When Bishop had arrived with Jacob Kulek, Jessica and Edith Metlock earlier that morning, the hotel lobby had been filled with clamorous groups of scientists, medical experts and parapsychologists. Outside had been an even larger gathering of media people, many of these too, from other parts of the world. Bishop was unsure if the conference was being held merely for cosmetic reasons to show that the government was taking some action, or out of sheer desperation because they had no solution to the problem. Probably for both reasons, he decided.

Jacob Kulek had become adviser to the special action committee formed to deal with the crisis, his Institute suddenly becoming almost another branch of the Civil Service. Just as Winston Churchill had introduced an occult bureau into the Secret Service during World War Two, so had the Home Secretary adopted what he considered was a similar, ready-made organization. The government was not convinced it was dealing with a paranormal phenomenon but, because it had not found any other answers, it was not ruling out the possibility. Hence the conference with its diverse groups of experts. At the moment, the 'trouble' in London was being contained, although the city was too vast to be effectively policed for long. New disturbances broke out every night, more victims were found cowering in the streets each morning. The sewer exits were being watched.

How long the police and troops could maintain control was anybody's guess; the night was already beginning to catch up with the mopping-up exercises of the day. And how many more victims affected or infected – still nobody was sure of the correct term – by the Dark could be kept under lock and key was another problem that was reaching crisis point. The exodus of London residents was relatively small so far, but the sudden influx of outsiders gave cause for alarm. Why would men and women flock to the city when such danger stalked the streets at night? And why were so many flouting the 'lights-on' regulations? It was almost as if some welcomed the phenomenon that had become known as the Dark. Bishop sat in the bar, pondering over the imponderable. Were they faced with a crisis that could be dealt with by scientific means, or a crisis whose cause lay in the paranormal and therefore, could only be answered by psychic means? He, himself, felt they were about to discover there was a definite link between the two.

He drained his glass and waved it at the barman for another.

'I think I need the same,' came a voice from behind him.

Bishop turned to see Jessica had entered the bar. She perched herself on the stool next to him and he ordered her a Scotch.

'I saw you leave the conference theatre,' she remarked. 'I wondered if you were okay.'

He nodded. 'Just weary. The discussion doesn't seem to be getting far. Too many fingers in the pie.'

'They feel it's necessary to get as many views as possible.'

'Some of those views are a little eccentric, wouldn't you say?' Bishop passed Jessica's drink over to her. 'Water?' he asked.

She shook her head and sipped the Scotch. 'Some are fanatical in their beliefs, I agree, but the others are well respected in their particular fields of psychic research.'

'Will any of it help, though? How the hell can you beat something that apparently has no material form?'

'The idea of germs being living organisms was unknown not too long ago. The Bubonic Plague itself was at first thought to be the work of the Devil.'

'I thought you believed this was.'

'In a way, I do. I think our terms are wrong, though. Many think of the Devil as a creature with horns and a long forked tail, or at least, a living creature who pops through the gates of Hell every now and again to create havoc. It's a belief the Church has done nothing to discourage!'

'And the Devil is behind all this?'

'As I said, our terms are wrong. The Devil is within us, Chris, just as God is.'

Bishop sighed wearily. 'We are God, we are the Devil?' There was disdain in his words.

'The power for good and the power for evil is in us. God and Devil are just symbolic names for an abstraction.'

'That's some abstraction if, as you're implying, it's the root cause of everything good and everything bad that's happened in the world.'

'It's an abstraction that's fast becoming a reality.'

'Because Pryszlak has found a way of using it?'

'He's not the first.'

Bishop stared at her. 'This has never happened before.'

'How do you know? Read your Bible, Chris; it gives us plenty of indications.'

'But then why this evil power? Why hasn't someone used the power for good?'

'Many have. Jesus Christ was one.'

Bishop smiled. 'You mean all those miracles were due to a force he knew how to tap?'

'Miracles are more common than you think. Christ may have been a man who knew the process of using that power.'

'Would that make Pryszlak the anti-Christ? I mean, he went for the other extreme.'

Jessica ignored the mockery in Bishop's question. 'There have also been many anti-Christs.'

The whisky on an empty stomach had begun to make Bishop feel slightly light-headed, but the earnestness in Jessica's eyes made him bite back his cynicism. 'Look, Jessica, if you say miracles are fairly common, why is it that no one else is using this other source in the way Pryszlak apparently is?'

'Because we're still learning. We haven't yet grasped it. When it is used, it's done unconsciously. When we learned to walk, did we think about it first, or did the realization come after? Once we were aware that we could walk, that it was physically possible, we could learn to do other things. Run, then ride, use implements, make vehicles to carry us. It's a gradual process, Chris, and only our own awareness can speed up that process.'

Bishop wondered why he was resisting the argument, for it explained much of his own thoughts regarding the paranormal. Perhaps it was because it all seemed too simple, too obvious an answer; but then, who said the answer had to be complicated? Everything came from the individual, no outside force was involved; and when each personal source was discovered, then, united with others, that collected power became massive. It did seem that the Dark affected those people who were in some way mentally disturbed, whether they were criminals, insane, or – his grip on the glass tightened – or had evil in their minds. Many of the cases he had heard of over the past few weeks concerned individuals who held some grievance against others – even mere dislike – and it seemed the madness around them had triggered off their own violence. If the Dark could seek out this evil, invade their minds and draw out that force, uniting with it, reinforcing its own strength like some giant, rapacious organism, then where would it end? As it grew stronger, would it be capable of swamping any opposing force for good in the mind, finding the evil that lurked in every living soul and using it? Was the reason for that power not having been developed more fully in the past because of the conflicting oppositions within everybody, only those rare beings who were truly good or truly evil being capable of harnessing it in their own way? And when you died, did that entity die with you or was it released into . . . into what? Bishop realized that Jessica's answer had not been simple at all: it was as complex as man's own evolution.

'Chris, are you all right? You've gone deathly white.'

Jessica's hand was over his own, and he became aware of the crushing grip he had on the glass. He placed the Scotch back on the bar, but still she kept her hand on his.

He took in a deep breath. 'Maybe it's all catching up with me.'

Misunderstanding him, she said, 'You've been through so much. We all have, but you more than most.'

He shook his head. 'I don't mean that, Jessica. Lynn's death is something I'll never really get over, but it's something I know I'll learn to accept, just as I've accepted Lucy's. The hurt will always be there, but it'll become controllable. No, what's shaken me is your explanation for the Dark. I take it Jacob shares your view?'

'It *is* his view. I agree with him.'

'Then there's no way we can overcome it.'

She was silent for a moment, then replied. 'There has to be a way.'

Bishop turned his hand over so that the palm joined with Jessica's. His fingers curled around her hand and gently squeezed; but he said nothing.

He was still awake, sitting in the uncomfortable armchair in his hotel room, facing the large picture window and wondering what fresh atrocities were breaking out in London, when the light rapping on the door disturbed his thoughts. He glanced at his watch and saw it was ten-thirty. The rapping came again. Crushing his half-smoked cigarette into the ashtray resting on the arm of the chair, he rose and walked over to the door. He hesitated before turning the twist-lock handle, apprehension having become a part of his life-pattern now. Jessica's voice dispelled his anxiety.

He opened the door and found himself looking into the sightless eyes of Jacob Kulek, Jessica standing just behind her father.

'May we come in, Chris?' Kulek said.

Bishop stood aside and Jessica guided her father into the room. He closed the door and turned to face them.

'I'm sorry I have not been able to speak with you during the day, Chris,' Kulek apologized. 'I'm afraid my time is governed by others nowadays.'

'It's all right, I understand. These people seem to expect a lot of you, Jacob.'

The blind man gave a small laugh, but Bishop noted there was a tiredness to it. 'The scientists and medical people on the one hand are sceptical, while most of the psychicists on the other are cautious – they see this as an opportunity to prove everything they have preached over the last few decades. The irrational ones among them have, thank God, been largely ignored. The authorities are stuck somewhere in the middle of both groups, naturally leaning more towards the logical or, if you like, the scientific, point of view. I believe it is only because the scientists have not as yet provided any clues, let alone answers, that our opinions are being sought. May I sit, Chris? It's been a wearisome day.'

'Please.' Bishop turned round the armchair he had just vacated to face the room and Jessica guided her father into it. She smiled warmly at Bishop as she sat in the chair provided with the room's dressing-table. He settled on the edge of his bed and returned her smile.

'Can I order you both some coffee?' he asked.

'No, thank you. I think a large brandy might help to ease my ageing bones, though.' Kulek inclined his head towards his daughter.

'Coffee will be fine for me, Chris.'

Bishop picked up the phone and ordered two coffees and one large brandy. When he replaced the receiver he said, 'Is Edith okay?'

'Tired, frightened, like all of us. Our smaller, more intimate meeting in which she was included, broke up only twenty minutes ago. The select committee had to discuss all the points raised at the conference today – the valid points, that is.'

'Who decided which were and which were not?'

'I suppose you could say moderation did. Our Home Secretary is not one for extremes, you know.'

'From what I hear, he's not one for actions, either.'

'Then his decision may surprise you.'

'Oh?'

'I'm not sure he's convinced, but he has agreed to – what shall I say? – to an experiment.'

Bishop leaned forward, arms resting across his knees, interested.

Kulek pinched the sides of his nose and squeezed his eyes tightly shut for a few seconds to ease the ache in his head. His face looked drained when he raised his eyes again. 'We are going back to Beechwood. That is, what's left of Beechwood.'

Bishop was stunned. 'Why? What good could that possibly do? As you said, the place is in ruins anyway.'

Kulek patiently nodded and rested his long, thin fingers over the top of his walking-cane. 'It was, and still is, a focal point in this whole affair. Every night, more and more unfortunate victims of this thing we call the Dark gather there. Some die, others are found the following morning either standing or lying helpless in the rubble. There has to be a reason for them to go there, something that draws them to it.'

'How could it help for you to go there? We tried it before, remember?'

'And something happened, Chris,' Jessica broke in.

'Jacob nearly got killed.'

'And you had a vision,' the blind man said quietly.

'You saw what went on in that house,' Jessica added. 'You saw how Pryszlak and his followers died.'

'Don't you see, Chris, there are strong vibrations around that area? Even though it is only a ruin, there will be those same energies.' Kulek fixed Bishop with his sightless gaze.

'But the danger. You . . .'

'This time we will have protection. The area will be guarded by troops, we will have powerful lighting . . .'

'You're not thinking of going back there at night?'

'Yes, that would be the only time for what we have in mind.'

'You're crazy. Jessica, you can't let him do this. The Army won't be able to protect him.'

Jessica looked at Bishop steadily. 'Chris,' she said, 'we want you to come with us.'

He shook his head. 'This is wrong, Jessica. There's no point to it. What can we do there, anyway?'

Kulek replied. 'The only thing that is left to us. We are going to make contact with the Dark. We will try to talk with Boris Pryszlak.'

The discreet knock on the door announced the arrival of the coffees and brandy.

26

It could have been daytime, the lights were so dazzling. Every house in Willow Road had been cleared of its occupants; not that there were many of them left – the road had attracted the attention of too many victims of the Dark for any residents to feel safe. Army vehicles were parked along the kerbside, all pointed in the same direction, and heavily guarded barriers had been placed across both ends of the road. Two powerful, wide-beam searchlights mounted on trucks and powered by their own generators, were directed into the open space that had once been Beechwood. Most of the rubble had been cleared to allow for an array of equipment to be set up, instruments ranging from sound and video recording machinery, to Geiger counters and other sophisticated gadgetry that Bishop had never seen before, let alone put a name to. Arc lamps, hooked into the main electricity system of the area, were placed at strategic points around the grounds. The whole scene had an unreal look and Bishop could not help feeling he had wandered on to a film set, the various cameras operated by army personnel adding to the illusion. Nearby, Jacob Kulek was having angry words with the Principal Private Secretary to the Home Office over the amount of machinery and reinforcements that were in evidence, all of which, Kulek claimed, might interfere with the energy patterns in the atmosphere and impede any mental contact that might be made with the Dark. The Private Secretary, a thin, waspish little man named Sicklemore, testily replied that they were conducting a scientific operation rather than a parlour seance and his instructions had been to gather and record all necessary data from the experiment while providing every protection possible to civilian life. He added that for decades parapsychologists had urged scientists to work hand in hand with them, so Kulek should not complain now that this was happening. The blind man had to concede the point, realizing the crisis was too grave for petty bickering. Jessica, standing by her father's side, looked relieved that the minor flare-up between the two men was over.

Bishop eased his way through the throng of technicians, police and army personnel, all of whom seemed to have some specific task to perform, and saw Edith Metlock sitting alone among the confusion in a canvas-backed chair. He went over to her and sat in the empty seat next to her.

'How do you feel?' he asked.

Her smile was faint. 'A little nervous,' she replied. 'I'm not sure this is the right way.'

'Jacob seems to think this might be the only way.'

'He's probably right.' Her mood was one of resignation.

'We've got plenty of armed protection,' he said to reassure her.

'You don't understand, Chris. I have to let this ... this darkness enter my mind. It will be like allowing an evil spirit to invade my body, only in this case there will be several hundred demons.'

He pointed towards two men a few yards away who were talking in low tones. 'They'll be with you.'

'They're both sensitives of high repute and it's a privilege to be working with them. But our combined strength is nothing compared to the evil influences that have accumulated. I can feel their presence already and it frightens me.'

'Maybe nothing will happen.'

'In some ways, I hope you're right. It has to be stopped, though, before it's too late.'

Bishop was silent for a few moments, his head bowed as if studying the dirt at his feet. 'Edith,' he said finally, 'back in Jacob's house, when we were being held hostage by those two crazy women. Before you arrived, one of them said that Lynn, my wife, was still "active". Can you tell me what she meant?'

The medium patted his arm sympathetically. 'She probably meant that your wife's spirit was tied to those others controlled by the Dark.'

'She's still part of it?'

'I can't say. She may be. Is that why you're here tonight?'

Bishop straightened his body. 'There's a lot I've had to accept recently. I admit I'm still confused by many things, but just the thought of how they murdered Lynn . . .' With effort, he controlled his anger. 'If there's anything I can do to help smash this thing, I will. Jacob said he was unsure of what caused the manifestations in Beechwood before – you, or me, or a combination of both of us. I suppose I'm just an ingredient he wants handy to throw into the pot.'

A shadow fell over them and they looked up to see Jessica. 'Everything's nearly ready, Edith. Jacob would like you and the others to take up your positions.'

Bishop helped the medium to her feet and could not help noticing how the robustness had left her demeanour. They walked towards Jacob Kulek who was talking to a group of people which included the Police Commissioner, a youngish-looking army major, and several men and women whom

Bishop knew to be scientists and metaphysicists. It's like a bloody circus, he thought grimly.

Kulek broke off his conversation when Jessica tugged at his sleeve and said something to him. He nodded, then spoke to the group around him. 'Anyone who is not necessary to this operation must leave the site. Will you please see to that, Commissioner? The very minimum of guards, the very minimum of technicians. Conditions for what we are about to attempt are poor enough without making them worse. The searchlights will have to be switched off, Major.'

'Good Lord, you're not serious?' came the immediate response.

'I'm afraid I am. The arc lamps, too, will have to be dimmed considerably. Edith?'

'I'm here, Jacob.'

'I'm sorry about these conditions, my dear, I hope they will not be too much of a distraction for you. Mr Enwright and Mr Schenkel, you are both ready?'

The two mediums whom Jessica had also brought over answered that they were.

'Is Chris there? Chris, I want you seated next to Edith. Could everyone please take their positions?'

Bishop was surprised: he had thought that he would be somewhere on the sidelines. Suddenly, he was even more afraid.

Six chairs forming a rough semi-circle had been placed in a flattened area of the site. To his further discomfort, Bishop realized they were in a spot close to where the main room of Beechwood would have been. Rough boards beneath his feet covered any gaps leading to the cellar below. Glancing at his watch, he saw it was just after ten. The medium called Schenkel sat in the end seat, Enwright next to him. Then came Edith Metlock, himself, Jacob Kulek, with Jessica sitting slightly back from the group just behind her father.

'Please, we must have complete silence.' Kulek's voice was barely raised, but everyone on the site heard. 'The lights, Major. Could we have them down now?'

The searchlights blinked off and the specially fitted dimmer switches of the arc lamps were turned down. The scene that had been brightly lit became gloomy and immediately sinister.

Kulek turned to Bishop. 'Think back to that first day, Chris. That first time you came to Beechwood. Remember what you saw.'

But Bishop already had.

He knew what he had to do. They had told him.

The inside of the power station was like a huge cavern, a giant's lair that roared and throbbed with the sound of the massive furnaces and turbines. He passed between them, monster steel-plated turbines on one side, furnaces and boilers that stretched up from the basement thirty feet below, almost touching the ceiling over a hundred feet above, on the other. The turbines were painted a bright yellow, each one equipped with an instrument console that kept a watchful eye on their activity. The furnaces and boilers were deceptively cool grey in colour, though the effort of burning a ton of oil per minute made them dangerously hot to touch. Heavily insulated pipes ran from them combining with the boiler pipes in the basement to carry the steam at a pressure of fifteen hundred pounds per square inch to drive the turbine blades.

He passed a technician checking the rows of dials which monitored one of the furnaces and he gave no acknowledgement to the waved hand. The technician frowned, puzzled by his colleague's unkempt appearance, but his thoughts quickly returned to the instruments before him; the loads were heavy these nights because of the government edict that every possible light in the city should be turned on.

The man headed for the stairs leading to the administration floors. And the main switching room.

For two days and nights he had hidden in his basement flat, the curtains drawn, the two rooms he occupied kept in a shadowy gloom during the day, a total darkness during the night.

He was a squat man of twenty-eight, his face still riddled with acne that should have disappeared years before, his hair already leaving his scalp in disloyal batches. He lived alone, not by choice, but because no others, male or female, had any inclination to live with him. His contempt for the human race in general was only thinly disguised and it was a feeling he had nurtured ever since he had realized the world was contemptuous of him. He had thought that leaving school would mean the end of being treated like some loathsome object by immature minds, only to find that the minds at the college he had gone on to, although older, were still as immature. By the time he had become a chemical engineer, the damage was entrenched within him. His parents were still alive, but hardly seen by him. They had never offered him real comfort. Their finding him spying on his rapidly-developing sister on several occasions had earned their early disenchantment with him. They had let him know that the thick lenses he had to wear which made his eyes look like black buttons swimming in silvery pools were a punishment from God. So did He also give him the spots because he couldn't stop abusing himself? And did He make his body smell more than others because he hated his sister, even though he spied on her? And now was He making his hair fall out because he never stopped having dirty thoughts? Did He do all that? Well forget Him, there were other gods to worship.

He climbed the stairs to the offices, passing no one else on the way; the generating station needed little more than a complement of thirty staff and technicians to keep it functioning, a small group of people who controlled the power used by millions. Being in charge of the energy used by so many was what had attracted him to the job in the first place. There were three ways of depriving people of their light and power in the area supervised by his particular station: one was to blow the whole plant up; two was to systematically shut down the generators and turbines, and cut the fuel supply; three was to turn off everything, apart from the furnaces, by the remote controls in the main switching room. He had no access to explosives, so blowing up the plant was out of the question. Shutting everything down and cutting the fuel supply manually would take too long and the other technicians would stop him before he'd managed one turbine. So the answer was in the control room. Cut the switches and everything would be black. Black as the night. A look of pleasure came into his eyes.

The main switching room was a large glass-fronted box projecting out into the generating hall, crammed with consoles containing dials, and a row of television screens that kept an eye on every part of the power station. The supervisors had been even more alert than usual over the past few weeks, for the danger of allowing a power failure in any area covered by their plant had been carefully explained to them. The danger within their own ranks, however, had been unforeseen.

The duty supervisor looked up in surprise as the man

entered the room and was about to ask where he'd been the last couple of days when the bullet from the Beretta punctured his forehead. The other supervisors were too stunned to react quickly and he carefully shot them, each bullet finding its mark with precisioned nonchalance. He was amazed at his own accuracy considering he had never handled a gun before, but not amazed at his own calmness. The stranger, the tall lady, had shown him how to use it when she had come to his basement flat earlier that day, but it was not she who had instilled the calmness in him. The Dark had done that.

He sniggered as the bodies of his colleagues tumbled to the floor and he took time to watch their twitching limbs for a few moments. His lips glistening, made wet by the tongue that constantly flicked across them, he stepped over the bodies towards the control panels. His hand was trembling as he reached for the first switch.

Bishop blinked his eyes rapidly. Was it his imagination or was it becoming even darker? He felt the tightness in his throat as he tried to swallow. It seemed as though there were four walls around him, transparent walls through which he could see the hazy figures of the others on the site. The walls grew more solid. A window to his left, curtains closed. Another window to his right, further down. Shadows moving like wispy smoke.

He resisted.

Edith's eyes were closed, muted sounds coming from her. Her head slowly sagged forward until her chin rested on her chest. The other two mediums were watching and Bishop saw their alarm. The one on the end, Schenkel, began to shiver. His eyelids fluttered and his pupils rose upwards into his head before his eyes closed completely. Enwright had not noticed what was happening to his colleague, for he was still watching Edith Metlock. Strong fingers curled around Bishop's arm and he snapped his head around to find Kulek's sightless eyes peering intently at him.

'Chris, can you see them again?' Kulek whispered. 'I can feel there is something malevolent here. Is it them, can you see those same faces again?'

Bishop was unable to answer. It was too sudden; no sooner had the lights been dimmed than the presence was with them. As though it had been waiting.

The room was solid and figures wafted before him, floating into focus then becoming vague again, blurred images. The room seemed smaller. Sounds buzzed in his ears, voices bursting forward then disappearing abruptly, replaced by others, as though a frequency dial was being aimlessly turned across the airwaves. He looked back at Edith and saw a black substance was seeping from her lips, dribbling down her chin and on to her chest. It could have been blood, yet he knew it wasn't. He reached out a hand to touch and there was nothing there, no black stickiness on his fingers, nothing on her chin. He withdrew his hand and the substance dribbled from her lips once more. Bishop looked up and the room seemed even smaller.

Schenkel fell from his chair and lay still on the rough boards and earth covering the cellar below. No one stepped forward to help him, for they had been warned not to interfere unless something drastic occurred. Enwright glanced at his companion but ignored him. Edith Metlock moaned aloud and something dark was expelled from her mouth like a billow of smoke. The voices inside Bishop's head were laughing now and he saw that the room was shrinking, the walls and ceiling reaching in towards him. He knew he would be crushed and he tried to rise from the chair. His body had become frozen solid and he could feel the frost heavy on his eyelids, sealing them tight. His hair prickled as each one became a brittle icicle. The walls were only feet away.

A cold hand touched his and somehow warmed it. Edith had reached out to him. His other hand was being held by someone else and, although his head was frozen tight, he knew it was Jacob Kulek who gripped him. The warmth returned to his body and he felt something falling away from him, something that had threatened to smother him. The walls and ceiling had vanished, but a swirling darkness filled his vision.

The sound came from Enwright, but it was not his voice, nor the voice of any living thing. It was a high squealing sound, a tortured wailing. The medium stood, his palms pressed against his temples, his head turning from side to side as though he were trying to shake something from it. His eyes looked wildly around until they came to rest on Bishop.

The after-image of those staring eyes stayed in Bishop's vision as the dim lights went out and everything succumbed to the crushing blackness.

27

The hands closed around Bishop's throat and began to tighten. He could only see a black shape before him, but he knew it was the medium, Enwright, who was trying to choke the life from him. He gripped the man's wrists and pulled at them, his chin automatically tucking itself downwards, neck muscles taut, to resist the increasing pressure. Even as he struggled, Bishop was aware of the confusion around him, the shouts, the running feet, the sudden small flares as matches or lighters were lit, then the long torch beams cutting out bright sections in the night.

A dizziness made the scene even more chaotic and he knew he would soon begin to lose his senses if he did not break the choking grip, but no matter how hard he pulled at the wrists, the pressure still increased. He did the only thing possible. Releasing his own hold, he grabbed the medium's clothing and pulled the man towards him, pushing his heels hard into the boards beneath them. His chair leaned back at a precarious angle, then both men went toppling over, Bishop increasing the momentum with an added thrust of his heels. They landed heavily, Enwright's head smashing on to the boards with a loud crack, his body immediately becoming limp. Bishop had curved his back and hunched his shoulders so the impact had little effect on him. He pushed the sprawled body away and sat up, looking quickly around, then closing his eyes for a few seconds to help them adjust to the darkness more easily.

'Get those bloody searchlights on!' he heard someone shout and almost immediately a broad expanse of light lit up half the site.

'The other searchlight!' cried the same voice and Bishop could now see it was the army major who was shouting the commands. 'Get it bloodywell on!'

But something was happening at the vehicle on which the second searchlight was mounted. Bishop could just make out struggling figures and he flinched when a shot rang out. Other soldiers began to run towards the vehicle, their 7.62 mm self-loading rifles held across their chests, ready for use.

More movement before him caught his eye and he saw Edith Metlock was tossing her head from side to side, her hands waving in the air as though warding something off. The other medium, Schenkel, was now on his knees, body bent forward and hands covering his face.

'Chris, help me!'

Jessica was trying to pull a man away from her father, a man who wore the dark blue uniform of a policeman. The realization struck Bishop in a flash of new dread: the Dark had penetrated the minds of some of those meant to protect them. He staggered to his feet and ran towards Jessica, but another figure reached them first. The policeman was behind Kulek and was dragging him backwards, an arm locked around his throat, Jessica in front of both men trying to wrench the arm away. The other man came up behind the policeman and dug rigid thumbs into the flesh points just under the uniformed man's jawline, digging them in deeply with a screwing motion. The policeman screamed and was forced to release Kulek; as he turned, the second man brought the heel of his hand sharply up beneath the policeman's nose, snapping his head backwards. A swift chop at the exposed windpipe sent the policeman reeling to the ground where he lay squirming and gasping for breath.

By then, Bishop had reached them and he recognized the man who had saved Kulek as Peck's DI, Roper.

'Bleedin' wollies,' Roper said, barely giving the injured policeman a second glance.

Just then, Peck himself emerged from the general confusion. 'Are you okay, sir?' he asked, a hand reaching out to steady Jacob Kulek.

The blind man drew in deep breaths as Jessica held on to him. 'I'm ... I'm learning how to resist such attacks,' he managed to say and Peck allowed a brief flicker of amusement to cross his face.

'We'd better get you out of here,' he said. 'It looks as if the power supply to half of London has been switched off. Anything can happen now.' He turned to Bishop. 'You all right? I saw that bastard ready to attack you just before the lights blew. Sorry I couldn't get to you in time.'

'I'm okay. How could the power fail?'

Peck shrugged. 'Overload, maybe.'

'Or sabotage.'

'For the moment, it doesn't matter. The main thing is to get you all somewhere safe.'

'Edith. Where is Edith?' Kulek was clutching at Jessica, frustrated by his own blindness.

'She's still in her chair, Father. She's in a trance state. I think she's trying to break free of it.'

'Quickly, take me to her before it's too late.'

'I think we ought to get away from here, sir,' Peck interjected.

'Edith first,' Kulek said firmly. 'We must take her with us.'

Jessica led him over to the agitated medium and Roper looked uneasily towards his superior.

'I don't like this, guv,' he said. 'We don't stand a chance if that searchlight fails.'

'Get over to the cars, Frank. I want all their lights on right away. Where's the bloody Commissioner? And the army major – he should have had things organized by now.'

But more gunfire told him that organization under those circumstances would prove difficult, and when the shattering of glass preceded the extinction of the remaining light, leaving the site filled only with individual torch beams, they knew it would prove virtually impossible.

'The cars, Frank, quick. Get those lights on.' Someone bumped into Peck and he roughly pushed the figure away. He reached inside his jacket for the Smith and Wesson holstered discreetly at his hip and drew it.

'Bishop! Where are you?'

'Right here.' He had been following Kulek and Jessica before the remaining light had blown and now stood midway between them and Peck.

The detective cursed the lack of moonlight. What a bloody silly night to choose! 'Can you reach Kulek?' He had to shout to make himself heard over the general clamour.

'Yes, they're not far . . . Jesus!'

Peck made his way towards the dark shape a few feet away when he, too, felt the coldness stab inside him. It blanked out his thoughts for a few moments, a numbing iciness that seemed to fill every secret crevice of his mind. He stumbled against someone.

'Bishop? What is it? Can you feel it, too?'

'Don't give in to it, Peck. Force it out!'

'What is it?' Peck was shouting, his free hand against his eyes and forehead, the gun held away from him.

'It's the Dark. It's probing your mind. You can resist, Peck, but you've got to want to.' Bishop's mind was clearing fast after the first paralysing assault on it and he suddenly understood that the Dark could only claim those who allowed themselves to be claimed. The Dark had to be accepted before it could take, like the mythical vampire who could not cross a threshold unless invited.

He grabbed Peck and shook him. 'Fight it!' he yelled. 'It can't touch you if you fight it!'

Bishop lost his grip as Peck slid to the ground. 'Get them . . . get them out of here!' he heard the detective say.

Bishop wasted no more time: only Peck could save himself now. More shots were ringing out and the brief gunflashes lit the scene into frozen actions. The darkness around them was heavy, cloying, but his eyes were slowly adapting to it and he was able to make out shapes more clearly. He moved towards Jessica and her father, finding them crouched beside Edith Metlock, who still writhed in her chair.

'Jessica,' he said, kneeling next to her, 'we've got to leave here. It's too dangerous to stay.'

'They're torturing her, Chris. She can't bring herself out of the trance.'

Kulek was clutching the medium's shoulders. He softly called her name over and over again. Her body heaved as she began to retch, the sound dry and agonized until she slid from the chair and vomit spurted from her mouth in an arched stream. Bishop felt warm, sticky particles spatter his face and a foul stench came to his nostrils. He brushed the speckles away with the sleeve of his jacket, then reached down for the medium and pulled her into a sitting position. Lights began to spring into life from the roadway and two sets swung their beams on to the site as drivers manoeuvred their cars. Edith's eyes were wide and staring and, although she still shook, the wild writhing had stopped.

Bishop stood and dragged her up with him. She offered no resistance and he was relieved she could stand albeit only with his support. 'Jacob, hold on to Jessica. We're getting out now.'

'We made a mistake. We did not realize the madness we were dealing with, the evil that is around us.'

'You're telling me. Now come on, let's go!' There was an anger in Bishop that he did not understand, but was glad to have; it somehow threw strength into him.

He half-carried, half-dragged Edith across the site, making for the road where the lights were, urging Jessica and her father to keep close to him. The soldier who stood in his way took his time in raising the rifle and aiming it at Bishop's head.

All Bishop could see was the black silhouette against the glare from the nearest car, but he knew the soldier's intention. He started at the shot that rang out and watched the soldier's body slowly crumple.

'You going to stand there all night?' said Peck, emerging from the shadows to one side of the bright twin beams. Bishop almost cried out with relief; he never thought Peck would have been such a welcome sight. He tightened his hold on the woman, who still stared blankly ahead, and moved forward, Peck joining him and helping to support her weight.

'I thought it had me back there,' Peck said loudly. 'Couldn't move, like being doped up for an operation but not as pleasant. Scared the life out of me. Keep up with us, Miss Kulek, we'll soon be out of this!'

The site was further lit by the first searchlight coming back into action again and, as Bishop swung his head to survey the scene, he saw there were many individual struggles taking place, soldier against soldier, policeman against policeman, and a mixture of both. There were others on the site now, men and women who had not been there before, and these people cowered under the naked glare, shielding their eyes with raised arms. Where they had come from, he could not even guess, but it was evident that they were victims of the Dark. Bodies of policemen or soldiers whom they had attacked lay at their feet. He couldn't be sure, but one of these recumbent figures looked like the Police Commissioner himself.

They stumbled over the rubble around the edges of the site and crossed the small concreted area that had once been Beechwood's car space. To Bishop it seemed like only yesterday that he had crossed that area for the first time, yet so much had happened since, it could well have been years ago.

Willow Road and the Beechwood ruin were a bubble of light in that broad section of the city, the glow tinging the night sky so that it could be seen for miles around. People were stirring, looking out from their windows at the bright glow, wondering why it was lit when their streets were in total darkness. Others left their homes, or emerged from sewers and other dark places to make their way towards the light, already knowing what they would find there.

Bishop squinted his eyes against the headlights, the shouts, the screams, the crackle of gunfire spurring him on. They reached the first car and almost fell against the bonnet in their haste.

'Over here, guv,' came a familiar voice.

Policemen, uniformed as well as those in plain clothes, were all around, and Peck led the small party through them towards Roper who was standing by another car.

'Bloody murder going on back there,' the Detective Inspector said. 'I didn't think you'd make it.'

'Yes, me too,' Peck replied. 'Have you been on to HQ?'

'Yeah, they're sending all available help. They've got their own problems, though; trouble's breaking out all over again.'

Peck called a uniformed sergeant over. 'I want one more car swung round to point its lights into the site. Back as many of the others as possible up against one another to give a circle of light around us. Let's keep any marauding maniacs away, or at least see them before they get too close.'

They ducked instinctively when a bottle shattered into the road near them. They tried to see who had thrown the missile, but were dazzled by the other car lights parked further down. Another bottle came sailing through the air and this one broke against the shoulder of a plain-clothes policeman. The man went down on one knee, then rose again, apparently not badly hurt. Shadowy figures flitted momentarily through the beams of light before disappearing into the surrounding darkness once more. Peck knew he would have to get his men organized quickly – their fear was becoming greater because of their confusion.

'Bishop, I want you and these people out of the area. My driver, Simpson, will get you over to the other side of the river.'

Bishop thought Kulek might offer some resistance to Peck's directions, but when he turned to the blind man he saw only a look of utter defeat on his face.

'Jacob?'

'It's become too strong, I did not realize.' The words were spoken to no one in particular; it was as if Kulek had retreated within himself.

'We must leave, Father. We can't do any good here,' Jessica urged him.

Peck was already opening the doors of the Granada. 'In you get,' he ordered crisply. 'Kulek and the two women in the back, you in the front, Bishop. Frank, grab a patrol car and go with them. Take a couple of wollies.'

Roper dashed off to commandeer a white Rover nearby, its driver immediately gunning the engine, relieved to be on the move. The car screeched over to the Granada as Peck slammed the door after Kulek and the two women. Other police cars were positioning themselves in the road, tyres screeching as they turned their vehicles so their headlight beams shone outwards. There were several muffled thuds as bodies of people lurking in the darker areas were struck by the fast-moving vehicles. Peck was surprised at just how many people were advancing on them, their forms frozen in the swinging lights reminding him of paralysed foxes caught on country roads at night. Whether or not they were all victims or some had merely come to investigate the lights and commotion, there was no way of knowing; there was no choice but to treat everyone as a potential enemy. He leaned into the Granada's passenger window and spoke across Bishop to his driver.

'Back to HQ, and don't stop for anything. Just follow the patrol car.'

Bishop called after Peck as the detective made his way towards the Rover. 'What will you do?'

Peck turned and said, 'We'll get the Commissioner and the civilians out of here, then head back over the river. The Army can sort themselves out!'

He turned and shouted instructions at the driver of the patrol car before Bishop could tell him he thought he had seen the Police Commissioner either dead or unconscious on the ground. Peck banged his hand down hard on the Rover's roof and the car shot forward. Bishop was thrown back into his seat as the Granada lurched after it. They had only travelled a hundred yards when the red brakelights of the car ahead blinked on and both cars screeched to a halt. Bishop poked his head out the passenger window and a wave of despair swept over him.

The end of the road was completely blocked by crowds of people. They moved forward, some running, others walking slowly as if by automation. He could see that many were in a bad state of deterioration, while others were alert, their actions quicker, the light not seeming to bother them as much. There was no way of knowing just how many were out there, but it seemed like hundreds, an unbroken mass of advancing bodies. As they drew nearer, he saw that many carried weapons ranging from iron bars to knives and milk bottles. One of the running men held what looked like a shotgun.

Jessica, directly behind Bishop, was leaning forward in her seat, unable to see clearly. 'What is it, Chris?'

He had no time to reply, for the driver in the car ahead had decided what to do: the Rover accelerated towards the mob and the Granada followed. If the policeman in the first car expected the crowd to jump aside and leave a path clear for him, he was mistaken: they stood their ground and the Rover plunged into them.

Jessica screamed when she saw the bodies tossed into the air, the headlights of the Granada illuminating the scene in shocking relief. Their car skidded as the driver turned the steering-wheel to avoid crashing into the back of the now stationary Rover; instead, the Granada's side smashed into the lead vehicle, throwing the patrol car's occupants forward and shaking Bishop and the others badly.

Roper's head appeared out of the white car's rear passenger window and he waved his arm in a forward motion at them. His own driver was quickly recovering from the shock of running down so many people and was starting his stalled engine once more when a man appeared near the bonnet of the Rover. He carried a shotgun and he aimed it at the windscreen.

Bishop heard the blast and saw the glass shatter leaving an irregular opaque fringe of glittering silver around the edge of the black hole it had created. Both policemen in the front of the patrol car jerked backwards, then their bodies slipped from view. Roper was already pushing his door open when eager hands grabbed at him. He raised his gun, but the weapon was forced aside as he was mobbed.

'We've got to help him!' Bishop cried as he reached for the door-handle on his side.

The driver grabbed him and pulled him back. 'No way. My orders were to get you lot out of here and that's what I'm going to do.'

'We can't just leave him!'

'We'd have no chance out there – there's too many!'

Even as he spoke, their own car was being surrounded, fists and makeshift weapons pounding on the roof. Hands reached in and tore at Bishop's arms and face; the driver had wisely kept his window closed throughout. Bishop pulled himself away from the grasping hands and struck out at them, feeling no pity for these people and what they had become, just a loathing fear. Metal scraped against metal as the Granada lunged forward once more, friction between the two cars sending a shower of sparks into the air.

Jessica watched with horror as one man refused to let go of the door on Bishop's side and was dragged along with the vehicle as it gathered speed. Slowly and deliberately, Bishop prised the man's fingers away from the door-frame until the hands fell away; Jessica felt the slight but sickening bump as the car ran over the man's trapped ankles.

Simpson headed towards the pavement which seemed less congested than the road itself. A woman leapt on to the bonnet and managed to cling there, staring with manic eyes through the windscreen before the car mounted the kerb and she was tossed off. Bishop looked back, but could see nothing of Roper, just a mass of black shapes swarming over the Rover. Another blast, then a great roar as the patrol car's tank exploded; someone – probably the same man who had shot the driver and his partner – had deliberately fired into the Rover's bodywork. A great ball of flames rose into the air, killing those too close, burning others. Most of the road was lit up by the explosion, but the shadows quickly regained ground, beaten back only by the red glow from the ensuing fire.

The Granada bounced back on to the road, the main body of the crowd having been skirted, and sped on, heading for the T-junction at the end of Willow Road. The headlights caught the figure of a man as he ran forward and hurled a milk bottle at the windscreen. Both Bishop and the driver raised their arms to protect their faces as their view became a web of fractured glass. Barely slowing, the driver punched a hole through the windscreen and shouted to Bishop, 'Take my gun – smash out the glass.'

He had flipped back his jacket and Bishop could just make out the gun butt protruding from the holster at the driver's waist. The policeman loosened the restraining grip, his attention still firmly directed through the jagged hole he had created. Bishop pulled out the gun and used it to smash a larger hole in the glass. The wind rushed through the gap, but they hardly noticed it. The car tore into the street at the end of Willow Road, the tyres flattening out and desperately biting into the road's surface for grip. Bishop was thrown against the passenger door and he grabbed the frame to hold himself there until the car had regained stability. He had one last look at Willow Road through the windows opposite him before they had turned the corner completely and houses blocked his view. Lights, flames and milling people were all he had seen. Now there was blackness around them, probed only by their own headlights.

Bishop became conscious of the cold steel he held. He proffered the weapon towards the driver. 'Here's your gun.'

The policeman's eyes were screwed into narrow slits against the wind rushing at his face and he did not take them from the road ahead. 'You keep it, I've got to concentrate on driving. Don't hesitate to use it if necessary.'

Bishop was about to protest, but thought better of it. The man was right: he could hardly protect them and drive at the same time. It was fortunate that all senior policemen had been issued with guns – the whole force would have been armed if there had been enough weapons to go round – for the number of victims claimed by the Dark was growing day by day. Or, more appropriately, night by night.

He wound up his side window, then turned to the three passengers in the back. 'Are you okay?' he asked above the noise of the engine and the wind rushing through the interior. Their shapes were barely discernible in the darkness. Jessica's face came close to his.

'I think they're both in a state of shock, Chris.'

'No, no, I'm all right.' It was Kulek's voice. 'It was just so . . . so . . . overwhelming. The power has become so great.'

Bishop sensed the blind man's utter weariness and shared in his feeling of defeat. How did you combat something so intangible, something that had no material form, no physical nucleus? How did you destroy energy from the mind? The living people who gave themselves up to the Dark could be controlled, killed, but the killing itself allowed that energy to become stronger.

A wild skid as the driver tried to avoid a group of people in the centre of the road caused Bishop to clutch at the back of his seat. The car swerved into a narrow sidestreet, leaving the group calling after them; they may or may not have been victims, but the driver had no inclination to stop and find out. Dull glows were coming from the windows of many houses they passed as though the occupants were lighting fires or candles to create a natural light. They saw that other people were leaving their homes, leading or carrying children, and jumping into their cars, switching their headlights on.

'Looks like we're not the only ones heading for the bright lights,' the driver remarked as he swerved around a car that was just pulling out ahead of them.

There were more headlights in the distance as people followed the example of neighbours and hurried out to their own cars, not understanding what was happening but knowing enough to realize the darkness around them was dangerous.

'It's going to be bloody chaos soon!' Simpson shouted. 'They'll all be trying to get to the other side of the river!'

'Who can blame them?' Bishop replied.

Their car was forced to stop when two cars on opposite sides of the road swung out and collided. Their speed had not allowed any serious damage, but the cries of anguish and panic could be plainly heard. Another car screeched to a halt behind the Granada.

'The silly bastards have blocked the road.' The policeman

looked behind, hoping to reverse away from the situation. Yet another vehicle had pulled up behind the car blocking their exit and horns began to bellow their annoyance.

The police driver looked swiftly from left to right, searching for a way out. 'Hold on tight!' he yelled, then jammed the gearstick into reverse and struck down hard on the accelerator pedal, braking almost immediately after. The Granada shot back a few feet, crunching into the car behind and pushing it back, allowing the policeman valuable room ahead to manoeuvre. He spun the wheel round and once more mounted the kerb. Bishop sank back into his seat, his heels pressing involuntarily into the flooring as though to brake, sure there was no way the Granada could pass between the lamp-post and the low garden wall on their left. They got through only because the car itself widened the gap considerably by taking much of the garden wall with it. The tearing of metal and crumbling brickwork on the passenger side made Bishop lean towards the driver, expecting his side of the car to rip free at any moment. The policeman found his way back on to the roadway, the two crashed cars successfully passed.

'Always wanted to do that,' he said, grinning despite the tension.

'Sunday drivers,' Bishop commented, relieved to still be in one piece.

'There's a main road ahead. We should be able to make better progress.'

The driver's optimism, however, was misguided, for as they tore into the wide road, they saw that the intersection ahead which was normally controlled by traffic lights was jammed solid with vehicles.

'The sideroad – there!' Bishop pointed at the narrow turning to their left and the driver directed the car into it without hesitation. At the far end they could see a building blazing, figures standing in the road watching.

'Right!' Bishop shouted, but the driver had already seen the turning and was reducing speed. The car struck something that made a dull thud against the metalwork; neither of the two men in the front had seen whether it was a man, woman or stray animal. The driver accelerated once more, saying nothing.

The sidestreet ran into another main road and the Granada came to an abrupt halt halfway across it. To their right was the jammed intersection they had just avoided and now they could see people being dragged from the cars and attacked. Again, there was no way of knowing whether or not the attackers were Dark victims or merely angry motorists frustrated at not being able to escape the lightless area of the city. As they watched, a man, lit by the headlights, leapt on to the roof of his car while hands reached up and clawed at him, trying to drag him down. His resistance came to an abrupt halt when his legs were swept from beneath him by a stick or iron bar of some kind; he fell on to his back, then slid from the roof, fists pummelling him as he went down. Screams directed their attention to another spot in the jumble of machines: a woman was being stretched across a car bonnet, her clothes ripped from her body, arms and legs pinned down by eager hands. The rush of others towards her obscured what followed, but as the screams became more shrill, there was little doubt as to what was happening to her.

Bishop's hand tightened on the Smith and Wesson as Jessica said, 'We've got to help her, Chris, please, stop them!'

He looked towards the policeman who shook his head. 'Sorry,' Simpson said, 'we'd have no chance. There's too many.'

Bishop knew the man was right, but he was unable to sit there and let the atrocity happen. The driver sensed his mood and quickly stabbed down at the accelerator pedal. He swung the car around in a tight quarter-circle, heading away from the intersection. Anger burst from Bishop and for a brief second he considered levelling the gun at the policeman's head.

Then Edith Metlock began to laugh.

He swivelled around to look at her, the gun poised, barrel angled towards the car's roof. Kulek and Jessica had recoiled away from the medium and were staring at the dark form sitting opposite them.

The laughter did not belong to her. It was deep, nasty, a man's heavy laughter.

The driver kept his foot down, knowing it could be fatal to stop in that blacked-out area, but he experienced the same dread as the others: the coldness seeping through him, the feeling of fluttering pressure just below the back of his neck, the loosening of sphincter muscles. The laughter was unnatural.

'Edith!' Kulek said sharply, the weariness now gone from his voice. 'Edith, can you hear me?'

Oncoming cars flashed by, their lights briefly casting beams into the interior of the Granada, the drivers unaware that the way ahead would be blocked by the jam at the intersection. Edith's face was momentarily illuminated as each fleeing vehicle swept by and they could see her eyes were full of a malice that was alien to the woman herself. Her mouth was open, but her lips did not curve upwards into a smile; the laughter rattled from somewhere deep in her throat.

Kulek blindly reached out towards her, his searching hand finding her immobile face. The wind blew in through the broken windscreen and howled around the interior of the car. Still she laughed.

'Force him from you, Edith!' Kulek shouted above the noise of the wind and the car's engine. 'He cannot take you unless you allow him to!'

But the laughter had become that of many now. And the wind had stopped.

It was as though they were in a vacuum; even the noise from the engine could not be heard. Only the hollow laughter of things that were dead filled their heads, mocking them and enjoying their fear.

The driver nervously glanced back over his shoulder, unsure of what was happening, the sounds making him hunch his body over the steering-wheel as if he were warding off something physical. 'For Christ's sake, make her stop! Hit her, do something!'

Kulek began to talk to her again, his voice low and soothing; the others could not hear him, but each time the interior was lit up, Bishop could see the blind man's lips moving, and he knew Kulek was urging the medium to rid herself of the demons using her body.

'Oh, no!' It was the driver again.

Bishop turned and saw the policeman was staring at the road ahead; he was heaved towards the smashed windscreen as the brakes were slammed on. The car skidded to a halt and rocked backwards and forwards on its suspension; the three passengers in the rear were thrown against the backs of the front seats.

Because of the remaining shattered glass in the windscreen, Bishop could not see what had made the driver stop. He quickly leaned over towards the steering-wheel and peered through the gaping hole in the glass. He drew in a sharp breath.

A line of vehicles stretched across the road, those at each end jammed into shop doorways so there was no possible gap for other cars to break through. The blockage had been deliberately set up to prevent the main road being used as a means of escape to the other side of the river. They saw the wrecks of other cars that had reached that point before them, their bonnets buckled and bent because the drivers had not braked in time. Faces peered over the top of cars at the Granada, then figures leapt over the barrier and appeared from doorways on either side of the road, streaming towards them. Their cries snapped the policeman into action, but not before the first man had leapt on to the car bonnet and was curling his fingers around the jagged windscreen glass for grip. Another joined in, this one a woman, her face black with dirt and her body emaciated.

The door on Bishop's side was pulled open just as the car shot backwards away from the blockade, swinging wide with the added momentum. Bishop felt Jessica's hands on his shoulder as he nearly tumbled out on to the road. A man clung to the door, his legs stretched out behind him as he was dragged along. The woman on the bonnet was thrown off and landed in the road, her piercing scream instantly cut off as her skull cracked against the hard surface. The first man still miraculously clung to the broken window and was hauling himself forward against the gravitational pull, his free hand reaching in and clutching the steering-wheel.

'Shoot him, Bishop!' the policeman cried and, almost in a reflex action, Bishop raised the weapon and pointed it at the gaping hole in the windscreen. Instead of squeezing the trigger, he brought the gun down hard on the man's knuckles. The hand opened and glass snapped from the windscreen as the man flew away from them.

The Granada gathered speed, the driver silently praying that no other vehicle would suddenly appear behind them. Without warning he jumped on the footbrake and spun the wheel into full lock. The car did a hundred and eighty degree turn, its nose ending up pointed in the direction from which they had come. The passenger door swung shut, sending the man clinging to it skidding and bouncing across the road.

Once again the accelerator pedal was pressed and the car leapt forward. Bishop was too breathless to make any comment on the driver's skill; he checked behind to see if the others were still in one piece, but even before he could ascertain whether or not they were, the car was screeching around to their right, the driver knowing it was useless to go back the way they had come. When Bishop had righted himself again he saw they were speeding along a street that had high-rise buildings on one side, a row of shops on the other.

Somehow, he knew there was something ominous about the headlights that swung into view ahead of them.

Simpson raised an arm to shield his eyes from the glare. 'Silly bastard – he's on full beam.' He flashed his own headlights to warn the other driver, but the advancing beams were not dipped in acknowledgement. Their faces were brilliantly lit by the oncoming lights and Bishop realized the vehicle coming towards them had to be a lorry or a truck of some kind – its lights were too high above the ground for it to be a car. The policeman steered over to his right, for the other vehicle was on the wrong side of the road. The other driver matched his direction, pulling to his left.

'Jesus, he's trying to hit us!' the policeman whispered, but the wind was back in the car and no one heard his words. The glare became even more harsh, the dazzle painful. It filled their vision, drawing closer like a fiery comet dashing across a black void. Bishop could hear Jessica screaming, the policeman shouting. The laughter of the dead.

He closed his eyes and pushed himself back against his seat, bracing himself for the impact.

28

For Bishop, there was no sense to the next few moments, just the shock of screaming noise and whirling lights. The police driver had spun his steering-wheel to the left in an effort to thwart the oncoming vehicle, but the other driver had altered his direction just enough to clip the Granada's right wing, sending the car into a screeching spin, the occupants violently jarred by the blow. The policeman was powerless to control the skid and the car turned completely around almost in its own space, before careering across the forecourt of a block of flats to their left. Most of the glass in the windscreen had been shaken loose and Bishop opened his eyes in time to see the entrance to the high-rise building tearing towards them; he jammed his feet hard into the footwell in front of the passenger seat and pushed both hands against the dashboard to prevent himself going through the windscreen when the car hit concrete.

Even though the driver had the brake pedal fully pressed and was turning the wheel to avoid hitting the building head on, the impact, when it came, was tremendous. The bonnet buckled upwards as it met the corner of the entrance, the radiator cut in half and each segment pushed back into the engine in a shower of scalding steam. Bishop was thrown forward, but was saved from going through the windscreen by the position he had taken up moments before; his chest hit the dashboard and he was thrown back into his seat. The driver clung to the steering-wheel which collapsed against his weight and he found himself out of the windscreen, his face against the risen metal of the bonnet, unaware of the body that slammed past him. Edith Metlock was saved from flying over the front seats because she had been knocked to the floor when the lorry had struck the wing on her side; Jessica had already been clinging to the back of Bishop's seat when they had first been hit and her grip had tightened so that when they plunged into the building she was able to prevent herself from being propelled forward. Jacob Kulek was less fortunate.

The total silence that followed did more to rouse Bishop than any voices or body-shaking hands could have; the screams, the laughter, the screeching tyres, had all culmi- nated in the strident cry of torn and crushed metal, and now the contrasting quietness seemed to prod him physically.

He pushed himself upright, his movements slow and delib- erate, waiting for sudden pain to tell him he was injured. None came, but a general numbness gave a hint of the pain to come from the bruising he had received. He heard a whimper from behind.

'Jessica?' He twisted his body to see. Somehow the head- light on the passenger side had remained undamaged, although its twin was completely shattered, and just enough light was reflected back from the cavern of the building's entrance to enable him to make out shapes in the car's interior. 'Jessica, are you hurt?'

He half-knelt on his seat to reach her. Her face came up from the top of his seat where it lay, her eyes still closed, beginning to open. She whimpered again and shook her head slightly as if to clear it. Her eyes opened fully and she stared blankly at him.

Movement on the driver's side caught Bishop's attention; the policeman was cautiously drawing himself back from the glassless windscreen into the car. He groaned aloud as he slumped back into his seat. There was blood on his forehead and Bishop could see tiny sparkles of imbedded glass. The policeman gingerly rubbed his chest then drew in a sharp breath when his probing fingers reached his ribs.

He groaned. 'Cracked one, I think,' he said turning to Bishop. 'Maybe just bruised. You okay?'

Before he could reply, Edith Metlock's head and shoulders came into view. 'Where are we? What's happened?' she asked.

Bishop and the policeman exchanged quick glances. 'It's all right, Edith. We've had an accident,' said Bishop gently, aware of the obviousness of his statement.

'Come on,' Simpson said abruptly. 'We'd better get out of here. We're sitting ducks. Did you lose the gun?'

Bishop felt around the floor of the passenger footwell and his fingers touched cold metal. 'Got it.'

'There's a torch in the glove compartment – get that, too.' He pushed open his door, grunting with the effort.

Bishop took the torch and stepped from his side of the car knowing they were lucky not to have been seriously injured: the damage to the front of the Granada was appalling.

'Father!' Jessica's scream sent Bishop rushing to open her door. She tumbled out and pushed past him, running towards the wrecked part of the car. He realized what must have happened when he saw only Edith Metlock in the back passenger seat: Jacob Kulek had been hurled through the windscreen.

He found Jessica kneeling beside the still body of her father. Slipping the gun into his jacket pocket, he knelt and shone the torch on to Kulek's face. The blind man had the look of death on him, his eyes narrow slits through which only the whites showed, his mouth partially opened, a faint, empty smile on his lips. Bishop frowned, for he could see no outward physical signs of injury. He probed the skin beneath Kulek's jawline with two rigid fingers and was surprised to find the pulse fluttering weakly.

'He's alive,' he told Jessica and her sobs subsided. She slipped her arm beneath her father's head, raising him slightly from the paving. The blood from his skull began to flow freely.

Bishop became aware that the driver and Edith had joined them.

'Dead?' the policeman asked brutally.

He shook his head. 'Unconscious. His skull may have been fractured.' Bishop took a handkerchief from his pocket and helped Jessica place it against the wound; the cloth immediately became a soggy, red mess. But Kulek moved and a murmuring came from his parted lips.

Jessica called his name, touching his cheek with her free hand and, for a moment, his eyelids flickered as though he were going to open them.

The policeman crouched low and said urgently, 'We've got to get going, Bishop, it's too dangerous to stay here.'

Bishop stood, passing the torch over to Edith who had replaced him by Kulek's side. Although still bewildered by her surroundings, she had the presence of mind to loosen the blind man's tie and shirt collar.

'We shouldn't move him,' Bishop said to the policeman in soft tones so Jessica could not hear. 'We don't know how badly he's hurt. Fortunately, most of the glass was out of the windscreen, but he must have gone through the opening with some force. Either the top of the car or the concrete pavement must have . . .'

The policeman cut in. 'We've got no choice – we'll have to

carry him. We'll need to find some other transport to get us away from here.'

'There are plenty of parked cars around, but how can you get one started?'

'That's no problem – it's just a matter of jumping the wires. I'm going . . .'

This time it was the policeman who was interrupted as the revving of an engine came to their ears. They turned and looked back in the direction from which they had come. Probing headlights lit up the street throwing elongated shadows from the many figures making towards the wreck.

'They're coming for us,' Bishop said quietly.

The sound of the lorry's engine grew to a roar as it began to gather speed, several of the walking people silently disappearing beneath its wheels as if they were unaware of the vehicle's presence, even when they were crushed. Bishop and the policeman guessed the driver's intention.

'Get back into the building!' the policeman ordered the two kneeling women. Jessica opened her mouth to protest, but quickly saw what was happening. Bishop and the driver reached down for the injured man, pushing the two women towards the swing doors just beyond the lifts in the entrance hall. They roughly pulled Kulek towards the doors, a hand each beneath his shoulders, allowing the rest of his body to drag along the floor.

The whole of the entrance became bright as the lorry drew nearer, the driver beginning to angle his vehicle towards the block of flats and the wreck in its forecourt. Jessica and Edith pushed at the yellow swingdoors; they were stiff and opened only slightly. The women used their shoulders and swung the doors wide, holding them open for the two men to drag Kulek through.

'Use the gun!' the policeman shouted. 'Try and get the bastard before he reaches us!' Bishop let go of the injured man and ran back to the entrance, drawing the Smith and Wesson from his pocket. The lights were blinding once more and he kept his eyes narrowed against the glare. With both hands curled around the butt of the gun he took careful aim, amazed at his own coolness, knowing he had to somehow divert the lorry – if it hit the entrance square on, the impetus would easily carry much of the bodywork straight through to the rear stairwell. He aimed the gun at a point just above and slightly to the right of one circle of light, to where he hoped the driver would be. The vehicle was no more than seventy yards away, going into a sharp turn that would bring it head on across the forecourt towards the entrance. Fifty yards away. Bishop squeezed the trigger.

Nothing happened. Forty yards.

He resisted the urge to run and fumbled at the safety catch. Thirty yards.

Squeeze. Recoil. Three times.

One of the headlights went out. Glass shattered. The lorry came on. Bishop ran.

He threw himself at the swingdoors that Jessica and the medium held open and heard the explosion of metal against concrete behind, his fully stretched body sliding on the tiled flooring and tipping over the few steps leading down to the building's rear exit. The two women fell away from the released doors which were slowly closing, covering their faces with their hands, more against the horrendous tearing noise than the flying wreckage. As Bishop rolled on to his back, the building itself seemed to jolt and he saw something bulky shoot from the cabin of the lorry and scrape itself along one wall of the entrance, leaving a large smear of red as it went. It smashed against the swingdoors, an arm becoming trapped between them, preventing them from closing completely. Bishop just had time to see the driver's bloody face peering at them through the reinforced glass, his neck propped up at an impossible angle, before flames billowed out and filled the entrance in a great, leaping ball of fire.

He drew his knees up and covered his head as a blast of hot air swept through the partially open doors; for a moment he thought he was alight, but the searing feeling quickly passed as the air was funnelled up the stairwell. Cautiously raising his head once more, he looked over the top of the three stairs he had fallen down and saw the flames had retreated, but the burning cabin of the lorry completely blocked the entrance. The hallway was filled with chunks of twisted metal, much of it smouldering and black, and the vehicle had struck the entrance at an angle, totally destroying the crashed Granada. Edith Metlock had fallen to one side of the swingdoors and had been protected by the solid wall facing the stairway leading to the upper floors. The police driver was half-sitting against the exit doors, the body of Kulek sprawled beside him.

Bishop put the gun back into his pocket and crouched beside Jessica whose legs were stretched out on the lower two steps. He helped her into a sitting position and when she saw the burning lorry in the entrance, she clung to him. His fingers sank into the soft hair at the back of her neck and he held her to him, her small, trembling body feeling vulnerable to his touch.

She pulled her head away from him and looked quickly around. She found her father and tore herself away. Kulek's eyes were fully open now and confusion was clear on his face, which was bathed in a flickering warm glow from the fire. His mouth opened and closed as if he were trying to speak, but no words came.

Bishop rose to his feet and pushed at the exit doors. They were locked.

The policeman looked up at him. 'Don't worry about them – we might be better off staying inside this building.'

'But the fire.'

'It won't spread. They built these blocks of flats to contain any fires. Let's get upstairs and find a phone – at least they shouldn't be affected by the power cut. We'll get some help sent to us.' He eased himself into a standing position, keeping his grip on the blind man. 'Right, let's get him up.'

Together, they managed to get Kulek on his feet. 'Jacob, can you hear me?' said Bishop.

Kulek slowly nodded, a hand trying to reach behind his head.

'It's all right. You've had a bad knock. We're going to try and get into a flat upstairs and find some help.'

The old man nodded, then managed to say his daughter's name.

'I'm here, Father.' She had found another handkerchief or a piece of cloth from somewhere and was holding it against the wound on Kulek's head. Fortunately, the blood was not flowing as badly as before.

Bishop put his shoulder beneath Kulek's arm, grasping the wrist around his neck, his other arm around the blind man's waist. 'Can you walk?'

Kulek took a tentative step forward, Bishop holding him tightly. The policeman held his other arm, supporting him, and between them they managed to get the blind man up the first three steps. Edith came forward from the corner she had been crouching in.

'Lead the way,' Bishop told her. 'Upstairs to the first floor.'

They half-carried, half-dragged the weak form of Kulek up the stairs, going fast, thankful that the lorry was partially blocking the entrance to the flats, the flames preventing anyone from passing through any gaps. Neither Bishop nor the policeman had forgotten the approaching figures.

The fire from below lapped over the balcony of the first floor, so they decided to continue upwards to the second. Edith led the way down the short hallway to the open landing, a four-foot-high balcony running in either direction along the length of the building. The block of flats seemed comparatively small against normal high-rise buildings. There were only three apartments to each floor and as yet they did not know how many floors there were, but Bishop guessed there were probably nine or ten. There were two flats on the landing to the left of the short hallway, one to the right. The policeman helped Bishop prop Kulek against the balcony, then hurried along to the single flat on their right. While he banged on the door, Bishop looked down into the forecourt and street below.

Smoke rising from the burning wreck stung his eyes and he quickly drew back, but not before he had seen the people standing just beyond the ring of light thrown by the flames. Their faces were turned upwards as though watching him.

'Police. Come on, open up in there!' the driver was calling through the door's letterbox.

Bishop left Jessica steadying her father with Edith helping her, and hurried over to the irate policeman.

'There's someone in there,' he said, turning to Bishop, 'but they're too scared to open the bloody door.'

'Have they said anything?'

'No, but I can hear them moving around.' He put his face to the letterbox again. 'Look, it's the police – we're not going to hurt you.' He rattled the flap when no reply came.

Bishop looked back over the balcony and did not like what he saw. The flames below seemed to have lost much of their intensity; soon they would be low enough for those waiting to get through to the stairs. And although they were only shadowy blurs, there were many more people down there than he had at first thought.

'Let's try another flat,' he said hastily to the policeman.

'Yeah, I think you're right; wasting our bloody time here.' He stooped for one more try. 'Look, if you won't let us in, at least call Emergency. Ask for the police *and* an ambulance – we've got an injured man here. My name's Simpson, driver to Detective Chief Inspector Peck. Got that? Chief Inspector Peck. Tell them I've got Jacob Kulek with me and to send immediate assistance. Please do it!'

He rose once more, shaking his head. 'Let's hope they listened.'

'Let's hope they've got a phone,' Bishop replied, leaving the policeman staring after him as he returned to the two women and Kulek.

'Shit,' Simpson said to himself, then followed Bishop. 'Let's get up to the next floor,' he said. 'These other buggers won't open their doors now they know their neighbours wouldn't.'

This time Jessica helped Bishop move her father as Edith and the policeman led the way, the medium shining the torch ahead of them in the darkened stairwell. On the next landing, Simpson went to the first door on their left and rattled the letterbox.

'Hello in there. This is the police. Open up, please.'

They leaned the injured man against the wall in the hallway, Bishop reluctant to be seen by the victims below.

'Edith, bring me the torch,' he called out softly, and the medium left the policeman to come round to them. 'Shine it on Jacob; let's see how he is.'

He looked a hundred years old, his face drawn and pale, the lines in his skin somehow more deeply etched than before. His sightless eyes blinked against the light, but there seemed to be little thought behind them. Bishop knew by the way his tall but frail body sagged that he would collapse without their support. Just how badly he was hurt, there was still no way of knowing; he had known men to be conscious even with a fractured skull. Yet, it seemed impossible that Kulek could even be semi-conscious after being tossed through the windscreen with such obvious force.

'Father, can you hear me?' Jessica anxiously bit her lips when she received no reply, and looked across at Bishop pleadingly.

'He's a strong man, Jessica. He'll be okay once we get him to a hospital. Hold him, Edith, while I see how Simpson is getting on.' Bishop really wanted to find out what was happening below without alarming the two women. Allowing the medium to slide into his position without losing grip on Kulek, he turned the corner, then peered warily over the balcony. The area of light below had become smaller, the blaze on the lorry and the Granada having become several separate, weaker fires rather than one large inferno. The ring of waiting people had drawn closer. Bishop shuddered at the thought, but it seemed as though these people knew who had been in the Granada, knew that Jacob Kulek was in the block of flats. Was it possible? Was there some telepathy between them and the Dark? This strange force possessed and directed them; did it really have an intelligence?

Someone stepped into the area of light below and looked directly up at him; it was a woman and there was something vaguely familiar about her. He reached for the spectacles he used for driving, pulling them from his breast pocket and slipping them on. For the first time that night, anger became more dominant than his fear. It was she, the tall woman, the one who had helped kill his wife. His fingers tightened around the balcony rail and for one wild moment he wanted to run back down the stairs and throttle the life from her. How had she known where to find them? Had it been what Pryszlak had wanted all this time – to trap them in an inescapable area of darkness? And why? Was it just revenge on a man who had refused to help him so many years before? Or was Jacob Kulek a threat? The questions flooded his mind, but they remained mere questions, for he had no answers at all.

'Someone's coming!'

The policeman's voice brought Bishop back to the situation behind him.

'Will you open the door please?' Simpson said, this time keeping any harsh authority from his request. 'There's nothing to be afraid of. I just want to use your telephone if you have one. Look, I'll put my identification card through the letterbox, then you can examine it under any light you've got in there.' He lifted the letterbox flap and slid his wallet through. 'Okay. Now please have a look at it, then let me in. We've got an injured man out here and we've got no time to waste.'

Bishop could just see a vague shape through the window next to the flat's hallway, in a room that was probably the kitchen. It moved from view and again there seemed to be movement behind the reeded glass of the hall door.

Simpson looked across at Bishop and said, 'I think we're in luck this time.'

There were noises inside, a bolt being drawn back, a doorchain being loosened. Finally the lock turned and the door opened fractionally. Bishop thought he could see a face peering out at them, but it disappeared when the policeman moved closer.

'Hello?' Simpson said. 'Don't be alarmed, no one's going to hurt you.' He reached towards the door and gave it a gentle shove. It opened a little wider and he poked his head into the gap. 'Have you got a phone?' Bishop heard him say.

The policeman pushed the door all the way open and stepped into the blackness of the hallway. For a moment, Bishop lost sight of him; then he appeared again, backing out of the doorway. He slowly turned, his eyes looking pleadingly at Bishop, who now saw the hilt of the carving knife protruding from a point just below the policeman's rib cage. Simpson sank down the door-frame to the floor, one leg buckling awkwardly under him, the other sprawling outwards so he was propped there. His head gently lowered itself to his chest and Bishop knew he had died.

The shock had dulled Bishop's reactions, for he was not even reaching for the gun in his jacket pocket when the figure came lurching out of the blackness. He reached up automatically to ward off the thin clutching hands. The glasses he had just donned were knocked away, the lenses having prevented his eyes from being raked by sharp-nailed fingers. The creature he struggled with hissed and spat at him and he realized that it was an old woman. Her wrists felt brittle in his grasp and although she only had the feeble strength of the aged, she fought with an intensity that was frightening. She pushed him back so that his shoulders were over the balcony, her fingers curling closed then open like talons. It was Jessica who ended the battle by coming up behind the old woman, reaching both arms around the scraggy neck, and pulling her away from Bishop. He felt no remorse when he clenched his fist and struck the ranting woman's jaw as hard as he could; to him, she was no longer a human being, just a shell, a host for an energy that was pure evil. She gave a sharp cry and staggered from Jessica's grip, falling backwards over the sprawled leg of Simpson into her own hallway. Her head cracked against the wall inside and she went down in a heap, her body crumpled like a bundle of old rags.

Bishop had to draw Jessica away from the still form of the policeman and she moaned softly as she leaned against him.

'How many, Chris? How many more will it take?'

He was afraid to reply for the answer depended on how much evil existed and in how many minds. Who knew what dark thoughts a friend, neighbour or brother kept hidden? And who didn't possess such thoughts? He led her back to Edith and her father.

'Let me have the torch, Edith. I want you to wait for me here while I search the woman's flat for a phone.'

'Can't we lock ourselves in there?' said Jessica. 'We'd be safe, wouldn't we?'

'If I can call the police from there, maybe.' He hesitated before deciding to tell them the truth of the situation. 'There's a crowd down in the forecourt – I think they want us, or at least, Jacob. It wouldn't take them long to break down the door or smash the windows. We'd be trapped.'

'But why should they want my father?'

It was Edith Metlock who answered. 'Because they fear him.'

Both Bishop and Jessica looked at her in surprise, but the sound of footsteps prevented any further questions. Someone was coming along the landing from the single flat on the other side of the hallway; a faint glow preceded the footsteps. Bishop pulled the revolver from his jacket pocket, and pointed it towards the approaching light, hoping there were still bullets left in the chamber. The man peered cautiously around the corner, holding the candle well before him. He was dazzled by the torchlight.

'What's goin' on 'ere?' He blinked his eyes against the light.

Bishop relaxed slightly; the man seemed normal enough. 'Step out where I can see you,' he said.

'What's that – a gun?' The man raised the long, iron bar he was carrying.

'It's all right,' Bishop assured him. 'No one's going to harm you. We need some help.'

'Oh yeah? Well put the gun down first, mate.'

Bishop lowered the pistol, holding it by his side, ready to be raised if necessary.

'What 'appened to the old lady? I saw her run out at you from me door.'

'She killed a policeman who was with us.'

'Bloody 'ell. I'm not surprised though – she was always a bit crazy. What did you do with her?'

'She's unconscious.' He decided not to tell the man she was probably dead. 'Can you help us?'

'No, mate. I'm looking after meself and the family, that's all. Any bastard who comes through my front door cops this.' He brandished the iron bar in the air. 'I don't know what's goin' on lately, but I ain't trustin' no one.'

'My father's hurt, can't you see that?' Jessica pleaded. 'You've got to help us.'

There was a short silence, but the man had made up his mind. 'I'm sorry about that, miss, but I don't know who you are or what you are. There's too many nutters around for me to take any chances. I mean, who crashed the bleedin' lorry down there, for a start? Thought the building was coming down.'

'We were being chased.'

'Oh yeah? Who by?'

Bishop was beginning to grow irritated by the man's doubting attitude. 'Look, we wanted to use that woman's telephone. That's what I'm going to do now.'

379

'You'll be lucky: she ain't got one.'

'What about you? Have you got one?'

The man was still cautious. 'Yeah, but I ain't lettin' you in.'

Bishop raised the gun once more.

'I'll 'av you with this first, mate,' the man warned, holding the iron bar in front of him.

'Okay,' Bishop said resignedly, knowing it was pointless to argue; any man who thought he could beat a bullet with an iron bar either had to be very dim or very sure of himself. 'Will you ring the police for us? Tell them where we are and that Jacob Kulek is with us. We need help urgently.'

'They're likely to be a bit busy, aren't they?'

'I think they'll make the effort. Just remember to tell them Jacob Kulek is here.'

'Kulek. Right.'

'Tell them to get here fast – there's a mob downstairs after us.'

The man took a quick peep over the balcony. 'Oh my Gawd,' he said.

'Will you do it?' Bishop persisted.

'All right, mate, I'll get on to 'em. You ain't comin' in though.'

'Just keep your door locked and barricade yourself in. You should be okay – it's us they want.'

The man backed away, the iron bar still pointed forward, his eyes never leaving the group in the hallway. They heard his front door close and the bolt being drawn.

'Nice to see the old blitz spirit coming back,' Bishop remarked wearily.

'You shouldn't blame him,' said Edith. 'There must be millions like him, totally confused by what's going on. He has no reason to trust us.'

'Let's hope he at least rings the police.' Bishop glanced

towards the balcony and saw the glow from the fire had dimmed considerably. 'We'd better move on,' he said to the two women.

'Where can we go to?' Jessica asked. 'We can't get out.'

Bishop pointed upwards. 'There's only one place to go. The roof.'

Inside the flat, the man was trying to calm his terrified family. 'It's all right, it was just some people in trouble – nothin' for us to worry about.'

'What are they doin' 'ere, Fred?' his wide-eyed wife asked, clutching her ten-year-old daughter to her. 'Were they in that crash downstairs?'

'I dunno. They wanted me to get the police.'

'Are you goin' to?'

'I'll 'av a go, won't do no 'arm.'

He pushed past his wife and entered the sitting-room, walking over to the telephone resting on a sideboard. 'Keith!' he called back to his teenage son, 'get somethin' up against the door – somethin' solid.' He laid down the iron bar and leaned close to the telephone, using the candle to see the dial.

He let it ring for a full two minutes before replacing the receiver. 'Would you believe it?' he said incredulously to his wife who had followed him into the room. 'It's bloody engaged. Their lines must be jammed solid. Either that or they're out of order.'

He shook his head regretfully. 'Looks like those poor beggars out there are on their own.'

29

They had only reached the sixth or seventh floor – Bishop had lost count – when they heard footsteps on the stairs below.

He leaned against the rail, gasping for breath, trying to listen. Jacob Kulek was now over his shoulder in a fireman's lift, and with each step Bishop took, the blind man seemed to grow heavier.

'They're in the building.' He looked into the blackness below and could see nothing. The acrid smell of smoke from the burning wreck seemed to fill the stairwell even though it was apparent that the worst of the fire was over.

Edith Metlock shone the torchbeam downwards and they saw what looked like tiny white creatures sliding upwards along the stair rails; they soon recognized the shapes as the hands of ascending people, the rest of their bodies hidden by the overhanging staircases. It was an eerie sight, for the hands seemed to be disembodied, a nightmare army of marching claws.

'We'll never make it!' Jessica cried. 'They'll catch us before we reach the top!'

'No, they're moving slowly – we've still got a chance.' Bishop pushed himself upright again, adjusting the weight of the semi-conscious man on his shoulder. 'Take the gun from my pocket, Jessica. If they get too close, use it!'

They went onwards, Edith leading the way, shining the torch ahead of them. Bishop felt his legs weakening, his body slumping more and more under the load. His teeth bit into his lower lip with the effort and the muscles in his back protested their agony. They reached another floor and he fell to his knees, unable to stop himself. Kulek slid from his shoulder and Jessica just caught her father's upper body before it touched concrete. Bishop drew in sharp breaths, his chest heaving. He leaned his head against the bars of the stair rail, his face wet with perspiration.

'How far down are they?' he asked between gasps.

Edith shone the torch downwards once more. 'Three floors below us,' she said quietly.

He grabbed the rail and jerked himself to his feet. 'Help me,' he said, reaching down for Kulek.

'No,' Kulek's eyes were open and he was pushing himself into a sitting position. 'I can walk. Just get me to my feet.'

The way in which the blind man was drifting in and out of consciousness was somehow more worrying to Bishop than if he had just remained unconscious. Kulek groaned aloud and clutched at his stomach as they lifted him. His body was stiff as he forced himself upright.

'I'll be all right,' he reassured Jessica as she held on to him. A trembling hand reached for Bishop's shoulder. 'If you will just bear my weight,' he said.

Bishop slipped the blind man's arm around his own neck and they turned the bend to the next flight of stairs. They began to climb and he felt Kulek wince at every step. 'Not far, Jacob,' Bishop said. 'We're nearly at the top.'

Kulek hadn't the strength to reply.

'LEAVE HIM, BISHOP. HE'S NO USE TO YOU NOW!'

They froze on the staircase as the words spiralled upwards.

It was a woman's voice, and Bishop knew it was the tall woman, the one called Lillian.

'He's dying, can't you see that?' The words were no longer shouted, echoing up from the stairwell like a hissed whisper. 'Why be hindered by a dead man? Leave him, otherwise you'll never escape us. We don't want you, Bishop; just him.'

As Bishop stared down into the blackness, he knew the Dark was all around them, carried in the night air like some invisible parasite. He could feel its coldness caressing his skin, freezing the beads of perspiration into tiny globules of ice. He saw pale blurs that were faces in the black pit below.

'Leave him. Leave him,' other voices inside his head told him. 'He's no use to you. An encumbrance. A dead weight. You'll die if you keep him with you.'

His grip tightened on the rail. He could make it without Kulek. He could get on the roof. They wouldn't be able to reach him there. He could hold them off.

A rough hand snapped his head around. 'Don't listen, Chris.' The torchlight stung his eyes as Edith Metlock spoke sharply to him. 'I can hear the voices. They want me to help them, too. Don't you see? It's the Dark – the voices are trying to confuse us. We must go on, Chris.'

'I hear them,' said Jessica. 'They want me to shoot you, Chris. They keep telling me you're leading my father into worse danger.'

'BISHOP, IT'S NOT TOO LATE – YOU CAN JOIN US!' the tall woman screamed. 'YOU CAN BE PART OF US!'

'Take the light out of my eyes, Edith,' he said, turning away from the stairwell.

Both women sighed with relief and, once more, they resumed their arduous climb. The footsteps below grew louder, became more hurried. Through sheer willpower, Bishop increased his own speed, almost lifting the injured man clear of the steps and dragging him upwards. They reached the next floor, turned the bend, began the next flight upwards. But the footsteps were drawing closer, running, scrabbling up the staircase, other sounds accompanying them, noises that could have come from frenzied animals. They were now below the floor Bishop and the others had just left, scurrying up from the darkness like creatures climbing out from hell.

Jessica felt weak with fear. She pushed her back against the wall, her legs still climbing, but her movement slow. She held her arm out rigid, pointing the gun towards the terrible scuffling noises that were drawing closer and closer.

A light appeared at a point between her and those approaching, growing stronger, beginning to fill the darkness in the bend of the stairs. Cold air blew in from the landing as the swingdoors were pushed open, and suddenly there were voices, more lights adding to the brightness of the first.

'Who's down there?' a gruff voice demanded to know.

'Look, Harry, there's someone up there on the stairs,' another voice said.

Jessica was suddenly bathed in bright light.

'Christ, she's got a gun!' the same voice exclaimed.

Edith, who had been concealed around the bend halfway up to the next floor, quickly descended a few steps and shone her torch towards the voices.

A group of men and women stood in the entrance to that particular landing staring up at Jessica and now her. They were obviously neighbours who had banded together for safety when the power had been cut.

'Go back!' Edith called out to them. 'For your own safety, go back into your homes and lock yourselves in!'

Someone pushed past the first man in the doorway. 'You tell us what's goin' on first, lady.' His flashlight was powerful and threw out a wide, undefined beam. 'What's this girl got a gun for?'

'They must've had something to do with the crash downstairs,' another voice murmured.

Bishop was close to Edith, but still out of sight of the people below. 'Shine the torch down the stairs, Edith,' he whispered. 'Show them the mob coming up.'

The medium leaned over the rail and did as he said. The figures crouching below were suddenly lit up.

'There's more of 'em down there!' All the lights were pointed downwards and the people on the stairs covered their eyes, moaning in pain.

'Jesus, look at that lot. They're all the way down the stairs.'

One of the men cowering under the glare began to creep upwards, keeping his head tucked down. Another man followed, moving in similar fashion.

'They're coming up!' a woman's voice screamed out.

The man carrying the flashlight stepped forward, descending a few steps and bringing a heavy boot down hard on the creeping figure, sending it reeling backwards. 'I've had enough of this,' was his only comment.

All hell seemed to break loose at that point. Other men and women who had come to a halt on the stairs suddenly surged forward, shielding their eyes from the light, shrieking their demented cries, and swamping the man who had been foolhardy enough to defy them. His friends ran forward to help and more lights appeared on the floors below and above, almost as though a signal had been given for many of the residents to venture out from their separate flats, curiosity overcoming their previous caution. Many rushed back indoors as soon as they saw the people on the stairs, while others decided enough was enough: if the Law wouldn't do anything about intruders, then they, the residents would.

Perhaps they would have stood more chance in the confused and brutal battle that ensued if a number of their own neighbours had not already succumbed to the Dark as they had waited in the blackout. The residents of the tower block had no way of telling who was friend and who was foe.

The swingdoors on the floor above Bishop opened and lights were flashed through it. He grabbed Edith's arm and said, 'Get Jessica – we're going on.'

The medium did not bother to protest, for she saw his logic: the roof – if they could get on to it – was still the safest place to be. She reached Jessica and pulled her upwards, leading her around the bend in the stairs, catching up with Bishop and Kulek. They reached the next floor and the people waiting there watched them curiously.

'You'd better lock yourselves in until the police get here,' Bishop told them. 'Don't try to fight those people downstairs – there are too many.'

They looked at him as though it were he who was mad, then peered down into the confusion of sounds and flashing lights below. He didn't bother to see if they had taken his advice, but kept onwards, the cool air that was rushing in through the open doors helping to revive him. Kulek was trying to help their ascent, his legs moving haltingly over each step, his thin frame trembling with the exertion.

'We're nearly there, Jacob. Just a little further.' Bishop could almost feel the remaining dregs of strength draining from the blind man. Kulek's left arm was tightly clamped against his stomach.

Jessica cried out in relief when she saw that the stairs ran out on the floor above: they had nearly reached the top of the building. Her arm encircled her father's waist and she pulled and lifted with Bishop, urging her father on to the last flight of stairs. Edith's steps were heavy, her breathing laboured. It had been a long climb and her body was in no condition for such stern exercise. One plump hand grasped the stair rail and dragged the rest of her body forward, the movement slow, the effort exhausting. Not far, she kept telling herself, not far now, a few more steps, just a few.

The man who waited for them at the top was the caretaker of the flats. He lived, in fact, on the ground floor, but earlier that evening had gone up to the tenth floor of the building to give a warning to the elderly couple who lived there. He had warned them before – or at least, he had warned the old man. The Council did not, *absolutely* did not allow urinating in the lifts. The old man had always denied it had been him, blaming it on the kids who roamed the estate, vandalizing property, making the lives of the residents miserable. The little bastards broke windows, scribbled graffiti four-foot-high on walls, and generally created pandemonium up and down the stairs. The lifts were a particular source of joy to them and the all-too-frequent breakdowns were due to the kids tampering with the buttons, blocking the closing doors, opening the doors between floors, or jumping up and down while the lifts were in motion. Certainly, they messed in the lifts, but they were not the main culprits of this misdemeanour. Oh no, the old man had a lot to answer for in this respect. Why they put elderly people at the top of these flats, God only knew. When the lifts were out, either through the misdoings of vandals, the normal and not infrequent mechanical malfunctions, or – as was the case tonight – general power failures, these old folk were stranded. Another problem – and this was the relevant one – the two lifts had been engineered to move slowly, for too swift ascents and descents scared the life out of the residents. If you were aged, and if you liked to drink a lot, and if your bladder was no longer the sturdy water carrier it used to be, then a trip up in the lift could take a lifetime.

Unfortunately, the old man was well past his prime, and had a weak bladder. Other residents had complained more than once that the lift doors had opened revealing the old boy standing in a puddle of liquid. The way in which he always doffed his hat and bade them a pleasant good day or evening could never disguise the foul smell of piss as he swayed past them. The caretaker had warned him three times so far, ignoring the protested denials, and now he would warn the old lady as well. Either she kept rein on him, or they were out. O.U.T. No nonsense. No more pissing in the lift. Putting up with the other tenants with their carping complaints about the heating, the plumbing, the vandalism, the rent, the lifts, the refuse collectors, the noise and their neighbours, was bad enough, but having to mop up the mess left by some incontinent old imbecile was too much. Sometimes the caretaker fantasized about planting a time bomb in one corner of the tower block, setting it for one-thirty and retreating to the pub further down the road, sitting there with his pint of bitter, checking the second hand of his watch as it crept up to the thirty minute mark, chomping on his veal-and-ham pie, studying the building through the pub window, ordering a fresh pint, having a joke with the landlord as the fatal seconds ticked away; then the lovely bang, the floors of the tower block crumbling like playing cards or like those films you saw of industrial chimneys being demolished, blown up at the base so the bricks tumbled down in a straight line, the structure resembling a telescope closing in on itself. All those tenants off his back once and for all, no more complaints, no more running around after them. All crushed, all dead. Lovely.

The caretaker had been halfway up when the lights went out and the lift came to a shuddering halt. He had groped around in total darkness, cursing loudly as his index finger finally found the alarm button. He hoped his silly mare of a wife would hear it in their ground-floor flat, but after ten minutes of constantly stabbing at the button and banging on the metal walls of the lift, he decided the breakdown was probably due to something other than just mechanical failure in the drive motor. Bloody power cut, he told himself.

It had been creepy sitting there in the dark, sightless and unseen. Yet it was strangely comforting, like being back inside the womb, still unborn and still untouched. *Or like being dead, nothing for companionship but nothingness.* Soon, though, he had found he was not completely alone in the darkness.

After a while, the caretaker had forced open the lift door and, feeling with his hands, had discovered he was almost on the next floor, the step-up no more than three feet. Opening the shaft door which would let him out into the hallway beyond was a little more difficult, but he persisted, summoning up the reserves of strength the voices inside his head told him he had. The strange thing was that once you knew you could do something, it became easier to do.

He had continued his journey to the top of the building, using the stairs, no longer bothered by the blackness around him. The wind had howled around him when he had pulled open the swingdoors to the tenth floor landing, but he was grinning as he walked the length of the short hallway, then round to his right to the old couple's flat. They hadn't wanted to open the door at first, and he'd had to insist, telling them it was official business. The old lady had been the first to go and for her he had made use of the broom she kept in the hall of the flat, knocking her down, then forcing the broom-handle into her throat as far as it would go, blocking it so she could not draw in air. He had taken his time with the old man who had not tried to help his wife, but had cowered in his bedroom beneath his bed. The caretaker had merely laughed as he splashed through the foul-smelling puddle that was spreading out from under the bed, and had dragged the old boy out, enjoying the croaking screams as he hauled him back down the hallway and into the kitchen where so many innocent implements of death were waiting. Unfortunately, his victim's heart had given out before he could finish the job, but at least it had been pleasurable up until that final moment. No more pissing in the lifts for the old boy any more. No more pissing.

The caretaker had sat on the floor next to the warm corpse and continued to enjoy himself, free now to do whatever he pleased, free to indulge in new, forbidden experiences. The freedom tasted good. The sound of the crashing lorry came not long after and the sky outside briefly flared orange. The caretaker selected one of the bloodied kitchen tools he had been using and walked out on to the landing. He stood at the top of the stairs and waited.

Edith Metlock sensed his presence before she saw him. She was nearly at the top of the stairs when she stopped, her mind abruptly cutting out the screams, shouts and sounds of struggle below, to direct itself towards what lay ahead. One hand still gripping the iron stair rail and one knee resting on a step, she slowly shone the torch upwards – slowly because she dreaded what the beam would reveal, an inner sense fearing the worst – and found the man's legs, his knees, his waist. He was dressed in the blue overalls of a workman and, as the torchbeam came higher, she saw he was holding a stained, short-bladed chopper across his chest, the kind used in a kitchen for chopping meat; and as the beam reached higher still, she saw he was grinning, his teeth were red, and his mouth was red, and the redness ran down his chin and she now noticed it had splashed on to his overalls. She knew he was insane, for what normal person would eat raw meat. He came down a step and she screamed.

The first swing of the small chopper missed because he was blinded by the light, but the second scythed across the arm she had put up to protect herself. The whole of her arm went numb, as though it had been struck with a hammer and not a sharp instrument; she tumbled backwards, the torch in her other hand, sending its beam careering upwards, then around the walls as she fell. Bishop used his body to block her descent, gripping the handrail tight and still maintaining his hold on Kulek. His legs nearly went from beneath him with the medium's weight, but he managed to steady them. She had collapsed sideways on the stairs, her stout legs sprawled across one step, her body against the uprights of the stair rail; mercifully, she had not released the torch. Sure she would fall no further and sure he had regained his own balance, Bishop quickly snatched the torch from her grasp and pointed it upwards again. The man was slowly walking down, his grin made even more obscene by the sticky blood around his lips and on his teeth. The weapon was held high over his head, poised to strike.

Bishop tried to back away, but encumbered by Kulek's limp body, movement was awkward. Edith clawed at the man's legs, grabbing his overalls and tugging, trying to overbalance him. It was no use; the man was too strong.

The chopper was already swinging downwards when the bullet shattered his breastbone, the blast from the .38 made even more thunderous by the concrete walls around them. The caretaker screamed and fell backwards, the chopper dropping from his hand and slithering harmlessly off Edith Metlock's sprawled body. He turned over and tried to crawl away from them, but his legs kicked out spasmodically before he reached the top step and he slid back down, bumping

Jessica as he passed her on the stairs. The gun was still pointing at the empty space where the caretaker had stood when she shot him, smoke curling from the barrel, the smell of cordite heavy in the air. The noises below had ceased as though the single, reverberating blast had stopped all action. Bishop knew the silence wouldn't last.

With one hand, he helped Edith to her feet, catching a glimpse of the cut in her lower arm as he did so. It was a long wound, just below her elbow, stretching from one side to the other, apparently not too deep, for she seemed to have no trouble in using her arm. He pushed her in the direction of the landing above and followed, almost lifting Kulek with him. He gently sat the blind man down with his back against the swingdoors. The stairs ended on a small landing, separated from the short hallway leading to the other side of the building by the yellow swingdoors. The iron stair rail ran off to the left making the small landing Bishop was on a balcony overlooking the steep stairwell. At the end was a door, which he assumed was the fire exit to the stairs for anyone living in the top flats on that side of the hallway. He saw what he was looking for when he shone the torch towards the ceiling: a large trapdoor was housed there, the metal ladder leading to it running down the wall opposite the balcony railings. A wooden plank was chained and padlocked to the ladder, top and bottom, a simple device to prevent children or trespassers from climbing up to the roof.

The sounds of battle began again and he ran down the few steps to Jessica. He had to prise the gun away from her clenched fingers and forcibly drag her past the spot where the overalled man had been standing.

'See to your father, Jessica,' he said harshly, shoving her towards Kulek. He knew the killing had sent her into a state of shock and the only way to bring her out of it was to occupy her mind with other problems; after all they had been through, it would be too easy for her to crack completely. Jessica knelt beside her father and cradled him in her arms.

Bishop shone the torch on to the lower retaining chain on the ladder, tugging at it to feel its strength. He was surprised when it fell away in his hand; someone – kids probably – had already worked on one of the links, cutting through it, but leaving it in position until they had cut loose the chain near the top of the ladder. The second was just within reaching distance, too high for smaller children, but easy enough for the caretaker or maintenance men to get at. He gripped the chain and pulled. It held.

Bishop swore. Should they use the fire escape door and get into one of the flats beyond? No, they'd be trapped in there; a determined mob could easily force their way in. The roof had to be the best bet – an army could be held off from that position. He had to break the chain somehow, or bust the padlock; the gun he was holding would do it.

'Edith, get over by Jessica!'

The medium quickly did as she was told, realizing his intent. Bishop moved around so his body was between the three crouching figures and the target he was aiming at. He half-turned his head, keeping his eyes narrowed, praying there would not be a ricochet. The sound of shattered metal was smothered in the blast and the deflected bullet spun onwards, thudding into the wall just above the fire escape door. The chain fell to the floor and the wooden plank toppled away from the ladder, bouncing against, then resting on, the railing opposite. Bishop wasted no time; he climbed the ladder and pushed at the trapdoor. It would not budge.

He slipped the gun into his pocket and used the torch to examine the trapdoor; a small hole was set into a metal square at a point near the ladder. The caretaker obviously

had a special key to allow access for himself and any author-
ized person.

'Edith, quickly – hold the torch!'

She reached up and took the torch from him.

'Shine it on the lock,' he told her. His ears were still
ringing from the previous gunshot, but he was sure he could
hear footsteps mounting the stairs once more. He jammed
the .38 up against the lock, having no other choice but to
hope for the best. The recoil in the confined space jerked his
arm downwards and scraps of metal and wood spat into his
face. He clung to the ladder, his head tucked down, almost
losing his grip on the rung he was holding. Then, the gun
still clenched in his fist, he pushed at the trapdoor. For one
dreadful moment, he thought it would not lift, but he exerted
more pressure and grunted with relief when the door shifted.
He climbed another rung and pushed even harder; the trapdoor swung open and came to rest against something behind
it. Bishop jumped back down on to the landing.

'Up you go, Edith,' he said, once more taking the torch
from her. He watched her climb, telling her to reach inside
the opening for some kind of handhold. She had obviously
found something, for soon she was pulling her plump body
through the gap, her injured arm hardly impeding her progress. Bishop stepped up a few rungs and handed the light
back to her.

'Keep it on us,' he said, then jumped down and went to
Jessica and her father. 'We're going to get him up to the roof,
Jessica.'

Kulek opened his eyes at the sound of Bishop's voice. 'I
can make it, Chris,' he said, his words slightly slurred but still
coherent. 'Just get me to my feet, will you?'

Bishop smiled grimly at the blind man's willpower. He and
Jessica lifted the thin body and Kulek bit his lower lip in an

effort to contain a cry of pain; something was wrong inside, something deep in his stomach had been twisted or torn. Yet he had to go on; he could not allow those creatures of the Dark to take him. Despite the weakness he felt and the pain he suffered, a thought was pounding in his brain, a thought that was struggling to surface, to sweep through his mind and . . . and what? Even as he tried to concentrate his head swam with a nauseating dizziness. The thought was close, but the barriers seemed impenetrable.

They helped him to the ladder and Bishop told Jessica to go first. 'I'll support him from down below, you try and pull him through.'

She swiftly climbed the ladder and disappeared into the black hole above. Bishop guessed there was some kind of box room built on to the flat roof of the tower block, the kind that usually housed the lift motors and drive pulleys, or water tanks. Jessica leaned her body back through the hole and reached down.

Bishop guided Kulek's hands on to the ladder and immediately knew the blind man would never make it. Kulek clung to the metal frame but did not have the strength left to move his legs. And the footsteps closing in from behind told Bishop that time was running out.

The first man was nearly at the top of the stairs, his two companions almost halfway. In the wide angle of light from the opening above, Bishop saw that all three were in a dishevelled state, a condition that had come to be recognized as belonging to the longer-term victims, those who had been affected perhaps weeks before. Their faces were black, their hands and clothes filthy and torn; no one could be sure where these people hid during the daylight hours, but it had to be somewhere dark, some place beneath the ground where nothing clean existed. The first man lurched forward, his deeply-sunk eyes fixed on Bishop, but dead and expression-less. The festering sores and scabs that corrupted his skin became clearly visible as he drew nearer.

Bishop drew the gun and pointed it at the advancing man who ignored the weapon, fearless because inside he was already dead. Bishop squeezed the trigger and the hammer clicked against an empty chamber. In panic, he tried again, knowing the gun was empty, the bullets all used.

The man spread his arms open to take him in his embrace, his eyes mere slits against the light, and Bishop struck out with the pistol, using it as a club, the blow cracking against the bridge of the creature's nose. The man still staggered forward as though the pain meant nothing to him, blood pouring from his injury and adding to the grotesqueness of his appearance. Bishop ducked beneath the clawing arms and used his shoulder against the man's chest, sending him reeling back towards the stairs. The gun was useless to him and he let it drop when he saw the only other object on the landing that could be used as a weapon. He picked up the heavy wooden plank that had been resting against the balcony rail and hurried towards the subhuman teetering at the top of the stairs, smashing it into him and pushing with all his strength. The man toppled backwards, falling on to his fellow victims, who were almost on to the landing, all three going down, their deteriorated bodies glancing off the concrete steps as they went, the heavy board following. They did not stop until they had reached the broader bend in the stairs where the tall woman stood gazing upwards.

Bishop saw her there in the gloom and hate surged through him. Again he wanted to rush down and kill her, not as punishment for what she had become, but for what she was and always had been; instead he hoisted Jacob Kulek over his shoulder and began the strenuous climb up the ladder. Just when he thought he would never make it, his last reserves of strength almost depleted, helping hands reached down and lightened his load. Jessica and Edith pulled together, grasping the blind man by his clothes, beneath his arms – anywhere they could get a grip. Bishop made one final effort and heaved upwards, almost willing the injured man into the opening, and the two women gained firmer grips, lifting Kulek's upper body through, pulling him to one side so he could not fall back. The relief to Bishop was short-lived, for other, hostile, arms were wrapping themselves around his legs and pulling him down. His feet slipped from the rungs and he fell, the people beneath him cushioning the blow. He flailed out at the bodies trying to smother him, using his arms and feet to clear some space for himself, hearing Jessica's scream from above, the sound somehow making him even more desperate.

He felt himself lifted and then knew what they were about to do; the railings of the balcony rushed to meet him and suddenly he was looking directly down into the terrifying black depths below.

30

His body was slipping from them, going over the rail, beginning to slide forward; and the receding floors below were like a square-shaped whirlpool, its dark centre eager to suck him down. He started to scream, but his own instinctive reaction took over from his petrified mind. He grabbed at the handrail that was only inches away from his face just as they released him. His body went over the top, but he maintained his grip, falling back against the other side of the rail, feet dangling in empty air. He gasped at the pain as his shoulder socket was wrenched, his fingers almost opening at the shock. In one movement he swung round and grasped a metal upright, both hands now taking his full weight. He managed to get a foot on to the sill of the landing and there he clung, pausing for brief seconds to recover his strength and senses.

A hand smashed down against his and he looked up to see the tall woman standing over him. Bishop knew who it was even though her features were in shadow, and, despite his helpless position, the anger flared once more. A man was reaching over to grab at his hair, trying to push him down, away from the rail. Bishop twisted his head, in an attempt to break the grip, but the hand merely moved with him, pushing, forcing him away. Someone else had a foot through the metal supports and was kicking at his chest, trying to dislodge him; through the fury of the attack, Bishop was vaguely aware that this third person was a young girl, no more than a teenager. Another shadowy figure, unable to reach Bishop because of the others, stood at the rail and shouted encouragement.

Bishop felt his fingers becoming numb and he knew they could not resist the constant hammering for much longer. The tall woman changed her tactics and began to prise them open one by one. His body was well away from the rail, the girl's foot forcing him outward, the man's vicious grip on his hair pushing his head backwards. The tall woman cried out in triumph as she finally broke his hold on the rail; only his grip on the upright prevented him from plunging downwards. He knew he had only seconds left.

And then Jessica was down among them, kicking and clawing, merciless in her desperation to help Bishop. She pulled the teenager away and thrust her hard against the wall, the impact stunning the girl. Then she was on the man who held Bishop's head, tearing into him and raking his face with her fingernails. He let go of Bishop and tried to grab her, but was powerless against her fierce onslaught; he fell back, his arms covering his face. Jessica had her back towards the man who had been watching and now he moved towards her, arms outstretched.

'No!' the tall woman screeched, knowing Bishop was the more dangerous. 'Help me!'

He stopped, then leaned over the rail and began to smash his fist down against the clinging man's head. The blows stunned Bishop and he did the only thing possible: he jumped.

Using his grip on the rail and his foothold to thrust himself sideways, he snaked out a hand to grab the descending stair rail to his right. He seemed to be suspended in open space for an eternity and Edith Metlock, in the hatchway overhead, closed her eyes, unable to watch the frightening leap. His fingers curled around the slanted rail as his body slammed into the uprights and the side of the concrete steps. His other hand found purchase and he pulled himself up instantly, tumbling over the stair rail with a speed that owed much to panic. Without pausing, he raced back up the stairs, reaching up for the collar of the man Jessica had been forcing backwards and who was now near the top step. Bishop pulled hard, twisting sideways as he did so, and the man hurtled past, his body only striking concrete when it was three steps from the bottom. He screamed as he made contact, then was silent as he rolled down. He came to rest in a crumpled heap among the groaning bodies of those who had fallen earlier.

Still Bishop did not stop; he was on the landing, running past Jessica and slamming his shoulder into the other man standing next to the tall woman. They both went down, but Bishop's mind was his own and he was able to move quickly. His fist smashed down into the upturned face, knocking the man's head against the concrete. Bishop dug both hands into the man's hair, then lifted the head almost a foot off the floor and pushed it back, the sickening smack telling him the man would not be a problem for a while.

Hands closed over his eyes, digging into them, and he knew it was the tall woman who was trying to tear them from their sockets. He threw his head back and the pressure eased slightly. Then he was released and, as he staggered forward on his knees, he saw that Jessica was holding the tall woman from behind, one arm around her waist, the other around one shoulder. The tall woman was too strong, too cunning; she brought an elbow sharply back, driving it into Jessica's ribs. Jessica doubled up and the woman whirled around, aiming two swift punches to her breasts. Jessica screamed and collapsed to the floor. The tall woman's eyes were hidden in the dark shadows, but Bishop could feel the hatred in them.

She rushed at him like a thing possessed, her teeth bared in a snarl that was primitive, the sound ascending to a high-pitched screeching as she closed in on him.

He rose to meet her and failed to stop her clutching his throat, her strength no longer normal, her savagery no longer her own. But he remembered her evil, the horrible deaths of Agnes Kirkhope and her housekeeper, the near-killing of Jacob Kulek, the murder of the policeman. The burning of Lynn. She was the willing tool of the unclean force that was in every man, woman and child; she was its servant and its instigator, a creature who worshipped the dark side of the mind. He pushed her back against the rail, her eyes visible now, tiny black pools in muddy brown irises, shrunken apertures to something darker and boundless inside. She squeezed his throat, spittle from her open mouth splattering his face, her own neck straining forward in an attempt to tear his flesh with her bared teeth. His whole body quivered with the fury he felt and blood rushed through him, swelling veins and arteries with their torrent. Then he was lifting her, scooping her legs up in one mighty heave, the movement fast but drawn out in time so the action was slow and dreamlike. Higher, her back on the rail, her shriek becoming that of fear, her hold on him loosening. Higher until she was tilted over the black void as he had been earlier. Higher until the balance was drawing her down. Then her body slipped from his grasp and she was screaming and flailing at the air as she plummeted, bouncing against the sides of stairs, an arm snapping, a leg torn from the hip, her back breaking even before she disappeared from sight and squelched against the concrete below.

Bishop hung over the rail, the strength finally drained from him. He could no longer think, no longer reason; the urge to sink to the floor and lie there was almost overwhelming. But the shouts below grew louder and footsteps drummed on the stone steps. He saw faces peering up at him, disappearing, hands snaking up the stair rail, the crowd now ascending as one, the battle with the tenants of the tower block over. A hand pulled him away from the railing and towards the ladder reaching up into the roof. Jessica implored him to climb to safety, her face stained with tears of anxiety and exhaustion.

'You first,' he told her.

'Hurry!' came Edith's voice from the open hatchway. The mob were on the last flight of stairs, the strongest of them coming fast, the torchlight growing strangely weaker as though the darkness of night were approaching with them.

Without further hesitation, Jessica climbed the ladder and disappeared into the hole above. Bishop leapt upwards, forcing his weary legs to climb, knowing the desperation of the hunted. He felt a hand close around his ankle and he stamped down hard with his other foot, the heel scraping down his pursuer's face, causing the man to drop to the floor. And then Bishop was rolling over the side of the opening, the hatch slamming closed behind him. Edith and Jessica fell on to the covering as fists pounded against it. Fortunately the hatch was solidly made and they knew that no more than one person at a time could climb the ladder to push against it. They lay in the gloom, the torch on its side and pointing towards the machinery that operated the lift, Edith and Jessica slumped over the hatch, Bishop on his back panting for breath and totally spent, Kulek sprawled on one side near a wall. They listened to the muted howls of anger below, the drumming of fists against the hatch, and they were aware of the oppressive darkness that was there with them in the small box room on top of the ten-storey building. The wind tore round the corners outside as though it were an unseen force trying to enter and Edith Metlock rejected the probing she felt at the edges of her mind, refusing to hear the anguished voices that whispered their threats. She thought only of her three companions in the machine room, keeping an imagined wall of light between her and the Dark.

After a while the noise from below faded away and there was no more pressure against the hatch. Bishop breathed more evenly as he raised himself on one elbow.

'Have they gone?' he asked, not daring to hope.

'I don't think so,' the medium said. 'I don't think they'll give up until they have Jacob.'

'But why do they want my father?' said Jessica. 'You said before that they feared him. Why should they? What can he do against them?'

'Because I'm close to the answer, Jessica.'

They swung their heads around at the sound of his weak, quavery voice. Edith picked up the torch and shone it towards where Jacob Kulek sat, his back propped up against the wall, his hands pressed down against the floor to keep his body erect. He seemed strangely shrunken, as though his body were slowly crumbling in upon itself, his cheeks collapsed inwards, eyes half closed as though resisting sleep. Jessica quickly crawled towards him, not having the strength to rise, and Bishop followed.

Jessica took one of her father's hands and tenderly touched his cheek. The lids of his eyes briefly opened wider and he tried to smile at her. She pressed her face against his, afraid for him without knowing why; it had nothing to do with the physical danger they were in, and concern over his injuries was only part of it. He opened his mouth to speak again, but she softly placed her fingertips against his lips.

'Don't, Father. Save your strength. Help will be here soon, I'm sure of it.'

A trembling hand took hers away. 'No, Jessica ... there will be ... no help ... for us this night.'

'We managed to get a message through to the police, Jacob,' Bishop said. 'They'll try to reach us.'

Kulek wearily turned to him. 'They have no ... control over this ... terrible thing, Chris. Only people as individuals ... can fight against it. But it can be defeated.' Strength seemed to be returning to his words.

'How, Jacob?'

'Pryszlak ... Pryszlak knew how to unleash the evil inside him. At the moment of death, he knew how to direct that evil. Don't you see, his death was like opening a box, releasing the contents. The content his own psyche, and his will was strong enough – even in death – to control that psyche.'

'It isn't possible.'

'Years, Chris, years of conditioning his mind for that final moment.' Kulek sucked in a huge breath and began to cough, his body doubling over and shoulders jerking spasmodically. They lifted him upright when the seizure had passed, resting his back against the rough brickwork; they were alarmed to see the speckles of blood on his lips and chin. He breathed slowly for a few moments, then his eyes opened. 'Don't you see? He built up the power of evil around him over the years through his own practices and those of his followers, their minds communicating, joining as one, directing their separate forces so they merged; all that remained was the barrier of life.'

'And he knew he could go on even after his own death?'

Kulek's eyes closed again. 'He knew. He was an extraordinary man, his mental development stretched far beyond that of normal men. He could use areas of the brain that we know nothing of. The mind is a mystery to us; he had unravelled some of its secrets.'

Edith Metlock spoke from the darkness on the other side of the torchbeam. 'Jacob is right. They fear him because he knows the truth.'

'But I do not have the answer!' Kulek said loudly, anger and frustration in his voice.

Edith was about to say more when she suddenly looked down at the hatch beneath her and listened. 'They're still there,' she said in a whisper. 'Something is being moved – I can hear a scraping noise.'

Jessica and Bishop moved towards the hatchway and listened, fighting to keep their own breathing as soundless as possible. They did not see the thin line of blood appear at the corner of Kulek's lips, running down his chin, forming a pool around his jawline before falling in spots on to his chest. The flow thickened and then ran from his chin in a steady stream.

The scraping noise below had stopped and for a moment there was only silence. All three jumped when something crashed against the hatch. It rose several inches before slamming shut again.

'Christ, they've found something to batter against the hatch!' Bishop said, his nerves beginning their frenetic dance once more.

The crash came again and both Bishop and Jessica combined their weights with Edith's to keep the hatch closed. It slowly began to rise beneath them.

'They must have got a table or something from one of the flats to stand on. There's more than one person pushing now.' Bishop grabbed the torch from the medium and shone it quickly around the machine room, looking for a weapon of some kind, anything he could use to beat back someone climbing through. There were small windows set in the walls and a door leading out to the roof itself; the drive pulley and the lift motor were nearby, the opening to the shaft black and menacing. There were no tools lying around, nothing at all that could be used as a weapon. The hatch beneath them opened a few millimetres wider and a stout, metal bar was pushed through to keep it open. Bishop pulled at the bar, but it was jammed into the gap. Fingers curled around the edges of the hatch opening and the pressure below became even more intense. The gap widened and they heard another object being scraped through to be used as a lever by the person on the other side. They tried to prise away the fingers around the edges but they merely returned in another position. Their arms and shoulder muscles were taut with the effort of pressing down, yet they could feel the hatch rising higher each second. An arm came through the gap and Jessica screamed when the hand closed around her wrist.

It was at that point that the power came back on.

Light flooded in through the opening, blinding them with its suddenness. The lift machinery clanked into life and the pulley turned as the car resumed its interrupted journey. There were cries from below as the hatch dropped and came to rest on the objects that had been pushed through; the arm and the hands around the opening had already disappeared. They heard scuffling on the landing below, the sound of footsteps running down steps, screams as people fell in their haste to escape the dazzling lights.

The two women fell away from the hatch, both crying with relief, praying that it was finally over for them – for that night at least. Bishop cautiously swung the hatch open wider, the metal bars sliding away and bouncing off the table below before clanging down on to the concrete landing. The upper stairs were empty apart from the sprawled bodies of those who had been injured before. He could hear the others scurrying down, many moving fast, knocking aside those who had been victims for a longer period and who were totally blinded by the lights.

'They've gone,' he quietly told the two women. He shivered as the wind rushed into the machine room and turned to see the door was open wide. Jacob Kulek was no longer sitting against the wall.

The two women looked up when he dropped the hatch and rushed to the door. They, too, realized the blind man was missing.

The wind hit Bishop like a physical blow as he ran out on to the roof, tearing at his clothes and whipping at his face so that he had to half-close his eyes against its force.

The lights of the city spread out before him like a vast silver and orange constellation and, for a moment, he could only gaze at its manufactured beauty, for the first time truly understanding its potency. He panicked when he could not see Kulek; the roof was completely flat apart from the machine room and another similarly shaped building that he guessed housed the tower block's massive water tank. Jessica and Edith joined him and all three apprehensively scanned the rooftop.

'Jacob!' Edith Metlock called out.

Jessica and Bishop followed her gaze and saw the blind man standing just ten yards away from the edge of the building; they could only make out his shape because of the lights blocked out behind him. He turned to look at them as they began to walk as one towards him.

'No,' he warned them, 'it's dangerous here. You must stay back.'

'Father, what are you doing?' Jessica cried against the noise of the wind, her arms reaching imploringly.

Kulek clutched at his stomach, but refused to bend to the

pain. His face was just a vague whitish blur against the night sky, but they could see the blackness spreading down from his mouth on to his lower jaw. There was a thickness to his words as though the blood was filling his throat.

'They wanted me dead! They wanted to kill me before I found the answer ... before I learned how I could use my own ...' His words were lost as he stumbled towards the lip of the roof.

'No!' Jessica screamed, breaking away from Bishop and Edith Metlock and running towards the blind man. 'No!'

Kulek turned to look at Jessica and his words were whipped away by the wind. Then he plunged into the night.

31

Jessica brought the car to a halt and once more Bishop leaned out the window and showed the special pass card to the soldier. The sergeant examined it then ducked his head to scrutinize Edith Metlock sitting in the back. Satisfied, he signalled to another soldier standing by the red and white striped barrier, which was then dragged to one side. It had been the third time their car had been stopped since entering the area around Willow Road. The group of soldiers idly standing around an army truck watched them as they drove through, their curiosity apparent, their weapons even more apparent. The military were taking no chances with this operation, not after the total disaster of three weeks before. Many men had been lost that night, police and civilians, as well as soldiers, their brains infected or affected by whatever chemicals the scientists said the Dark contained, turning on each other, damaging the lights that had been their ultimate protection. Their defence against the hordes who poured into the area had been hampered by the confusion within their own ranks. The battle that had taken place had been horrendous and only the swift arrival of reinforcements had prevented those unaffected from being completely overcome. A nightmare action, but one brought about by their own underestimation of the unseen enemy. Tonight they would be better prepared.

Jessica swung the car out to the middle of the road, avoiding the lorry bearing the huge searchlight parked at the kerbside. They had passed many such machines on their journey, many of which had been in service for the past two weeks, others brought in for that night's particular operation. Most had been adapted so they did not throw directional and defined beams, but shed a broad and powerful area of light. Smaller lights had been fixed to roofs of houses or hung from their eaves; that area, which seemed to be the worst affected in London, had been literally flooded with lights. The curfew was still imposed throughout the city and lighting-up time had taken on a whole new meaning. Veterans of the wartime blitz thought it ironic that now it was unlawful not to show a light at night-time, whereas in the war years it had been a punishable offence to do so.

Bishop's uneasiness grew as they approached Willow Road and he looked across at Jessica to see her features were also strained, her hands clamped tightly around the steering-wheel. She felt his gaze on her and turned to give him a quick, nervous smile. Since the death of her father, they had grown close, the earlier attraction they had felt for each other developing into a strengthening bond of friendship – and something more. They were not yet lovers, but both knew that when their separate wounds had healed, their mutual stress subsided, then their intimacy of feeling would be matched by a physical intimacy. It was a desire in both of them, but one that could not – and would not – be hurriedly fulfilled.

She braked as a military vehicle carelessly turned the corner from Willow Road and swerved across their path, the driver obviously taking advantage of the empty streets. He waved an apology and sped on. Jessica took her foot off the brake and guided the car into Willow Road.

Bishop's eyes widened at the sight ahead, even though the details were not clear because of his slight short-sightedness. The road was filled with vehicles of all kinds, most of them military, others belonging to the Metropolitan Police, and also many civilian cars. Open-topped lorries bore more searchlights and armoured scout cars kept a watchful eye at each end of the road. There seemed to be uniformed figures everywhere, blue mingling with khaki, soldiers lining the pavements as though they were a guard of honour. Houses were being entered and searched for any hiding victims undiscovered in the earlier searches. He could just make out the bright red of fire tenders at the far end of the road, and the ominous white shapes of ambulances told him the authorities were prepared for the worst. But the sight that astonished Bishop most of all as Jessica eased the car past the parked vehicles and scurrying men was that of the strangely naked area halfway down. The houses on either side of the Beechwood debris had been completely demolished, leaving a wide, empty space. He had no clear view into the extended site because of the confusion of machinery and vehicles around its fringes, but he guessed what lay inside the boundary, for the intentions of that night's operation had been fully explained to him. The authorities had been forced to involve Edith Metlock and himself, albeit reluctantly, for they had unsuccessfully repeated their experiment for the past three nights and, as yet, the Dark had not returned to the site. Sicklemore, the Principal Private Secretary to the Home Office who had been fortunate to survive the disaster of three weeks before, had suggested that Bishop and Edith Metlock be called in to assist once more. There were protests, for the scientists and technicians involved claimed that the Dark had nothing to do with the paranormal, that it was merely the carrier of some unknown and, as yet, untraced chemical that in some way triggered a reaction in the hypothalamus region of the brain, creating electrical charges that manifested themselves in acts of extreme aggression. The Dark was a physical entity, a chemical catalyst, not some mystical and incorporeal leech, and therefore could be overcome by scientific means, not by spiritualistic mumbo-jumbo. Since Jacob Kulek's death, the uneasy alliance between scientist and parapsychologist had become a disdainful non-alliance. But Sicklemore had insisted. Three nights of failure and three days of the Home Secretary bellowing for results had made him desperate: Bishop and Metlock were thin straws to clutch at, but at least *something* had happened when they had last been present.

Edith Metlock stared out at the military and scientific paraphernalia from the darkness of the back seat and her heart sank into further depths of despair. Had it all been for nothing? Had Jacob died in vain? The Dark had only grown stronger after that night, nothing happening to dissipate its power. She had tried to make contact with him, but now it seemed her powers as a sensitive had left her, for nothing came to her any more, no visions, no voices. It was as though the thin veil between herself and the spirit world had become an impregnable barrier. Perhaps it was because she had lost her own beliefs.

Peck saw their car approaching and walked out into the middle of the road, waving his arm at them. He leaned in the window when Jessica brought the car to a stop.

'You'll find a space to park further down, Miss Kulek,' he said, then directed his attention towards Bishop. 'If you and Mrs Metlock could come with me?'

They stepped from the car and Jessica went on searching for a gap by the kerb in the congested street.

'How is she?' Peck asked, nodding towards the departing vehicle.

'She's come to believe her father's death was pointless. It's made it worse for her,' Bishop replied.

Peck mentally sighed. He remembered how he had found them on the tower block rooftop weeks before, almost frozen, physically exhausted. It had been dawn before he and a couple of squad cars had made their way to the high-rise building, only the persistence of one of the block's tenants alerting them to Kulek's whereabouts. The tenant had tried all night to get through to the Information Room, phoning in every hour but, because the lines had been flooded with emergency calls, his message had only been taken when daylight was approaching. Peck and his officers had been halfway to the top, checking each body on the stairs as they passed, not allowing themselves to spare time on the injured, when they had met Bishop coming down. He had looked dazed, his shoulders slumped in a weariness that was both physical and mental. He told them the two women were still on the roof, that Jacob Kulek was dead. It was only when they had all been brought down to the safety of the ground that he learned that Kulek had deliberately jumped; Edith Metlock had said that Kulek's death would provide the answer to the Dark. The medium hadn't appeared to be hysterical – she spoke softly, calmly – and Kulek's daughter seemed to see some sense in what she told them, although the girl's grief was apparent. When Peck had walked around to the side of the building and had found Jacob Kulek's smashed body, his rage burned inside. The blind man had been badly injured when the police car had crashed – from what Peck had gathered, Kulek had been busted up inside as well as concussed. He had obviously been delirious when he had jumped, they should have seen that. Now, the medium was making him out to be the new Messiah, someone whose death was for the benefit of mankind. Peck had turned away from the misshapen body, barely disguising his anger when he returned to the waiting group. The blind man had been thrown through the windscreen of a car, dragged up ten flights of stairs, chased by a mob of zombies and madmen, and then had fallen from the roof; what glory could there be in such a death? Even Bishop had seemed to listen to the medium's crackpot assertions. But now three weeks had passed and nothing had happened to diminish the power of the Dark. They had been wrong and Peck could only feel sorry for them.

'I'll take you over to the site,' he said to Bishop and Edith. 'The Private Secretary wanted to see you as soon as you arrived.'

They followed the detective, carefully stepping over the thick electric cables and avoiding the white-coated technicians who were making last-minute adjustments to various pieces of equipment. Dusk was not far away and already many of the smaller lights had been switched on. Bishop looked incredulously at Peck when he saw the newly expanded site. A huge pit had been dug out in the area that had once been Beechwood and its grounds, and seated within it were four massive light machines, each rectangular in shape, their Perspex surfaces pointed towards the sky. Similar machines, but smaller, more compact, were placed in positions around the pit. Further back, on the flattened land that Beechwood's neighbouring house had been built on, stood a prefabricated steel hut, a dark-tinted window stretching along its entire length and overlooking the site. On the opposite side stood the generator which would supply the power for all the apparatus.

'They're taking no chances this time,' Peck explained as he guided them towards the hut. 'They've got backup generators and lights, and enough guards to fight off an army. The power stations are heavily guarded too, by the way, so there's no chance of someone doing the same as that madman three weeks ago. He held out for hours before they finally got to him.'

They had just reached the squat, metal-walled building when Sicklemore emerged followed by a bespectacled man in shirtsleeves, whom Bishop recognized as the chief scientific adviser to the government, and who, at the Birmingham Conference Centre, had openly rejected any paranormal connotations regarding the recent disasters.

'Mr Bishop, Mrs, uh, Metlock,' Sicklemore briskly acknowledged. 'Perhaps your presence tonight will bring us more luck.'

'I don't see why it should,' Bishop replied bluntly.

The Private Secretary regarded him speculatively, then said, 'Nor do I, Mr Bishop, but you seemed to last time. You remember Professor Marinker?'

The scientist gave them a grudging nod of his head.

'Perhaps you'll explain tonight's operation, Marinker?' Sicklemore said, having privately made it clear that he was no longed prepared to put up with petulance over the use of what the scientist termed as 'bloody cranks'.

'Your part is simple enough,' Marinker said gruffly. 'You just do the same as three weeks ago. I, personally, don't see why the Dark should return just because you're here – it makes no sense at all to me – but that's the decision of others.' He looked meaningfully at Sicklemore. 'Although the Dark seems to be an insubstantial thing, we have managed to detect a denser area at its centre – a nucleus, if you like. We believe the chemical which reacts on certain other chemicals present in the hypothalamus region of the brain is strongest within that centre. Our intensive tests on living victims have now made it clear that the disturbance is certainly in that region of the brain, and further tests have shown that minor radiation disperses those chemicals. Unfortunately, the radiation, slight though it is, damages brain cells to a degree where the victim can no longer function as a living person.'

Bishop shook his head, no humour in his smile. 'You mean your experiments kill them.'

Sicklemore hastily interjected. 'We have no choice but to be brutal in our tests. Those victims would not have lived long, anyway.'

Marinker continued as though there had been no interruption. 'It explains why the Dark can only exist at night, why the radiation in the sun's rays causes its disappearance. It goes to ground, if you like.'

'You said you believed it was a chemical. How could it react in such a way unless it were a living organism? Or something else?'

'I used the term loosely, Mr Bishop, to keep the conversation in layman's terms. Certain chemicals do have negative reactions to opposing properties, you know. We are sure it's the ultraviolet rays from the sun that are harmful to the chemical and further tests on victims bear this out. The tiniest exposure to ultraviolet makes them try to hide, to cover their eyes. You've seen our light machines set beneath ground level, the others angled around the excavation. Unfortunately, the ultraviolet wavelength does not travel far, but our specially constructed machines are extremely powerful and, so that the area will be fully saturated we will have several helicopters mounted with similar but obviously smaller lights overhead, their beams directed at the ground. Gravitation itself will give them a longer wavelength so the helicopters will be fairly high and in no danger. Of course, gamma rays or X-rays would have been even more effective, we believe, but then, that would have been highly dangerous for everyone in the immediate area, too.'

'Lasers?'

'Too defined an area. They would penetrate, but not saturate.'

'But surely too much exposure to ultra-violet rays is harmful to us.'

'You will be protected and we will be inside the hut. Those outside will wear gloves and hoods and stand behind shields. Their normal clothing will give them added protection.'

'How will we be protected?'

'Special suits with oxidized visors.'

'And if nothing happens? If we don't attract the Dark?'

'Let me speak plainly, Bishop: I don't expect you to. I think that what took place three weeks ago happened by mere chance. The fact that the victims seem to be drawn to this place each night indicates that there is a fundamental source of energy in this area; we have no idea what that source is nor have we been able to locate it specifically. But we know it's here, we're sure this thing that everyone calls the Dark will return to it. It's just a matter of time.'

'Which we don't have,' Sicklemore snapped. 'The point is this, Mr Bishop: your presence will not hinder the operation, and it might just do some good. I mean no offence, but I personally find the argument for psychic phenomena far from convincing, but at this particular moment, I'm ready to try anything if it will mean our success. In fact,' he said, turning his eye on the scientific adviser, 'I shall even indulge in a few prayers when I'm inside that hut.'

Marinker opened his mouth to speak, but thought better of it.

'Now,' Sicklemore continued. 'The light is fading fast. Can we please make our final arrangements?'

Marinker called through the hut's doorway and an agitated youngish man appeared, a sheaf of papers in his hands, a well-chewed pencil clenched between his teeth.

'Get these two kitted out, Brinkley,' Marinker said. 'Full gear, they'll be fully exposed to the light.'

Brinkley waved the papers in the air with one hand and grabbed at the pencil in his mouth, pointing it behind him into the hut. 'But I . . .' he began to protest.

'Just get on with it!' Marinker pushed past him and disappeared through the doorway. Brinkley stared after him, then turned to inspect his two charges.

'Right, I'll leave you to it,' Sicklemore said. 'Will you stay with them, Peck, see that they have all they need?'

'Yes, sir.'

'I'll see you both presently, then.' Sicklemore strode hurriedly away from them, his small, waspish figure soon swallowed up by the crowds of technicians and soldiers on the site.

'Gone to report to his superiors,' Peck said, enjoying the fact that the man he had to be servile to had to be servile to others. 'He's had his own little department set up in one of the nearby houses, with a direct line to the Home Secretary. Poor bastard's been popping in and out every half-hour all day.'

'Er, if you'll come along with me we'll find you a couple of suits to put on,' Brinkley said, eager to get back to his work. He led them through the site to the road. 'You're Bishop and Edith Metlock, I take it,' he said, forced to slow his brisk pace so the others could keep up. 'I heard what happened three weeks ago; sounds to me as if the whole operation was too hastily put together.'

Peck looked at Bishop and rolled his eyes upwards.

'Still,' the scientist went on brightly, 'that won't happen tonight. I think I can promise you we've found the answer. All very simple really, but then aren't most things if you approach them correctly?'

As Brinkley babbled on, Bishop looked around for Jessica and saw her making her way towards them along the pavement. He waved an arm and her pace quickened.

'Here we are then.' Brinkley had stopped beside a large, grey-coloured van. The back section was open and they could see the shelves inside were filled with white garments. Brinkley stepped in and checked the sizes marked on the shelves. He soon returned with the appropriate uniforms. 'They're pretty loose and very light – you can slip them on over your normal clothing. Helmets are separate, but they're not at all cumbersome. There we are, the light will just bounce off you.' He gave them a cheerful grin, then frowned at the medium. 'That's a nuisance – you're wearing a skirt. Never mind, you can change in one of the houses – they're all empty.'

Jessica had joined them by now and Peck noticed how close to Bishop she stood, almost leaning against him. It gave the detective some satisfaction, for he knew the ordeal both had been through; perhaps they could at least give a little comfort to each other. He was worried about the medium, though: she seemed lost, confused.

'Are you all right, Mrs Metlock?' he asked. 'You look a little pale.'

'I ... I don't know. I'm not sure that I can be of any help tonight.' She looked down at the pavement, avoiding their eyes. Jessica went to her.

'You must try, Edith,' she said gently. 'For my father's sake, you must try.'

There were tears in the medium's eyes when she looked

up. 'But he's not there, Jessica. Don't you understand? He's gone, I can't reach him. There's nothing there any more.'

Brinkley appeared to be embarrassed. 'I'm afraid we don't have too much time. Could I, um, ask you to put the suits on now, please? I've rather a lot to cope with in the operations hut, so if you'll excuse me . . .?'

'Go ahead,' Peck told him. 'I'll bring them over when they're ready.' He turned to the medium and his voice was hard. 'I know you're frightened, Mrs Metlock, but they're only asking you to do what you've been doing professionally for years.'

'It isn't fear . . .'

'All right, maybe it's exhaustion. We're all bloody tired. I've lost some good men over the past few weeks – two of them trying to protect you – and I don't want to lose any more. Now, all this may be nonsense, I don't know – I don't have to judge – but they . . .' he waved his hand at the site in general '. . . see you as a last resort. I've seen things recently that I never thought possible, so there may be something in it. The point is, we've got to try anything, and both you and Bishop *are* our anything! So will you please help us and get into that ridiculous spaceman's outfit?'

Jessica took the medium by the arm. 'I'll help you, Edith.'

Edith Metlock looked at Bishop, her expression a mixture of helplessness and pleading, but he could only turn his head away. 'Go with Jessica, Edith,' he told her.

The two women left, Jessica leading the medium by the arm as if helping a very old, and very tired woman. Bishop struggled into the white suit, surprised at its toughness despite its flimsy appearance. The helmet itself, with its stiff, black visor, hung loosely over his back; it could be pulled forward like a hood, the visor snapped into position by two clips on either side. The arms ended in close-fitting gloves, elasticated at the wrists, the feet made to the same principle. He zipped the suit up to a point just below his chest and looked up to see Peck watching him, his face grim.

'Bishop,' the detective said, then hesitated.

Bishop raised his eyebrows questioningly.

Peck looked uncomfortable. 'Just watch yourself in there.'

They sat side by side, the huge, square lights set out before them, lifeless yet threatening. Two lonely, white-clad figures, the centre-piece in an outward spreading array of technical equipment, weaponry and manpower. They were afraid, and those around them were afraid, for the tension among them was steadily increasing, feeding upon itself and touching them all as they watched. The sun had disappeared from the sky an hour before, its sinking hidden by dark clouds that had formed on the horizon, and now the site was lit only by subdued lights. The men around the perimeter were all shielded by metal screens and they wore special glasses already positioned over their eyes, making them look sinister and emotionless; a certain number were equipped with full protective headgear and gloves. They waited as they had waited for three previous consecutive nights; but this time they sensed it was different. This time, each man would occasionally look up at the sky, removing his dark glasses to study the black rolling clouds for long moments before turning his attention back to the two figures sitting in front of the open pit. Something would make each one shiver, but not outwardly; it was more like a sudden shudder of internal organs. It passed from man to man, mind to mind, an infection whose carrier was their own thoughts. Even the scientists and operatives inside the squat steel hut, surrounded by their own technology, felt particularly uneasy that night. Marinker's mouth was dry, the palms of his hands wet. Sicklemore kept clearing his throat and tapping one foot. Brinkley could not stop blinking.

Outside, behind a screen, Peck jangled the loose change in his trouser pocket, while Jessica, who stood by the detective's side, bit on her lower lip until her teeth left deep indents. The minutes passed and all casual chatter ceased; if anyone did speak, it was in a whisper just loud enough to be heard over the steady hum of the generators. The air seemed to be growing colder. And, of course, through their protective glasses, the night looked even darker than usual.

Bishop found it difficult to think clearly. He tried to remember, as he had done before, the first day he had come to Beechwood, the terrible sight that had confronted him. But it was all vague, all misty and remote, as though it had only been a dream which could not be brought into focus. He looked over at Edith sitting two feet away, but her features were barely visible through the darkened visors they both wore. Her hands were clasped across her lap and he could see them clinging tightly to each other.

'I can't think, Edith. It's all a blur to me for some reason.'

She said nothing for a few moments, then her visor turned in his direction. 'Don't try to think of it, Chris. Leave your mind blank. If the Dark really is what we believe it to be it will seek you out. It doesn't need your guidance.'

'Can you . . . can you sense anything?'

'I see Jacob's face, but I can't feel his presence. I feel nothing, Chris, only emptiness.'

'Did he really believe . . .?'

The medium turned away. 'I don't know any more. Jacob's perception was stronger than any man's I've ever known; even stronger than Boris Pryszlak's.'

'You *knew* Pryszlak?'

The black visor made her inscrutable. 'I was once his mistress.'

For a few moments, Bishop was too stunned to speak. 'His mistress? I don't understand . . .'

'It was a long, long time ago. Twenty years, perhaps more. So long, it sometimes feels as if it never really happened, as if the woman who slept with him was someone I knew vaguely, but whose name or face I can no longer remember. Boris Pryszlak was an astonishing man, you see; his very wickedness made him attractive. Do you understand that, Chris, how a malignant thing can be attractive?'

Bishop did not answer.

'I found him fascinating. At first, I didn't see the deepness of his corruption, the depravity that was not just part of him, but *was* him, his very being. It was he who recognized my powers as a sensitive, who encouraged me to develop those powers; he thought he would be able to use me. It was Jacob who finally drew me away from Pryszlak's influence.' She smiled almost wistfully beneath the mask. 'Jacob and I were never lovers – he has always been faithful to the memory of his wife. You of all people will realize that in our world, nobody dies; they merely pass on to something more enduring.'

'But why didn't Jacob tell me this at the beginning?'

'Because I asked him not to. Don't you see it wasn't important? It had nothing to do with what was happening. Boris Pryszlak's immorality was like an infectious disease – it tainted anyone close to him. For a while I wallowed in the filth he thrived on and it was only Jacob who tried to help me. Perhaps he saw I was being used, that I was a victim of evil rather than a perpetrator. Jacob once told me he had tried to lure away other followers of Pryszlak, but had come to see those people were as sick and twisted as the man they idolized, and it was my own desire to leave – to be saved, if you like – that made me different from them. Even so, Pryszlak hated Jacob for having taken away just one of his followers.'

'Yet he came to Jacob for help.'

'He needed him at that time. He wanted to combine his own extraordinary mental powers with Jacob's; that combination would have been formidable. But Jacob had no desire to become involved in the ultimate aims of such a man. Besides, he knew that involvement would mean eventual subjection. Jacob bitterly regretted not having tried to destroy Pryszlak's plans all those years ago before they had become fully formed; but then, he was a truly good man and failed to recognize the extent of Pryszlak's malignancy. Even I failed to see that and I had shared his bed for almost a year.'

Bishop drew in a deep breath. He was disturbed by Edith's revelation, but not shocked; too much had happened for his emotions to be jarred by any fresh disclosure. 'Is that why Jacob called you in at the beginning of all this – because you had some connection with Pryszlak?'

'Yes. He felt it would be easier for me to reach Pryszlak. I knew something of his mind, something of his intentions. I had never visited Beechwood before, but I felt his presence as soon as I entered the house. It was almost like walking into Pryszlak's mind, each room a different, dark cell. He used to experiment with his own telepathic powers when we were ... together ... using me as his receiver. He never failed to penetrate my mind with his evil thoughts. For him it was a new kind of eroticism, a fantasy of imagined deviant sexual acts yet, because of the strength of his mental powers, experienced as though physically performed.'

Bishop saw her white-clad figure shudder.

'Those thoughts are still with me, burned deep into my

brain. Only Jacob could help me subdue them and now he's gone. That's why I'm so afraid, Chris.'

'I don't understand.'

'Jacob poured his strength into me. Here, when we first gathered at Beechwood and you saw the vision, I was the one who made contact, but Jacob was helping me resist Pryszlak, preventing him from dominating my mind completely. Even when you found me at my home in a trance state, Jacob, who was lying injured in hospital, was using his mental powers to keep Pryszlak from taking possession. He was my protector, the barrier between myself and the full force of Pryszlak's parasitical soul.'

'But the Dark *can* be resisted, Edith. The reaction is only against those who have some imbalance in the brain.'

'We *all* have that imbalance. We all feel hate, aggression, jealousy! As the Dark grows stronger – as Pryszlak gathers his spiritual army – it will seek out the evil inside all of us and use it to destroy! Those it can't overcome – and they will be few – will be killed by its still-living physical legions. There will be no escape for any of us!'

'Only if the Dark is what you say it is. The scientists claim otherwise; they'll destroy it with their machines.'

'And with all you've seen, all you've been through, can you believe the Dark is just a chemical reaction?'

Bishop's voice was firm. 'I don't know any more. I almost came to believe in what you and Jacob told me, but now . . .' He looked away from her, his gaze falling on the huge light machines before them. 'Now I hope you were both wrong.'

Edith's body seemed to slump further into itself. 'Perhaps we were, Chris,' she said slowly. 'Perhaps I hope so, too.'

'Bishop?' The call came from the tiny radio receiver fixed into Bishop's ear. The voice had a metallic sound to it, but he assumed it was Marinker from the control hut speaking. 'Our helicopters are in the air. Anything happened with you two out there?' The question had a cynical edge to it, but Bishop sensed the underlying tension.

'Nothing so far.' His reply was picked up by the small microphone clipped to his chest. Slight static in the receiver made the scientist's next words hard to grasp. 'I'm sorry, what was that?' Bishop asked.

'I said we've just had a report . . .' more static '. . . trouble near here. Nothing for us to worry . . .' static '. . . being dealt with. More victims on the loose, that's all.'

Another voice came through the earpiece and Bishop guessed it was Sicklemore. 'You'll let us know the moment you feel anything, um, strange happening?'

Marinker spoke again. 'The build-up from the ultraviolet lights will be gradual, Bishop, so you needn't worry about any sudden flare. Just give us some warning . . .' more static, then, 'Can you hear us all right, Mrs Metlock? We seem to be getting interference from somewhere.'

There was no reply from the medium and Bishop anxiously turned towards her. Her body was rigid in the chair, her black visor facing straight ahead.

'Mrs Metlock?' the metallic voice came again.

'Be quiet, Marinker,' Bishop said harshly. Then, more softly, 'Edith? Can you sense something?'

She continued to look ahead and her voice sounded faint. 'It's here, Chris. It's . . . oh my God!' Her body shuddered. 'Can't you feel it? It's growing. It's all around us.'

Bishop tore his eyes away and quickly looked around the site. He felt nothing and the tinted glass he stared through made everything seem darker. He quickly unclipped the visor and lifted it back over his head.

The soldiers and technicians positioned around the site glanced uneasily at each other, sensing something was finally about to happen. Jessica felt a weakness spread through her, a weakness born of dread. A perception that was akin to intuition but stronger, more certain, told her that the menace was even greater than before, that they were all more vulnerable, their resistance against the Dark a fragile thing. She clutched at Peck, afraid she would sink to the ground. He turned in surprise, beads of perspiration on his forehead despite the coldness of the night. He supported her weight, then turned his attention back to the two figures sitting near the open pit. Bishop was looking around him as though searching for something, his visor pushed up from his head.

Inside the control hut, Marinker was speaking agitatedly to his radio operator. 'Can't you cut out this bloody static? I can't hear what they're saying out there.'

'I'm trying, sir, but there's not much I can do about it. I'm afraid it's atmospherics – it's interfering with our contact with the choppers, too.'

Marinker avoided Sicklemore's eyes, afraid he would give away the alarm he was strangely feeling. He cursed himself inwardly for being stupid and hoped no one noticed his hand trembling as he stabbed at the speaker button once more, 'Bishop, is something wrong out there? Can you hear me?' A constant crackle of static was his only reply.

Bishop tore the earpiece away, the interference becoming unbearable. His eyes narrowed as he searched the site. The general gloom was because only a few lights had been switched on, but was the air becoming heavier with something more than just nightfall? He blinked, but still he could not make out any definable difference in the lighting. He began to wonder if an hallucinatory tension had built up in the minds of everyone present on the site, a muted form of mass-hysteria that was creating a false fear.

'Edith, I can't see anything.'

'It's here, Chris, it's here.'

Something swirled in the corner of Bishop's vision and he snapped his head around to see what it was. Nothing there. Another movement, to his right this time. Nothing there . . .

Edith was pushing herself back against the chair, her hands tightly gripping the seat. Her breathing was heavy, laboured.

Bishop felt the coldness on his exposed face, a prickling sensation of closing pores, tightening skin. The coldness crept through to the rest of his body. More movement, and this time he caught sight of something shadowy. It flitted across his vision like a tenuous veil, gone when focused upon. A sound, the kind the wind makes when it suddenly sweeps around the corner of a house. Gone. Silence. Lights dimming.

Bishop spoke, hoping the microphone would pick up his words. 'It's beginning,' was all he said.

But in the control hut they only heard the irritating noise of static. All eyes watched the two white-uniformed figures through the long, shaded window until Marinker said, 'Check those lights – they seem to be fading.'

A technician turned a dial and the lights grew bright again. But slowly, almost imperceptibly, the brightness dulled.

A low moaning sound came from Edith and Bishop was about to reach out to her when his movement froze. Something was touching him. Something was running a hand over his body.

He looked down at himself and saw the loose folds of the white suit becoming smooth, flattening out. But the material moved on its own; nothing pressed against it. The whiteness of the suit which had been subdued under the poor lighting now became a dark grey in colour. The coldness that was in his body began to creep into Bishop's mind, a numbing frost seeking corridors to chill, and the familiar welling up of fear encouraged its progress. He tried to speak, tried to warn the others of what was happening, but his throat was too constricted. The darkness was descending, a shadowy blackness that threatened to extinguish all light.

Bishop tried to stand, but felt a crushing weight pushing against him, the same cold hand that had explored his body and which had now grown into a giant, invisible claw holding him captive. He knew it was only his own confused mind lying to him, making him believe what was not possible, but the pressure existed as though it were real. Once more, he tried to reach Edith, and his arms were held down by his sides, too heavy to lift. He saw the medium begin to slide from the chair, her own moaning rising to a piteous wail. Then the figures began to appear.

Inside the control hut, Sicklemore was speaking urgently to Marinker, years of civil-service breeding preventing his voice from rising to a shout. 'For God's sake, man, turn on the machines. Can't you see what's happening out there?'

Marinker seemed uncertain, his eyes switching from the array of controls before him to the barely visible figures outside. 'Bishop hasn't got his visor in position. I can't risk turning on the machines while he's exposed like that.'

'Don't be stupid, man! He'll use the mask as soon as the ultraviolet lights begin to come on. Do it now, that's an order!'

The figures were just dark, ethereal shapes, their forms having no clearly defined image. They drifted closer, converging on the two people by the pit, black shapes that were part of the blackness around them. They drew near, looming over Bishop and Edith, the man locked into his seat by an unseen force, the woman cowering on the ground. Bishop gasped for breath, feeling as though he were sinking into thick, slimy mud, his mouth and nostrils choked by the foul-smelling substance. He forced his arms up, slowly, tendons straining, fists clenched and trembling. He tried to grip the invisible thing that pushed against his chest and found nothing there, no shape, no substance. But the pressure still remained.

The soldiers around the site, those in the road, and those in the streets beyond the road, held their self-loading rifles and Sterling submachine-guns at the ready, knowing the inactivity had come to an end and that the danger had finally presented itself. The policemen felt comforted to be under the protection of their weaponry. In the distance, they could hear shouts, the occasional burst of gunfire; elsewhere trouble had already started.

Jessica tried to dodge round the metal shield, wanting to reach Bishop and Edith, but Peck grabbed her wrist and held her back.

'Leave them,' he said gruffly. 'You can't help them! Look.'

She followed his gaze and saw the sudden white glow emerging from the pit. The ultraviolet lights had been switched on, their brilliant light slowly spreading upwards and out. Other lights around the site began to glimmer, growing stronger second by second. Overhead could be heard the whirring blades of helicopters and the sky itself began to glow with the spreading white light.

'Chris hasn't got his visor down!' Jessica cried, struggling to free herself once more.

'He soon will have, don't worry. Just keep still, will you, and watch!'

Jessica stopped and Peck released his grip. 'Good girl. Now keep behind the screen.'

Bishop was dazzled by the rising brightness. He closed his eyes against it and tried to reach the visor lying flat over his head. He forced his hands towards it, sucking air in wheezing gasps, the black slime clogging his throat. Suddenly the pressure on his chest was gone; his arms felt free. He snapped the visor down and opened his eyes. The glare was still strong, but the silver chloride in the photochromic glass of the visor steadily counteracted the brightness, enabling him to see around him. Edith was half-crouched, one arm on the seat of her chair, looking towards the pit, her other arm shielding her eyes even though her visor was down. Bishop thought he could see the dark shapes falling away from the light, the images disappearing as though swallowed by the brightness.

The intensity of the light grew, becoming bluish in colour, a red tinge tainting the hue as it became more powerful. Soon the whole site was flooded with the blinding glare, shadows dispersed completely because of the positioning of other lights. The glow merged with the lights from above, the Gazelles maintaining their position, careful not to infringe on the air space of their fellow helicopters.

The area was completely bathed in the peculiar blue-violet light, every shadow quenched by it; even the man-made metal screens were lit from the back with less powerful lights so that no darkness could linger behind them.

Bishop felt his mind soaring, his fear leaving him. 'They've done it!' he cried to Edith. 'It's gone, they've destroyed it!' The scientists had been right all along: the Dark *was* a material thing, a physical property that could be obliterated as any other chemical, gas or solid matter could be. Jacob, poor Jacob, hadn't realized what it was; his mind had been too steeped in the paranormal to understand that the Dark was nothing more than an unexplained phenomenon and not a spiritual entity. Their own minds had fed the exaggeration, making them see things, imagine things, that did not exist. He, Bishop, had received the telepathic thoughts of Edith when he had had the 'visions' at Beechwood; she had known Pryszlak, had associated with his followers, known their cravings, their degeneracy, and he was receptive to her thoughts because he had discovered the dead and mutilated bodies. Everything else was the madness inflicted by the thing known as the Dark, and the earthly evil of those who had been followers of Pryszlak when he had been alive. The knowledge was overwhelming, for it was not just the answer to the terrible, catastrophic events that had recently passed but a reaffirmation of his beliefs over many years.

Bishop staggered towards Edith, his arms reaching out to help her. And it was as he was leaning forward over her, a hand beneath her shoulder to pull her upright, that the shadow fell across the glaring blueness of her clothing like a dark blemish on fresh-fallen snow.

He stumbled away from her and fell, going down on to his knees and staying there, the mask hiding the horror on his face. Edith was rising, looking down at the shadow spreading across her body, her arms outstretched, her legs wide. She lifted her head and screamed up at the skies.

Then the blue-violet glow began to dissolve under the swift-falling darkness.

The shapes came back with the shadows, like wisps of black smoke, twisting, spiralling above the light machines in their pit as though taunting their power. The lights could clearly be seen receding back into their source as though forced by some invisible, descending wall. The generators on one side of the site began to whine, reaching a pitch, slowing, then rising again. Technicians leapt away from them as sparks began to shower outwards. Every glow, whether it was from floodlight, searchlight or handheld torch began to fade, bulbs popping and glass shattering. The instruments inside the control hut became erratic, needles bouncing across dials like metronomes, switches shutting themselves off as though operated by invisible fingers, noises booming from receivers and transmitters. The hut was plunged into darkness as all the lights failed.

Overhead, a helicopter had pulled sharply away from the confused scene below, its broad, ultraviolet beam of light fizzling out as had the others in the companion helicopters. The pilot felt the Gazelle dip suddenly and struggled to maintain height; but the power was no longer there. It hit the helicopter which was rising from below and had inadvertently crossed the former's flight path. The roar of the explosion was deafening, the swirling ball of flame blinding. The tangled machines plunged to the ground, the red flames trailing behind like the tail of a comet. Because both Gazelles had veered away from the site their death fall took them into the troop-filled road. The screams of the soldiers were drowned in the second explosion as the machines struck the ground. Scalding metal and burning petrol splattered towards the exposed men.

The third pilot was more fortunate, for he was able to direct his machine into a clear space two streets away as it lost power. It crashed to the ground, but neither the pilot nor his companion was badly hurt. As they climbed shakily from the damaged machine, they failed to notice the people who moved in the shadows towards them.

Bishop tore the mask from his face, the site now lit only by faint light from the machines in the pit and the red glow that came from the fire in the road beyond. His cheeks were wet from tears of rage and frustration – and new-found fear. Other small fires had started, caused by dropping flames when the helicopters had first made contact, their height spreading the fallout wide. Edith Metlock was silhouetted against the feeble light in the pit, her arms still held wide, the screams still bursting from her. He tried to push himself upright, but the oppressive weight was on him again, bearing him down, crushing his limbs. The black shapes swirled towards him, growing out of the darkness, seeming to become solid as they approached. He felt something hit him and he fell to the ground, shocked rather than hurt. He raised himself on one elbow, but there was nothing near him. Another blow, glancing off his forehead, and the skin where he had been touched burned as though ice had been smeared across it. The man he knew had been Pryszlak was before him, his malicious features clear even though they were totally black. The head came forward and his breath was fetid as he revealed his black teeth in a grin that made Bishop cry out and try to cover his eyes. There were others with Pryszlak, familiar faces that had become distorted with their own corruption. The man who had tried to kill him with the shotgun. The bearded man he had seen in his visions at Beechwood. The tall woman, her eyes ablaze with triumphant hate. And her short companion, cackling derisively. Others he did not recognize. And one who could have been Lynn, but the distortion was too great to tell. They moved closer to him, touching his body, prodding him. Yet he could see through them; he could see Edith, still hear her screams; he could still see the dimming glow from the pit.

Then the glass from the lights was bursting upwards, sparks, then flames leaping from the machines as they exploded, destroyed by something that had come to know no limitations, something that could only become stronger. The glass spun in the air, the shards flashing redly as they turned and reflected the distant fire; huge sheets specially strengthened to protect the delicate but powerful filaments beneath them. He saw a piece flying towards Edith, its glistening surface the size of a door, saw it slice her body in half, and closed his eyes before her legs, standing on their own, slowly toppled over.

The hands that were smothering him clutched at his throat and it seemed that each figure had a grip, their faces swimming before him, the mass that was the mind of all of them sucking at his own mind, no longer probing, searching, instead drawing out what it desired, what it needed to exist, to propagate. Just before the blackness became total he saw that crowds had invaded the site, screeching maniacs who attacked anyone who was not of their kind. Jessica was running towards him, her face hardly visible in the darkness. The shroud descended and there was nothing more to see. He could only close his eyes against the Dark.

And then he opened them, wondering where the blinding white light came from, the light that grew from nothing and washed the area on which the house called Beechwood had once stood with its vivid radiance, scouring out every rut and crevice with its brilliant intensity, making every brick and stone shadowless, casting out the darkness.

The light that burned into his eyes even though he had closed them once more.

... The dreams have left me; time has numbed the horror of those terrible days. Even Jessica is no longer afraid of the night. We're together now, not yet as man and wife, but that will come. We need to adjust more fully to our new existence; formal rituals can take their turn.

After two years, we still remember that night at Beechwood as though it were only yesterday. The events have been discussed, analysed, written about, but still no one can explain the phenomenon that took place. The Church tries, of course, and now the scientists are prepared to listen to us, to consider what we tell them, for it was they, the technologists, who were proved wrong, they who came to realize that evil is a spiritual power and not a biological malfunction of the brain. Jacob Kulek would have been pleased – is pleased – that a true bond has been struck between the scientist and the parapsychologist, a working relationship no longer grudging, the alliance opening new doors to our self-discovery. It's everything he worked for when he was alive, only his death achieving those aims. Jessica frequently communicates with him, and I am slowly learning to. Edith is helping, acting as my guide.

She has spoken to my daughter, Lucy, and has promised she will bring her to me soon. She tells me Lucy is very happy, and Edith, too, is content in her own death.

The Dark never returned after that night, but Jacob has warned us it has not been truly vanquished. He says that as long as there is evil in the minds of men, it will always exist. One day, I suppose it will manifest itself again.

There are many of us who are aware now. All those who

*were at Beechwood and saw the Light form and grow until its
effulgence destroyed every dark shadow have gained this unique
extra-sensory perception. Only those who could not cope with the
new powers they found they possessed have suffered, for their
minds have retreated from it, hidden within themselves so they
can no longer function as people. The scientist, Marinker, was
one such person. But they are being cared for, and have not
suffered the same fate as the victims of the Dark, who were left
empty and alone, their bodies becoming weak shells that no
amount of medical attention could save from wasting away and
eventually dying. Some who were present that night say the Light
was like a ball of fire, a new sun rising from the earth itself;
others claim it had no form, no visible shape, but was a tenuous
gas, expanding in sudden flashes, filling the air with its charges.
Several say it grew in the shape of a cross, losing its outline as
the brightness became too intense. For myself, I remember seeing
only the brightness, no shape, no structure, just a brilliant light
that flooded my mind.*

*We've heard reports that the Light has been seen since, in
different parts of the world where oppression is prevalent. Jessica
tells me Jacob is strangely uncommunicative about this. She has
also asked him what part God has played in all this, but again,
Jacob will not answer the question. He has told her that our new
perception is at too fragile a stage for us to know, that even in
death we are still learning, no truth fully realized.*

*Jacob had known he was dying from internal injuries that
night on the rooftop; but he also knew his own mind had to
maintain control as death eclipsed his life. The Dark, with its
growing power, had endeavoured to fill him as he died, to
swamp his thoughts, to destroy his spiritual will; the swiftness of
his death prevented that. These black, incorporeal beings knew
that as the body died, so the will, the essence that is within
everyone, faded too, only to be restored, reawakened, when the*

tenuous strands that tied it to its earthly shell were finally broken. A metamorphosis that, in our terms, took three days. But Jacob had not allowed his will to deteriorate with a slow death; he had controlled his spiritual power in his last fleeting moments, aware of and playing a wilful part in his own rebirth. As had Boris Pryszlak. Both had chosen different paths.

Jacob had found himself among an awesome realm of energies, a new dimension that was partly of this world, but ultimately a doorway to something greater, something that could be glimpsed, but not fully perceived. He had been confused, lost, and not alone. Others awaited him.

He had become part of them, joined the flow that never ceased growing, moving, yet which, again in our terms, had no reality; and eventually a part of that flow was allowed to return to its beginnings and combat an opposite energy that threatened its embryo. We are that embryo. The Dark is that opposite energy. The Light is the power we will become.

None of us who saw the Light resents the affliction it dealt us, for the blindness isn't a burden but a release from our lack of vision. Jessica is carrying our child and we both know that he – it will be a boy – will be blind, like us. The thought makes us happy, for we know he will be able to see as we do.

 **Ash**

JAMES HERBERT'S LATEST NOVEL

James Herbert's best-loved character, David Ash,
the sceptical detective of the paranormal, returns in the
long-anticipated novel *ASH*. There are reports of
strange goings-on in an isolated castle.
Many suspect that it is haunted . . .